COLLECTION

*When courageous knights risked all
to win the hand of their lady!*

Don't miss any of this stunning collection!

Medieval
LORDS & LADIES
COLLECTION

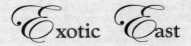

Exotic East

Anne Herries & Claire Delacroix

MEDIEVAL LORDS & LADIES COLLECTION
© Harlequin Books S.A. 2007

The publisher acknowledges the copyright holders of the
individual works as follows:

Captive of the Harem © Anne Herries 2002
Pearl Beyond Price © Deborah A Cooke 1995

ISBN: 978 0 263 85885 3

53-1107

Printed and bound in Spain
by Litografía Rosés S.A., Barcelona

Captive of the Harem

by

Anne Herries

Anne Herries, winner of the Romantic Novelists' Association's Romance Prize 2004, lives in Cambridgeshire. After many happy years with a holiday home in Spain, she and her husband now have their second home in Norfolk. They are only just across the road from the sea and have a view of it from their windows. At home and at the sea they enjoy watching the wildlife and have many visitors to their gardens, particularly squirrels. Anne loves watching their antics and spoils both them and her birds shamelessly. She also loves to see the flocks of geese and other birds flying in over the sea during the autumn, to winter in the milder climes of this country. Anne loves to write about the beauty of nature and sometimes puts a little into her books, though they are mostly about love and romance. She writes for her own enjoyment and to give pleasure to her readers.

Don't miss Anne's brand-new
Mills & Boon® Historical novel,
available in December 2007!

Chapter One

'I shall miss you, my teacher. The days will seem long without the benefit of your words of wisdom, Kasim.'

'I shall be sorry to leave you, Suleiman—the years we have had together have been truly a blessing for me, but the time has come for me to prepare to make my peace with God, my lord. I must go home to my own land to die…'

'Yes, I know. I would not hold you. Go then…and may Allah guide your footsteps to Paradise.'

Suleiman Bakhar felt the sting of the unmanly tears that would shame him as the old man left and he knew that it was for the last time; they would never meet again in this life.

He moved away to gaze down at the gardens of his apartments in his father's palace, his fierce, wild eyes lit by a silver flame in their depths. His expression for those who dared to look was at that moment much that of an untamed creature frustrated by the bars of its cage. The palace of Caliph Bakhar was a perfumed, luxuriously appointed cage—but nevertheless a prison to the man whose spirit wished to soar like the hawks he lavished with so much love and attention.

He was a strong, handsome man, though his features were at times harsh, his mouth capable of looking as cruel as the sharp beaks of his birds of prey. At other times his dark, mysterious eyes could be bright with laughter, and his mouth, slackened by desire, could look soft and deliciously sensuous—as was his voice when he chose to entertain the court with his singing. Now was not one of those times. He was bored, restless, and conscious of a growing anger inside himself that he did not understand. And he was losing the man who had been his teacher for many years, a man he revered and loved almost as a father. His life would be that much the poorer for the teacher's going.

Yet he would not have held Kasim for he loved him as dearly as he loved his own father. He must seek elsewhere to fill the emptiness the teacher's going would leave in his life.

Fluttering about the scented walks of the gardens below, the women of his harem twittered like brightly coloured birds in their scanty clothes as they paraded through sunlit walks. Here and there stone benches were placed in the shade, and the sound of tinkling water from fountains echoed the laughter of the women. They were all aware that Suleiman was watching them from his windows above. He was making his choice and one of them would be sent to his bed that night.

The favoured one would spend the afternoon being pampered by the other women. She would be washed in soft warm water in the baths of the harem, then perfumed lotions and creams would be massaged into her body and hair so that her skin would be smooth for the touch of her master, and finally she would be dressed in the finest silks…layer upon layer of diaphanous materials that he would either remove himself, or instruct her to remove as suited his whim.

It was an honour to be chosen by the Caliph's favourite son, and also a pleasure. Suleiman was young and virile, his body honed to masculine perfection by hours of training in the courtyards with the Janissaries. His love-making was legendary amongst the ladies of the harem, and word had spread to the other harems, some of which had less well-favoured masters, and there were many sighs as envious eyes peered at him from behind pierced screens. It was forbidden for the ladies of one harem to mix with those of another, of course, but it happened—as other forbidden things happened in secret places: things that could bring a swift beating or worse if they were discovered by the eunuchs.

Sometimes, the ladies of the Caliph's court were allowed to watch Suleiman at sport in the great courtyard of the palace. Suleiman delighted in trials of strength with the officers of the Janissaries, and it was very seldom that he lost his bouts.

'He will choose me. I know he will choose me,' Fatima said to Dinazade, who was her chief attendant. As Suleiman's favourite, Fatima had her own rooms and slaves to wait on her. 'He always chooses me.' She gave a satisfied smile as the chief eunuch beckoned to her. 'There, I told you so. Come with me, Dinazade. I must be beautiful to please my lord tonight.'

Suleiman moved back from the window as his chosen partner was led away. He had selected Fatima again because there was fire in her. Most of the concubines had been given to him as gifts, either by his father or merchants wishing to gain favour with the Caliph, and were too obedient to please him. He had dined too much on honey and wanted something with more spice.

His features were set like iron, his mouth thinned to a severe line. Sometimes he felt he would go mad if he were confined to this idle life for many more years. He could fight, ride out into the countryside beyond Constantinople with his hawks or spend the afternoon pouring over his manuscripts—but none of these pleasures held any real appeal for him that day. There was a hungry yearning in his soul—but for what? Suleiman did not know, unless it was simply to be free…to travel the world?

Such an idea was forbidden to him. His father had refused to let him enter the Janissaries in case he might be injured in a real battle—for his tussles with the elite guard could only ever be play-acting. No one would dare to inflict harm on the Caliph's son for fear of the punishment that would certainly follow—not from Suleiman, but from his father.

'Your place is here with me,' the Caliph had told him when he had asked permission to leave and join the Sultan's personal bodyguard. 'Together we are strong. I am getting older, Suleiman. Soon you must prepare to take over from me.'

Caliph Bakhar was known for his wisdom and fairness throughout the empire. It was he who dispensed justice and kept the common people in order in the city for his royal master Suleiman the Magnificent. The Sultan was the supreme ruler of the great Ottoman Empire, and under his rule the empire had reached new heights of power and splendour. Suleiman Bakhar had been named for him.

'Forgive me, my lord.' One of the eunuchs approached, his slippered feet making no sound on the marble floors. 'Your honoured father, the great Caliph Bakhar, requests your presence in his apartments.'

Suleiman's eyes were very hawkish as he let them sweep over the fleshy face of the eunuch. It was necessary to have such creatures to guard the women of the harem, but he did not like or trust them. They were sly, calculating creatures—especially this one.

'Very well,' he said curtly. 'I shall attend the Caliph.'

For a moment Suleiman thought he saw a flash of resentment in the eunuch's eyes. Abu was the child of one of his father's older concubines, and perhaps resented the fact that Suleiman and he shared the same blood but were treated in very different ways. Abu's mother had been a Nubian slave and of very little value, while Suleiman's mother had been the daughter of an English nobleman and the Caliph's favourite wife.

Taken from a shipwreck more dead than alive, Margaret Westbury had been presented as a gift to Caliph Bakhar. He had found her fascinating and taken her as his wife, but after she had given him a son he had offered to return her to her homeland. Margaret had preferred to stay on as his chief wife, and though she had been allowed little say in her son's upbringing, she had been allowed to see him twice a week in the gardens.

Yet another soft-footed eunuch with doe-like eyes conducted Suleiman into his father's presence. He fell on his knees before the Caliph as was the custom, but was immediately told to rise.

'The Caliph wished to see his unworthy son?'

'Suleiman is a most worthy son,' Caliph Bakhar replied after the ritual salute. 'I have a problem, Suleiman. The Sultan has made it clear that he is displeased over certain disorders in the city—there was a riot in the streets and the mob passed close to the palace walls.'

'The disturbance was swiftly quelled by the Janissaries.'

'But it should not have been allowed to happen so near the palace,' his father said. 'I have displeased our master, therefore, I must find gifts to regain favour in his eyes.'

'What does my father have in mind?'

'Something of rare beauty—an important piece of Venetian glass, perhaps?'

'Or a beautiful woman?'

'She would have to be an exceptional woman. The Sultan has many Kadins.'

The Kadins or Sultanas were women who had pleased their royal master and were given their own luxurious apartments—much as Fatima was favoured in Suleiman Bakhar's much smaller harem.

'Of course.' Suleiman frowned. 'Does my father wish me to visit the slave markets of Istanbul—or travel to Algiers?'

'You are not to leave our shores,' the Caliph said with a frown. 'We have too many enemies. Send word that we are looking for something special. She must be lovely beyond price and untouched.'

'It would be rare to find such a jewel,' Suleiman

replied. 'Perhaps I should look for some other treasure that would please the Sultan?'

'It would be wise,' the Caliph said, nodding. 'And now, my son—will you hunt with your father? I have a new hawk I would match against your champion.'

'None can match Scheherazade—she flys higher, swifter and her bravery puts all others to shame.' His pupils were lit from within by a silver flame as he spoke of his favourite hawk.

'She is truly a bird to prize above all others. Find a woman as beautiful, clever and brave as your hawk, Suleiman, and the Sultan will forgive me a hundred riots.'

'If such a woman exists, she would be a prize above all others,' Suleiman replied. 'I do not think we shall find this woman, my father—though we search all the markets in the Ottoman Empire!'

Eleanor stood at the top of the cliff gazing out towards the sea. The view was magnificent—sparkling blue water, gently wooded slopes and a dazzling variety of oleander and wisteria. The wisteria had spread from the gardens of the villa behind her, she thought, and inhaled its wonderful perfume.

Such a glorious day and yet her thoughts at that moment were of the house they had left behind five months earlier. It would be autumn in England now, the mists just beginning to curl in from the sea, swirling into the Manor gardens. The Manor was the home she had shared with her father and brother for the first eighteen years of her life, and she doubted she would ever see it again.

'Why so sad, Madonna? Does the view not please you?'

Eleanor turned to look at the man who had spoken, her deep azure eyes seeming to reflect the blue of the Mediterranean sky. Beneath the severe French hood she wore, her hair was long and thick, the colour of ripe corn in sunlight. She kept it well hidden, even though she had thought herself safe from being observed here, but wisps had escaped to tangle betrayingly about her face. She could do nothing to disguise the loveliness of her classic features, though she chose dark colours that did nothing to enhance her beauty.

'I was thinking of my home,' she replied, unable to hide a wistful note in her voice. 'It will be misty now and the fires will be lit in the library.'

'You cannot prefer the cold damp climate of your country to Italy?' His eyebrows arched in disbelief. 'But perhaps there was a lover…a young man who holds your heart in his hand?'

For a moment Eleanor was tempted to invent a handsome fiancé, but she was an honest girl and did not wish to lie.

'No, sir. I was thinking of my books. We were unable to bring many with us. As my father has told you, we were forced to leave in a hurry.'

Count Giovani Salvadore nodded, his expression sympathetic. He was a man of moderate height, not fat but well built with rather loose features. His hair and small beard were dark brown, his eyes grey and serious. Eleanor supposed he would be considered attractive, and his wealth made him an important man in the banking circles of Italy.

'It was an unpleasant experience for you,' the Count replied. 'Fortunately, your father had already placed much of his fortune with the House of Salvadore for safe keeping.'

'Yes, that was very fortunate,' Eleanor agreed, hiding her smile behind her fan. He was so pompous, so sure of himself! Yet she should not be ungrateful. He had generously made his villa available to her family until they should find somewhere they wished to settle. Sir William Nash had spoken of this part of Italy as being *pleasant* but Eleanor knew that he meant to travel on to Cyprus very soon. He had friends there: an English merchant who had settled on the island some years earlier and had offered both a home and an opportunity for Sir William to join him in business.

'Shall we go in?' The Count offered Eleanor his arm. 'Your skin may suffer in this heat if you stand in it too long.'

Eleanor had come out to be alone for a while. The Count's mother and sister chattered like magpies all day long, and they did not speak much English. She had hoped to escape for a while, so that she could have a little time to herself—but he had pursued her.

As she had feared, the Count was too interested in her for comfort. At home in the west of England, she had been allowed to do much as she pleased, and it pleased her to keep her distance from any gentleman she had considered a threat to her peaceful existence.

Eleanor had no wish to marry. She had become the mistress of her father's home when her mother died. She had been fourteen then, already a pretty girl but inclined to solitary walks and study. Lady Nash had spoken often of her lovely daughter's future marriage, but after her death it had been forgotten. Eleanor liked it that way.

To be a wife meant servitude. As a much-loved and indulged daughter, Eleanor had a freedom she might lose if she married. Sir William was an enlightened man. He had taught his daughter to enjoy study for its own sake, and her intelligence delighted him. She spoke French fluently, a little Italian, and could read some Arabic and Latin, of course. Her main interest was ancient history, which she could discuss at a level above most men of equal rank, and she had thought that when the time came for them to leave England, she would enjoy seeing the places of which she had only read.

Indeed, she had enjoyed her visits to Venice and Rome, drinking in the beauty of old palaces and wonderful scenery. It was only since they had come to the villa that she had begun to feel restless.

Count Giovani Salvadore was too attentive! He made Eleanor feel as if he were trying to smother her with his generosity and his compliments caused her to be uneasy. She was afraid he meant to ask for her hand in marriage. Eleanor was almost sure Sir William would consult her in the matter, but she could not be certain. She would not feel comfortable until they were on the ship taking them to Cyprus!

'There you are, Eleanor! Father sent me to find you.'

Eleanor saw her brother coming towards them and went forward eagerly to meet him. At fifteen, he was slight and fair, a merry, happy boy—and she loved him dearly.

'I am sorry if I worried you, Dickon.'

'Father wants to talk to you,' Richard said, his smile shy and engaging. 'He has something to show you— an illuminated manuscript. He wants you to help him decipher it.'

At last! Eleanor felt her spirits lift. She had missed working with her beloved father on his collection of old manuscripts. He was beginning to build them up again. When they had their own house, everything would be as it always had been. Sir William would not force her to marry. He cared for her too much!

She glanced at the Count and smiled. 'Forgive me, *signor*. I must go. My father waits for me.'

'Oh, Father!' Eleanor cried as she saw the manuscript for the first time. 'I do not think I have ever seen anything quite as lovely.'

The manuscript was tiny, and when rolled could be stored in a space no larger than the handle of a woman's fan. Its container was made of pure gold and inlaid with emeralds and pearls, and there was a loop to suspend it from a chain or a ribbon so that it could be worn on the person.

'It is writ in Arabic,' Sir William said. 'But my eyes are not good enough to make out the words.'

The script was very small, though the decoration of gold leaf, rich crimson and deep blue was as clear and bright as the day it had been painstakingly inscribed.

'It is a part of the Qur'an,' Eleanor said. 'Or the Koran, as the Western world would name the Muslim's holy script. But there is an introduction…it praises the goodness of Allah, and asks for his blessing…' She paused. 'I think it says for the Abbey of the Far Cross…surely that cannot be, Father? I do not understand—would an Islamic prayer ask for Allah's blessing on a monastery?'

'Yes, that it is correct,' her father said and she saw the gleam of excitement in his eyes. 'It is the work of Abbot Gregorio. He was a very learned man who lived at an Abbey on an isolated island in Greek waters some three centuries ago. The monks were a silent order, but they had many secrets and there were legends of their fabulous wealth—though where it came from no one knew. According to the story, the Abbot believed that all religions stemmed from the same source and it is said that he was very interested in Islam—but his great wisdom did him little good. Not long after this manuscript would have been created, the Abbey was burned to the ground by Saracens and all the monks were slaughtered. No one knew what had happened to the treasures of the Abbey. They were thought lost…' Sir William's excitement was intense. 'This was discovered in an iron pot in the ground on Cyprus—on our land, Eleanor. Who knows what more we may find hidden away?'

'No, indeed, if the story be true—we might find untold treasures.' Eleanor caught her father's excitement. 'It is very intriguing,' she said and smiled at him. 'This must be worth a great deal in itself. Did Sir John send this to you?'

'He writes that it was discovered when the gardeners were working near to the house he purchased in my name. Knowing of my interest in such things, he sent it with his warm wishes for our speedy arrival.'

'Does that mean that we are to leave Italy soon?

'Yes. It pleases you that we are to leave this house?' Sir William's eyes were a faded blue, his hair silvered by age but showing traces of the gold it had once been. 'Have you not been happy here, daughter? The Count has been kind…'

'Very kind, Father—but I shall be happier when we are in our own home and may begin to gather our things about us again.'

'My poor daughter,' Sir William said, tenderness in

his eyes. 'You miss your books, I dare say. It was a pity we could not bring more of them with us.'

'We dare not seem to be packing everything,' Eleanor replied, a flicker of fear in her eyes as she recalled the way they had been forced to flee in the night. 'You were likely to be arrested at any time. Your life is more important than books—however precious.'

'England is a dangerous place for a man who was known to be a friend to Cranmer,' Sir William said. 'Queen Mary senses treachery in the actions of any man not of her own faith.'

'But you took no part in any plot against her.'

'No—yet I knew those who did,' Sir William said and shuddered. 'Several of my friends had been seized and put to the torture. I was warned that the same was planned for me. Had it been myself alone...but I had you and your brother to consider, Eleanor. Better a life in exile than a painful death. Fortunately, I have long traded with the merchants of Venice, and much of my fortune was safe in Italy. We have good friends here and in Venice—and Cyprus. But it is there that I believe we should settle. Sir John is brother to your mother and a good, kindly man. If anything should happen to me, he would take care of you and Richard.'

'Pray, Father—do not speak of such things,' Eleanor begged him. A chill wind had seemed to blow across her heart as he spoke and she was afraid, though she saw no reason for it. 'You are safe from those who would see you burned.'

She shuddered as she thought of the cruel deaths suffered by the Archbishop Cranmer and others—and all done in God's name. She did not believe that the God she knew in her heart would demand such wickedness—for it was surely wicked to kill a man simply for worshipping in his own way. She thought that she quite liked the ideas of the Abbot, who had embraced both Christianity and Islam, though of course she would never dare to voice those opinions aloud. The question of religion had caused fierce fighting all over this region of the Mediterranean for centuries, Christian against Muslim, west against east—and, indeed, she could not condone the culture of the Eastern potentates!

'Yes, we are all safe, child,' Sir William said and smiled at her. 'So you do not wish to marry Count Salvadore? You know that he means to ask you before we leave?'

'Please do not allow it,' Eleanor pleaded. 'Tell him that you wish to settle in your own home before you consider the question of my marriage.'

'Very well, Eleanor.' He was not displeased by her decision, because there was no hurry for her to marry. Sir John had a son of twenty years. It was possible that the two might please each other. 'We leave the day after tomorrow. Sir John has sent his own ship to carry us to our new home. It is a stout vessel and will have a precious cargo of rare treasures. Sir John trades much with the ruler of the Ottoman Empire and he has spent some months collecting pieces he thinks will tempt the Sultan.'

'Surely my mother's brother would not trade with such a man? From what you have told me, the Turks are barbaric! To keep others as slaves for their benefit is a terrible sin, Father.'

'Yes, Eleanor. It is a terrible sin, but you must remember theirs is a different culture. These people are not all barbarians by any means, though the Corsairs that plague these waters most certainly are. I believe that amongst the ruling class there are extremely clever men—and they have wise teachers. The rich live in wonderful palaces; they are also advanced in many things…medicine, for instance.'

'Because they have Arab slaves,' Eleanor replied scornfully. 'You told me that it was the Arabs who had wonderful knowledge and skills in such things—not the Turks!'

'In the Ottoman Empire there are many races blended into a melting pot of talents and wisdom. These people have developed the Devisherme system, Eleanor. That means that slaves—and the children of slaves—who convert to the faith of Islam are accepted into their society and allowed to prosper from their various talents.'

'Yet they remain slaves, subservient to the whim of their master!'

'In theory, yes,' Sir William admitted, his eyes alight with amusement. Such debates with his daughter were the bread of life to him. He was more tolerant than Eleanor, who could lose her temper when passionate about something—as she was now. 'But I believe many of them rise to become powerful men—even Bey of a province.'

'But they are still bound to their master!'

'Every man, woman and child in the Empire is bound in some way to the Sultan,' her father replied. 'He could order the death of any subject who has displeased him—so the free men are no more at liberty to do as they please than the slaves.' His eyes twinkled at her. 'Are they so very different from us, Eleanor? We were forced to leave our home because of the whim of a Queen. I could have been seized, tortured and condemned for a crime I had not committed.'

'Yes, I know, Father.' She shuddered. 'I am aware that your life was in danger and I thank God we escaped unharmed. But at least in England they do not shut women in a harem all their lives.'

'No—but some Western women suffer as much as their Eastern sisters. Disobedient women have been sent to a nunnery against their will, Eleanor, which is perhaps an even more harsh life. I believe the Kadins are rather spoiled, pampered creatures.' He chuckled deep in his throat. 'If ever you find yourself in a harem, daughter, you must make yourself indispensable to your master—that is the way to an easy life.'

'Never! I would rather die. I wonder that you can even say such a thing, Father.'

'It was but a jest, my dear,' Sir William said. 'I pray that you never will find yourself in such a place. You are right. I should not have said anything of the kind. Please forgive me. Though I would rather you fought for your life, my child, always remember that whatever may be done to your body, your mind and soul remains your own. Be true to yourself and to God and nothing can harm you.' He touched her head as if in blessing.

Eleanor closed her eyes and whispered a prayer. She had felt that chill wind again, but her father's words comforted her. If she kept her faith and her pride, she could face anything.

Yet why should anything terrible happen? They had only a relatively short journey ahead of them, and were to travel on board a ship belonging to Sir William's kinsman and friend. Surely they would arrive safely within a few days?

* * *

They had been sailing for twenty-four hours when the storm suddenly hit the ship. It came from nowhere, a great, swirling wind that whipped what had seemed to be a calm blue sea into huge waves. The merchant vessel was tossed about like a child's toy, lurching and rolling in the grip of the atrocious weather.

'You and your children must stay below,' the captain had warned Sir William. 'If you come on deck, I cannot be responsible for your safety.'

Eleanor had been forced to obey, though she would have preferred to be up on deck. It was terrifying to feel the ship shudder and buck, and she feared that they would all die.

She felt ill and was sick constantly, managing only to whisper a prayer between bouts of vomiting. Surely they would all drown!

It was a terrible end to their voyage of hope, and Eleanor touched the heavy silver cross and chain she wore around her neck, together with her father's precious manuscript, which she was wearing beneath her gown for safe keeping.

'Oh God, let us all live' she prayed. In her terror she reached out to whoever was listening. 'Whether you be Our Lord or Allah—let us live…'

All night the storm raged around them, but suddenly just before dawn it died and the silence was even stranger than the wind that had preceded it. The ship was not moving at all. It seemed that the god of the sea had worn itself out in its fury and was resting.

Their captain told Sir William that they were becalmed and could do nothing but drift until the wind returned.

'How long before that happens?' Sir William asked.

'Perhaps hours…or days.'

There was nothing anyone could do except wait for a benevolent wind. At least the ship had survived the wild night. The sailors would spend their time clearing up the debris of a broken mast; the passengers could do nothing but sleep and wait.

Eleanor was woken by the sound of shouting from the deck above. Immediately, she sensed that something was wrong and struggled into her gown, which fastened at the front to make it easy for travelling. Although she had a maid, the girl was in the next cabin and still terribly ill from the sickness she had suffered during the storm. Eleanor did not know her well, and felt that it would be better to manage alone for the moment.

She paused, then took a few seconds to don her ugly cap, tucking all her hair beneath the veil at the back. She was already wearing her father's treasure, but her cross and chain were lying on the chest beside her. She was about to snatch them up when her brother came rushing into the cabin.

'Forgive me,' he cried, clearly frightened. 'But Father says you must come. We must all be together. He means to bargain with them…'

'Bargain with whom?' Eleanor asked. 'I do not understand you, Dickon. What is happening?'

'Corsairs,' he said, his cheeks pale. 'They have a fast galley and are bearing down on us hard. We cannot move, Eleanor—which means they will board us.'

'May God have mercy!'

Eleanor knew what this meant. Every vessel feared an attack by the fearsome pirates who roamed these waters—but their ship was fast and powerful and would usually be capable of outrunning the pirates' galley. Not without a wind! They were helpless, caught in a trap!

Now Eleanor understood what her father meant about bargaining with the Corsairs. Their only chance was that the captain of the galley would be prepared to sell them to their friends—rather than either killing them or selling them in the slave markets of Algiers.

She was trembling inwardly as she went up on deck. Their lives were truly in the hands of a higher being now. They could be dead within minutes—or prisoners. She held her head erect as she went to join her father. He kissed her on both cheeks.

'Forgive me, child. When I jested with you, I never dreamed this would happen.'

'Your jest did not make it happen, Father,' she replied, refusing to show her fear. Her eyes flashed with anger. 'The storm brought us to this—and these barbarians take advantage of our plight. Now tell me they are civilized people, Father!'

The galley had drawn alongside as she spoke and she could see the grinning faces of the men who had begun to swarm up the sides of the ship. They were strange, fearsome faces and she felt close to fainting— but she would not give in to such weakness! She would stand up to these heathen devils if she died for it.

The screaming and killing had begun as the sailors prepared to defend themselves from the invaders. They knew their fate if they were taken, and many preferred a swift death to being chained in a galley until they were flogged to death or starved at the oars. Eleanor watched the carnage about her, her face remarkably unmoved—but inside she was shocked and horrified by the cruelty of the invaders. They gave no mercy... even when a cabin boy, who had at first tried to fight, sank to his knees and begged to live.

Eleanor put her arm about Richard's shoulders. If they were to die, then they would die together.

One of the Corsairs—a tall man with swarthy looks and cruel eyes—had seen them. He appeared to be the leader of these men and he pointed towards Eleanor, giving what was obviously a command.

She lifted her head, meeting those cruel eyes proudly, daring him to touch her. He grinned suddenly as if he recognized the challenge and said something more to his men. Three of them were coming towards them, their manner purposeful.

'Do not be frightened,' she said to Richard. 'Be true to your inner self whatever they do. Remember, you are Richard Nash, and—'

The men had arrived and started to grab at her. She pushed her brother behind her, trying to shield him, but one of the men swooped on her, lifting her and throwing her over his shoulder.

'Father!' she cried. 'I love you—I love Richard.'

She kicked and struggled for all she was worth, but knew it was useless. The man carried her as though she were a sack of straw. He was taking her towards the side of the ship where she was lifted over into the arms of their leader, who was waiting to receive her. The pirates were gathering what they could now and retreating to their galley. Eleanor looked back and saw her father. He was trying to talk to one of the pirates, but the man struck him a blow to the side of the head and he fell to the deck, bleeding profusely.

'Father...' she cried despairingly. She saw that another of the pirates had her brother, who was kicking and struggling valiantly against his captor. 'Don't fight, Richard…try to live…' It was her father's instruction to her and she vowed that she would try. 'I love you, Father,' she murmured. 'I wish they had killed me too…but I shall try to do what you asked of me…'

She could hear the Corsairs shouting and pointing. Glancing out towards the sea, she saw another, larger, faster galley approaching them swiftly. It was a Spanish war galley—and the Spaniards were sworn enemies of the Corsairs.

'Oh, please God let them be in time,' Eleanor prayed. 'Let the Spanish captain of the galley wreak vengeance on these murdering devils. Let us be rescued…'

Tears were trickling down her cheeks as she was dumped on board the galley and then dragged off to what was clearly the cabin of the Corsairs' leader. She was thrust inside what was an airless hole and she fell to the ground, hitting her head against an iron chest as she did so.

Eleanor was claimed by the merciful blackness and did not know that the Spanish galley had chosen not to pursue their enemy. Its captain was even now climbing aboard the crippled merchant vessel, intent on rescuing the remaining crew of a Christian ship, unaware that the Corsairs had taken prisoners before they ran…

Chapter Two

Eleanor could not be sure how long she had lain in the stuffy, airless cabin. When she first came to herself, she had been aware of pain in her head and very little else. She lay in a state of semi-consciousness, drifting in and out of awareness. Hours passed before she felt her shoulder being roughly shaken and then found herself looking up into the bearded face of the man who had captured her. His fierce eyes snapped with what she thought was anger, sending a ripple of terror winging through her. She gave a moan of fear and shrank back, but instead of cruelly ravishing her as she half expected, he thrust a cup of water into her hand.

'Drink, woman,' he muttered in French.

'You speak French?' Eleanor asked in the same tongue. 'Please—tell me what has happened to my brother. Is Richard alive?'

'Be silent, woman. Drink now—food later.'

Eleanor sat up as the door of the officers' cabin closed behind him. She sipped the water gratefully. It was cool, fresh and sweet on her lips, taking the taste of ashes from her mouth. For the first time she was able to think clearly and began to wonder how long she had been on board the galley—was it merely hours or days?

Gingerly, she put a hand to the back of her head and found that her hood had been removed, and that there was a patch of dried blood in her hair. Someone must have taken the headdress off while she was unconscious, probably to see what had rendered her that way. It was the blow to the side of her head as she fell that had done the damage, but she ached all over and wondered if she had suffered some kind of a fever. Perhaps the effects of the storm combined with the terror of the pirates attack had... *Her father was dead!* The pain of knowledge returned like the thrust of a sword in her breast.

Tears welled up in her eyes and fell in a hot cascade down her cheeks. She sobbed for several minutes as her grief overwhelmed her. It was hard to believe that the man she had loved so dearly was lost to her forever...but she had seen the blow that had felled him and believed he must have died of it.

What of her brother? Eleanor's eyes were becoming accustomed to the gloom of the cabin now, and she began to glance around her, trying to make out what the shapes were. There were no bunks or divans here, merely a collection of sea chests—one of which had caused her to have a nasty headache—and a table and stool pushed hard against one wall. Did these men never sleep? But was a roll of blanket spread on the ground near her—perhaps that served as a bed on this war galley?

One thing was clear: she was alone. Her brother had not been thrown in here after her. Where was he? What had happened to him? Their captor had so far been gentle enough to her...but had Richard been treated differently? Was he still alive? The questions tortured her, increasing her own fear of what was to happen.

She tried to get up and found that she could stand, although her head was still spinning and she felt sick, but she kept upright and did not fall. After a moment or two she managed to walk towards the table on which were spread what she realised were charts and maps of the sea, also various instruments for calculating distance by the stars. Clearly the captain of this vessel was more educated than his appearance allowed, and with that knowledge came a lessening of her fear.

If he was intelligent she might be able to reason with him herself, to arrange for a ransom to be paid. Sir John often traded with the Sultan of the Ottoman Empire. A message could be sent to him...he would pay for her and Richard's release. Perhaps all was not yet lost.

She finished her water and sat down to look at the charts before her. The captain had clearly been plotting a chart—and seemed to be heading for the great city the Christians still called Constantinople, though it had been renamed Istanbul by its conquerors, which lay on the shores of the Bosphorus Straits. She was being taken there to be sold in the slave markets! She had imagined the galley's base would be Algiers, perhaps because the captain spoke French so well.

The French were more at home in these waters than most of the other Western countries. Some years earlier the Turks had signed an agreement that they would allow only the French flag to trade freely and safely in their waters, though of course there were other merchants who made individual agreements. There were also those who roamed where they would and took the consequences, as their kinsman's ship had—but only the French had the protection of the Sultan himself.

Her fate would be the same wherever she was taken!

Eleanor shivered as the realisation hit her. It was easy to make the decision to be bold and demand she be ransomed, but why should the Corsair captain listen? He could quite easily sell her—perhaps to the Grand Turk himself—and then she would disappear into a harem, never to be seen again. She shuddered at the thought of what her life would be like in such a place.

The idea of being a man's concubine appalled her. No! It must not happen. She would not let it happen. It was all a question of money. The Corsairs had taken prisoners to sell them in the slave market. What would her value be on the auction block? She had no way of knowing—but surely it could not be so very much? Her mother's cousin would pay twice as much to have her back.

Eleanor had no doubts that Sir John would do his utmost to recover both her and Richard. If he had heard of the fate of his ship, he might even now be trying to trace them. Her head lifted, her expression proud and determined. No matter what happened to her she would fight—she would live as her father had bid her—and perhaps one day she would be returned to her family.

But where was Richard?

Mohamed Ali Ben Ibn frowned as he thought about the woman they had captured; she had lain in a fever for several hours after they had taken flight from the

Spanish war galley and at first he had thought she might die. That would have been a great loss.

He had seen her quality immediately and ordered her taken as his personal share of the plunder from the merchant ship. Unfortunately, they had not managed to snatch much else of value before they were forced to abandon their prize.

There was the boy, of course. His delicate features would appeal to certain men in the slave markets of Constantinople, and another woman. She was young but not beautiful and would fetch a moderate price—but his woman was more of a prize than he had imagined when he first spotted her.

That glorious hair! He had been shocked when he removed the hood that covered it to attend to her wound, and at first was elated by the value of his prize. But now there were rumblings amongst the crew because their prize was so small. He had been determined to bring the woman to Istanbul at once—and he knew exactly what he was going to do with her—but the crew was dissatisfied with their share.

He must make sure that none of them got near enough to her to see what a beauty she was. Not a hair of her head must be touched—and she must not be violated, for then her value would be lost. He would take her to a certain house on the shores of the Bosphorus where she would be safe from prying eyes—and then he would begin his bargaining.

In the meantime he must find a way of pacifying the crew. He took out the gold ornament he had discovered tucked beneath the girl's dress when he tried to loosen her bodice—Western women wore such ugly, restricting clothes it was a wonder any of them could breathe!

He saw that the little cylinder of gold was studded with precious stones, and noticed the stopper at the top. Opening what he had imagined was a scent flask, he discovered the tiny manuscript and drew it out. His face paled as he discovered what it was and he dropped it as though his fingers had been burned.

Mohamed Ali Ben Ibn was a Corsair by necessity, not birth. He had been educated in the best schools of his homeland before being captured by Spaniards, and forced to work in their galleys for long years before he had escaped, vowing revenge on the men he hated. Since then he had roamed the seas in search of prey—and he had been successful. He was now a wealthy man and owned a beautiful house, to which he would one day take a woman of his own beliefs, and make sons with her.

His brow furrowed as he looked at what he knew to be cursed. That manuscript was a part of the treasure of the Abbot of the Far Cross—and the legend was that anyone who sought to benefit from the sale of this treasure was doomed to a terrible death. The Saracens who had looted the Abbey and killed the monks had all died violently soon after and it was said that the treasure was scattered far and wide. How had the woman come by it? And why did she wear it around her neck like a talisman? Was she of the true faith and not a Christian as he had supposed?

He was a superstitious man. The treasure must be returned to the girl! Mohamed would find some other way of satisfying his crew. He would give them gold from his own coffers—and he would make sure he recouped his loss from the sale of the girl!

Eleanor was visited twice a day by the captain of the galley. He brought her food and water, and he

returned her father's treasure to her. She had not noticed its loss at first, and was surprised when he gave
it to her.

'Why have you returned this?' she asked. 'It is valuable. My family has money. My kinsman will pay a
high ransom for me—twice my price in the slave market.'

He glowered at her. 'Drink and eat, woman.'

It was all he ever said to her

She had begun to wonder if she had overestimated
his intelligence. Perhaps they were the only words of
French he knew? The next time he came she spoke to
him in English, then Italian and finally she spoke the
only words she could think of that might reach him.

'*Insh'allah*…may the will of Allah prevail. And his
blessings be upon you for your kindness…if you will
ransom me and my brother to my family. My brother
is Richard Nash…son of Sir William and—'

'You speak too much, woman,' Mohamed said
harshly. 'A woman should have a still tongue if she
does not wish to be beaten.'

'You are an educated man!' Eleanor cried. 'Why
will you not listen to my requests? My family will
make you a rich man if you ransom me to them. My
uncle is Sir John Faversham of Cyprus—'

His look darkened to one of anger. 'I do not trade
with infidels! I kill them. You are not to question me,
woman. Be thankful that I do not give you to my men
for their sport.'

Eleanor shrank back, the fear writ plain in her face.
'You would not…be so cruel?'

'Thank Allah that I am not the barbarian you think
me,' Mohamed said. 'I have plans for you, woman—

but I may still beat you if you do not still your clacking tongue.'

Somehow Eleanor did not believe him. If he had meant to harm her, he would have done it by now. It was clear that he did not like to be questioned by a woman, but she would not give up. If she kept talking about a ransom he was bound to at least think about it...

Suleiman Bakhar was laughing. He felt exhilarated by the sport he had just had with the man he knew was considered to be the champion of the Janissaries. It had been a fierce fight that could have gone either way, pressing each man to the limit—and he had won!

'Come, my friend,' he said, laying an arm about the shoulders of the man he had vanquished. 'We shall bathe, drink and eat together—and then I shall give you a woman for your pleasure.'

'You honour me, my lord.'

Suleiman nodded, accepting that he was being generous in victory, but he felt pleased with himself. His astronomer had that morning told him that he was about to enter a new cycle of his life—one that would bring him both torment and pleasure.

'You will gain your heart's desire,' the old man had told him after consulting various charts, 'but only if you are prepared to learn and to suffer.'

'To learn and to suffer?' Suleiman's expression had caused the astronomer's pulses to race for a moment. 'Explain your predictions.'

'All is not yet clear,' Ali Bakr told him. 'I see only that a bright flame has moved into the heaven of your chart. This flame will burn you and yet it will eventually bring you all that you long for in the secret places of your heart.'

'You speak in riddles as always.' Suleiman dismissed the astronomer with a handful of silver. 'Come to me when I send for you—and give me a clearer reading next time.'

Suleiman had dismissed the old man's ramblings as a misguided attempt to please him. It had happened often enough in the past. Most of his kind were charlatans and liars, pretending to a knowledge they did not have—yet he had heard much good of this one.

Suleiman had trained and fought for most of the day, and now his body was free of the restless energy that so often plagued him. The afternoon would be spent eating and drinking the rich dark coffee he enjoyed, talking with the men he knew as friends. Then perhaps he would send for Fatima…and yet he had no real desire for her.

Perhaps he should visit some of the better slave merchants? The Circassian women were beautiful and much prized; if he were lucky, he might find one that tempted him.

It was as he was being massaged with perfumed, healing oils by one of the eunuchs that the news came.

'There is a message from Mohamed Ali Ben Ibn, my lord,' the slave said. 'He asks if you will grant him the favour of seeing him.'

Suleiman rose from the massage bench, wrapping a cloth around his waist. His back and shoulders glistened with the oil that had been rubbed into his skin, enhancing the honed beauty of his muscular torso. He had a presence, an air of power and confidence that kept others in awe of him, but also created a distance so that he had few true friends.

What could the Corsair want with him? Suleiman was aware of a tingling sensation at the nape of his neck and experienced the first prickles of a strange excitement. The Corsair's reputation was known to him, though they had never met.

'Ask him to come to my private room.' He glanced at the officers who were also enjoying the benefits of being massaged by Suleiman's slaves. 'Excuse me, my friends. This will not take long. Please, eat, drink— and the women will entertain you.'

He gave an order to the eunuchs for dancing girls to be brought as he retired to his inner chamber, where only a very few were ever permitted.

'Bring coffee and food,' he told one of the slaves, 'then leave us.'

Suleiman was seated on a silken divan, clad now in simple white trousers and a long white caftan belted at the waist, when the Corsair captain was shown into his presence. He fell on his knees but was immediately told to sit, which he did on the cushions provided.

'We are both men,' Suleiman said, his eyes narrowed and intent on the other's face. 'We shall speak as equals. You will take coffee with me?'

'You honour me, my lord.'

'You have something for me?'

Mohamed smiled. The Caliph's son wasted no time. 'I have been told you seek something rare and beautiful?'

'This is true. What have you to sell?' Suleiman frowned. It was said of this man that he had an eye for quality. When he had merchandise for sale it was always the best—always highly priced. Again he felt that tingling sensation in his spine and was conscious of excitement. 'Is it treasure—or a woman?'

'Some would say this woman is a treasure beyond price.'

'Why?' Suleiman's hard gaze intensified. 'There are already many beautiful women in my harem—what makes this one worthy of special attention?'

'Her hair is the colour of ripe corn in the sunlight and reaches to below her waist,' Mohamed said. 'Her body is perfect, her eyes are azure like a summer sky and—'

'And?' Suleiman was demanding, imperious, dismissive of such details. 'What else?'

'She is clever. She speaks three languages, and I believe she reads Arabic. She is the daughter of an English baronet—curse all unbelievers!'

The prickling at Suleiman's nape had become almost painful. He felt as if a thousand hot pins had been stuck into him, and it was all he could do to stop himself gasping. A feeling of intense excitement had come over him, but he had no intention of showing it.

'Her mind is of little account,' he said with a studied carelessness. 'If her body is perfect, I may be interested. Where did you find her?'

'I attacked the ship of a merchant of Cyprus,' Mohamed said. He was not in the least put off by Suleiman's apparent indifference. It was expected that they would bargain. 'The ship was damaged and becalmed after the storm, and we thought it ripe for plucking—but a Spanish war galley bore down on us. We were able to take only the woman, her servant and a boy before escaping.'

'How do you know she is the daughter of an English noble?'

'She told me, my lord—in three languages. She insists her family would pay twice her price in the market for her return.'

'And yet you come to me?'

'I would not sell this woman in the market, my lord. Nor would I entrust her to the slave merchants, who might defile her. She is safe in a house I know of— and will stay there until I sell her.'

Suleiman nodded, his face expressionless. 'What is your price for this woman?'

'One thousand gold pieces, my lord.'

'For a woman?' Suleiman laughed scornfully. 'No woman is worth a third of such a sum.'

'Forgive me for wasting your time, my lord.' It was clearly the Corsair's intention to leave as he rose to his feet. Suleiman rose too, matching the Corsair for height and build. 'I was told you sought something rare, a treasure beyond price but—I see I was misinformed.'

'Stay!' Suleiman's face was very hawkish at that moment, his pupils more silver than black. 'We have not yet concluded our business.'

Mohamed Ali Ben Ibn smiled inwardly. He had not thought for one moment that he would be allowed to leave.

'She is truly beyond price, my lord. I would not have offered her to you if I had not thought the woman a rare prize. I swear you will not be disappointed in her.'

'Eight hundred if she is what you claim.'

'One thousand gold pieces—her family would pay more.'

'For a woman?' Suleiman scorned and yet he knew he would pay the price asked if she was all this man claimed. 'A thousand then, but I will take the boy you spoke of, too.'

'He has been sent to the slave market.'

'Get him back,' Suleiman commanded, determined that he must assert his authority in some way. The boy was of little importance, but a Corsair must not best the Caliph's son in business. 'One thousand for them both or you may send the woman to the market too.'

'Come with me, child,' the woman said to Eleanor in a soft, melodious voice. 'You must feel so dirty after being on the galley for so many days. Bathe and rest and you will feel better.'

'Who are you?' Eleanor asked. She had been too weary to notice much as she was brought to this house that morning, but she had been given a delicious meal of rice and vegetables in a sweet sauce, and allowed to rest in a room by herself and was feeling better. 'And where am I? What is going to happen to me— and where is my brother? Has he been brought here too?'

'So many questions! I cannot answer the half of them.' The woman laughed. 'I am called Roxana and I am what some people call a Morisco—but I have mixed blood. My father was a Moor but my mother was Spanish.'

'Are you a Muslim or a Christian?'

'I am of the true faith,' Roxana replied, but did not meet her eyes as she spoke. 'Mohamed thought you might be of the Muslim persuasion—are you?'

Eleanor hesitated. She might be spared much if she was thought to be a Muslim, but she did not wish to lie to this woman, who had treated her kindly.

'No. I was raised as a Protestant—but I believe that

everyone should have the right to worship as they please. How can any of us know that we alone are right in our religious beliefs?'

Roxana looked anxious. 'You should not speak so openly, child. Men are fanatical about such things—you could be put to death for those words. In Spain you would have been given to the Inquisition for questioning. Here too you could be punished for voicing such an opinion. It is always best for a woman to be silent.'

'But why?' Eleanor sighed. Was there no one left to whom she could open her mind? Now that her father was dead she would never be able to speak freely again. But Roxana was only speaking the truth. 'You are right, of course. But you have not answered my questions.'

'You are in my house,' Roxana said. 'I was given it by Mohamed Ali Ben Ibn for saving his life some years ago. I have some skill with herbs and I nursed him when he was close to death. He comes here sometimes and I live because he lives. If it were not for him, I would have to sell myself to a master—and I would prefer to die.'

'I do not think him a bad man. He was not unkind to me.'

'That is because you will fetch a good price,' Roxana told her. 'You are very beautiful. Your skin is soft and smooth, and your body is comely—though a little thin for perfection. Good food will soon cure that. Come, now, and cleanse yourself. Then we shall sit and talk until your master comes for you.'

'You are kind, Roxana.'

'I have known what it is like to be in your position. I was sold by my family to an old man. He was...not kind.' Roxana shuddered at the memory. 'But he died and I ran away before his possessions were sold. I lived in a hut by the river and it was there I nursed Mohamed...'

'You love him—don't you?'

'Yes.' Roxana smiled at her. 'My wish is only to serve him, but one day he will take a wife and go far away. Then I shall not see him again.'

'He will not marry you?'

Roxana shook her head. 'He will take a young girl of his own...class. He came from a good family. He has suffered much at the hands of the Spanish—in their galleys as a slave.'

Eleanor nodded. She had been terrified of her captor at first, but she was beginning to see that she had been lucky. Instead of being taken directly to the slave market, she had been brought here to this house to rest and refresh herself. It could have been so much worse, and her mind shied away from what might have happened to her. She was safe here for the moment with this kind woman.

Yet she would escape if she could! Her mind was frantically looking for a way of escaping as her hostess led her into a walled garden, which was planted with many bushes and flowers that gave out a heady perfume. They walked through little paths between the bushes and wooden trellises, up which scrambled flowering shrubs. At a sunlit spot in the middle of a very secluded area, they came upon a sunken bath.

'You may wash here,' Roxana told her. 'There is soap in the jars and towels to dry yourself when you have finished.'

'I have never bathed in the open air before,' Eleanor said, glancing round nervously.

'No one will disturb you.' Roxana smiled at her. 'I shall leave you to bathe in private—and bring clothes to you in a while.'

It was very warm as Eleanor removed her clothes. Her dress felt stiff with dirt and sweat and she was glad to be rid of it. The sun was warm on her skin as she stood naked at the edge of the pool, relishing the warmth on her skin. It was many years since she had swum naked in the river at her home, for when she assumed the duties of a woman she had left the pranks of childhood behind her—but it did feel so good to be free of her restricting gown for once.

She was of medium height and slender with slim hips and small, pert breasts, the nipples the colour of a dark pink rose. Her skin was a warm cream in colour, and seemed to have a slightly golden sheen in the sunlight. Seen in her naked glory she was truly magnificent, a goddess come to earth—or so it might seem to any who saw her thus.

She walked down the gently sloping steps into the water, which seemed to be perfumed and was cool to her skin. It felt delicious and she walked further into the shallow pool, dipping down into the water and splashing in it in sheer delight. She suddenly went right under, remembering that she had loved to swim beneath the water as a child. She was so dirty and her hair needed a good soaking to be rid of the filth of her imprisonment.

It was so good to relax here by herself. She would think about escape later. For the moment she was simply going to enjoy the luxury that had been granted her.

Suleiman caught his breath as he watched the woman bathing. She seemed to be content as she splashed and soaped her limbs, and then her hair. It *was* a wonderful colour. He did not think that he had ever seen such beautiful hair...so thick and wavy. Now that it was wet it had gone darker but he knew it would look even better once it was clean. It would be pleasurable to bury his face in hair like that, to stroke that skin and crush her to him.

He felt a stirring in his loins, and realised that she had affected him in a way no woman had for a long time. His breath caught in his throat, and for a moment he knew a fierce longing to take her there and then— but then his self-control asserted itself once more. He had not paid a thousand gold pieces for his own benefit. He needed something rare and beautiful to please the Grand Turk.

She was truly a gift fit for the Sultan, he thought as he continued to watch her. The money demanded for her price had been exorbitant, far more than he would normally have considered—but perhaps she was worth it. He frowned as she submerged beneath the water again, seeming to stay there longer than necessary.

Was she trying to drown herself? Such things were not unknown amongst infidel women—they did not always take kindly to the idea of becoming a slave. He had heard of women killing themselves rather than being forced to submit to slavery.

He moved out from behind the pierced wooden screen, which had served as his hiding place, just as the woman surfaced once more. At first she did not seem to see him, then, when she became aware that she was no longer alone, she stared at him for a moment, screamed and ducked beneath the water again.

Suleiman cursed loudly and waded into the pool.

The foolish woman *was* trying to kill herself. He saw her beneath the surface and bent down to grab her, but she shot out of his grasp, swimming beneath the water to the far side. Then she came up gasping for air. He caught a glimpse of her lovely breasts, the nipples a deep rose, peaked and tempting, and then she crossed her arms over herself, her eyes meeting his in a cold stare.

She was angry! Suleiman was also angry. He was wet and uncomfortable and he realised that she had no intention of drowning herself—which made what he had done seem foolish.

'Who are you?' Eleanor demanded as he waded up the steps of the bath. He had been wearing a long, heavily embroidered robe over loose white pants and the tunic dragged against him in the water. 'How dare you spy on me?'

'I thought you meant to drown yourself. I did not intend to frighten you.'

Eleanor realised that she had spoken in English and that he had replied in the same language, clearly as at home in her native tongue as she. She had not expected that somehow.

'Go away! You have no right to be here. Mohamed Ali Ben Ibn owns me and he will kill you if he finds you here.'

'I do not think so.' Suleiman was amused by her show of defiance. Did she not realise that she was completely at his mercy? He could strip off his wet clothes and join her in the bath… The temptation to do so made him harden beneath his robes. He could feel his manhood burning and throbbing with a fierce need—a need he had not felt in a long time. 'Come out and dry yourself, woman.'

'Not while you're watching!'

'Foolish one! You have nothing to show that I have not already seen a thousand times.'

'I don't care how many concubines you have!' Eleanor retorted, stung by his mockery. How dare he speak to her so! 'I am not one of them and I am not coming out until you go away.'

'You will turn cold.' Suleiman sat down on a tiled bench, his eyes intent on her face, his mouth softened by amusement. 'I have no intention of leaving.'

'You are also wet.'

'But I shall dry in the sun.' He laughed huskily, the cruel mouth softened and suddenly appealing. 'What a fierce one you are, my little bird. You are truly worth the price asked. You will make a fine gift for the Sultan.'

Eleanor was chilled. So she was to be sold after all!

'Have you bought me?' He inclined his head, sending strange little sensations down her spine as she saw the brilliance of his eyes. 'Who—who are you?'

'My name is Suleiman Bakhar. I am the son of Caliph Bakhar—chief justice minister to the Sultan.'

Eleanor was silent, fighting her desire to weep. It seemed that all her hopes were at an end. She had hoped so much that she would be able to persuade her captor to ransom her—but it was already too late. There was something masterful about this man, an air of arrogance that told her he would not easily give up what was his.

Suleiman relented as he saw her shiver. 'Come out, foolish woman. I shall turn my back.'

He stood up, turning away so that he could not see her. He heard her moving in the water and was tempted to turn as she left the bath, but resisted.

'You can look now.'

Suleiman turned. She had wrapped a towel around her body, leaving her shoulders and arms bare, and was clutching the cloth to her as if her life depended on it. He smiled, feeling oddly moved by her need for modesty. Most of the women were only too eager to show off their charms. He picked up the second towel.

'Come here. I shall dry your hair.'

She made no move to obey, simply staring at him with her head up and her eyes proud. No one disobeyed Suleiman! To do so could mean instant punishment—even death. He was stunned by her obstinacy. Was she mad or merely foolish? Had she no idea how important he was—or what he could do to her if he chose?

'You must obey me. I am your master.'

'You may have bought me, but that does not mean that you can make me your slave.'

Suleiman saw the pride and defiance in her eyes and felt a surge of excitement. She was like one of his hawks—when they were fresh from the wild and untamed to the touch of his hand. Most of the birds succumbed to gentle persuasion in time, but now and then one would attempt to tear out his eyes. If that happened the bird was returned to the wild. Some men would have ordered it killed, but Suleiman understood the wild spirit that could not be tamed—and respected it.

He had never met a truly spirited woman before. They were always trained in their duties by the eunuchs and older women long before they were presented to their master.

'What makes you say that? Do you not understand

that I have absolute power over you? I can do with you as I will.'

'You can do as you will with my body,' Eleanor retorted, head high. She ought to be afraid of this man but she wasn't. 'But you cannot command my mind— or my soul.'

'Ah…' Suleiman nodded, enjoying this verbal tussle. 'Yes, I see. You think you can rise above the indignity of being a slave. I understand. But you do not. You are fortunate that I paid a great deal of money for you—or you might even now feel pain. I do not think you have ever experienced true pain, Eleanor.'

'Who gave you permission to use my name?' Her eyes flashed blue fire.

Suleiman moved towards her, towering above her, menacing her with the power of his strength and masculinity—yet she did not flinch. Her hair had begun to dry at the edges in the hot sun, little wisps curling about her face. He could imagine what it would look like properly dressed in its natural waves, cascading down to the small of her back. He was pleased with his purchase and inclined to indulge her for the moment.

'Here…' He put the second towel around her shoulders to protect her from the fierce heat. 'Go into the house and let Roxana help you to dress. We have a ride of some distance to my father's palace.'

Eleanor was torn between anger and caution. This man was a noble of his own country. A barbarian, of course, but better than many she might have been sold to. She was foolish to antagonise him. If she tried persuasion instead, he might ransom her to her family.

'I shall obey because I have no choice for the moment,' she said with dignity. 'But you do not under-

stand either, sir. I am the daughter of an English baronet. I have powerful friends. They will look for me
and they will pay a high price for my return—twice
what you paid for me. You may name your own price,
sir.'

'You do not know how much I paid…' A smile
curved his mouth. 'Would your family give ten thousand in your English gold coin? I might sell you for
such a sum.'

It was a king's ransom and her family could not pay
anywhere near as much—and he knew it.

Eleanor paled from shock. 'That is impossible. You
did not pay any such sum!'

Suleiman laughed, much amused by her reaction.
She had not tried to lie, and that pleased him. 'No, I
did not—but I am beginning to think I paid too much.
You have too much to say for yourself, woman. Have
you no respect for your betters? Do you not know that
it becomes a woman to remain silent in the presence
of her master—at least until she is given permission
to speak?'

'When I am in company that deserves my respect I
give it.' She felt a flash of temper. How dare this barbarian try to teach her manners? She was an English
gentlewoman! 'Here, I see only barbarians.'

'Be careful, woman.' Suleiman's mouth hardened
as he took a step towards her. 'My patience wears thin.
Go to the house before I drag you back in the pool
and drown you!'

'You wouldn't…' Eleanor began, but the look in
those fierce eyes made her think he just might. She
gave a little squeak of alarm, turned and fled.

Suleiman watched her flight, his eyes bright with
laughter. He had won the first tussle—but what a fight

she had put up. She was indeed a fine prize. A worthy gift for the Sultan…and yet perhaps she needed to be tamed a little first. She was too fiery, too defiant. From what he knew of the Sultan, her spirit would not be particularly appreciated.

Perhaps Suleiman would keep her for a while…

Chapter Three

'You are beautiful,' Roxana said as she brushed Eleanor's long hair. She sighed and looked at her with sympathy. 'It is a pity that you are destined for the Sultan's harem and not Suleiman Bakhar's own household.'

'Why?' Eleanor frowned at her.

'Suleiman Bakhar is young and strong—and they say that to be loved by him is like dying and going to paradise. Though perhaps this is only gossip brought by servant women to the markets.'

'I do not care if he is young and handsome,' Eleanor said, shivering as she remembered the look in those fierce eyes when he had threatened to drown her. For a moment she had truly believed he might do it. 'I do not want to be his concubine.'

'He might marry you—if you are clever. Until now he has taken only concubines. They say he must marry soon, because he must give the Caliph an heir…'

'I have no wish to be his wife!' Eleanor stared at her in horror. 'I can think of nothing worse.'

'That is because you do not know what it is like to be the wife of an old man.' Something flickered in the older woman's eyes. 'If you did, you would do all you could to make Suleiman notice you and want you for himself.'

'Was it very hard for you, Roxana?' Eleanor looked at her with sympathy. It was easy to see that the older woman had once been lovely—and that she had suffered.

'Sometimes I prayed that I might die before night came.'

'Is that why you left me alone in the garden? Did you think I might escape? Were you trying to help me?'

'It is not in my power. Had you tried to escape, you could not have done so,' Roxana replied. 'The walls are high and there are guards outside. Besides, if you had got out you would have been noticed immediately. The clothes you were wearing marked you as an infidel and an unbeliever. You would have been chased and caught by the mob—then, when they saw how beautiful you are, they would have begun to quarrel over you. Unless Mohamed's men rescued you, you might have been raped again and again…'

Eleanor turned pale. She held up her hands as if to ward off the pictures Roxana's words had brought to life in her mind.

'Enough! It is clearly useless to try and escape in the city—but if I managed to slip away outside its walls dressed like this…'

She was wearing a pair of drawers, very full, which reached down to her ankles; they were of a fine green material brocaded with gold. Over these, was a smock of a paler green silk gauze, edged with pearls; it had loose sleeves which covered as far as her elbows and closed at the throat with a cluster of pearls. And to

Eleanor's disgust, her breasts were clearly visible through it! The waistcoat fitted her close to her body and had very long sleeves fringed with gold tassels, and the buttons were again clusters of pearls. On top of all these was what Roxana had called a caftan, and that was a straight robe that covered her to the ankles. A girdle of gold threads woven with what looked like precious stones, but must surely be crystals, was fastened with a heavy clasp of gold, again set with jewels. If they were jewels. But Eleanor was certain they must be false. On her feet she wore soft boots that reached just to mid-thigh and were embroidered with gold thread.

It all felt very strange and she protested when she was told that she must put on a casacche before she went out. Since this was a huge cloak that would envelop her in its folds, and she must also wear a veil and a talpock to cover her head, she felt she would suffocate.

'It is too much,' she said. 'I thought my own gowns were restricting enough—but this cloak thing is ridiculous.'

'You will become accustomed to it,' Roxana said. 'When you are in the gardens of the harem you will be able to dispense with some of these layers if you choose. However, you will never be allowed to leave the palace wearing less.'

'Shall I be allowed out? I thought that was forbidden—that once in a harem women disappeared forever.'

Roxana smiled. 'You Western people do not understand our culture. Men of good family guard their women for their own protection. You would not be allowed to leave at will, of course, but the Sultan grants his favourite wives certain indulgences. You may be taken on a shopping expedition—or to some grand ceremonial occasion.'

'But what of those women who do not have their master's favour? What is it really like in a harem?'

'You will discover that soon enough. Come, Eleanor, you must not keep your master waiting or he may become angry.' The look Eleanor gave Roxana at that moment was so full of despair that the older woman's heart was touched. She embraced her. 'It is not always so very terrible. Try to please Suleiman Bakhar. If he keeps you for himself, you will not regret it.'

Eleanor nodded but said no more. She knew that Roxana could not help her, that she was free but had no power, no way of earning her living other than by selling herself. She lived here because she pleased Mohamed Ali Ben Ibn, and was as much at his whim as Eleanor would be at her master's.

It was terribly unfair, but it was the way of the world. She had been spoiled, petted and indulged all her life—and now she had no loving father to protect her. She was completely alone. She did not even know if her dearest Richard was still alive, and her heart wrenched with pain at the thought of what might have happened to him. Richard might already be dead—but she would live and she would win her freedom one day.

She saw Suleiman Bakhar waiting for her in the courtyard, and her heart caught for one terrifying moment and then raced on. He was truly one of the most impressive men she had ever seen, and he looked...wild, an untamed creature and dangerous. She should be afraid of him, and yet...there was something that drew her to him, some thin, invisible thread that seemed to bind her to him as surely as any cruel chains they might put upon her.

She lifted her head as she reached him, eyes bright and challenging. 'Am I to be chained?'

Suleiman's gaze narrowed. 'Should I chain you, Eleanor? Are you planning to try and escape?'

She had hoped there might be an opportunity to slip away from him and now realised that she had been foolish to put him on his guard. 'What would you do—if you were in my place?'

'I should kill my captors and run away,' Suleiman replied truthfully. He laughed deep in his throat, a soft husky sound that Eleanor discovered was very attractive. 'Foolish woman. I have never put chains on anything—beast or man—let alone a woman with skin as soft as yours.'

'What has the softness of my skin to do with it?' She gave him a haughty look.

'Chains would mark you and mean you were worth less,' he replied, his expression inscrutable.

'Of course—I should have known.' For a moment she had thought he was being compassionate. He was a barbarian and a savage—she should not expect anything from such a man. 'How am I supposed to ride in this ridiculous thing?'

Suleiman looked at the cloak that enfolded her. 'You could not ride like that. You will be carried in a litter. It is the usual mode of travel for a woman of class here. I did not know that you could ride.'

'I would prefer to ride.'

'Then perhaps I shall allow it one day,' Suleiman replied. 'However, today you will be carried in the litter. Come, I am ready to leave.'

Eleanor looked round for Roxana, but she had slipped away as soon as she had delivered her charge. Besides, there was nothing the Morisco woman could have done to help her.

'Are you afraid?' Suleiman asked as he saw her hesitation. 'You have no need to be. You are being taken to my apartments for the moment. I have decided I shall let the older women of my father's household school you in the manners you need before you are fit to grace the harem of any man.'

At that Eleanor's head came up, eyes flashing with anger. 'Afraid—of you? Why should I be? You are merely a man...'

'Truly, this is so. Why should you be afraid of me? You have no need to be—if you please me.' Suleiman's smile flickered deep in the silver depths of his strange eyes. His remarks had had their desired effect. Her pride had leant her courage. 'Your escort awaits you, lady.'

She felt a tingle at the base of her spine. He had addressed her as a woman of quality at last, and he was behaving as though she were his equal instead of a slave he had bought. Perhaps she might yet persuade him it would be better to ransom her.

'Thank you, my lord,' she responded graciously. If he thought she needed to be taught manners, she would show him how an English gentlewoman behaved. 'Will you see that Roxana is rewarded for her kindness to me, please?'

'It has already been done.' Suleiman smiled. What a proud beauty she was! Already he was beginning to regret that his father had need of a gift for the Sultan. 'We should leave before the sun begins to set. It can come suddenly in this land, and my father's house is outside the city…at times there are bands of lawless bandits who roam the countryside looking for unwary travellers to rob. We have guards to protect us, but I would not have you frightened by these rogues on your first night in your new country.'

'You are considerate, my lord,' she said and inclined her head. 'But this is not my country—it is merely a place I must live in until I can regain my freedom.'

Suleiman's gaze narrowed, but he refused to be drawn. She was like the hawks that fluttered desperately against the bars of their cage. When she had learned to be obedient to her master's voice, she would learn that she could fly high and free once more—provided that she returned to his hand when called.

Had he really made up his mind to keep her? It was a risk, for the Sultan might learn of Suleiman's treasure and be angry because it had not been given to him. If Suleiman kept this woman for himself, he must find another treasure for the Sultan—but not a woman. It would be an insult to give their lord an inferior treasure. Something else rare and precious must be found to take her place…

He was lost in his thoughts, and turned carelessly aside to speak to one of his men as they emerged into a street that was already beginning to fill with the shadows of night. Until one of his men gave a shout of alarm, he did not realise that Eleanor had dropped her casacche and started to run. What did she think she was doing? Foolish, foolish woman! Had she no idea of the dangers of this city? Alone and at night she would disappear into some stinking hovel and never be seen again.

'Eleanor! Come here at once!'

He began to run as he shouted, sprinting after her down the narrow alley. She was fast, but she could not outrun him and it was not long before he caught up to her. He grabbed her arm, but she struggled and wrenched away again; he lunged at her and brought her down into the dust of the street. She scratched his face, fighting and kicking as she fought to throw him off, but he held her as easily as he would a child, laughing down at her as she raged in frustration.

'You would make a fine Janissary, my little bird—but do not make me hurt you more than I already have.' His eyes gleamed with triumph as he gazed down at her and Eleanor experienced the oddest feeling deep down inside her—it was as if a tide of molten heat had begun to rise up in her. 'Come, defy me no more.'

'You have not hurt me!' she said defiantly, but it was a lie because the fall had hurt her shoulder and his weight had crushed the breath from her. 'I hate you! You are a barbarian and a savage!'

Yet even as she lay beneath him and gazed into his fierce eyes, she felt the pull of his power and charm. He was not what she had named him, for if he had been she would have been treated more harshly. Her breath caught in her throat and she experienced a strange longing—a desire to be held in his arms and comforted.

Comforted by this man! What foolish idea was that? Her wits must be addled!

'It was your own fault,' he said as he pulled her roughly to her feet. 'You were foolish to try and run from me—there are worse things than being in a harem. You would have been taken a dozen times before this night was out and worse…'

'Nothing could be worse!' She flung the words at him. 'You will never take me willingly. No man will take me willingly…I shall fight to my last breath.'

'Then you will suffer,' Suleiman replied, his features harsh and unforgiving. 'If I wanted you…and I do not think you worth the bother…I would soon have you eating from my hand like a dove.'

'Hawks kill doves for their food,' Eleanor retorted. 'And you are a hawk—wild and dangerous.'

Suleiman's anger faded as swiftly as it had flared. He considered her words a compliment rather than the insult she had intended and was amused. He smiled and took her arm, leading her firmly back to where the litter and horses were waiting.

'I'm not going to wear that thing,' Eleanor said as she saw that one of his men had picked up her cloak. 'And I am not going to be carried in that stupid litter.'

'Then you will ride with me,' Suleiman said, a glimmer of amusement in his eyes. 'And you have only yourself to blame for this, Eleanor.'

He picked her up and flung her over his saddle so that she lay face down, then mounted swiftly before she could attempt to wriggle free. His knees were pressed against her, the reins firmly gripped above her head and she knew she could not free herself.

'You devil! Let me down at once! You cannot treat me like this! I am a lady…if you know what that means.'

'Be careful, Eleanor,' he warned, but there was laughter in his voice. 'I may have to beat you if you continue to flaunt my orders. My men are watching and I cannot allow a woman to dictate to me. You will lie there quietly until I decide to let you up—or you will be sorry.'

As he kicked his horse into a sudden canter at the same time as he spoke these words, Eleanor was unable to do anything. She was fuming, but she was also very uncomfortable. How dare he do this to her? She was indignant.

'You are a brute,' she muttered into the blanket that lay beneath his leather saddle. 'I hate you. You are just like those murdering pirates who killed my father. I would have killed them if I could—I will kill you if I get the chance!'

'Speak louder, Eleanor,' Suleiman said. 'I cannot hear you.'

She could hear the mockery in his voice and knew that he was laughing at her. He did not believe she could touch him—because he was too arrogant and sure of himself. He was accustomed to being obeyed instantly, and thought himself all-powerful. Well, just let him wait! One of these days she would make him sorry!

They had left the city walls behind before Suleiman stopped and lifted her into a sitting position, his arm about her waist pressing her to him, as much his prisoner as before. She had seen nothing but a blur of stone walls and dirt streets, keeping her eyes closed most of the time because she had been afraid of falling if she did not concentrate.

'Is that better?' he asked softly against her hair. 'I am sorry, little bird. That was unkind of me—but you made me angry. Besides, I had to make sure you could not get away from me. Constantinople is a dangerous place for a woman—especially one as lovely as you.'

'I know…Roxana told me.' Eleanor was leaning back against him; she had been feeling dizzy when he raised her, but now the unpleasant sensation was beginning to fade and she was oddly comforted by the feel of his strong arms about her as they rode. 'I would not have run…but I was afraid.'

'You told me you were not.'

'How could I not be?' Eleanor turned her head to glance at his face. 'You are going to give me to the Sultan. I cannot bear to be the concubine of a man I do not know—a much older man…'

'Would you prefer to be my concubine?' Suleiman whispered huskily against her hair, his voice so soft and low that she was not sure she had heard him correctly.

'I—I do not—'

What she was about to say was lost, for one of Suleiman's men gave a warning shout and, looking over his shoulder, Suleiman cursed. A small group of black robed men were riding fast towards them.

'Bandits,' he said. 'Hold tight, Eleanor. If you are taken by these men, you will wish you had died…'

Suleiman kicked at his horse's flank and they set off at a tremendous pace across the open countryside. She could see the pinkish stone walls of a great sprawling palace looming up ahead of them in the gathering darkness. Behind her she heard shouting and screaming as Suleiman's men joined battle with the bandits to allow him to reach the palace in safety, and then, as they drew close to the huge wooden gates they opened and a small troupe of horsemen raced out to join the escort guards.

'You are safe now, little one,' Suleiman whispered in her ear. 'You must not be afraid. Do what the women tell you and no harm will come to you. I give you my word.'

'The word of a barbarian?'

'The word of Caliph Bakhar's son,' Suleiman replied. 'You will discover soon that that means more than you might imagine…'

Eleanor waited as he leapt down from his horse's back and lifted her to the ground. Men had come running, and also an older woman dressed all in black. At a command from her master, she took Eleanor's arm and led her away. Eleanor looked back and saw that Suleiman had mounted a fresh horse. He was going back outside the gates to fight with his men. She wanted to stop him, to beg him not to risk his life, but he would not have listened. She was nothing, merely a slave he had bought as a gift for another man.

'What is happening?' she asked the old woman, who was pulling at her arm. 'Is the palace being attacked? Why has Suleiman gone back out there?'

The woman shook her head, clearly not understanding a word she said. Eleanor tried the same question in French, but there was no response.

The woman began to talk to her in what was probably Arabic. Eleanor thought she recognised a few words, but was not certain—though it was obvious that the woman wanted Eleanor to go with her. There was no point in resisting any further for the moment; besides, all the fight had suddenly gone out of her. Oddly, her fears at this moment were more for the man who had brought her here than for herself.

He had told her she would not be harmed if she did as the women told her and somehow she believed him. But what of him? It was obvious that those men who had followed them were armed and dangerous—would Suleiman be killed in the fighting? She suddenly discovered that the thought appalled her.

Nothing must happen to Suleiman Bakhar! He was her only chance of ever being allowed to return to her family. She had called him a savage and a barbarian, but in her heart she knew he was not that—though she did not know what kind of a man he really was. He looked fierce and proud, and undoubtedly he was— but she believed there was a softer side to him. If she could reach that inner core, then there might be a faint hope for her…nothing must happen to him.

'May Allah keep you safe,' she whispered. 'And may God be with you this night.'

Let her prayers be heard by his god or hers. It did not matter at this moment as long as he lived. For, despite her attempts to escape him, and her anger at the way she had been treated, something deep inside her told her that she had been fortunate to be bought by this man…

'Allah be praised!' Caliph Bakhar said when they brought him the news that Suleiman had returned to the palace triumphant with his prisoners, who would be speedily dispatched the next morning at dawn. 'These bandits have been a thorn in my side for too long. My son has done well.'

He had been furious that Suleiman had put his own life at risk, but now that he was safe and the bandits taken, the Caliph's pride knew no bounds. Suleiman was a worthy son!

'Ask my son to eat with me this evening,' Ahmed Bakhar said to the chief eunuch. 'I wish to tell him of my pleasure in his victory.'

Suleiman was emerging from his bath as the request was brought to him. He frowned, wrapping himself in a large white towel and waving the slave away.

'Tell my honoured father that I will come soon,' he said. 'Ask him to forgive me that I do not come at once.'

Another eunuch was waiting to help him dress. He allowed the creature to help him on with a simple white tunic and trousers. He would put on his costly robes when he went to his father's apartments—but for the moment he must visit the injured. His men had fought bravely against the bandits and one had died. Suleiman must make arrangements for him to be given a funeral worthy of a hero, and for recompense to be sent to his family.

He would have liked to send for Eleanor this evening, to talk to her—for he understood how strange it must be for a Western woman to suddenly find herself cast into an alien world. His mother had spoken to him of her own feelings when she first entered his father's harem, and although she had been very different from Eleanor—a quietly spoken, gentle woman—she had feared what she did not understand.

'I had been told that all Turks were savages,' she had said to her son as they sat talking together during their privileged afternoons. 'I was afraid that my new master would rape and beat me—but your father was kind and considerate and very soon I came to love him.'

Before he went to see his men, he must make sure that Eleanor was being treated as a woman of her class was entitled to be, even in a harem. She ought to have her own rooms and a servant to wait on her. He believed there was an Englishwoman in the palace…an old crone who had long since been put to work in the kitchens. She must be fetched and told to wait on her new mistress, and the older women must take care of Eleanor…prepare her for her new life.

He was not yet sure what her new life was to be. If she was not to be given to the Sultan he must find another gift…something rare and unusual that would pacify their illustrious master. For the moment he had other things on his mind. She would come to no harm within the palace—and he would have her sent for when he was ready to decide what to do with her.

Eleanor looked round the large chamber, which was the main one used by the harem for relaxing, talking and, perhaps, in the case of those concubines who did not have their own rooms, sleeping. There were divans covered in silks and satins, and piled with cushions for taking one's ease, also little tables on which were placed what looked like dishes of nuts and sweetmeats, fountains that played into small pools and various chests or cabinets. One girl was strumming on a musical instrument, the music strange and sounding off key to Eleanor.

The women gathered in small groups, talking, whispering and looking at her curiously. None of them had as yet approached her though she had been sitting on a cushion since the old woman had brought her here and then vanished.

What was she supposed to do? After the terror of her capture and the drama of that ride to the palace, it all felt rather like an anti-climax, simply sitting here watching several lovely women idle the hours away. One girl was brushing the hair of another and braiding it with flowers or ribbons, others were painting their toenails with some kind of a dye—and one was having her body painted with a pattern in some black stuff.

At the far end of the room, Eleanor could see there was a door leading out to what looked like pleasant gardens. Was she allowed to go out there? She had certainly had enough of sitting here by herself. Oh, well, if it was forbidden, someone would stop her. She got up and wandered towards the door, thinking that the floors of mosaic tiling were very beautiful, as were some of the pierced screens that were painted in bright colours of red, blue and gold.

No one shouted at her to stop, so she went out into the garden. It was evening now and quite dark, but there were lanterns hanging amongst the trees and she was able to find her way along a winding path towards the sound of water. She found a stone seat by a pretty pool and sat down, staring into the darkness. Was she really going to be forced to spend the rest of her life in a place like this? If she were reduced to living the way the other women did, she would go mad.

Tears came to her eyes as she thought of her father and brother, and the evenings they had spent playing games of skill together. Her poor father! Her throat closed with emotion. How could she bear to live without the two people she loved most in the world?

Where was Richard? She had not seen him since they were both captured and did not even know if he were still alive. His fate was probably far worse than hers! She thought that he might have been tortured or beaten. Poor, poor Richard! She prayed that he was not in pain or desperately afraid. He was only a youth, and he would have had no chance against his captors. Her head went up as she renewed her vow not to give way to self-pity or despair. She would fight to survive and somehow she would win her freedom one day.

'Are you there, my lady?'

The sound of a woman's voice speaking to her in English brought her head up. How could that be? The old woman that had first taken charge of Eleanor and then abandoned her had not understood when she had tried to talk to her.

'Who are you? Please come forward.'

A woman stepped out of the shadows and approached diffidently. She was obviously quite old, her face lined and her hair deeply streaked with grey.

'I am Morna, my lady. I came to the palace many years ago as a gift to the Caliph, but he was never interested in me as one of his concubines because I was not beautiful. I was sent to the kitchens and I have worked there ever since.'

'Morna?' Eleanor looked at her. 'I do not think I have ever heard that name before—it is pretty.'

'My mother was English, but my father came from the hills of Wales,' Morna replied. 'I think it is an ancient Celtic name, though I cannot be sure.' She smiled at Eleanor. 'I am sorry Shorah deserted you earlier. I do not think she knew what to do with you, so she left you with the other concubines—and they ignored you because they were not sure why you were there either. It is dangerous to form relationships in the harem unless you know the status of those you befriend.'

'Shorah—that is the old woman who took charge of me? I think she could not understand what I said to her.'

'No, she understands only her native tongue,' Morna replied. 'When I was told you were here I was not sure I would remember how to speak English. It is so long since I have used our language—but as you see, it came back to me.'

'Have you been here many years?'

'Oh, yes, much of my life has been spent in this palace. But I am fortunate. I am not important, merely a servant—so I am allowed to come and go as I please. I visit the market to buy food and trinkets for the women sometimes. They repay me by giving me some of their food—so I live very well.'

'Can you help me to leave the palace?' Eleanor asked eagerly. 'Is there any way I could escape?'

'They would kill us both if you tried to leave,' Morna told her gravely. 'It seems that you have caught the eye of the Caliph's son. You are to be given your own rooms and I am to wait upon you—as befits a lady of your rank.'

'What does that mean?' Eleanor asked. 'Am I to stay here, then? I thought…' She let the words die unspoken. Roxana had told her she would be lucky if Suleiman Bakhar kept her for himself, and she was beginning to believe that that might be the case. Better a young, intelligent master who spoke her tongue and might just be persuaded to let her go home, than the Sultan who would scarcely notice her amongst his other women. 'No, it does not matter. You could not know what is in *his* mind. Please take me to my rooms. I am tired and I should like to sleep now.'

'Would you like me to bring you food from the kitchens?' Morna asked, sounding eager. 'Surely you are hungry, my lady?'

Eleanor was about to reply that she had eaten earlier and was not hungry, but she realised that Morna might not get enough to eat and was hoping that some of her mistress's food might be left for her.

'Yes, bring me something,' she said. 'You can share it with me.'

'Thank you, my lady. You are generous.'

Eleanor nodded, but did not reply. She supposed there were probably hundreds of servants in this vast palace, which sprawled over a large area of land and consisted of a mass of different buildings. Many of the slaves were probably forced to live on the scraps left by others. The world was a cruel place, especially for slaves, and she was angry that people like the Caliph and his arrogant son believed they had the right to dispose of the lives of others as they chose.

'Where is the Caliph's son?' she asked. 'Has he returned to the palace?'

'Oh, yes, some time ago,' Morna replied. 'It is by his order that you have been given your own rooms.'

'He has not asked for me?'

'Our master's son has not chosen a woman this night,' Morna replied. 'They say he is with the physicians who tend the wounded—and that he has spoken to the family of the man who died. The Janissaries are all Suleiman Bakhar's friends. He trains with them every day. Sometimes there is much sport in the courtyard, and you may be allowed to watch him wrestling or fighting with the others if you are lucky.'

Eleanor was astonished. 'Why should I wish to watch that barbarian at sport?'

'Hush!' Morna glanced over her shoulder nervously. 'You should not say such things—ears may be listening. We are always watched in the harem. There are spies everywhere. Fatima will have heard that you have arrived by now and she will not be pleased that you have been given your own apartments.'

'Who is Fatima?'

'She is the lord Suleiman's favourite. She rules the harem and all the other women are afraid of her.'

'Why—what harm can she do them?'

'Many unpleasant things can happen in this place,' Morna warned. 'Fatima is jealous of any woman she thinks might take her place as Suleiman's chief concubine. She is hoping he will take her as his wife— but she has not yet given him a child, and they say he will not marry her unless she does.'

'I have no wish to lie in Suleiman Bakhar's bed,' Eleanor said. 'Besides, the other women will not understand what we say if we speak in English—will they?'

'Most will not,' Morna agreed, 'but there are those who do—some of the eunuchs understand English, French or Spanish as well as many other languages. It is the eunuchs who spy on the harem all the time. Some do it from idle curiosity, some to discover what they can for their masters—but others have their own reasons.'

'What do you mean?' Eleanor looked at her curiously. 'They…cannot desire a woman for themself, can they?'

'No—not a true eunuch,' Morna replied in a whisper. 'But sometimes…no, I dare not say. It is forbidden and would cause trouble if it were discovered.'

Eleanor saw that the old woman was frightened and did not press her further, though she thought Morna must be hinting that the women were not as protected as their master imagined. It was clear that there were many mysteries and intrigues in the harem, and that life there was not quite as it had seemed as she'd watched the women amusing themselves earlier

Morna had led her to a room that was slightly apart from the main one that she had seen earlier. There were actually three small interconnecting rooms. One had a little pool for bathing and a place for relieving the bodily functions, one for sleeping (with a couch for her servant at the foot of her own divan) and one for sitting. All of them were luxuriously tiled and hung with silken drapes of pink and silver. There were cabinets of dark wood inlaid with silver, mother of pearl and small semi-precious stones, also stools and little tables.

'The rooms are very nice,' Eleanor said. 'At least I shall be able to be private sometimes—but what am I supposed to do? What are my duties, Morna? Am I to be given no work—no occupation?'

'The ladies of the harem are here to please their master,' Morna replied. 'You simply amuse yourself until you are called to the bedchamber and then...well, then you do as you are told, and smile if you do not wish to be beaten.'

A little shudder went through Eleanor. 'That is truly a savage custom! I refuse to obey the whim of a man simply because he paid another man money for me.'

Morna shook her head at her sadly. 'You will learn soon enough,' she said. 'I shall fetch food, my lady. You should eat and rest—for tomorrow you will meet the important women of the harem, and they will begin to school you for those duties you say you will not accept...'

Eleanor stared in frustration as the servant left her. She could not stay here! She would die of boredom. How could all those women out there be content to sit around and wait patiently until their master decided to send for them—and what if he never did?

What if she never saw Suleiman again? She would not be able to win her freedom unless she could persuade him to ransom her...

* * *

Fatima glared at the woman who had brought her the information that the new arrival had been given rooms of her own. She gave a little scream of rage and struck Shorah across the face, leaving a nasty red mark.

'I told you to leave her with the other concubines. I gave orders that she was to be ignored!'

'It was the order of Suleiman Bakhar himself,' Shorah replied, her head bowed before the favourite, hiding the gleam of resentment in her eyes. 'I had nothing to do with it, mistress.'

Fatima swore beneath her breath. Word had been brought to her that Suleiman had gone to the city to see a beautiful woman and that he had paid a fabulous price for her—but she had believed the woman was to be a gift for the Sultan. Now it looked as though Suleiman might be planning to keep her for himself. He might even take her as his wife…and that was a position Fatima wanted for herself. As a concubine she could be sold or given away to another man, but as the lord Suleiman's wife she would be safe and ruler of the harem.

'Is she beautiful?' she demanded suddenly of the old woman. 'This new woman—more beautiful than me?'

'No one could be more beautiful than you, mistress.'

Fatima nodded. She knew that her dark hair was shiny from all the oils rubbed into it, and her skin was soft and smooth to the touch, exuding a heavy perfume that was guaranteed to drive men wild. And her lord had shown himself no different from others in that respect. She spent most of her time bathing and being prepared for the moment she would be sent for—but Suleiman had not sent for her that evening.

It was most unusual. He always sent for a woman after he had won one of his games of skill—and he was always in a good mood at these times—but he had not sent for Fatima that night. Her one consolation was that he had not sent for the new woman either, choosing to waste his time in comforting the family of the man who had died, and in visiting the wounded.

Yet she feared this woman she had not yet seen. It was said that she was an English gentlewoman—and therefore more dangerous than any of the other concubines. Suleiman's mother had been English, and Fatima knew that he had fond memories of his childhood.

Suleiman was hard to fathom. When he fought with the Janissaries, Fatima understood the excitement and his feelings of triumph when he won—and she knew that he was a skilled and passionate lover when he chose. However, he often spent his evenings talking, either with his teacher or his friends…they spoke of strange, intricate matters that Fatima would have found boring had she been allowed to listen. She was not, of course. Women were for pleasure, and when Suleiman sent for her she knew how to please him…except that he had not seemed pleased on the last few occasions he had sent for her.

Indeed, she had felt that he did not really want her, and that he would have preferred to be talking with his teacher. She had been glad when she learned the teacher had gone away, thinking that Suleiman would want her more often. Instead he had chosen to invite his friends from the Janissaries to eat and drink with him, and, though, he ordered the dancing girls to perform and he allowed his friends to take their pick of them, he had not sent for Fatima.

She had feared that her lord might have heard whispers concerning her and yet that could not be—he could suspect nothing, for her creature would have told her.

Fatima knew everything that went on in Suleiman's private apartments, because she held one of the eunuchs in the palm of her hand. He was her dog, less than dirt to her because he was not a proper man—but he was also useful. She held the power of life and death over him, could expose him as a traitor to his master if she chose—and so he reported everything that went on to Fatima.

She would soon know what Suleiman intended for his new woman—and she would make her own plans accordingly.

Chapter Four

Eleanor was roused by the sound of a disturbance. She had been dreaming happily of a certain misty morning in England, when she had ridden out with her father, and was startled by the noise of screeching voices. Waking suddenly to the unfamiliar surroundings, she had wondered where on earth she was. As realisation dawned on her she was swamped with a feeling of intense unhappiness; then, before she could gather her thoughts, a very beautiful, dark-haired woman, dressed in a rich red tunic and pants embroidered heavily with silver and pearls, rushed into the bedroom.

'How dare you tell your servant to keep me out?' she demanded in excellent French. 'No one tells me I may not enter anywhere within the harem!'

Eleanor stared at her as the mists of sleep began to clear, and she remembered what Morna had told her the previous night. This must obviously be Fatima, Suleiman Bakhar's favourite concubine—and she was clearly in a temper.

'I believe you would not appreciate a visit from me without some warning?' Eleanor replied in the same

language Fatima had used. She lifted her head proudly
and assumed the haughtiest manner she could. 'While
you are always welcome in my apartments, Fatima,
politeness shows good breeding.'

Fatima's mouth opened in surprise. No one addressed her in such a manner! Had they dared, she
would have ordered Abu to flog them. For a moment
she could not speak, then her dark brown eyes narrowed to suspicious splits, and she was tempted to
order this woman beaten, but caution held her back.
Suleiman had only recently bought her, and he might
notice if her skin were accidentally marked.

'Who are you?' she demanded imperiously. 'And
why are you here?'

'Because I was brought here much against my will,'
Eleanor said, remaining calm despite her instant dislike of the other woman, 'I have no wish to be in this
place and would leave this minute if I could. Believe
me, I am no threat to you, Fatima—nor would I wish
to be. My only desire is to be returned to my home. I
am the daughter of an English baronet, and my family
is wealthy—they will be searching for me even now.'

Fatima's dark eyes narrowed in suspicion, her
lovely face still reflecting sullen anger. 'How do you
know who I am?'

'I have been told of Suleiman Bakhar's beautiful
favourite,' Eleanor said. 'Who else would you be?'

Fatima nodded. Put that way, it sounded like a compliment. She knew that the other women were afraid
of her—and that the servant woman Morna was firmly
on this upstart's side. Before long, the women of the
harem would start to take sides, especially now that
this Englishwoman had been given special status.
They would believe that Fatima had begun to lose

Suleiman's favour, and once that happened they would not hesitate to follow a new leader. That could be dangerous for Fatima, for she had enemies who would use any chance to strike at her. Perhaps it would be wiser to get to know this woman better.

'Tell your servant not to bar my way in future—but do not punish her. She will be no use to you if she cannot work.' Fatima's expression changed subtly. 'I do not like to be thwarted, but if you truly mean that you do not wish to become Suleiman's favourite, we may be friends. You are more my equal than any of the other women here. I am the daughter of a French nobleman and an Arab dancing girl. Until my father was lost at sea we lived in a beautiful villa in Algiers, then my mother was cast out and she sold herself to a master so that we could live. I was trained all my life to give pleasure to the man who would one day own me…that is why Suleiman sends always for me. I am the only one who really knows how to please him. He will never put me aside for another.'

'I am very glad to hear it,' Eleanor said immediately. 'I have no wish to be bad friends with you, Fatima. Nor do I wish to be sent for in the way you speak of. Indeed, if you could help me to escape, I would leave the harem.'

'That is impossible,' Fatima said and frowned. 'We can none of us leave here unless Suleiman grants us freedom.'

'Does that ever happen?'

'Sometimes…' Fatima gave her a long hard look. 'The Caliph would have freed Suleiman's mother after she gave him a son, but she preferred to stay here and became his favourite wife. They say he still mourns her.'

'Tell me more about her, please?'

'Why do you want to know?' Fatima's mood altered once more. She would tell this woman nothing that might help her to secure Suleiman's favour. 'I have no time to talk with you. I came only to make sure you understood your place here…'

Eleanor watched as the other woman left the room abruptly. It was clear that Fatima still did not trust her; she probably imagined Eleanor was scheming to become Suleiman's wife.

'Forgive me,' Morna said as she came in after the favourite had left. 'I could not stop her bursting in on you. I told her you were sleeping, but she would not listen to me.'

'It doesn't matter,' Eleanor replied. 'Do not risk her temper again, Morna. Just ask her to wait one moment while you wake me—but it was unusual for me to sleep so deeply. What time is it? It feels as if half the day has gone.'

'You were exhausted,' Morna replied. 'The refreshing drink you enjoyed last night was a tisane I made to help you pass a peaceful night. I knew that you needed rest or you might have lain awake all night thinking and weeping.'

'That was a kind thought,' Eleanor said, 'but do not give me such a drink again unless I request it.'

Eleanor had been sitting up against a pile of silk cushions, but now she put her feet to the floor, a feeling of hope and determination surging through her. She had been at the edge of despair when Fatima broke in on her so rudely, but for some reason the other woman had aroused her fighting instincts. She was not going to be put down by Fatima or anyone else! Nor did she wish to be lulled into a false sense of security by drugging drinks designed to dull her senses. She did not wish to be here and she would escape or win her freedom some other way if she could, but until then she would set herself to making what she could of her life.

'Is it possible to have writing materials brought to me, Morna?'

'Perhaps…but you would not be allowed to send a letter to anyone, my lady.'

'It is not for writing a letter,' Eleanor said. 'I must have something to occupy my mind or I shall go mad. I thought that perhaps you would teach me the language and customs you have learned. I could write the words down and practise them when I am alone.'

'I could bring you a slate and marker,' Morna said. 'We have them in the kitchens for noting down what is needed from the markets—but pen and paper would have to be authorised by the eunuchs.'

'And how do we ask them for things?'

'Fatima is usually the one to approach,' Morna said. 'But you have been given rooms and a servant of your own…you might be given other things if you ask.'

'Bring the slate for the moment,' Eleanor said. 'We can begin my lessons after I have bathed and eaten. What shall I wear? Surely I do not need all the garments I was made to wear yesterday?'

'Karin brought clothes for you earlier,' Morna said. 'She is the most important woman after Fatima…but much older. If Suleiman's mother still lived, she would rule over his harem until he took a chief wife, but Karin is one of the Caliph's older wives. She was visiting with relatives yesterday, but you will meet her later today. She will explain many things to you, much better than I could, my lady.'

'Very well.' Eleanor smiled at her. 'It was very fortunate for me that you were here, Morna. At least I feel that I have one friend in the palace—one person that I may trust.'

'I am happy to be your servant, my lady.'

'I would rather that we were friends,' Eleanor said and smiled. 'We must try to help each other, Morna. If there is something I can do for you—you must tell me.'

'I am always hungry,' the old woman replied. 'All I ask these days is food to eat and somewhere to sleep. To serve you, my lady, is much easier than the work I was put to in the kitchens.'

Eleanor nodded. 'Then I shall see that you share my food—and if ever I am able to leave here, I shall try to take you with me.'

'No, I do not wish to leave,' Morna replied. 'I have no life other than here. I am content to remain in the Caliph's household until I die…there is nowhere for me to go now. I am too old. I should be forced to beg on the streets for my food.'

Eleanor's eyes stung with tears as she turned away. How sad that this woman's life had been wasted in such a terrible way. Morna's hopelessness made Eleanor even more determined that whatever was forced upon her, she would not let herself become enslaved…

Suleiman spent the morning exercising with the Janissaries. After he had bathed and received a brisk massage from one of the eunuchs, he ate sparingly of dates and rice mixed with spiced lamb, then drank several cups of the rich dark coffee he enjoyed. The afternoon stretched emptily before him, and he felt the loss of his old teacher keenly. There must be other clever men, with whom he could share a pleasant afternoon, but Saidi Kasim had understood him so well, and they had been friends. There were few within the palace that Suleiman could truly call his friends—he could not even be sure of the loyalty of his half-brothers Bayezid and Hasan, for there was always rivalry between the sons of important men.

Suleiman's thoughts turned towards the woman he had brought to the palace the previous evening. She would have spent the morning with Karin, being taught how to behave in the harem, and what to expect of her new life. It was too soon to send for her if he expected her to please him as the other women did—and yet he wanted to speak with her.

All at once, Suleiman realised that he did not want her to be the same as the other women. He would send for her now and talk to her himself, explain that he would like to know her better before she became one of his concubines...no, perhaps his wife.

Suleiman must marry soon and give his father the grandsons the Caliph longed for, and Eleanor was the only woman he had so far found that he deemed fit to be the mother of those sons. She had spirit and intelligence, and she would surely accept her fate if it were properly explained to her. He would tell her that she was to be honoured above all the other women, and that he would give her time to adjust to her new life. She had accused him of being a barbarian, but he would show her that she was wrong.

He was pleased with himself as he summoned the eunuch and told him to send for Eleanor.

'She is to be brought to me at once,' he ordered.

'There is to be no ritual of the bath—no special pampering.'

The eunuch nodded and went away to execute his master's orders, which were most unusual. Indeed, no woman had ever been sent for in such a manner. Suleiman always made his choice early in the afternoon and the woman was prepared for him in the time-honoured way—to send for her so abruptly must mean that she was to be punished. Which would please Fatima, of course.

A little smile touched Abu's mouth. It would not suit him if Fatima were to be displaced by this new woman. Fatima was a bad-tempered, spoiled cat—but she suited Abu. She believed she held the power, and he allowed her to dictate to him while she kept his secrets. It was an arrangement that gave something to them both—and placed both in equal danger. For if Suleiman ever guessed what sometimes took place in the secret places of his father's palace, both Fatima and Abu would be put to death.

So Abu would help Fatima to overcome the challenge of this new woman—and Suleiman had unwittingly helped them by showing his displeasure in this way.

Eleanor was fascinated as she listened to Karin talk of life in her country, telling her of simple family life and the way the common folk lived, which was very different from the noble lords in their rich palaces.

The older woman had come to her after she had bathed, taking her into a secluded corner of the gardens so that they could talk in private. Speaking in French, which was the foreign language spoken most often in the harem, she had told Eleanor a little of the history of the Turkish Sultans and their Sultanas, and found her an apt pupil.

'I have been told that you speak three languages,' she said in her soft, musical voice. 'And that you may understand a little Arabic.'

'I can read it a little,' Eleanor said. 'But I do not understand the language the other women speak…'

'That is because they have so many different tongues and dialects and they have found their own way to communicate. The perfection of pure Arabic is only found in the written form, and that is what you have learned—but here you will soon begin to understand what is being said to you.'

'I have asked Morna to bring writing materials so that I can write down the words and learn them when I am alone.'

'But you must not spend all your time alone,' the older woman told her. 'You should learn to enjoy the pleasures offered you in this place, Eleanor. There are many more than you might imagine. Once you learn to relax you will enjoy having sweet oils massaged into your skin, and it is pleasant to bathe in the pools—there are large pools both in the garden and inside the palace. Also you may have music lessons and you may learn to dance if you choose; it is good exercise and a skill that may be helpful to you. The other women will be friendly towards you after I have spoken to them, and you may pass your time in playing games or helping each other to braid your hair.'

'But what of my mind?' Eleanor replied. 'I have been used to study—is it possible for me to have books?'

Karin frowned. 'I am not sure if this would be permitted. I cannot grant you such a favour, Eleanor—

you must wait until you are sent for—' She broke off
as she saw the eunuch striding purposefully towards
them. 'Perhaps you will not have to wait so very
long…'

She rose to her feet as the eunuch approached. 'You
wish to speak with me, Abu?'

'The woman is to come with me!'

'Now?' Karin was startled. This was unheard of!
Suleiman never sent such a message—unless he was
very displeased. He must be angry with Eleanor for
some reason. 'Where are you taking her? Is she to be
punished?'

'That is for Suleiman Bakhar to decide—he has sent
for her.'

Abu grasped Eleanor's arm, pulling her roughly to
her feet. She stared at him haughtily as she felt his
fingers dig cruelly into her arm. Something in his eyes
sent shivers through her and she knew that this man
liked to punish others.

'How dare you?' she said. 'Take your hand from
me, sir.'

Abu looked into her eyes, and for a moment he felt
compelled to obey her, and then he recalled
Suleiman's orders. 'You are to come with me at once!'

'Unless you take your hand from my arm, you will
have to drag me there.'

'Disobey me, woman, and it will be the worse for
you!'

'Go with him, Eleanor,' Karin told her, looking anxious. 'Let go of her arm, Abu. It is not necessary. She
will not try to run away—where could she go?
Besides, if she resists you, you may bruise her skin,
and that would not please your master.'

Abu's eyes narrowed. Most of the women obeyed

him instantly. Indeed, they were all afraid of him—
afraid of his power—but Karin was not under his ju-
risdiction, and he could not threaten her. Besides, he
was not absolutely sure that this Englishwoman was
to be punished.

He glared at Eleanor, but let her arm go. 'You are
to come at once. My master wishes to see you now.'

'He wishes to talk with you, Eleanor,' Karin said,
seeking to reassure her. 'You have not been prepared
for him, nor received instruction—so there will be
nothing else required of you today.'

Eleanor looked at the older woman and nodded, understanding what she was telling her. She was not to
be taken to Suleiman's bed that afternoon. Perhaps he
had decided to tell her what he intended to do with
her—he might even have thought over what she had
said to him the previous day and was perhaps prepared
to sell her to her family. She lifted her head proudly
as hope flowed anew.

'Very well, you may lead me to Suleiman Bakhar.'

Abu thought of the soft whips he used so skilfully
that they left barely a mark on the skin of his victims,
and of how much he would like to teach this woman
a lesson she would not soon forget. He had been
robbed of the pleasures that were his right as a man
by the surgeon's knife, but he gained much pleasure
in seeing women on their knees begging for mercy.
One night he and Fatima would pay this haughty bitch
a little visit...

Eleanor was aware of evil in the man who walked
so softly just ahead of her, leading the way through
the women's apartments to an even larger and more
luxurious chamber which formed part of the harem,
but was used by Suleiman and not entered by the

women unless invited. This was furnished much as the harem, with richly patterned tiles on walls, floors and some ceilings, but also contained many items, which she knew had come from other lands. She was not allowed to linger and examine the curious items she saw placed in alcoves and on little tables, but she believed that some of them were scientific instruments for the study of astrology, and there were also several rather beautiful clocks.

Who used the astrological instruments? She had no time to wonder for they continued through this apartment into another, which was clearly used for sitting with soft cushions and divans placed here and there on gleaming marble floors. Her attention was drawn to the man who occupied the largest divan; he seemed to be interested in some object he was holding, which as they drew closer she saw was what appeared to be a fabulous clock. She thought it was made of gold and saw that it was shaped like a polygon, with intricate workings clearly visible at the top. Quite fascinating!

'On your knees, woman!' Abu hissed.

'No!' Suleiman countermanded the order instantly. 'You may remain standing, my lady.' He stood up and held out his hand to her. 'Come, sit with me.'

Suleiman drew her down to the divan beside him and, seeing that the object he had been looking at as she entered had caught her interest, smiled. 'It is a clock, you see,' he said. 'Made by the great French clockmaker Pierre de Fobis—it strikes the hour...'

'It is beautiful,' Eleanor said, marvelling at the beauty of the clock. 'Is the case of gold?'

'Yes—but it is the way the running mechanisms are arranged one over the other so intricately that is so fascinating. Do you see?'

She looked closer as he demonstrated the strike to her and nodded, thrilled by its wonders. 'It is truly magnificent, my lord. My father had a beautiful German clock at home in his study. Its case was of ebony, jasper, lapis lazuli and silver gilt—but the works were hidden and the clock was not as fascinating as this one. I have never seen anything to equal this. It must be very valuable? I noticed others as we came, and I think that you have quite a collection of them.'

Suleiman nodded, then, looking up, he saw that Abu was still standing there as though waiting for something, and he waved his hand impatiently to dismiss him.

'Do you think this clock a gift worthy of a Sultan?' he asked Eleanor when they were alone. 'I must give our master something rare and fine instead of the gift I had planned for him. To give him less than the best would be an insult—is this fine enough, do you think?'

'It is a gift any prince would appreciate,' Eleanor replied honestly. 'Such things are usually only found at the courts of rich and powerful rulers. I think it extremely fine and it must be rare. I dare say there is not such another anywhere in Christendom—or the Ottoman Empire either. You have a unique treasure, my lord.'

Suleiman nodded, his eyes moving over her with approval. She was as intelligent, as he had thought her at the start. The clock was the rarest of his own collection and he had prized it greatly—but he could offer nothing less to the Sultan since he had decided that he could not bring himself to part with Eleanor.

'Then it shall be given to him,' Suleiman said, a wicked gleam in his eyes. 'Which brings me to you—

what shall I do with you, my lady? I fear you are too wilful and disobedient to make a gift for the Sultan, which means that I have paid a great deal too much for you.'

'Ransom me to my family,' she replied eagerly. She had seen the gleam but missed its significance, for she did not yet know him. 'I should be so grateful to you, my lord. I know they would pay much for my safe return.'

'But I have no need of money,' Suleiman pointed out. He was enjoying himself toying with her, watching the emotions play across her expressive face. She was beautiful, but there was much more to her, and he wanted to know all. 'My father is very rich and I shall one day inherit all that is his...so what can your family offer me?'

'My father had many rare books at home in England...' Suleiman dismissed the offer with a dismissive shrug. 'He has other treasures...and I have this...' Eleanor took the little trinket she wore about her neck, which had been hidden under her clothes, and handed it to him. 'It has a little stopper, my lord—open it and see what it contains.'

Suleiman stared at the gold trinket suspiciously, almost as though he imagined it might contain poison, she thought, then he removed the stopper and took out the tiny manuscript inside. He looked at it in silence for several minutes.

'What is this? And why do you carry it with you?' He looked at her with interest. 'Do you know what is written here?'

'Yes, my lord. It is a part of the Qur'an, and the work seems to have been executed by a Christian Abbot. It was my father's and he gave it to me for safe keeping before we left Italy,' Eleanor replied. 'It is believed to be part of the treasure of the Abbey of the Far Cross and was found buried on my father's land in Cyprus. There may be more…and I believe it to be very rare.'

'I have heard of this,' Suleiman said and frowned. He replaced the tiny manuscript in its holder and returned it to her. 'The story escapes me for the moment. Kasim told me once of the Abbot of the Far Cross, but I cannot call his words to mind for the present.'

'The Abbey was burned to the ground by Saracens,' Eleanor replied, 'and the treasure stolen, but I do not know any more of the legend. My father was researching it…' She gave a little sob of grief and Suleiman's gaze narrowed.

'What happened to him?'

'He was killed when the ship was attacked.' She raised her head, her eyes bright with the tears she refused to shed before him. 'He was trying to defend me.'

'Ah…I see,' he said and nodded, understanding the terrible grief in her face. He would feel thus if his own father were killed before his eyes. 'And you were fond of your father.'

'Yes. I loved him very much—and my brother. I do not know what happened to Richard…'

'You grieve for your loved ones,' Suleiman said. 'I understand, my lady. It is hard for you—to come to a world that must seem alien to you after losing all that was dear. You thought us all like the Corsairs who attacked your ship, but I hope that you have begun to see that this is not the case?'

Eleanor was silent for a moment, then she nodded. 'I was wrong to call you a barbarian,' she said, 'but your ways are strange to me. I find it very wrong that one man should keep another as his slave. And why must you keep your women imprisoned?'

'Are your customs so very different?' Suleiman's brows arched. 'Your servants are treated no better than our slaves. We do not pay them money for their service, but they are housed and fed as well as your servants—perhaps better. Those who deserve it can rise to positions of importance—and we have a system by which men who convert to Islam can become persons of wealth and standing, no matter what their beginnings.'

'The Devishirme system? Yes, my father told me of it,' Eleanor replied. 'But they are still bound to a master in most cases—and women are not given the same privileges.'

'Women cannot expect to live as men,' Suleiman said and frowned at her. 'But they are protected and cared for and most are happy to live within the harem. Some become influential in their own right. My mother was one such woman. My father always asked her advice on anything that troubled him. She was granted many privileges and might have returned to her homeland had she wished.'

'Then she was fortunate,' Eleanor replied, a flash of anger in her eyes. 'But what of those who are never allowed to leave the harem? What are they supposed to do with themselves? What am I supposed to do? I shall die of boredom if I am forced to live as the others do, idling the hours away in vain pursuits. I need to be able to study…to use my mind…to think for myself.'

Suleiman nodded and smiled. 'These things may be arranged in time. Would you like to see my scientific instruments, my lady? I think they might interest you—and I have many ancient manuscripts, which we might study together if they please you.'

'They would interest me very much,' Eleanor said, caught by his promises despite herself. 'But will you not consider returning me to my family, my lord?'

'That is out of the question. I wish to hear no more of it.' He frowned at her, his mood of indulgence gone. 'Have you listened to nothing I have said to you? I have been trying to show you that you have nothing to fear here—that if you please me, I may choose to honour you as my mother was honoured.'

Eleanor's head went up, her eyes proud as she looked at him. 'No matter what honour you choose to give me, I should still belong to you,' she said. 'I should be no different from your other women—a slave and kept here in the palace against my will. I can never consent to such an arrangement, my lord.'

'If you had married in your own world you would have belonged to your husband. A woman is no freer in your country than here,' Suleiman said, a glint of temper in his dark eyes. Why would she not listen to what he was saying? Did she still scorn him as the savage she had named him? 'Where is the difference?'

'My father would never have forced me to marry,' Eleanor replied, tears in her lovely eyes. 'I would only have done so if I loved—and in love a man does not own, or demand, he gives himself. The woman also gives of her own free will. Only in this manner can true happiness be achieved by either.'

'And how do you know this?' He looked at her hard, his mouth drawn into a thin line. 'Have you known love—the love between a man and his woman?'

Eleanor blushed as she saw the accusation in his eyes. 'If you are asking if I have known a man in...*that* way, the answer is no. I am insulted that you should need to ask! I know because I have observed others—and seen unhappy marriages, some amongst my own friends and relations.'

'Do not lie to me. I can have the women examine you to discover the truth. It will go hard with you if I learn that you have deceived me!'

She could see that he was angry, and though tempted to lie in the hope that he would no longer want to keep her, something held her back. She did not want him to think her a loose woman.

'I swear by my father's love and all that I hold sacred that I have not.'

'If I thought...I would send you to the slave market,' Suleiman said harshly. 'But, no, I believe you...you would not be so foolish as to defy me. You know that I could have you punished. I still might. If you defy me too often I might decide to have you disciplined, to teach you to respect your master.'

'You will not break my spirit that way!'

The sudden defiance in her eyes made him smile inwardly. 'Oh, I think I could find a way to break you if I chose, Eleanor. Do not tempt me, woman—or I might have you whipped. Did you know that there are whips made of leather so soft that they can inflict terrible pain without breaking the skin?'

Eleanor flinched as she saw the way his eyes had suddenly become as cruel and bright as a hawk's about to pounce on its prey. He was an intelligent man, perhaps even clever, but there *was* a streak of savagery in his character. It was a part of his birthright, and though he had learned discipline and respect for others, something warned her that it might be possible to push him too far.

'If you want me to beg you not to punish me, my lord, I shall not. I cannot pretend to feel other than I do. As yet, I have been shown only generosity at your hands. I know this—even though I cannot but resent the fact that you bought me as if I were a horse.'

'Not as if you were a horse,' he said and laughed deep in his throat. There was such fire in her! She burned him while she amused him—and he had not been amused this much in an age. 'I would never pay so much for a horse, my lady—however noble its breed.'

Eleanor felt the power of his smile, and it made her gasp. She felt that she was being mesmerised by something in those dark eyes as he leaned towards her. She could smell the cleanliness of his body, so different from the smells that attached to many men of her own race, and another more subtle perfume she could not name. The combination was intoxicating!

She was powerless to move as his eyes held hers in a compelling gaze, her throat catching with some strange emotion. His mouth touched hers softly and she felt herself swaying towards him, as if wanting his kiss to deepen and become something more, but she suddenly pulled herself back sharply, refusing to give into the wicked urgings of her sinful body. He would bend her to his will and then discard her.

'No! You shall not bewitch me, sir! I do not know what arts you would employ, but I shall not succumb to them.'

Suleiman's mouth twitched at the corners, releasing her as if her defiance amused him—and his amusement made her temper flare. Did he think himself too powerful to be resisted? She leapt to her feet, facing him defiantly.

'Please send me back to the harem—or to the kitchens. Since I am not to be returned to my family, I would prefer to work in the kitchens as Morna does.'

Suleiman's gaze narrowed. 'You do not know of what you speak, foolish woman. Is it that you would prefer to bed with one of the Janissaries? You would not long remain untouched in the kitchens—ask Morna if you do not believe me.'

'I wish only to be free!'

'My patience wears thin,' he replied. 'I have told you that you are to be honoured in a very special way—and yet you still refuse to be pacified. I could have you punished, woman. Shall I summon Abu?'

'Is that the eunuch who brought me here?' Eleanor shivered. 'I do not like him—he is evil.'

'What do you mean?' Her words echoed a feeling long held by Suleiman without truly knowing why. 'Explain yourself.'

'I—I do not know,' she confessed. 'It is only an intuition—but I sense that he likes to punish others. I think him cruel and sly…'

'Yes, he is sly,' Suleiman agreed. 'I have known it before now. I confess I do not like the creature—but I shall not have him frighten you. He shall be given other duties.'

'Thank you…you are kind, my lord.'

'I would be much kinder to you if you would be as kind to me.'

The husky tone of Suleiman's voice made Eleanor tremble inside. She drew a deep breath, knowing that he had already indulged her beyond what was normal for a man in such a position as his. Even in her own land very few men would show as much patience as this one had.

'I would be your friend if you wished it,' she said after a moment's thought. 'If you wished for someone to help you decipher your manuscripts, I would copy them in a fair hand. And I often helped my father when he was researching some legend he wished to authenticate.'

'You can write a legible hand—one that others can read?'

'Yes, my lord.'

'My own writing is very small,' he replied. 'Kasim told me anyone else would need spectacles to read it— he could not read it himself. Are you able to decipher small lettering?'

'Yes, my lord. I can read Latin and Arabic, but I fear I have not yet mastered Greek. It was my hope to learn when we were settled in Cyprus.'

'I might teach you,' Suleiman said. 'If it pleased me—but you would have to please me, my lady.'

Eleanor raised her head, her face proud and haughty. 'I do not bargain for my honour, sir.'

'You are too proud and wilful,' he cried, a flash of temper in his eyes because she still defied him after all the concessions he had made her. 'Go back where you came from before I change my mind and send for Abu to punish you after all!'

Eleanor knew that she had angered him as he turned and went into the adjoining chamber, leaving her alone. She hesitated for a moment, then she too turned and walked back the way she had come.

What would he do next? He had said that he would never ransom her to her family, but perhaps if she could do him some service—but he was angry with her now. He had called her proud and wilful, and she knew that was true—it had ever been her way. Her father had indulged her, and she had always shown him her obedient face, for she'd had no reason to defy him. Perhaps she ought to have spoken more diplomatically to Suleiman Bakhar. He was clearly a reasonable man—though she had caught a glimpse of the other side of his nature just for a moment.

He was capable of anger, that she knew. How close had she come to being punished? She could not be sure. He had walked away from her after his threat, but supposing he changed his mind—supposing he had her beaten with the whips he had spoken of?

A shiver ran through Eleanor and she knew a moment of fear. Would she be as brave if her master had her beaten? Would she be able to face him so proudly in the future?

And yet there was a little voice in her head that told her Suleiman admired her spirit. She had seen his eyes gleam with inner amusement when she defied him. Why was that? He had absolute power over his harem. Why should he have tried to persuade her?

He could simply have had her prepared for his bed and then he could have forced her to become his concubine. Why had he not done so?

Eleanor sensed that he was a complicated man, that perhaps there was a battle going on inside him. He was, after all, the son of an English gentlewoman. Could it be that he was not completely at ease in the world in which he lived?

Was it possible that he saw the evil of slavery, but could not deny his heritage?

Suleiman was the Caliph's favourite son and his heir. To deny the very foundations of his life would be to throw all the benefits of rank and privilege away—to deny his very being. And yet she had sensed restlessness in him, a desire for something more than he had...yet what was there that a man like Suleiman Bakhar could not have with a snap of his fingers?

It was clear that the Caliph was extremely wealthy, and that his son was equally so—and yet she had sensed a need in him. Perhaps if he sent for her again she would try to reach that inner being...through talking of things that must interest him.

Eleanor knew much that might catch the attention of a man who wished to learn more of the world outside his own—but would he listen to a woman?

Women were considered so much less than men in this world to which she had been brought against her will. Even in her own world there were few men who were interested in a woman's thoughts—it was beauty that was prized and a sweet temper.

Her own father had been an exception, and she should not look to find his like again, especially here. It was foolish to imagine that Suleiman Bakhar might respect her for her intelligence—might choose her company simply to study and talk.

Eleanor's heart was heavy as she recalled the times she had ridden and played with her brother when they were both much younger. In later years she had studied with Richard...where was he now? She felt tears sting her eyes. She had been lucky to be brought here and she could only pray that Richard had also found a master who would be kind to him.

She blinked back her tears, knowing she must not dwell on her brother's plight or the happiness they had known as children. She might never see Richard again, but perhaps she might find companionship with

Suleiman. No, that was only a dream. She would be a fool to let herself be swayed by it.

If Suleiman sent for her again…it would be to force her to his bed.

And what would she do then?

Chapter Five

Eleanor was sitting in the gardens with three of the other women that evening when she saw Karin coming towards them. The older woman smiled and nodded approvingly.

'You are beginning to make friends,' she said as she reached them. 'That is good, Eleanor.'

'Yes, it is,' Eleanor said and smiled at the three women who had been brave enough to ignore Fatima's orders and approach her. 'Anastasia has been telling me of her life in Russia, and Elizabetta is from the north of Spain—and Rosamunde is Venetian. We have much in common, and since we all speak a little French and a little Italian there is no barrier.'

'That is fortunate,' Karin replied. 'I am glad you have taken my advice, Eleanor. You will need friends if you are to be happy living here—but I am pleased to tell you that your request has been granted.'

'My request?' Eleanor looked puzzled for a moment, then nodded as a feeling of excitement gripped her. 'I asked for pen and paper—have I permission for these items?'

'It is much better than that,' Karin replied with an

indulgent look. 'Come with me and I shall show you. You may return to your friends later if you wish.'

Eleanor followed her obediently. Karin was in charge of the harem ladies, but she did not try to assert her authority in an unkind way, and Anastasia had told her that the older woman was very kind when any of the women were ill or distressed.

'She is our comforter,' Anastasia had told her. 'When I was brought here I wanted to die, but Karin showed me that life in this place can be good and now I am content. My lord has only sent for me once, and since then I have been left to live a life of ease. If I had remained in Russia I would have been servant to a lady of the nobility, and here I have a much better life.'

'But do you not miss your family?'

'They were all killed in the raid on our village,' Anastasia replied simply, with no sign of emotion. 'Only the young women and boys were spared to be taken as slaves.'

'Did that not make you hate the people who took you prisoner?'

'Yes—but they were pirates and thieves. Our master is a good man and we are treated fairly.' Anastasia sighed. 'I was a gift from a merchant to the Caliph, who gave me to his son—but I did not please Suleiman and he has no use for me. I content myself with helping the others—and Karin sends for me when anyone is ill, because I have a little skill in nursing. My life is full, for though I have no children of my own I sometimes see the children of others playing. I should have liked to give the lord Suleiman a son— he has two daughters, but no woman has yet given him a son.'

It was obvious that Anastasia was saddened that her master did not summon her to his bed, and Eleanor wondered at it. Why was it that most of the ladies seemed eager to please Suleiman Bakhar? They had told her that he often watched them from a window above their garden, and that they all paraded back and forth along that particular path in the hope that he would notice them and send for them that night.

For a moment Eleanor recalled the treachery of her own body as he had kissed her softly on the lips. The sweetness of that kiss had surprised her, and aroused a longing for something that she did not understand, robbing her of the will to resist him. She had felt as though he cast a magic spell over her by some sorcery—was it this that made so many of the harem women eager for his notice? It was certain that every woman in the harem would have felt honoured to be sent for by her master. Yet did they not feel the shame of being his concubine—did they not fret at being bound to him by slavery?

Eleanor's ponderings were brought to an abrupt end as she saw what had happened in her absence. An exquisite desk and chair of French design had been placed in her sitting room, and upon it lay a leather-bound journal with pristine pages of cream vellum, writing quills, ink in a pewter pot, and a large pile of papers with close writing upon them.

'What are these?' Eleanor cried, pouncing on them with glee. 'They are in Latin, I think—and the writing is very small.'

'Our master has sent these scripts for you to decipher and copy into a fair hand,' Karin told her. 'They are his own work, done some years ago when he was a student, and he can no longer make out the lettering.

He asks that you transcribe them for him—into English or Latin, whichever pleases you.'

'Oh, what treasure,' Eleanor exclaimed joyfully clutching the papers. 'I wish to thank Suleiman Bakhar—how may I do so?'

'By doing what he has asked,' Karin replied, an odd smile on her lips. It had seemed a strange request to her, and even stranger that Suleiman should choose to answer it in this way—but now she saw that perhaps he had found a way to soften Eleanor's heart. 'I have been told by our new chief eunuch that it was not an order but a request.'

She sounded a little puzzled and Eleanor looked at her curiously. 'Is it usual for our lord to request such things?'

'He always asks respectfully when he wishes to speak to me,' Karin replied. 'But I am not of his own harem. It is more usual for Suleiman to order than ask…and there is another strange thing. Abu has been transferred from his duties in the harem to the Caliph's storehouses, where he is to be in charge of ordering supplies for the palace.'

'Is that a demotion to a less important position?' Eleanor asked, remembering the odd expression on Suleiman's face when she had said she did not like the eunuch.

'No—for it involves much responsibility, and a chance for Abu to better his standing. He might even become wealthy if he chooses to trade with the merchants on his own behalf.' Karin's eyes narrowed as she looked at Eleanor. 'I have long distrusted Abu and I would have had him removed from his duties here before this had I dared—but he is a dangerous enemy, Eleanor. If he believes that this change was due to interference from one of the women…she might have to watch her back very carefully in future. Especially if she should lose the favour of our lord, for then no one would care or notice if she disappeared.'

'I only said that I did not like him,' Eleanor replied. 'Our lord asked me what I meant, but I could not tell him—it was just a feeling that Abu liked to hurt others.'

'Yes, that is very true,' Karin replied. 'I have suspected him of inflicting punishment for his own pleasure in the past, but the victims were always too afraid to speak. If I had had proof I could have gone to Suleiman—but it seems you have achieved more in one hour than I in six years…'

'Oh, no…' Eleanor blushed and looked down. 'I am sure it was not a chance remark of mine that made Suleiman Bakhar change Abu's duties—he must have had it in mind to do so.'

'Yes, perhaps you are right,' Karin said. She knew that Suleiman had sent for Fatima that night, and that surely meant that Eleanor had not appealed to his sensual nature. He would not have moved his chief eunuch from the harem simply because a woman had voiced a dislike of him—or would he? The gift of writing materials was a very generous one, and Karin had never known it to happen before. 'I dare say it was as you say—and it would be best to mention nothing of what has passed between us here. I shall tell others that you have been ordered to do this work, because Suleiman has no other scribe fit to do it since his teacher left.'

'The lord Suleiman's teacher…was his name Kasim?'

'Yes. What do you know of him?'

'Suleiman mentioned his name, that is all,' Eleanor replied. 'I had the feeling that something had happened...something that made him sad.'

'Saidi Kasim is dying of an incurable disease,' Karin told her. 'He was in great pain and asked permission to go home. The lord Suleiman granted it to him—but he misses him, for they were great friends.'

'Was Saidi Kasim a slave?'

'In the beginning,' Karin replied. 'But he was a wise man and had much learning. Suleiman valued him and gave him great honours. Kasim was a humble man who did not wish for the riches of life, but he could have had whatever he wanted had he asked. They spent many hours together, I believe. He was closer to Suleiman than anyone—except the Caliph.'

'It is sad to lose such a friend,' Eleanor replied and, despite herself, felt that she would have liked to offer comfort to the man who had lost his best friend, though she knew he would not have wanted such words from her. 'But a man like Suleiman must have many others?'

'He has many friends amongst the Janissaries,' Karin replied. 'But so far he has not replaced Kasim. I do not think he can bear to do so...though he has summoned an astrologer on two occasions.'

'Ah, yes,' Eleanor replied. 'I saw the instruments such men use for reading the stars in his hall. They looked interesting.'

Karin nodded, and her expression was thoughtful. 'It is very rare for a woman to be appointed to the position of adviser,' she said. 'But it has been known. You might please our master in many ways if you do your work well, Eleanor. You should not despair that he has sent for Fatima and not you this evening.'

Eleanor stared at her. She was conscious of a very odd feeling; it was like a pain in her chest and she did not understand it, though she knew what had aroused it. Yet she could not be jealous because Suleiman had sent for his favourite! After all, she did not want him to send for her in that way… Even so, there was a feeling of disappointment that he should have summoned Fatima to his bed.

'It is good that he has sent for her,' Eleanor said when she could form the words. 'She was afraid that I might take her place and it made her spiteful—now she will be happy again.'

'And you—you are not disappointed that you did not please him?'

'No…' Eleanor knew that she was not telling the whole truth. 'I told him that I would never consent to be his concubine willingly.'

'You told the lord Suleiman that?' Karin stared in astonishment. She could scarcely believe that Eleanor had been so bold or so foolish. 'And he sent no word that you were to be punished? Instead, he grants your wish to have pen and paper…I do not understand this, Eleanor.'

'Perhaps it as you say,' Eleanor replied. 'I am useful in other ways.'

She did not tell Karin that Suleiman had promised to favour her above all others if she pleased him—or that she had defied him when he kissed her.

'In that case I must leave you to begin your work,' Karin said, clearly still mystified. 'You may send for fresh lamps if you need them, but do not work too long into the night—or you will overtire yourself and lose your looks.' Her gaze narrowed thoughtfully. 'You are very lovely, Eleanor. I cannot believe that

you do not stir Suleiman Bakhar. I do not know what
is in his mind concerning you—but I think he may yet
surprise us all…'

Suleiman watched as Fatima performed one of her
dances for him. She was extremely graceful, and there
was no other woman of his harem who was more
skilled in the arts of pleasing a man—both with her
dancing and in bed.

He had enjoyed her performance many times, and
been roused to make love to her after the dance, but
tonight it left him unmoved. He could still appreciate
her skill, yet there was no burning in his loins, or any
desire to lie with her.

'Come,' he invited as the music ended and she sank
to a position of supplication before him, arms stretched
out as if in entreaty. 'Sit on that cushion next to me
and talk to me.'

Fatima obeyed, though she was puzzled by this odd
request. Always before he had raised her up and taken
her into his private room and made love to her. She
had looked forward to it eagerly through all the ritual
of the bath and preparation. It was her reason for living, for she was a passionate woman and relished the
act of physical love. He had never asked her to talk
to him before, and she did not know what to say.

'What would my lord have of me?' she asked.
'Would you have me sing to you?'

'No. I wish for conversation,' Suleiman replied and
frowned. 'Tell me what you do with your days,
Fatima.'

'I wait for you to send for me, my lord. I bathe and
perfume myself—and sometimes I dance so that I retain my skill for your pleasure.'

'But what do you like to do yourself?'

'I live to please you, my lord.'

Suleiman stared at her. Was her life so empty? And what of the other women in his harem—those he had not sent for in months? Some that he had never asked for in all the time they had been here—what did they do with their time?

'Have you no friends? Do you not laugh and talk—walk with them in the gardens or bathe together in the pools? Do they not gossip with you or tell stories?'

'I could not say what the others do,' Fatima replied with a look of disdain. 'I seldom bother with them—they are jealous of me because you send only for me.'

Suleiman saw the look of spiteful delight in her eyes and was disgusted. She was an empty vain woman—and he had created her. She was this way because he had taken his pleasures carelessly without thought for what he did, not loving her but using her to slake the physical urgings of his body.

He knew that he did not desire her, that he would probably never want her again. His first thought was that she should return to the harem at once, but he checked it before the words were spoken. If he sent her back so soon, the other women would know that she had not lain in his bed—and they would despise her for losing his favour. She did not deserve that, for she was as lovely and graceful as she had always been—the change was in him

'So…you wait all day for me…' He stood up and Fatima's heart raced. Surely now he would take her to his bed and she would make him forget this strange mood that troubled him. 'I do not want you to pleasure me this night, Fatima—but I shall not send you back to the harem. You may stay here in this room until the morning and return at your usual hour.'

'But, my lord…' Still on her knees, Fatima caught at the hem of his tunic as he would have passed her. 'What have I done to displease you?'

'You have not displeased me,' he replied coldly. 'Your dance was excellent—but I do not desire you in my bed. You will sleep here and leave in the morning as soon as it is light.'

'Forgive me…' Fatima threw herself to the floor at his feet, abasing herself before him. 'Whatever I have done I will make amends, my lord.'

'You displease me by this display of temper,' Suleiman said, guilt making his voice sharper than need be. 'If you persist, I shall send for the eunuch to take you back now.'

He walked on past her, leaving Fatima stretched out on the tiled floor, her body shaking with the tears she could not hold back despite his threat to send her back at once. She longed to follow him, to plead with him again, but she dared not for he would surely send her back to the harem in disgrace. And then the other women would laugh at her. She had flaunted herself over them and some of them would not lose their chance to make her suffer now that she had lost their master's favour.

Suleiman felt both guilt and pity for her as he looked down on her misery. He had not truly understood how empty were the lives of the women in his harem until…until one of them had asked him how she was to pass her life. He had sent her work to do since it seemed that this was what she required, but it would be useless to offer such a boon to Fatima, for she would neither appreciate nor be able to do such intricate work. He doubted that she could write, let alone read Latin...it was a rare thing in a woman. Even his own mother had not been able to read Latin, but Eleanor could.

He wondered what Eleanor was doing at that moment. He wished that he might send for her—but to do so would be to offer a grievous insult to the woman he had left sobbing on the floor of his outer chamber. He would not choose to be that cruel, even though it was only now that he had begun to realise his actions could be cruel...that he hurt those he did not send for by omission. It was a heavy burden, and one that must be given careful consideration.

Tomorrow must suffice for his own pleasure. He would sit and read some of his manuscripts, though of late he had noticed that it was something of a strain to decipher his own lettering. The scripts he had sent to Eleanor for transcribing were some he had written long ago and concerned matters of astrology that he wished to consult again, so that perhaps he might be able to interpret his own charts and not have to trust the words of the astrologer.

He took the scripts to a stool by a table where a lamp was burning and began to read the fair hand inscribed for him by his old teacher, sighing as he did so. He missed Kasim so much...and there was no one else he could talk to in the same way, for his father was not interested in ancient teachings and mysteries. The Caliph was a man much concerned with the daily administration of justice in the Sultan's capitol, and had no time for the kind of work that gave Suleiman so much pleasure.

The mysteries of the stars, of medicine and ancient knowledge, some handed down from empires now lost to mankind, held a special fascination for Suleiman Bakhar. He had many books, which came from the printing works of Germany, France and Venice, which were easy enough for him to read—but it was the ancient manuscripts that he found difficult to decipher these days. He was forced to hold them at a distance and that was uncomfortable, and sometimes made his eyes ache if he worked too long into the night.

For the moment he must content himself with the books that showed pictures of medical practice and were self-explanatory, depicting lumps and sores on various parts of the body. He had been visiting at the bedside of one of the Janissaries earlier; the unfortunate man had developed a lump on his side. And, after consulting with the physicians, Suleiman was trying to ascertain whether it would be best to cut the lump from the man's body or treat it with powders to try and burn it off.

The sobbing from the outer chamber had ceased at last. Suleiman forgot the woman as he read his medical books, his mind now fully concentrated on a cure for his friend.

Eleanor had spent many happy hours poring over the scripts sent to her and had begun her transcription into both English and Latin, copying a page of each at a time. She had slept afterwards and woke feeling so much happier than she had in an age. At least now she had some purpose to her life—and she could almost imagine herself back at home with her father.

The memory of Sir William's death lay heavy on her heart. She knew that she would never cease to grieve for him, and for her brother—who was as lost to her as her father. Yet perhaps if she asked Suleiman, he might be able to give her news of Richard... It would require some payment, of course.

Eleanor knew that she had already been granted a considerable favour. Why had Suleiman done so much for her? She had thought him angry when he sent her back to the harem...and yet he had granted her request for some occupation. She was very grateful to him, and she was being very careful in her copying so that he would be pleased with what she had done.

'Come into the garden,' Anastasia said from the threshold of her sitting room. 'It is a lovely day, Eleanor. Karin bid me tell you, you have worked enough for now. You must take a walk in the air.'

'I am glad to do so,' Eleanor said and rose with a smile. 'I do not wish to study all the time. It is good to have friends and I like to talk with you and the others.'

'Fatima is in a bad temper this morning,' Anastasia said. 'It is unusual for her to be so cross after spending the night with our master.'

'It does not matter about her,' Eleanor said linking arms with the other woman. 'Tell me about the dancing lessons, Anastasia. I think I should like to learn. I can play a harp and the virginals—but I do not know how to play the instrument you were using the other night.'

'It is a dombra, and comes from the province of Kazakhstan.' Anastasia smiled at her. 'It is very like a lute in some ways, but the music it makes is different. I could show you how to play it if you wish?'

'Yes, I think that would be pleasant,' Eleanor replied. 'I am so glad that we are to be friends. I felt so alone the night I came to the harem—and no one spoke to me.'

'That was because Fatima forbade it,' Anastasia replied. 'The three of us decided the next day that we would disobey her—especially now that Abu is no longer in charge of the harem. He used to punish us for her if we did something that displeased her… He was cruel and it was his pleasure to whip us for some imagined slight of her.'

'Why did you not tell Karin?'

'Because she is not of the harem,' Anastasia replied. 'If we had told her, something might have happened while she was not here…women have disappeared without trace from the palace. I think Abu sold them to slave merchants.'

'But did no one notice they had gone?'

'Who would care?' Anastasia frowned. 'The Caliph hardly ever sends for a woman these days, and it would only be Karin or one of his other wives who have given him children—none of the concubines are ever requested. Unless the Caliph sent for someone who had disappeared he would never know—and then he would probably be told she had sickened and died of some mysterious ailment. No one could prove otherwise, for those who knew would not be asked.'

'That is terrible,' Eleanor said. 'Do you think Suleiman knows of this?'

'No—for who would dare to tell him? Abu was in charge of the harem and the only woman Suleiman sends for is Fatima—and I believe she knew what was going on. She helped Abu and he saw that she was obeyed in the harem… It was a strange partnership, but of mutual benefit.'

'Yes, I see,' Eleanor said. 'It is a happy thing for us that Abu has been sent to the stores.'

'Yes…' Anastasia nodded. 'And yet I think…' She

shook her head. 'No, I cannot be sure and it is safer not to notice. I shall say no more and nor should you.'

Eleanor looked at her curiously but did not press her to continue. Karin had told her it was dangerous to speak too openly in the harem, and although some of the women had shown themselves willing to be friendly with Eleanor, others remained aloof.

As they entered the main hall, Eleanor saw Fatima seated on one of the divans. Several of the women were hovering about her, offering dishes of sweet-meats and fruits. It was clear that she was displeased about something and her eyes snapped with temper as she looked at Eleanor. However, before she could speak Karin came up to Eleanor.

'Suleiman has sent for you,' she said. 'You are to bring your journal. He wishes to see what you have done so far.'

'Yes, of course. I shall fetch the journal at once.'

Eleanor left Anastasia with a smile of regret and a promise that they would talk later. She collected the journal from her apartments, then hurried after Karin.

Just before they reached the first of Suleiman's halls, Karin stopped and turned to her with a worried expression.

'I have heard strange whispers,' she said. 'One of the women from the palace kitchens died horribly last night. They say she was beaten and then strangled; there was no attempt to hide her body. I do not know why but this makes me afraid...for you.'

'But why?' Eleanor's eyes opened wide with surprise. 'You do not believe it was Abu...but, yes, you do!'

Karin nodded. 'I think it may have been anger or spite on his part, because he was stripped of his powers to punish. I may be wrong about this, but please be careful, Eleanor. I would not have anything unpleasant happen to you.'

'Yes, of course I shall take care. I thank you for your care of me, Karin.'

'I like you,' the older woman replied. 'And you are in my charge. I would not have you disappear or die mysteriously, as others have. Now you must go. Our master seems impatient to see you.'

Eleanor's heart was beating very fast as she continued on into the grand chamber, which contained all the cabinets and scientific instruments. Suleiman was not there and she ventured into the next room. She saw him at once. He was standing by a trestle and board, on which were spread several manuscripts and seemed intent on what he was doing.

'You sent for me, my lord?'

Suleiman swung round at her words, a flame of pure silver shooting up in his dark eyes as he saw her. Eleanor's heart caught and for a moment she could not breathe. How magnificent he was! He frightened her with his overpowering masculinity, yet she felt drawn to him against her will. He must not look at her so! As if he were pleased to see her, had awaited her coming eagerly. She could not bear it—it terrified her and excited her too, making her feel as if she had been running very fast.

'You brought the journal?' His gaze narrowed as she held it out to him wordlessly, unable to speak. He opened the first page and then turned to the next, his brow furrowing. 'You have translated into English and also given the original Latin transcription—why?'

'I thought it might please you,' Eleanor replied. 'In English the meaning becomes clearer—the Latin script was somewhat ambiguous. I gave it a literal interpretation…'

'Which makes it easier to understand how a chart should be drawn and understood…' His mouth curved into a smile that set her pulses pounding. 'Very clever…and exactly what I needed. How did you know that I wished to read my own horoscope?'

'You had made such detailed notes,' Eleanor replied. 'I saw the instruments used to take readings of the stars in your hall…a rather fine astrolobe and others I was not sure of. And I knew you had spoken recently with an astrologer.'

'Indeed? I suppose Karin told you that?'

'Yes, my lord.'

Suleiman nodded. 'I am pleased with your hand, my lady. It is easy for me to read. I find these difficult to decipher.' He waved his hand towards the scripts he had been studying. 'It was always my chief pleasure of an afternoon, but of late…' He shrugged and frowned. 'My eyes ache from trying to make out this lettering.'

'It is a medical treatise,' Eleanor said. 'Writ in Arabic. It tells of a bark that must be ground into a powder and mixed with wine. If used in the treatment of a bowel disorder it is promised most effective.'

'Then it is not the remedy I seek.' He sighed as if he were weary after many hours of study. 'I am looking for a treatment for a swelling of the body.' He squinted at the next script. 'I am sure it is here somewhere.'

'Would you like me to look for you?'

'If you will. I am sure there is a certain powder that may save my friend from the evil of having a lump cut out of his side by the surgeon's knife…'

'I think this may be what you are seeking, my lord.'

Eleanor had seen that the text he needed was just beneath the one he had been studying. She handed it to him and he held it out at arm's length, then nodded.

'Yes, the very one. I shall copy it and give it to the physician.'

'May I do that, my lord? Here is paper and ink. It will take but a moment.'

'As you wish.'

Eleanor sat on the stool and wrote the name of the bark used in the treatment of swelling and lumps, and the way in which it must be used, then handed it to Suleiman. He had been staring down at the various scripts and his difficulty was obvious.

'Perhaps you should wear spectacles for reading, my lord?'

'I have eyes like a hawk.' He glared at her indignantly. 'I can see small objects from a distance. My eyes are perfectly sound.'

'But you obviously cannot see to read properly. My father's eyes were much the same. He thought it was because he studied so much, but when he bought some magnifying lenses he discovered that it was much easier for him.'

'I am aware of these things…in the Arab world we have known of their properties for a long time. In your country they are far behind us. Besides, I do not need them. It is merely that my eyes are tired after too much work.'

'Yes, my lord. My father said the same until he tried them. And in China they have used these glasses since the tenth century. It is an old wisdom and not something you need to feel ashamed of using to your advantage.'

Suleiman gave her a hard stare, then, seeing the gentle smile on her mouth, he laughed. 'You think me too vain to use such aids? Well, I have been told before it would help me. Kasim advised the use of them, but I thought it a passing thing. It seems that I may have been wrong.'

'My father was sent his glasses by a Venetian friend, but I dare say he would not have bought them for himself.'

'Your father had a wise daughter.' Suleiman nodded, his eyes intent on her face. 'Are you pleased with the work I have sent you?'

'Yes, my lord. It was my habit to study with my brother at home.' She sighed as she thought about Richard, as she so often did in the privacy of her own rooms. 'We were very close…' She held back a sob, then lifted her head. 'We shall not speak of that—it was kind of you to send me the work, my lord.'

His gaze narrowed as he looked at her. Was it his eyesight or was she even more lovely than he had thought her? 'Karin tells me you have begun to make friends—is that true?'

'Yes, my lord. I have three friends in the harem. Anastasia, Elizabetta and Rosamunde.'

'What do you talk about with your friends? Come, sit with me. I have ordered sherbet and sweetmeats for your pleasure. Drink and eat as we talk. I would know more of how the women spend their time.'

Eleanor looked at him in surprise. Did he really not know or was he merely testing her?

'I can tell you only of those women I have begun to know, my lord. Anastasia plays the dombra, and I thought the music very strange for it is different from the music I play.'

'What instruments do you play?'

'At home I had a harp and the virginals that were my mother's—but Anastasia has promised to teach me to play the dombra.'

'And will that please you?'

'Oh, yes, my lord.' Her face lit up with eagerness. 'I could not bear to sit in idleness as some of the women do, but I am to learn to dance—and to sing in the manner of your own people…a kind of chanting, I understand. And then it is pleasant to hear about the other women's homes and their lives before they came here…'

'What of your land, Eleanor? Tell me of your home—describe it to me in detail and the countryside around it. Make me see it through your eyes.'

'Willingly, my lord.' She smiled at him. 'My father's house is timber framed and the upper level protrudes out over the lower. The walls are of a grey stone and panelled inside with English oak, the roof deeply sloping and thatched with straw. It is not a large house, though gracious and well built—but to you it would seem very small. Your father's palace is so huge…'

'Too large,' Suleiman said and frowned. 'It is impossible to know what goes on everywhere. But continue—tell me of the gardens and the landscape. What do you do when you are at home?'

Eleanor began to describe her home in detail, leaving out nothing that she thought might interest him. She spoke of woods and meadows and the creatures that inhabited them, of misty mornings and the beauty of the English countryside, of the autumn when the leaves began to change colour. She told him also of the winter when the snows came, filling the roads and ditches, and sometimes cutting them off for days. She described her father's collection of books, maps and manuscripts, and his other treasures that they had been forced to leave behind, her words eloquent and flowing like beautiful music.

Suleiman listened entranced, the sound of her voice holding him spellbound, and wishing that her tale might never end, but when she reached the part where they had been forced to flee England, he interrupted.

'You were unfortunate that your Queen has set her heart on Spain—those Catholic devils are without mercy.' Suleiman frowned. 'You called me a savage—but my people are no worse than the murderers of the Inquisition. Our justice is often harsh, but we can also be generous. We are neither savages nor barbarians, even though our customs are strange to you.'

'No, perhaps not.' Eleanor blushed. 'I was wrong to judge without knowing you, my lord. I thought you the same as the men who murdered my father and I hated you as I hate them.'

'And now?' His eyes seemed very bright and intent. 'Do you still hate me?'

'No...I do not hate you.' Eleanor took a deep breath. 'I know that you are not like the men who raided our ship. But I still ask that you will ransom me to my family.'

'No!' Suleiman got to his feet and reached down to pull her up to stand before him. 'You must learn to accept your fate, Eleanor. You can never leave here.'

'Then I shall hate you!' Her temper flared suddenly. 'Why will you not listen to me? Why can you not—?'

Before she could say more, Suleiman reached for her and crushed her against him in a powerful embrace. His mouth sought hers in a hungry, ravaging kiss that seemed almost to burn her. For a moment she was close to surrendering to the need she sensed in him, then she pushed against him with the flat of her hands, turning her head to one side. For a few terrifying seconds he held her and she sensed that he was close to losing all control, then he released her so abruptly that she felt she would fall. Daring to glance at him, she saw that his nostrils were flaring and he was breathing hard as though he laboured beneath some extreme emotion. She thought that he might be very angry—for what else could cause him to look like that?

'Why do you fight me?' he demanded. 'I have given you what you requested. What more can I give you? Do you want jewels? Silks…larger apartments?'

'No! How can you think these things would buy me?' she asked, her eyes bright with accusation. Her body felt as if it was on fire, and her limbs trembled with weakness. 'I am a woman of honour. To give myself to a man who was not my husband…' She stopped as she saw the gleam in his eyes. 'No! I do not ask for marriage, only that I might be free.'

'You ask too much!' His anger flared out of him now. 'I tell you that you shall never go from here. You belong to me and I shall never give you up.'

'Then you will never take me willingly.'

'Then I shall force you to succumb.' His eyes darkened, and she saw that his hands clenched at his sides as if he were struggling to control his temper. 'Next time I send for you, be prepared to obey your master, Eleanor. Now go before I lose all control and have you punished for your wilfulness.'

Eleanor gasped. His features might have been carved from granite. How foolish she was! As they talked, she had felt that he was inclined to be understanding of her feelings—but this was a different man. A more primitive, savage product of his culture and birthright—a man used to being obeyed.

'Forgive me,' she whispered, but he had turned back to his manuscripts and was ignoring her. She was not even sure he had heard her plea.

What had she done? Eleanor regretted her hasty words. They had seemed to be reaching a far better understanding before she had so foolishly defied him. Why had she not spoken more softly to this man who held the power of life and death over so many?

She was close to tears as she retraced her route towards the harem. Suleiman had been pleased with her when she read the ancient script for him. He had even accepted her advice about the matter of his eyesight—but she had rejected his embrace and now he was angry again.

When she walked into the main hall of the harem, she heard the excited chatter and laughter going on and wondered what had happened to cause such a stir in her absence.

'Oh, do come and look,' Elizabetta called to her. 'See what our lord has sent us!'

'What is it?' she asked. 'What has pleased you all so much?'

'There is a parrot that talks,' the other woman cried. 'And a monkey on a chain—and a cage of pretty singing birds in the garden.'

'Oh, let me see,' Eleanor said, catching Elizabetta's pleasure in the pets they had been given. 'Does the monkey do tricks?'

'He is such a naughty little fellow,' Anastasia said,

coming up to them. 'He keeps stealing things, but he is so sweet and pretty.'

'He seems to be causing quite a stir.'

Eleanor saw that most of the ladies were playing with the monkey, who was clearly going to be spoiled by them. Several of them were talking to the parrot—which was swearing at the top of its voice. And in English!

'Oh, dear,' Eleanor said and laughed. 'He is not a very polite parrot, is he?'

'What is he saying?' Anastasia asked. 'No one understands him.'

'Perhaps that is just as well, for he is very rude. I think he was brought up in the stables. We must teach him better manners.'

Eleanor glanced around the room. She thought that she had never seen the women so animated and happy. The new additions to the harem were very welcome, it seemed—and the thought to send them was a kind one.

It had been Suleiman's idea, of course. He must have given some considerable thought as to what might please and amuse the ladies. Eleanor wanted to thank him, but she doubted she would get much opportunity.

He had told her she must be prepared to submit to him the next time he sent for her—but when would that be?

'Are you pleased with your gifts?'

Karin had come up behind her. Eleanor turned to her with a frown.

'Surely the monkey and birds are for everyone to enjoy?'

'I was not speaking of them. Have you not been to your own apartments?'

'I have but now returned from Suleiman's halls.'

'You have been with him all this time?' Karin looked surprised. 'Have you eaten?'

'My lord provided sherbet and sweetmeats. I am not hungry, thank you.'

'Go and look at your gifts.' Karin smiled at her. 'We were wrong to think that you had not pleased Suleiman. Such gifts as he has sent you are usually reserved for a favourite wife.'

Eleanor felt hot and then cold. She trembled inwardly as she remembered Suleiman's words. In turn he had offered her both gifts and threats—if he believed the gifts had not tempted her, he might resort to punishment next. She had imagined he spoke of the journal and scripts he had given her.

She went to her own rooms, followed by a curious Anastasia and Elizabetta, who had both heard what Karin had to say. There, spread out over the divans, were robes of silk and cloth of gold. A large casket had been placed against a wall, inside which were other items of the finest materials she had ever seen. On her desk was a small wooden casket inlaid with ivory and agates. Morna handed her a small key, and when she opened the casket she found a rope of beautiful emeralds and pearls strung on gold wire. There was also a chain of emeralds for her wrist, and a huge emerald pendant suspended from a headband of pure gold.

'Oh…' Elizabetta breathed in awe as Eleanor lifted them out to examine them more closely. 'I have never seen such jewels. They are much finer than anything Fatima has.'

'No!' Eleanor was aware of a feeling of terror as she realised what the gift represented. 'I cannot accept these—they must be returned at once.'

'Do not be foolish,' Karin said from behind her. 'Suleiman has sent these things because he wishes to see you wearing them. He is obviously planning to send for you soon—which means there is no time to be lost. You will spend this evening with me. I shall explain to you exactly what will happen when Suleiman sends for you.'

'Please…do not,' Eleanor whispered her throat tight with fear. 'I cannot. I cannot be what you and he want me to be.'

'You must—for your own sake and ours,' Karin told her with what was a severe look for her. 'Suleiman has always been generous, but he is a man and men have a lurking beast in their nature. A clever woman knows how to subdue that beast, to have it tamely eating from her hand. You are the one Suleiman has chosen to be his wife…'

'His wife? How do you know?' Eleanor looked at her with frightened eyes. 'Has he spoken of this to you?'

'No, not yet—but I know. These jewels are priceless. He would not give them to a mere concubine. Suleiman will take you for his wife, Eleanor. You are the most fortunate of women, for he will give you all that your heart desires—even take you outside the palace with him. Your life will be so much better than it could ever have been as one of the concubines. You must accept the inevitable. You have no choice.'

Chapter Six

Eleanor was forced to spend the evening with Karin in her apartments. She was treated kindly, and the food served to her was the most delicious she had tasted either here at the palace or elsewhere, but she was here for a purpose and there was no escaping the lessons Karin was determined she must learn.

Her cheeks grew warm for shame as the older woman described things that their master might ask her to do—and others he might do to her if he chose. It all seemed terribly wicked to Eleanor, and yet there was a very odd feeling in her lower abdomen as Karin described the pleasures Suleiman could give her. She found herself remembering the sensations his kiss had aroused in her and trembled. Surely such things were wrong—a woman was not supposed to take pleasure in what she had been taught was a sin unless sanctified by marriage.

'But I cannot allow…' She swallowed hard, unable to meet the other's eyes. 'I mean…it is not decent. Surely no respectable woman could do…all those things?'

Karin smiled gently. 'I know it must seem strange

to you, and perhaps sinful. You have not been taught these things as many of our women have by their mothers. Some have been trained for years simply to arouse a man's sexuality—some to give pleasure in other ways. But always to please, to obey without question.'

'I have thought…' Eleanor blushed. 'It was pleasant when he kissed me…'

'He has kissed you…nothing else? Nothing of which I have just spoken?'

'No! I would not allow it.' Eleanor was indignant! 'I pushed him away…and yet I did not truly want to stop him kissing me.'

Karin laughed at this confession. 'I believe I have been wasting my time, Eleanor. It seems you need no teacher. I suspect that Suleiman wishes to teach you himself. Yes…' She seemed struck by this thought and nodded to herself. 'Perhaps he grows tired of women who are skilled in these arts. Perhaps he looks for something different…'

'Perhaps you are wrong?' Eleanor looked at her anxiously. 'He may just forget me. Perhaps he will never send for me again.'

'No, I do not think so,' Karin replied. 'Fatima was angry when she returned to the harem this morning. I think Suleiman no longer favours her—he wants you. You must be careful of her, Eleanor. She will harm you if she can.'

'Surely not?' Eleanor frowned. 'I have done nothing to make our lord favour me above her. I believed he was angry with me. I know he was! He may yet send the eunuchs to take back his gifts.'

Karin shook her head at her. 'You foolish girl! Do not fight your fate, Eleanor. I think it was written in the stars that you should come here—and I think your destiny will affect all of us. Indeed, it has already begun to do so in small ways—but the choices you make may have far greater consequences for all of us.'

'What do you mean? Suleiman would not punish the others because he is angry with me—would he?' Eleanor stared at her in surprise. 'I had not thought him so unfair…'

'No, I did not mean that,' Karin replied. 'But my horoscope was cast some days ago and I was told that change was coming. Not just for me, but for others I cared for.'

Eleanor was silent. She knew that many people scoffed at such predictions, but her father had believed there was merit in them if honestly done. He had shown her how to read a chart, and she knew that predictions of a trend could be frighteningly accurate. She had known that her family would have to pass through a period of danger, and that they would be forced to leave their own land, long before it happened. There was more truth in the stars than any man knew.

'I pray that I do not bring bad fortune to you, Karin.'

'I believe that what happens here in the future is in your hands, Eleanor. You can bring good or evil…the outcome rests with you and you should think carefully before you reject your duty.'

It was a heavy burden to carry, and Eleanor was thoughtful as she returned to her own apartments later that evening. She found Morna working frantically to restore the rooms to order, and saw that some mischief had been done in her absence. Her clothes were on the floor, and ink had been spilled on some papers on her desk.

'What has happened here?' she asked, looking displeased at the confusion.

'Forgive me, my lady,' Morna begged. 'Fatima sent for me; when I returned, I found that naughty monkey making havoc amongst your things. I think nothing has been spoiled—except those papers. Are they very important?'

Eleanor looked at them anxiously, but to her relief the papers that had ink spilled on them were some she had already copied.

'I shall have to explain what happened to the lord Suleiman when I see him.' she said. 'It was not your fault, Morna. What did Fatima want of you?'

'She said she had not sent for me, that I must have been given the wrong message—but it was her servant Dinazade who summoned me.' Morna frowned. 'I think it was she who set the monkey loose in here, on Fatima's orders.'

'Yes, perhaps you are right,' Eleanor agreed. 'I shall ask Karin to order that the monkey be shut in its cage at night so that this does not happen again. Much precious work might have been lost had other papers than these been destroyed, and then the lord Suleiman would have been angry.'

'If you give the order it will be obeyed, my lady.'

'Why—what do you mean?'

'Everyone says you are to be Suleiman Bakhar's wife. You will then rule the harem. All the women will obey you.'

'What of Fatima?' Eleanor frowned. 'I do not think she will obey me.'

'Then you may have her punished. You could have

her beaten for this if you choose. I am sure the eunuchs would obey you.'

'I do not choose,' Eleanor replied. 'I believe that Fatima may have caused this to be done—but it is merely a spiteful prank. I would not have her beaten for it. Besides, if it is true—if she is no longer our lord's favourite—she is suffering enough. I believe she truly cares for him in her way.'

'Fatima cares only for herself.'

Eleanor frowned. She knew that the other women did not like Fatima, and she suspected that some of the bolder ones might now try to punish her.

'Fatima may yet regain Suleiman's favour,' she warned her servant. 'No one should assume that her rule is over. I think it would go hard with those who do if he should change his mind and send for her again.'

Morna was regarding her thoughtfully, and Eleanor knew that her words would be repeated in the harem. It was all she could do to help Fatima, and perhaps more than she deserved.

'Come into the garden,' Anastasia said persuasively. 'You work too much, Eleanor—and it is such a lovely afternoon.'

'Yes, I shall stop now,' Eleanor replied. She sighed and laid down her quill. 'I have finished all the work Suleiman set for me. I shall give the journal to Karin and ask her to deliver it.'

Standing up, she shrugged off a faint feeling of tiredness. She had worked hard this past week—a week during which Suleiman had been silent. No one—not even Karin—had been sent for. Some said that their master had been training even harder than usual, some said that he had been out with his hawks every day—and others thought he had left the palace for a hunting trip with the Caliph.

Karin had told Eleanor that this last was not true. The Caliph had been working as always.

'He is a good and just man,' she said to Eleanor. 'I was fortunate—though I was only his second wife. He loved Suleiman's mother and no other.'

'Did you give the Caliph children?'

'Two daughters—both are married now,' Karin said a little sadly. 'They married into good families, but I never see them. I should like to visit them one day.'

'Would that be permitted?'

'If they lived in this city, yes,' Karin replied. 'My lord is generous. I am allowed to visit my brother's family sometimes—but my daughters live far away. I have my duties here for the moment, and cannot be spared—nor would I wish to leave while things remain as they are.'

'And if Suleiman had a wife?'

'Then I might be granted permission to leave for a while.'

'I see. You must hope that he will marry soon.'

'Only if he chooses the right woman. Fatima would make life intolerable for the others if I were not here to restrain her.' She frowned. 'I do not understand why Suleiman has not sent for you before this.'

'Perhaps he is still angry with me?'

Eleanor had wondered why she had heard nothing more from Suleiman Bakhar. Did he think her ungrateful for his gifts? She would have thanked him had she been given the chance. Indeed, she was anxious to do so.

'Listen to the birds calling,' Anastasia said, recalling her to the present. 'Someone has been cleaning their cage…'

Eleanor's attention was drawn towards the aviary of singing birds that Suleiman had sent to them. Her nerves tingled as she looked at the servant who had been tending them, and something about the slight figure who was now bending down to fasten the cage securely touched a chord in her.

'Richard!' she cried, her relief and pleasure in seeing her brother again leaping up in her. He was alive! Alive! Oh, God be praised! Her brother was alive and here in the palace. She forgot caution, and all that Karin and the others had taught her. 'Oh, Richard, my dearest!'

She was racing towards him as he turned and saw her. His face lit up with pleasure as he heard her call his name again and knew her for his sister. He moved towards her, his arms opening to receive her as she flung herself at him.

'Eleanor,' he choked, emotion welling over. 'My beloved sister. I have thought you dead long since. How are you—have these devils harmed you?' His eyes went over her and she saw understanding dawn as he realised how scantily she was dressed. 'You are one of our master's—' but she was pressing her fingers to his lips, kissing his cheek and hugging him, cutting off the terrible thoughts. 'It does not matter. Father would not think ill of you, Eleanor…he loved you too much. He would want you to live no matter what you were forced…'

'I am not yet…' she told him as soon as she could bear to stop kissing him. 'But I think Suleiman may soon take me as his wife…'

'Those murdering devils deserve to boil in oil for

what they have done,' Richard said bitterly. 'I hate them all and would kill every last one of them if I could.'

'No, no, my dearest,' she choked. 'You must not say such things. Suleiman Bakhar is not like those men who…' The words died on her lips as she saw three of the eunuchs coming towards them. There was no mistaking their purpose, and Eleanor suddenly realised what she had done. 'Oh, no! It is forbidden for a man to be within these gardens. How did you come here? They have not altered you? You are not as they are?' Her fear was that he had been made less than a man, and given the work here, but he shook his head, denying it. Then, seeing the approaching eunuchs, he realised that he was in danger and she saw fear in his face. 'Who sent you here?' she asked, sensing some mischief.

'I think his name was Abu…he is chief eunuch of the harem…'

'No! No…no longer…'

It was the last thing either of them managed to say to each other before they were both seized. Eleanor's arm was taken in a firm grasp, though she was not roughly handled, but Richard resisted fiercely and was knocked to the ground and then dragged to his feet by the two eunuchs. She heard his stifled cry of pain and turned to her captor, begging him to save her brother.

'Please…he did no harm. He did not know where he was…he was sent here by…'

'Be quiet, woman! You will not speak until your master tells you!'

'You are taking us to Suleiman?'

Eleanor looked at his harsh face but there was nothing more to be gained from him. She glanced back at her brother and saw that he was fighting his captors, which meant that they were dragging him along the ground much of the time. She wanted to tell him not to fight, but knew that anything she said might result in him being struck again.

It was all her fault…all her fault. She ought to have remembered what Morna had told her on her first night in the harem—the women were always watched. By her impulsive action she had brought this trouble on them both, and she was very afraid for her brother. She might be beaten, but her brother—Richard could be put to death simply for being in the harem.

She held back a sob, praying that they would be taken to Suleiman. If the eunuchs decided to administer punishment themselves…but surely Suleiman would hear for himself what Eleanor had to say?

Suleiman watched from his window as the eunuchs laid hands on the woman and the man she had taken as her lover. He had never felt such a cold rage as that which possessed him now—that this woman who had resisted his embraces so fiercely should throw herself into the arms of another!

The man should die and she—she should learn to know the power of her master. His first reaction had been to order them brought to him, but now his anger was such that he was almost inclined to have them tossed into the darkest cell the palace possessed and left to rot. The man should die most horribly and Eleanor… Pain pierced through his rage as he thought of her being beaten with the cruel whips the eunuchs used to such terrible effect. How she would suffer…she might even die of such a beating.

Yet she deserved her punishment. His eyes were

hard, his mouth set in a cruel line that told of the blood
of his ancestors swirling in his heated brain. She must
have known that what she did was forbidden, and yet
she went unheeding to her lover's arms. Did she love
him so much then that her life was nothing to her?

Suleiman was aware that his anger was turning to
jealousy and pain—pain that she did not love him as
she did this man, who looked to be a poor puny thing.
She had rejected his embraces and yet went eagerly to
this dog of an infidel. He was angry, but also curious
to see what kind of man it was that had aroused such
love in the woman he desired above all others.

They should be brought before him. He would let
Eleanor see that he was capable of justice. If she
begged for the man's life it might be spared—he could
be sent to the galleys as a punishment and she... He
would think of something more suitable for her punishment.

He heard the noise as they approached—the man
was shouting and yelling defiance at his captors. He
had spirit, then, despite his slight appearance. It would
be interesting to see what kind of man Eleanor loved
so much that she would spurn Suleiman for him.

His face was harsh as they were dragged before
him, and sent roughly to their knees. He did not immediately give Eleanor permission to stand this time,
for he wanted to make her suffer for her wilfulness.

'You have betrayed me with your lover,' Suleiman
said coldly. 'What have you to say before I condemn
you, woman?'

Eleanor looked up, gasping as she saw the rage in
his eyes. She had never seen him like this! He was
beside himself with anger and she thought that he
might be capable of anything in this mood.

'He is not my lover...'

'Do not lie to me,' he said. 'I watched you embrace him. You ran to his arms as soon as you saw him—why? You must know the punishment for your actions. Did you wish to die? Are you so miserable that your life is nothing to you?'

'Please, my lord,' Eleanor said. She was terrified of this stranger, but she would not let him see her fear. 'I beg you to hear me...' He glared at her but did not tell her to be silent. 'Richard is my brother...I told you he was taken when the Corsairs attacked our ship. He is my only brother and he is a youth of fifteen, not a man.'

Suleiman's gaze narrowed suspiciously as he looked at her and then the man. Indeed, the youth could not be older than she claimed—and there was a faint likeness about the eyes. Her brother, then, in truth. His rage abated a little. He bent down, gripped Eleanor's arms and pulled her to her feet, propelling her roughly towards the inner chamber, and thrusting her towards the sleeping divan so that she fell against it and slipped to the floor.

'Stay there!' he commanded fiercely. 'Don't you dare to move!'

'What are you going to do to my brother?'

'Be quiet or you will feel the sting of the whip. I shall do what I please with both of you!'

'Have mercy, I beg you. Richard was sent to the gardens by Abu—it was a deliberate act on his part, meant, I believe, to cause trouble.'

Suleiman paused, eyes narrowed in suspicion. 'He told you it was Abu? You are sure of this?'

'Yes, my lord. Richard believed the man was chief eunuch of the harem. He did not know that it was forbidden for him to be there. He was merely obeying orders. How could he have been there if it was not so?'

'But you were aware that what you did was forbidden?'

'Yes, my lord. I forgot in my excitement at seeing him—but I knew.'

His eyes gleamed with some strange emotion she could not read, though she did not think it anger. 'Wait here, Eleanor, and prepare yourself for your punishment.'

She hung her head as he left her. What would he do to Richard? It no longer mattered what happened to her—but if Richard were made to suffer unspeakable torture because of her impulsive behaviour she would not be able to bear it. Then, indeed, she would rather die than continue to live here as a slave.

Her mind went back to the times she had Richard had played together as children in the gardens of their home, and of one particular day when he had dared her to climb the old apple tree and she had fallen and hurt her arm. Richard had been so contrite, so loving, as he picked her up, wiping her tears…and there was nothing she could do to help him now that he was in trouble. She felt so helpless, so guilty because there was nothing she could do for her beloved brother. He would be punished because she had kissed him.

She could hear only a low murmuring from the other room and knew that Suleiman must be questioning her brother about how he came to be in the harem gardens. He must have been sent there for a purpose— and he could not have gained access without the key to the gates, which were always kept locked. Eleanor believed she knew what was in Abu's mind. He blamed Eleanor for his removal from the harem, and must somehow have learned that Richard was her brother—or at least that they were captured together.

Yes, yes, that must be what had happened. Abu had gambled that she would know the youth captured with her, and that she would react to seeing him there. Richard had been sent to clean out the birds' cage in the hope that she would see him and do something unwise—and she had fallen straight into the trap that had been set for her. The eunuch's plan had succeeded better than he could have hoped. How could she have been so foolish?

What was going on out there? What would Suleiman do to her brother—and to her? Her fear was mainly for her brother, but she tried to control it. She thought that Suleiman seemed to be questioning Richard at length…but there was silence now. What had been decided? Oh, please God, let her brother not suffer for her folly. She feared the worst. Suleiman had been so very angry. Had he accepted her explanation—had it swayed him towards mercy?

She had been sitting on the edge of the divan as he had bid her, not daring to move less she anger him further, but as he came back into the room she rose to her feet and faced him proudly. She had begged for Richard, but she would not do so for herself.

'I see that you are ready to accept your fate, Eleanor.'

'Punish me as you wish, my lord—but spare my brother.'

'Your brother's fate is out of my hands now.'

Eleanor gasped, her face turning pale. 'What have you done to him? He is but a boy—an innocent child.'

'You wrong your brother, my lady. He told me he

had a great desire to kill me and all my kind—those are a man's words, not a boy's.'

'He—he is bitter over our father's death. He does not know you. He thinks you as evil as those devils who captured him. I did not have time to ask him, but I believe he suffered at their hands far more than I...'

'Yes, I do realise that. I may be a savage, but I am not a fool.'

Eleanor bit her lip as she saw the way his mouth had gone hard, his eyes as bright as a hawk's before the kill. 'No, my lord. I have never thought you a fool.'

'No? That is good, because you will learn to respect me. I had hoped to spare you much, but it is time you accepted your position here. You are my property. I can dispose of you as I wish—have you beaten, sell you to the slave merchants.'

'I know that, my lord.'

'Do you, my lady? That is something. I had thought you incapable of accepting your fate. I hope you have learned your lesson today. I have perhaps indulged you more than I ought. You might do better with some discipline.'

'Yes, my lord. I have all my life been indulged. My father often told me that I must learn more humility, but—but he liked me as I am. What happened was my fault and mine alone. I accept the blame. Punish me as you wish—but spare my poor brother.'

'What—shall I not cut off his head with my scimitar? Or perhaps he should be roasted over a slow fire and the Janissaries may eat him for their supper. Or shall I be merciful and send him to the galleys?'

Eleanor stifled her gasp of horror. There was something in Suleiman's manner that alerted her. He was mocking her—deliberately baiting her to see her reaction.

'He is yours to do with as you will, my lord. I ask only for justice.'

'Ah…' A wicked light danced in his eyes. 'Now you change your tune, Eleanor. You ask for justice from a savage! Think you I am capable of justice?'

'If you are like your father, yes. I have heard that he is a truly great man and that his words are always wise. I believe that you will do none of these things you threaten for they are not just in this case.'

Suleiman tossed back his head and gave a shout of laughter, as his rage began to abate. 'I vow you are a sorceress, Eleanor. How did you read my mind?'

'There was a look in your eyes that gave you away, my lord.' She met his gaze with a proud stare as she began to realise that he was mocking her for sport, taunting her to punish her for her defiance. 'I think you would make game with me, sir. So, what would you consider just for my brother?'

'We have a school for the sons of the Janissaries in the palace. There the boys study and also learn the skills of war. If your brother wishes to kill his enemies, it is just that he should learn how it may be done— do you not think so?'

Eleanor could hardly believe her ears. He was sending her brother to school! She had expected many things, but not this.

He was watching her expectantly. 'You do not speak, my lady. Has something happened to your tongue?'

'I was thinking that it was the judgement of Solomon.'

'Ah, yes…that is a story from the book of fables your people call the Bible, is it not?'

'Yes, my lord. It is a story from the Bible. Have you read a Christian Bible, my lord?'

'Such a thing would be forbidden to one of the Faithful,' Suleiman said. 'Another day you shall tell me the story of this wise judge you call Solomon—but now we have other things to discuss. Your brother was blameless and has been treated accordingly, but you have admitted your fault and stand convicted of your crime.'

Eleanor sensed that he was lying when he said he had not read the Bible or at least looked inside its covers, but her heart quickened as she saw the expression in his eyes.

'Yes, my lord. There is the matter of my punishment.'

Suleiman nodded, his eyes narrowed so that the thick dark lashes veiled his thoughts from her. 'What would you think a fitting punishment for a woman who betrayed her lord in the arms of another man?'

Eleanor gasped as she saw the expression on his face—which was clearly jealousy. Her heart pounded and she felt as if she could not breathe. 'He was my brother, my lord. It was but an innocent kiss. I meant no harm—nor disrespect to you.'

'Women have been executed for lying carnally with their brother before this, Eleanor. In your case I believe it was innocent—but nevertheless such embraces are forbidden unless your lord is present and permits a decorous embrace. Yours was not restrained or decorous—indeed, so free was your passion that I think I can be forgiven for mistakenly believing he was your lover.'

Her cheeks were hot as she looked at him. 'Indeed, I have never kissed a man other than my brother or father—and if my kisses seemed passionate it was because I was so glad to see my brother alive and well. I had no intention of betraying you with any man, my lord. I beg you to believe me—I would not do that! I would not willingly lie with any man other than my husband.'

'Yet you spurned me when I said that I would honour you above my other women, that I would make you my wife—why was that, Eleanor? Am I an ignorant, cruel savage and not worthy of you?'

'No! No, of course not—I think you a good and generous man at heart and I have wanted to thank you for your kindness in sending the monkey and the birds...' Her voice faltered as he looked at her with narrowed eyes and she blushed. 'And the gifts you sent me...they were too generous, my lord. But I do thank you for them, and for treating my brother so fairly. Indeed, if I wished to marry any man...' She faltered and blushed as she realised what she had so nearly said, hoping he would not guess what had been in her mind, but she saw from the gleam in his eyes that he knew.

'So we make some progress,' Suleiman said, nodding to himself. 'I should end this nonsense now, Eleanor. You are a foolish child and do not know yourself. I would swear there was passion in you...' His eyes narrowed and glinted. 'Shall I show you how foolish you are to fear the loss of your maidenhead?'

Eleanor shook her head wordlessly. How could she explain that it was not fear of the physical act that held her back from giving herself to him—but the need to retain her freedom of spirit?

'I know you can take me here and now if you wish it, my lord. I cannot fight you, for your generosity prevents me. You make me your slave by your generosity, and if the price I must pay is to be your concubine then I shall accept as best I can…'

'But I must take for you will not give—is that it, Eleanor?' He looked deep into her eyes and she trembled at the fire she saw burning within them. 'If I force you to my bed, I shall never have you willingly—I shall never have that part you keep sacred within you—that is what you are telling me, is it not?'

Eleanor hung her head, for there was something in his manner at that moment that made her ashamed of her churlishness. He had given her so much, both in material gifts and understanding, and yet she had made no move to understand him or give anything in return.

'I—I hardly know you, my lord. I am beginning to admire and respect you, but…I cannot do what you expect of me…what Karin says I must do. I—I would be your friend if you—'

'You would be my friend?' Suleiman's gaze narrowed and he appeared to be considering. 'Why should I need a friend, Eleanor? Do you not think I have many about me who would call themselves my friends?'

'Yes, my lord. Forgive me for my presumption. It was only that we share an interest in ancient manuscripts. I—I enjoyed our talk when you asked me to help you read them and—and I have finished the work you set me. I would like to do something that would be of use to you. There are other women more skilled in the arts of love. I think I would provide poor sport for you, my lord.'

Suleiman nodded, a faint smile curving his mouth. 'You argue convincingly, my lady. Yet I wonder…'

Before she knew what he was about, he suddenly thrust her back across the bed and lay down with her, his body pressing hers into the softness of the divan. Eleanor felt his weight crushing her and then his mouth sought hers and he was kissing her…kissing her with a savage hunger that took her breath away. His tongue pushed inside her mouth, darting at the soft inner flesh, arousing strange sensations in her so that she felt her body beginning to melt in the heat of his passion. Oh, what was happening to her? She had never felt like this before, never experienced such pleasure. She moved her head restlessly on the bed, her breathing thick and fast as a little moan escaped her and she felt herself drowning in this new and wondrous feeling that was flooding through her. She knew that she did not want him to stop kissing her, that she wanted him to do all the things Karin had told her he would do—and yet if he did he would truly possess her. And she was afraid of that—afraid to surrender herself to him completely.

'No! No…' She suddenly began to fight him. 'No! I shall not let you…I shall not be your slave…'

'But supposing I refuse to release you?' His dark eyes seemed to devour her. 'Supposing I take my fill of you now? What then, my dove?'

'I—I cannot prevent you, but I beg you not to force me to submit like this…' She drew her breath sharply as he glared down at her and closed her eyes, knowing she could not fight him further. He would do as he wished with her.

Suddenly, Suleiman released her and stood up. She gazed up at him fearfully, expecting to find anger in his eyes, but instead she saw laughter. Why was he laughing? She had defied him yet again. Surely he ought to be angry? He held out his hand to her and when she took it, pulled her to her feet. The grasp of his hand made her tremble inwardly and she could not look into his eyes.

'That was just a little reminder, my lady,' he murmured. 'I wanted to test your obedience—for you promised to obey me out of gratitude, but it seems you forgot your promise as soon as it was given.'

'It isn't amusing,' she said, her feathers ruffled by his mockery. 'I—I am sorry, my lord, but I cannot be as submissive as your other women. It is not in my nature. I am too independent.'

'And is it this you fear to lose if you come to my bed, Eleanor?' He nodded as she remained silent. 'Yes, I begin to understand you, my lady—and I find you most amusing. You do not see why, but that is no matter. It is not for you to know everything—you are merely a woman. You should try to remember that and your place in the world. Remember that I am your lord and master—and tell me again why you think you are qualified to be my friend.'

He was provoking her, trying to make her lose her temper! She was beginning to know him now, to understand the quixotic nature of this man who called himself her master.

'You are a wicked, teasing man!' Eleanor cried. 'No one has ever mocked at me before.'

'Have they not?' Now she could see the laughter in his face. 'Then perhaps it is time they did. Now, tell me—what would I enjoy if I made you my counsellor and friend?'

'I have read much of ancient histories and the se-

crets of the art of astrology are known to me. I know
how to cast a chart and how to read it—I could draw
yours if it pleased you.'

'Indeed?' Suleiman looked at her, amusement dying
to be replaced by a new interest. 'Can you use the
instruments you saw in my hall?'

'Yes, my lord—at least, some of them. Some are
new to me, but I know how to take the angles of the
stars and to interpret what is meant by the alignment
of one to another.'

'Then I might find a use for you…' The laughter
was back in his eyes again. 'I agree that you would
probably be poor sport in bed, Eleanor. You do not
have the arts and skills a woman should properly have.
It is Karin's duty to teach you these things, but I think
in your case it would be a waste of her valuable time.
There are other women for pleasure, but I doubt that
any of them could cast a horoscope for me.' He nodded, seeming highly pleased with something. 'I shall
send for you again tomorrow afternoon. Be ready to
come to me every day, Eleanor—and make sure you
read the books I send you. I shall expect you to be
able to discuss the work I have set you.'

'Oh, yes, my lord,' she agreed eagerly. 'You will
not find me lacking in diligence, I promise you. I shall
try to please you—and I do thank you for your for-
bearance in the matter of my brother.'

'I have behaved well for a savage, have I not,
Eleanor?'

Her cheeks flamed as she caught the mockery in his
voice once more. 'I beg you will forgive me for my
ignorance in so naming you, my lord. You are more
intelligent and better educated than most men I have

met in my life. Indeed, I think you the equal of my father.'

'Then I am truly honoured,' Suleiman replied, bowing his head. 'For I believe that you could not give a higher compliment, Eleanor. Go now—I have important business awaiting me and I have wasted too much time on a mere woman already.'

Eleanor's temper sparked, then she caught the flicker in his eyes and knew that once more he was baiting her—deliberately emphasising a woman's lowly state to make her fly into a rage. He could read her far too easily! But he should not have best of her. She smiled and curtsied to him in the manner she would employ at an English court.

'I am sure that a man of your rank must always have important business, my lord. Forgive me for having given you so much trouble by my foolish thoughtlessness—but as a woman I must be forgiven for such lapses. I can know no better.'

Suleiman chuckled deep in his throat and she sensed that she had pleased him. 'That is very much better, Eleanor. If you continue to improve your temper, we may yet reach this state of friendship on which you set so much store. Go now—before you push me too far. Remember always that though I may choose to assume the manners of a civilized man—the savage lies just beneath the surface. Rouse him at your peril.'

Eleanor left, her heart racing madly. This new mood of the lord Suleiman was very odd and yet it pleased her—it pleased her very much. She had begun by fearing and hating him, had learned to respect him for his generosity and had now begun to like him.

The women gathered round Eleanor as she returned to the harem. From their faces it was easy to see that they were amazed she had returned, apparently un-touched and none the worse for her adventure.

'What happened?' Anastasia cried. 'I was so afraid for you, Eleanor. I thought you would be beaten—or put to death. You were so foolish. Kissing and hug-ging that man in full view of our lord's window. Did you not know what might happen to you if Suleiman saw you?'

'He did—he witnessed everything,' Eleanor replied. 'But, you see, the youth I kissed was my brother Richard. He was taken when our ship was attacked and I thought never to see him again. I did not think of what I was doing when I hugged and kissed him. When I saw him bending down to fasten the cage I simply felt such joy and relief that I ran to him without considering the consequences of my actions.'

'Were you taken to our lord?' Anastasia asked, looking at her curiously. 'Did he not punish you?'

'Oh, yes, he punished me in his way,' Eleanor said ruefully remembering his teasing. 'But I have discov-ered that the lord Suleiman is not by nature a cruel man, though his position in this place may lead him to be so at times—he was just to both me and my brother.'

Anastasia stared at her in awe. No other women would dare to say such things. 'But what did he do to your brother? It is forbidden for a woman of the harem to embrace any man other than her lord—even a brother.'

'Yes, our lord explained that to me,' Eleanor said. She was determined not to disclose Richard's fate, for she believed that Suleiman would not wish it com-monly known that he had been lenient. Some might think it weakness on his part and try to abuse his generosity. 'He has done what he thought right and it is not for us to question that. I am to be given more scholarly work to do and I shall be sent for each afternoon to perform those tasks our lord requires.'

Anastasia was stunned into silence. Suleiman was not known for his cruelty, but other women had been punished in the past for less than Eleanor had done. It was clear that she had special influence with him, and that meant the other women must look up to her.

'Fatima has been eagerly anticipating news of your demise,' she said after a moment or two of reflection. 'She will be disappointed to learn that you have not been punished.'

'Yes—but I do not think our lord intends to take me as his wife. It may be that he will send for her again soon. For your own sake, you must do nothing to antagonise her, Anastasia. She is still his favourite.'

'Perhaps…' The other girl looked at her doubtfully. 'Has…has he not taken you to his bed?'

'I think that our lord requires other things of me,' Eleanor replied, though in her heart she knew it was not quite the truth. Suleiman was playing a game with her, but in the end he would win and then she would have no choice but to submit. 'We shall see what happens in the future. I cannot tell…'

Nor could she tell her true feelings concerning these matters. She had been so close to succumbing to those odd feelings that had flooded her whole being as she lay beneath him on the divan. For a few minutes she had wanted to please him—had wanted him to pleasure her!

Surely she had not come so far in such a short time? Eleanor knew that she was gradually losing her fear and dislike of the world to which she had been brought forcibly. She quite enjoyed being in the harem with her friends sometimes, and though she also needed her privacy and her work, Suleiman had made both these things possible. Though she fought against the truth, she knew that the time she spent with him was a joy to her.

Why, then, was she fighting what she knew must be inevitable? He could take her whenever he chose and she would be powerless to resist him—and yet he had waited. Why? What more did he want of her?

She had told him she had come to respect and admire him, and she was beginning to like the man she suspected very few others ever saw—but what was this other feeling he had aroused in her?

Chapter Seven

The expression in Suleiman's eyes was harder than granite as he looked at the creature before him, his fury leashed only by the thinnest of threads. His treatment of Eleanor and her brother earlier had been very different from the punishment he intended for Abu now that his inquiries were complete.

'Do you deny that you sent the youth to the harem gardens?'

Abu looked into the unforgiving eyes of his half-brother and trembled inwardly as he saw the contempt there. 'No, I do not deny it,' he said. There was little point in lying for his plan had somehow gone wrong, and the woman went unpunished despite her crime. 'I saw no harm in it—he was but a youth and I wanted to show you that the infidel woman would betray you given the chance.'

'So it was done for my benefit?' Suleiman's gaze narrowed in contempt. Did the eunuch think he was so easily deceived? Well, he was about to discover his mistake. 'I am not such a fool as to believe that, Abu. You did it because you blamed her for your removal from the harem. You should know that she had nothing to do with that—I have had it in mind to remove you for some time. Rumours have come to my ears…tales that, if true, would mean your death.'

'You may do with me as you will,' Abu muttered sullenly. 'You have the power. Our father gave you everything—while I was given the choice of remaining here as half a man or being sent to work in the galleys. I know that you have always despised me— and now you have your chance to kill me. So be it— my life is worthless to me anyway. I shall not beg you for mercy.'

'Had I been given your choice I would have gone to the galleys,' Suleiman replied harshly. 'You would have had your chance to earn your freedom after five years and could have perhaps become master of a ship yourself. Better to risk death in the galleys than live as you do now.'

'I have not your strength. I should have died chained like a dog,' Abu said and looked at his half-brother with hatred. 'You do not know what it is like to be a slave—you have always been the favourite son…'

'But you knew that before you made your choice. You stayed and you abused your position of trust. And now I may punish you as I see fit. Our father has left the choice to me—what shall I do with you, Abu? What would be a just punishment—not only for the folly you committed in giving the key to the harem gardens to that youth—but for your other crimes?' He saw a flicker of fear in Abu's eyes. 'Did you really imagine that I would not discover what you did, my brother? Did you believe that you could dispose of your master's property without being discovered? You might have succeeded had you been content to indulge

in your sly little deals once or twice, but like all
thieves you became greedy. You were noticed coming
from the slave merchant's house and it was reported
to me some months ago. I did nothing for a time,
waiting to see if it was just a single mistake—but I
know all now. I know that six women and two youths
have disappeared without trace from the palace.'

'Then kill me...' Abu's eyes flared with defiance.
'Do it yourself, Suleiman. Give me the honour of
death by your scimitar—or have you no stomach for
it?'

Suleiman looked at him consideringly for a moment, then he walked over to a little cabinet, opened
a drawer and took out a wicked-looking knife with a
long curved blade. He removed its sheath and walked
back to Abu, the blade revealed in all its deadly
beauty. Then he threw the knife to the floor about three
feet from Abu's feet, which was an equal distance
from his own.

'Pick it up and try to kill me,' he said. 'You complain that I have all the advantages—now I am offering you the chance to live. Kill me and you will be
granted your freedom.'

Abu's eyes narrowed in suspicion. 'You lie to trick
me,' he cried. 'The moment I move towards the knife
your guards will rush in and kill me.'

'No, they have orders not to interfere,' Suleiman
said. 'But they are aware of what we are saying, make
no mistake. I, Suleiman Bakhar, grant you your life if
you can kill me.'

'It's a trick...' Abu shook his head. 'No, you cannot
force me to fight you. I should lose anyway. I have
no chance of winning against you. Everyone knows

you are skilled in these arts. It is a sham and I shall die whatever I do.'

'So you are still a coward?' Suleiman's mouth curved in a sneer of contempt. 'You are brave when you hold the whip and the woman is defenceless, but when it comes to fighting a man you have milk in your veins. You are not worthy to be my brother and I shall not treat you as one. You will be sent to the galleys for five years, and you may earn your freedom by the sweat of your back—it is more than you granted to those women you sold into a life of misery in the lowest brothels.'

Suleiman turned away to pick up a bell that would summon the guard, and in that moment Abu sprang for the knife. He had it in his hand and was aiming for his half-brother's back when Suleiman turned, grabbing Abu's forearm and jerking him so that he went flying over his shoulder. The movement was so fast and so unexpected that the eunuch lay winded and bewildered wondering what had happened, the knife now in his half-brother's possession.

'Kill me, then,' he cried. 'Kill me now. You intended it all the time.'

'I do not lie or cheat,' Suleiman said. 'You had your chance to fight me fairly. Had you done so, I would have spared you and set you free even had I won—but now your punishment is set. Take him away…'

Three guards had come into the room as they spoke, and they laid rough hands on Abu, dragging him to his feet and carrying him off as he screamed abuse at Suleiman's back, which was now turned against him.

'May Allah curse you…may you never reach paradise…may your entrails be eaten by wild dogs.'

Suleiman ignored Abu's curses as he was taken

away. A swift death by beheading would perhaps have been kinder than five years in the galleys, but Abu deserved his punishment. Yet even so the whole incident left a sour taste in Suleiman's mouth. Had there been another way…but to have simply banished Abu would have been considered weakness in the eyes of others.

Suleiman understood the nature of the world in which he lived; it was often cruel and even savage as Eleanor had claimed, but a firm hand was needed to keep order. Caliph Bakhar had told him that it was not always easy to hand out the harsh punishments necessary, but it had to be done if the order of the empire was to stand.

For how long would such an empire continue to flourish? Suleiman Bakhar had pondered it often, for although Suleiman the Magnificent was a just and wise ruler he was no longer young—and after him, what? The Ottoman Empire had ruled by blood and fear, and when weakness was added to that it could become corrupt and brutal.

The Caliph's son might never have left his father's palace, but he knew that there was hatred between the outside world and the empire. This hatred was grounded in differences of religion and culture, but it had been compounded by the many victories of Suleiman the Magnificent over his rivals and enemies—yet one day he would be gone and then the empire would begin to crumble. It had been predicted by astrologers and it would come to pass if no lessons were learned from the past.

It was Suleiman Bakhar's opinion that the time had come to try and make peace with the Christian world. If this were not attempted, one day the forces of

Christendom would unite to drive their enemies from
the sea. Perhaps not while the Sultan lived, but after
his death. The Sultan's son Selim was rumoured to be
weak and marred with the cruelty of his kind, and if
he were to rule in his father's place it could lead only
to the gradual downfall of the empire.

Yet there was nothing to be done, for Suleiman
Bakhar was tied to his father's palace, kept from any
valuable work he might have done for his country by
his father's fear of losing him. Besides, his opinion
counted for less than a single grain of sand and there
was none to heed it.

'May it be as Allah wills it,' he murmured to himself and dismissed the problem from his mind. There
were far more pressing problems to be solved for the
moment…not least the delicious one of how best to
tempt Eleanor to his bed.

Eleanor pored over the book Suleiman had sent her.
It had come from the great Venetian printing presses
and concerned the benefits of mixing astrology with
medicine. Certain remedies were said to be more effective if used when the stars were in a particular conjunction, and although she did not really see how this
could be so, it made fascinating reading. How she
wished that she might consult her father, for he had
known far more on the subject than she. She wished
that Sir William could have talked to Suleiman, and
believed the two men would have found pleasure in
each other.

Once again her thoughts returned to her brother.
Richard hated Suleiman and all he stood for.

Knowing her brother was in the palace and attend-
ing the school was both a pleasure and a torment to

her. As children they had spent much of their time together, and even when they were older they had shared the same delights and pastimes. Richard had often come to seek her out when she was at some female duty and coaxed her into going out with him.

How it must irk him now that he had no freedom to do as he pleased. Like her, Richard would find life very different here to the one they had known at home. They had been fortunate in their father, their lives rich and fulfilling...but at least they were luckier than many who had suffered a fate similar to their own.

Eleanor was growing more content with her lot, though her defiant spirit still struggled against the fact that she was a slave, the property of her master. Yet she knew that she must make the best of things and count her blessings.

Besides the book, Suleiman had also sent her a new journal to replace the one she had almost filled with his own work, and she had transcribed passages of the book she thought might interest him. She thought that he was still concerned about his friend in the Janissaries who had developed a lump in his side, for he had marked one section and she paid particular attention to this so that she could discuss it with him when he sent for her as he had promised.

She could hardly wait for the afternoon to come, and was conscious of excitement when Karin told her that she had at last been sent for.

'You are to take the book you have been studying.' Karin looked at her in a slightly puzzled way. 'All this is most strange, Eleanor. I have never heard of it happening before—older women are sometimes asked to become an adviser in domestic matters, but never a woman of your age and beauty.'

'I think the lord Suleiman likes to talk to me,' Eleanor said. 'Besides, I have been able to help him with some texts he found difficult to read.'

Karin nodded. 'Yes, I see that, but it is still a little strange.' She frowned and looked thoughtful. 'I tell you this in confidence, Eleanor—and beg that you will speak of it to no one else. It is my lord's wish that none of the concubines should know this… I have been told that Abu has been sent to the galleys as a punishment for what he did—and they also whisper that he tried to kill the lord Suleiman.'

'No!' Eleanor felt a sudden shaft of fear. 'Was he hurt—the lord Suleiman?'

'No, not at all. He disarmed Abu instantly.' Karin smiled at her. 'You have never seen your lord fight, have you? He is both clever and strong, and he always wins in the arena.'

Eleanor nodded, her cheeks warm. She had heard this from others, and found herself thinking that she would enjoy watching such a test of skill. 'Does he often fight?'

'It is one of his main pleasures to train and fight with the Janissaries,' Karin told her.

Eleanor made no reply. It seemed to her that Suleiman Bakhar was a man of extreme contrasts— the fierce competitor who delighted in the arts of war and the clever, studious man who had made his eyes ache looking for a cure for a sick friend.

She knew that this man interested her as no man ever had before, and the thought of seeing him, of being with him, made her heart beat faster so that she walked more quickly. By the time she arrived at his apartments she was flushed and a little out of breath.

'You look warm, my lady,' Suleiman said, offering

her his hand. 'Come, we shall walk in the shade of the garden for a while before we begin our studies. If you would like it, I shall show you my hawks.'

'Do you go hawking, my lord?' Eleanor asked. 'It is a pastime my father greatly enjoyed when in the north of our country. We did not live there, for as I have told you our estates were in the west—but my father had a sister he dearly loved and her husband had a great estate in the north. My uncle had a wonderful falconry, and sometimes he would let me stroke the birds.'

'Did you fly the hawks, Eleanor?'

'Once,' she replied, smiling at the memory. 'My cousin was training a new bird and he showed me how it was done. I was thrilled when the bird came to my lure.'

'It is truly a magnificent sight to see the hawk fly free and then have it return to your hand,' Suleiman said. 'Perhaps one day we shall ride out into the countryside together, Eleanor. You might like to hunt with me when I fly my birds?'

'It would be a pleasure and an honour, my lord.'

Suleiman had been leading her towards a door that opened out into an enclosed garden. She caught a glimpse of shaded walks and fountains playing into little pools, very much as in the gardens of the harem. But now he stopped and glanced at her, a flicker of amusement in his eyes.

'What has caused this transformation, my lady? Have you no objections to my plans today? No obstinacy?'

'Why should I object when you suggest only that which would give me pleasure, my lord?'

'I am glad that you share my pleasure in the hawks,

Eleanor.' He smiled at her, and they continued on in silence until they came to the falconry at the end of a shaded walk. This was a magnificent structure with both open and closed areas, so that the birds might fly free as well as perch inside when night fell.

Suleiman took a key on a chain he wore on his person and unlocked the door, going inside to bring out a fine peregrine falcon. 'How do you like my darling?' he asked in soft husky tones, stroking the head of the bird with his finger. 'Is she not beautiful?'

Eleanor looked at the glossy feathers and dark, glittering eyes of the female falcon, and knew that she was perhaps the most magnificent she had ever seen. Female peregrines were faster and stronger than the male of the species and much prized for their strength in hunting.

'Very beautiful, my lord. What is her name?'

'Scheherazade,' he replied and looked at her expectantly.

Eleanor laughed and met his look with a sparkling one of her own. 'I have heard the name,' she said. 'It is a legend long told amongst the peoples of Arabia, is it not?'

'It has been told for centuries past, and I believe was Persian in origin, though the story is set in India. As perhaps you know, it is the story of the betrayed Sultan who vowed to cut off his wife's head at dawn and take a new one every day,' Suleiman said. 'By her cleverness in telling stories Scheherazade was able to prolong the day of her execution for one hundred and one days, by which time the Sultan had fallen in love with this clever woman and could not bear to be parted from her.'

Eleanor nodded, recognising the humour and wit

shown by his choice of the name for the bird. 'Is your peregrine so clever that you could not bear to part with her?'

'She is both brave and clever,' Suleiman replied, 'and yet she has learned to love her master. She will fly free and return to me without a lure.'

'Then she is an exceptional bird,' Eleanor said. 'I do not think my uncle had such a hawk in his aviary.'

'It is very rare to find such loyalty, such devotion— in any female,' Suleiman replied. 'That is what makes her beyond price.'

He lifted his wrist suddenly, giving the peregrine her freedom to circle the gardens. She flew high and circled several times before settling in a tree high above them, but when Suleiman held out his arm and called to her in the soft husky voice that held such fascination for both the bird and the woman who watched, Scheherazade flew back to him.

'I have never seen that before,' Eleanor said and there was a kind of awe in her words. 'Always, the birds come for the lure, for food—but she came to the sound of your voice.'

'She knows that I love her,' Suleiman said softly. 'And she has learned to love her master—though at first she longed to be free. Now she rejects freedom for love.'

Eleanor felt her spine tingle as she met the dark intensity of his eyes. What was he telling her? That she too would have a certain freedom if she gave herself to him in love? To be truly loved would be a wondrous thing. Her heart seemed to catch with an odd pain, and she knew a deep longing within her, but she suppressed it fiercely. She was a woman, not a bird of prey!

She turned away to inhale the perfume of a musk rose and Suleiman left her to return the hawk to its perch in the aviary. When he returned to her, it was as if the incident had never happened.

'Well, my lady,' he said in his mocking tone. 'And what have you learned since we met? I hope you have not been idle?'

'No, my lord. I have been translating the work you set me into English and trying to discover exactly what circumstances are necessary for the cure to work.'

'And what have you discovered?'

'It seems that the stars must be in a certain alignment when the powder is applied—but I fear that particular conjunction will not come about for some weeks yet.'

'That is a pity,' Suleiman said, and his expression was grave. 'The surgeons tell me that if they are to cut it must be soon or the sickness will be too advanced. I had hoped to spare my friend the knife, but I fear there is no hope for it. I shall give the order this evening.'

'I am sorry, my lord.'

'Yes, so am I. Too often the knife leads to infection and death—besides the pain of bearing it.'

'But if there is nothing else to be done…' She saw that he was distressed by the idea of his friend's suffering. 'I have copied out a recipe for an ointment that I know to be helpful in the treatment of wounds. It is made from cobwebs and might prove useful…if your physicians would care to have it made up.'

'Give it to me,' Suleiman replied. 'We shall try everything that may help him—for he is a brave soldier and does not deserve to die in such a way.'

'Surely no one does, my lord. Medical science can do only so much—the rest is in God's hands.'

Suleiman nodded, his expression thoughtful. 'But whose god, Eleanor—yours or mine?'

'Who can know that for certain?' she asked, wondering that he should voice his thoughts so openly to her, for surely it was forbidden to him to think in such a way? And even a powerful man could be brought down by the jealousy and spite of others. To discuss such matters with her was to make himself vulnerable to bigotry and prejudice. 'When the ship I was on almost floundered in a storm I prayed to all the gods for help—yours, mine and the god of the sea.'

'You should not say such things,' Suleiman warned her, though he himself had begun the discussion. 'Do you not know that you could be put to death for such wickedness?'

'But not by you, my lord,' she replied, her eyes meeting his steadily. 'I believe you have thought more on these matters than most.'

'I am one of the Faithful,' Suleiman answered. 'But it is correct that I have considered other religions to discover what is truth. I remain loyal to my father's faith for it is the basis for my life and any other would make it impossible for me to live here. If I believed in your god and accepted the teachings of your faith I should have to leave—and that would break my father's heart. He is a good man, Eleanor, and I would rather die than bring harm to him.'

'Yes, of course. I knew it must be so.'

Suleiman frowned. 'I think you see too much, my lady. Be warned—a still tongue makes a wise head. There are those who would use what you say to destroy you.'

'Yes, my lord. But I have been used to speaking my mind with my father who, like you, was a man of vision, with the understanding to question and not accept blindly all he was taught. It is pleasant sometimes to open your heart and mind to the one person who will understand.'

'And you believe you can open your mind to me, Eleanor?' His eyes danced with amusement. 'What is this? It is not many days since you thought me beyond any feeling or decency.'

'My lord is pleased to mock me,' she said and blushed. The look in his eyes was making her heart race like the wind and she found herself longing to be held in his arms, her lips parting as if in invitation of his kiss. 'We have reached a new plane of understanding.'

'Have we, my lady?' Suleiman smiled. 'That is good…I think. Now, are you prepared to cast my chart? Think you, you can do it accurately?'

'I can draw up your chart and explain what is the meaning of the angles and alignments,' Eleanor said. 'But I am not sure that it is always easy to interpret their precise meaning—but I will willingly show you how it is done.'

'Then we shall begin at once. I was born on the fifteenth of August at the hour of midnight…'

'Then you are a Leo,' Eleanor said and smiled. 'I might have known it would be so—for the lion is king of the heavens, is he not? He has the power of the sun and was born to be a leader of men.'

Suleiman's eyes gleamed as he caught the hint of mockery in her voice. 'I have been told this many times, my lady. Now tell me, under which sign were you born?'

'I was born under the sign of Sagittarius,' Eleanor replied, 'I believe that is the sign of the archer or hunter.'

'And does the hunter capture and kill the lion?' Suleiman asked with a lift of his fine dark brows.

'I am told that the two are perfect partners,' Eleanor replied, but would not meet the gleam in his eyes.

'Indeed,' Suleiman said. 'I shall test your skill with the art of astrology, my lady—but I warn you that I shall know if you seek to flatter or deceive me. Give me only a true reading, for I value honesty above all things.'

'Then I shall not seek to deceive you, whether the readings be good or bad, my lord.'

Suleiman frowned over the chart Eleanor had drawn for him. His own skill in the art was sufficient for him to know that she had been as accurate as most who called themselves astrologers, and that her reading was very similar to that of the last man he had summoned to cast his horoscope.

She had not mentioned the flame that would burn him, or that he had lessons to learn, but she had told him that the stars seemed to forecast change for him.

'This alignment of Jupiter with your star seems to indicate that there will be a struggle, my lord. I see…some danger for you in the near future, but after this you will gain something you have long desired.'

'I have been given a similar prediction before this,' he replied. 'I was inclined to doubt the astrologer's words for many have tried to lie to me in the hope of gaining favour. The trouble is, no one can explain exactly what the signs mean. A man may desire many things…'

'Indeed, that is true, but I do not think it is in the power of any man to predict the future exactly, my lord—though I think trends are often very accurate. I believe that your life may be going to change in some fundamental way.'

'Thank you,' Suleiman said and smiled at her. 'You have done well, Eleanor. You may return to your apartments now.'

'Will my lord send for me tomorrow?'

'I shall send you more books,' he replied. 'But I am leaving on a hunting trip with my father in the morning. When I return I shall send for you and we shall discuss what you have learned.'

'Yes, my lord.' She turned to go, feeling a sense of loss though she did not understand why. 'Take care on your trip…'

'Stay a moment.' He caught her arm as she turned away, swinging her round to face him. 'You sounded as if you cared what happened to me. Would it distress you if I did not return, Eleanor?'

'Yes, my lord…' She hung her head and would not look at him for fear that he should gaze into her eyes and read too much. 'And—and I shall miss our talks while you are away.'

'Then perhaps I should take you with me?'

'Take me with you?' She stared up at him, startled by his suggestion and her heart began to pound with excitement. 'Do you mean that, my lord?'

'It would mean that you have to wear the veil and the casacche you hate so much. You would also have to be carried in a horse-drawn litter—my father would be outraged if I threw you across my saddle, Eleanor. There must be no attempts at escape, no wilfulness. If

I took you with me on this outing, I would expect you to behave with all the respect due to the Caliph.'

'Oh yes, yes,' she breathed, her eyes lighting with excitement. 'I promise to behave just as you would wish, my lord.'

'Not as I would wish,' he replied in the soft husky voice that he had used when handling Scheherazade. 'I would let you fly high like my hawks, my lady, trusting you to return to my hand—but my father expects certain behaviour of a woman. It is for his sake that I ask your promise not to try to escape.'

'I give you my word,' Eleanor said, looking into his eyes. 'I shall not abuse your trust, my lord. I swear it on my father's honour.'

'Then I accept your good faith,' he said and reached out his hand to trace the line of her cheek and then the smooth arch of her throat. 'I believe we begin to know one another, my lady. It is good.'

'Yes,' she replied, her throat tight with emotion. She could scarcely breathe and her senses swam as she felt the warmth spread through her whole body. 'It is good, my lord.'

Her heart was singing as she retraced her steps towards the harem. For some reason she was feeling happy—happier than she had ever felt in her life before. She could not believe that her feelings had changed so soon. Was she a fool to let herself like Suleiman so much?

Was his kindness to her merely a honeyed trap? She knew that he was playing her, drawing her to him on a gossamer-fine thread, and that eventually she would be bound by it like a fly in a spider's web. What she did not know was how she would feel then. Would she struggle against it and regret her lost freedom—or would she fly back to the hand of the man who had tamed her spirit like the peregrine?

Her thoughts were rudely interrupted by Fatima, who grabbed her arm as soon as she entered the harem. It was clear that Suleiman's ex-favourite was in a temper, her dark eyes flashing as she glared at Eleanor.

'You lied to me,' she cried viciously. 'You swore that you did not wish to become Suleiman's wife—and yet you go to him every day. He has not sent for me in over a week. It is because of you—because you have turned him against me as you did against Abu.'

'I have said nothing against you,' Eleanor said. 'I do not know why Suleiman has not…'

She broke off as Karin came up to them. The older woman was looking thoughtful and a little anxious.

'Suleiman has asked for you, Fatima,' she said. 'You are to go to him at once.'

'At once?' Fatima looked surprised. 'But I have not bathed or perfumed myself. Surely you have got the message wrong?'

'His order was that you should go at once,' Karin replied. 'I should obey him if I were you, Fatima. He did not seem best pleased.'

'But he was in such a good mood when I left…' Eleanor said and then bit back the words as she saw the flash of anger in Fatima's eyes. 'At least, he seemed to be…'

'Word has come that Abu has escaped his guards,' Karin said as Fatima flounced away, clearly annoyed by the preemptory order from her master. 'Suleiman was very angry. It is said that someone within the palace must have bribed them…'

'But surely…the lord Suleiman's guards are loyal to him, are they not?' Eleanor looked at her anxiously.

'Could this mean danger for our lord? He—he is to leave on a hunting trip with the Caliph tomorrow and…and I am to go with him.'

'Yes, I know. He had sent for me to tell me—that is how I knew about Abu's escape. I was there when the news came.'

'It is very strange that he should be allowed to escape,' Eleanor said. 'Has the lord Suleiman enemies in the palace?'

'There are always intrigues and petty jealousies in a place like this,' Karin told her. 'Suleiman is his father's favourite son—but he is not his only son. Abu is his half-brother and there are others.'

'Abu was my lord's brother?'

'Yes—though because his mother was never a favourite of the Caliph he's been treated no better than any other slave, and I believed he deeply resented this. There are others who have been favoured more than Abu—but given lowly positions within the Caliph's household. Suleiman can do no wrong in his father's eyes, but if he should die the Caliph would have to appoint another son as his heir.'

'It would not be Abu…for the Caliph would want grandsons to carry on his line…'

'No, it would not be Abu—but he could have been promised his freedom and wealth if he brought about the death of the lord Suleiman.'

Eleanor shivered as the fear trickled like ice down her spine. 'I saw danger for him in the charts,' she whispered. 'And tomorrow he leaves on a hunting trip. Many things may happen at such a time.'

'Yes, that is true,' Karin said. 'You must watch and listen, Eleanor. Suleiman is a worthy successor to his father—but there are others who are not…some who would not hesitate to have all his concubines strangled if they took over his place in the Caliph's household.'

'You do not mean it?' Eleanor was horrified.

'Yes, I do,' Karin said. 'It is often done when a man dies. Sometimes the new master takes pity on the women and allows them to return to their homes—but that is not always the case.'

Eleanor's face went white as she saw the expression in the older woman's eyes. 'That is a terrible custom. I cannot believe anyone could be so cruel.'

'You have been fortunate,' Karin said. 'You were bought by a good master—had you been less fortunate you could have been treated very differently. Your stubbornness would have brought you a beating in many households.'

'Yes, I see that…' She looked at Karin with dark, anxious eyes. 'It would be best not to speak of this to anyone else. I would not have my friends upset by what you have told me.'

'I shall tell no one else what I have told you,' Karin agreed. 'But as Suleiman's intended bride I thought that you should be aware of what had happened. For if your lord is in danger, then so too are you. I fear that Abu would reserve your punishment to himself…'

Eleanor felt sick as she thought of the cruel eunuch who believed her responsible for his downfall. She could not begin to imagine her fate if he were to be in a position of power once more.

Suleiman cursed himself for a fool. He ought to have killed Abu when he had the chance. It was what his father would have done. Their overlord the Sultan Suleiman the Magnificent had put his own sons to death for less than the crimes Abu had committed. It had been a weak moment to spare him, and Suleiman knew that he might rue the day he had allowed himself to be swayed by the tie of blood.

He had felt guilt because he had been favoured so much while Abu had been forced to give up so much—though he knew that, presented with the same choice, he would have taken the galleys. He would rather have died than become a eunuch. It was a barbarous practice to maim a man in that way, to take his manhood from him and strip him of a man's natural pride—but it was necessary to their way of life. A necessary evil to uphold the system.

The eunuchs were thought to be more docile than true men, and they could not defile the women in their charge. It was common enough amongst the children of concubines, for without some form of control there would be constant fighting amongst the sons of important men. Suleiman's own father had had a favourite wife, whose son he had raised up above all others, but there were other sons who had not been dealt with in this way—and Suleiman was aware that some of them would be only too willing to take his place. Some would be willing to kill both him and his father to gain power for themselves.

It was because of this that Suleiman could not defy his father's wish to keep him close. The Caliph was still a strong man, but growing older—one day his other sons might try to wrest power and wealth from him, but not while Suleiman had the loyalty of the Janissaries. He knew that he was both feared and respected, and while this was so the elite guard remained faithful to their master.

Now it seemed that at least one or two of the men he had counted as friends had turned against him—

who had bribed them and in what coin had they been paid?

Suleiman had heard whispers concerning Fatima. He had been told that she had been in league with Abu in the matter of the women who were spirited away from the harem in the night—and of cruel punishments meted out at her command. There were also other tales, which were even more damning, and made him wonder just how far her betrayal had gone. Had she also been responsible for bribing the Janissaries?

He turned as she entered, throwing herself to her knees before him in her customary way, waiting for him to raise her up. She was smiling as he bid her rise, a confident smile on her lips as if she believed he had sent for her to pleasure him. Did she not yet realise that he no longer wanted her—or did she believe she could continue to deceive him?

As he saw the secret satisfaction in her eyes, Suleiman wondered what he had seen in her for so many months. She was sly and vain, and he must control his sudden dislike of her or he might judge her unfairly. Fatima was not liked by others in the harem and these rumours might be malicious and untrue. He would talk to her and discover what he could—but he would not punish her yet. He must be sure of the truth before he did anything for which he might afterwards be sorry...

Chapter Eight

'Suleiman and the Caliph must both die,' Abu said, eyes glowing like black diamonds. 'For, if one lived, retribution would be swift. Our only hope is to take them by surprise—and by taking this hunting trip together they play into our hands.'

He glanced round at the faces of the men who had been bribed to join him—the Caliph's second son Hasan, four of Hasan's guards and two of Suleiman's own men. Abu was not entirely certain of these two, though they were afraid of him. Both had lain with Fatima, which meant they would be put to death if their crime were discovered. She was insatiable, and even when she had been Suleiman's favourite, she had craved sexual pleasure with others. Abu had arranged for her to lie with these two in return for help with the disappearance of a woman from the harem.

'We shall kill them both—and when they are dead I shall rule in my father's place,' Hasan said, his cruel mouth narrowed in a sneer. 'And you shall be my chief adviser, Abu. You may have a free hand in disposing of Suleiman's concubines.'

Abu inclined his head, his features expressionless. He knew he could not hope to become Caliph himself, but he could control this weak fool and rule through him. He moistened his lips with the tip of his tongue at the thought of the power he would hold.

'I shall make you more powerful than your father,' he promised. 'Only play your part, Hasan, and within two days you shall be Caliph…'

'Yes, yes…' Hasan's weak face glowed with the thought of his triumph over the brother who had always taken precedence over him in their father's favour. 'And then I shall dispose of all my enemies…'

'Why do you come to me with this tale, Bayezid?' Suleiman's eyes narrowed as they fixed on his younger brother. 'I know well that you do not like Hasan— why should I believe your story? It might be that you wish to make trouble for him.'

'I cannot make you believe my story,' Bayezid said. 'I can only tell you that I have seen Hasan and Abu together. They thought they had concealed their meeting, but I came upon them behind the stables of the Janissaries, and I heard something. I do not know what it means, but I believe they intend to kill you during the hunting trip with our father.'

'And you do not wish to see me killed?'

'They would also need to kill our father, and I respect the Caliph because he is a good and just man— and I would like to be as he is one day if I can earn the respect of others and be given a position of trust.'

Suleiman nodded. Bayezid was young and studious and, although he knew there was envy and hatred between Hasan and Bayezid, he was inclined to believe his story—especially as he had known Abu must have had help from inside the palace to make his escape. He had thought Abu must have gone long ago, but now he realised the renegade was hiding somewhere within the palace grounds. Clearly he was waiting his chance to do more mischief.

Suleiman could instigate a thorough search, root out the culprits and punish them—or he could allow the conspirators to go ahead with their treachery and have them taken in the act. Perhaps this was the best course, since he would then catch all the birds in one throw.

'Thank you for your warning, brother.' He smiled at Bayezid. 'I believe it took courage to come and tell me—is there some way in which I might reward you?'

Bayezid shook his head. 'I have all that I need, brother. I want only a quiet life and to be left in peace to study. May Allah protect and guide your hand tomorrow.'

'Allah be with you.'

Left alone, Suleiman walked to the window that looked out on the harem gardens. They were deserted at this time of night, for his brother had waited until after dark to come to him in secret.

Suleiman was wrestling with his problem and frowned as he came to his decision. He had given his word to Eleanor that she might accompany them on their hunting trip, but it must be broken. Her presence in the camp would hamper him, for she would be vulnerable and he had no time to watch over her. He would need all his wits about him if he were to defeat his enemies.

Eleanor would be disappointed to be left behind. If it were not so late he would send for her and explain, but the women would be sleeping and anything out of the ordinary might alert the conspirators.

No, he must act as usual, but Eleanor must stay behind tomorrow.

'What do you mean—I am not to accompany the lord Suleiman?' Eleanor stared at Karin in dismay. She had looked forward to this trip outside the confines of the palace and to be denied at the last moment was a terrible disappointment. 'Why? What have I done to displease my lord?'

'I do not know,' Karin replied, frowning. 'He sent word early this morning that you were not to go after all. I am sorry, Eleanor. I suppose that he must have changed his mind.'

'He changed his mind...' Eleanor nodded, her eyes sparking with anger. Suleiman had changed his mind and so she was not to go. Her feelings on the matter were of no importance. He had not even bothered to send for her to tell her himself, merely sending a message at the last moment. It seemed he broke his promises as easily as he made them. 'Yes, I see—I see that he is faithless and cares little for his word.'

'You should not speak so of the lord Suleiman,' Karin said giving her a severe look. 'If it were reported to him, you could be beaten. I am sure he has his reasons for disappointing you.'

Eleanor's temper was at bursting point, but she held it inside. Her anger was almost as much against herself as Suleiman. She had begun to believe in him, to trust him—and now he had done this! It made her realise that he could not be trusted...ever. She would be a fool to let herself be swayed by his soft words and his

promises. He was, after all, nothing but a barbarian—
and next time they met she would keep her distance.

Her mood was not improved as she saw Fatima
preening herself in the harem gardens that morning.
She was wearing a satisfied expression that seemed to
say *she* was back in Suleiman's favour, and the news
that Eleanor was not after all to be taken on the hunting trip made an interesting piece of gossip for the
ladies of the harem.

Some of the women cast her pitying glances, others
made a fuss of Fatima as if wanting to assure her that
they had never even for one moment thought that she
had truly been set aside for this new woman.

Anastasia, Elizabetta and Rosamunde were sympathetic towards Eleanor, telling her that Suleiman must
have good reason not to take her with him. She smiled
and pretended to agree with them, but her heart had
begun to ache and it was difficult for her not to creep
away and weep. But she would not let Fatima see that
it mattered, and so she stayed with the others throughout the day, playing with the monkey and talking to
the parrot, which she was trying to teach to say a few
polite words in French.

It was not until the evening that she retired to her
own room to study and transcribe some of the latest
work that Suleiman had sent her—and then the heaviness of her heart was indeed hard to bear. She was a
fool to have let down her guard even for a moment;
if she once let herself truly care for him, she would
be the same as all the other women who sighed and
waited for him to notice them.

The attack came on the first night at the camp.
During the day the hunting had gone well and they

had killed a wolf in the forest above the plains, which was better sport than the wild boar which was seldom hunted by Muslims. It had been decided they would make deer their sport on the next day.

Suleiman had set his spies to watch Hasan and his guards, and he was warned long before the thin blade of a knife began to slit the side of his pavilion. He watched from the shadows in the far corner as the stealthy figure crept towards the sleeping pallet where he ought to have been lying asleep, and as the dagger was brought down into the bundle he had arranged to resemble a man beneath the blanket.

'Die, you dog!'

The voice proclaimed the identity of the assassin had Suleiman needed proof. 'Unfortunately for you, Abu—that was not me.'

The cloaked figure gave a startled oath, the knife still in his hand as he swung round, gasping his dismay. Suleiman moved forward out of the shadows so that the assassin could see his face. Abu cursed. He lunged wildly at his half-brother, the certainty of what would happen when the discovery of his full treachery was known making him lose his fear.

'So you live still!' he yelled. 'Yet I shall kill you— guards, to me! To me!'

His cry to the men who stood on guard outside the tent went unheeded. He had chosen the men who had once served Suleiman, but they had already sensed his plans had gone awry, hesitating about following him inside and slipped away into the night rather than face the fury of the master they had foolishly betrayed. Somehow the lord Suleiman had learned of the treachery planned this night, and their only chance now was to flee.

Suleiman met his half-brother's attack without hesitation, striking a blow at his arm, and then twisting it so that Abu cried out in pain as a bone cracked and his weapon fell uselessly to the ground. He swayed on his feet, half-fainting in his agony, his eyes sullen and disbelieving as he looked at Suleiman. He had known he was strong, but his skill was even more awesome than Abu had imagined. The cowardly dogs he had paid to help him had refused to enter the tent, saying that they would watch over him and he suspected them of betraying him.

'So now you will kill me,' he said as he looked into Suleiman's cold eyes. 'You will not be foolish enough to spare me again.'

'You made a mistake by throwing in your lot with Hasan,' Suleiman replied, his features set like iron. 'Had your attack been just against me I might have kept to my original plans for you, Abu—but you dared to lift your hand against my father and for that there can be only one punishment.' He raised his voice to summon his trusted guards. 'Take him away!'

Three guards entered the pavilion and laid hands on Abu, dragging him away as he cursed and screamed, for they did not and would not spare him. He would suffer horribly, for he had dared to plot against the life of the Caliph, and such a crime must be punished in a way that would deter others. Even Suleiman could not spare him what was to come—nor would he have considered it.

'My father?' Suleiman asked as a fourth man entered the pavilion after the others had gone. 'The Caliph is unharmed?'

'Your instructions were followed to the letter, my lord,' the captain of the Janissaries replied. 'I took your father's place and when they came to kill him my men were waiting—the traitors have been taken and will be punished in accordance with their crimes.'

'Good—I leave justice in your hands, Omar. And I thank you and your men for their loyalty.'

'The two who betrayed you with Fatima have been arrested—what would you have me do with them, my lord?'

'They may go to the galleys for two years and then be free to go whither they will,' Suleiman said. 'They confessed their crimes and told of the plot against me—and for that I shall spare their lives.'

'You are just, my lord,' Omar said. 'Allah be praised that this night went well—but what of your brother Hasan?'

'Has my father spoken?'

'He says that Hasan may be spared only if you grant him his life.'

'I do not,' Suleiman said, his eyes as cold as deep water ice. 'If he is spared he will plot against us again, and others will be foolish enough to follow. In order that no more lives may be lost, his is forfeit. However, he is not to be tortured and he is to be given a clean death by the sword. I trust you to see that my order is carried out as I have given it, Omar.'

'Again your justice is good, my lord. It is how it should be.'

Suleiman inclined his head, but did not speak as the captain of the guard bowed and left him. A deep shudder went through him as he thought of the fate of the traitors, and he knew that he had never felt so alone—so desperately alone.

The Caliph had felt incapable of ordering the execution of his second son, even though he knew it must

be and so he had left it to Suleiman, who had not
shrunk from his duty—but it was a hard duty, the hard-
est thing he had ever done. To condemn his half-
brothers to death… Abu he had never liked or trusted,
but as a small boy Hasan had been a delightful companion and they had spent much time together. He was
sorry that Hasan's life had come to this sorry end.

Yet it had to be, there was no other way open to
Suleiman. This world in which they lived was a harsh
one and justice must be seen to be done or the fragile
order would crumble about their ears. He had been
weak in allowing Abu to escape death the first time,
but he would not escape this time—and nor would
poor foolish Hasan.

And yet Suleiman felt as if it were he who was
being punished. He shivered again, feeling the darkness descend on him as he went to open the flap of
the pavilion and look out at the stars.

Did those same stars shine in the sky above
England? The land of his mother's birth, of which she
and Eleanor had told him—and would life be less
harsh in such a place?

He doubted it, for had not Eleanor been forced to
flee her home in fear of retribution from a harsh re-
gime? Why did human beings do so much harm to
each other and themselves?

Suleiman gave himself a mental shake. To dream of
a civilisation where people could exist in harmony
without spite or cruelty was to live in a fool's paradise.
Perhaps one day people would learn a new way, but
it would not come in his lifetime.

He smiled wryly at his own thoughts. Saidi Kasim
had taught him too well. He was beset with the doubts
that would best become a philosopher and were not

for the son of Caliph Bakhar, who must be strong and just. He would do better to think of something more pleasant…of a woman's soft limbs and a smile that made him want to drown in her arms.

'Oh, my lady,' he murmured. 'Would that you were here to lie beside me and drive away the demons this night.'

The hunting trip was due to continue for another day, but after that he would send for Eleanor and tell her what he had decided for her future.

Elizabetta was teaching Eleanor to dance, showing her how to sway her hips alluringly. Anastasia was playing music for them, and Rosamunde was standing by to comment and encourage. Some of the other women had also come to watch.

'Yes, you are beginning to get the idea now,' Elizabetta said 'you just need to put a little more feeling into it. Imagine that you are reaching out to your lover, begging him to take you in his arms and caress you…'

Eleanor shook her head, throwing herself down on the cushions and laughing. 'It is no good. I shall never be able to dance the way you do, Elizabetta.'

'That is because you have never learned,' her friend replied. 'It will come if you practise.'

'I will show you how to dance—how it should properly be done.'

Eleanor looked up in surprise as she saw Fatima, wondering how long the other woman had been watching them.

'I have heard that you dance more gracefully than anyone,' she said. 'Please dance for us, Fatima. I should enjoy it.'

'I need no music,' Fatima said. 'The music is in my head.'

She stood poised for a moment, her eyes closed, head down. Then her head came up, eyes open, a smile on her lips. Eleanor was fascinated by the graceful, sensuous swaying of the other woman's body. She had seen the other women dancing, but none of them had Fatima's magic or mystery. It was little wonder that Suleiman had found so much to please him in his beautiful favourite.

Eleanor clapped her hands when the dance ended with Fatima lying on the floor, her arms outstretched. 'That was beautiful,' she said sincerely. 'I have never seen anyone put so much into their dancing, Fatima. I could never dance half as well as you though I practised for years.'

Fatima looked up and her dark eyes were dark with spite. 'That is why you will never keep the favour of the lord Suleiman,' she said. 'He may find you amusing for a while—but then he will send for me again when he tires of you.'

Eleanor did not answer her. In her heart she feared that Fatima was right. Suleiman had seemed pleased with her, but how could she hope to hold him when he could summon any woman he chose? Fatima was beautiful, but so was Rosamunde, and the others were also extremely lovely in their own way. Why should Suleiman prefer Eleanor to his other women?

There was no reason she could see why he should want her more than half a dozen others, and since Fatima was his favourite it was natural that he would continue to send for her. Eleanor felt the sting of jealousy, though she tried hard to suppress it. She had no right to feel jealous! Had she not declared that she had no wish to be his concubine—and indeed she did not wish for it. But she did wish that she might be his love.

There was so much difference between the two things, but she knew that she was asking for the impossible. In Suleiman's world there was no such thing as love, and though he demanded complete faithfulness from his women, he did not give as much in return. Eleanor would be a fool if she allowed herself to care.

She looked up as Karin approached her. 'Your lord has sent for you, Eleanor,' she said. 'You are to go to him at once.'

Eleanor was about to obey, and then something snapped in her head. She was not his slave, even though he had paid gold coin for her, and she would not be sent for.

'Thank my lord for his attention, Karin, but pray tell him I cannot answer his summons for the moment—because I am not well.'

Karin stared at her. 'Are you refusing an order from your master?'

'Was it an order or a request?'

'He asked that you would go to him at once.'

'Then it was a request,' Eleanor said. 'Pray give him my regrets and tell him I am lying on my bed with a headache.'

'But you were dancing a few moments ago…'

'And that is why I now have a terrible headache. Excuse me, please, I must lie down. I am sure that my lord will understand if you explain why I cannot answer his request.'

She got up from her cushion and walked into her own apartments, leaving the other women to stare after

her in awe. How dare she refuse to go to Suleiman?
He would be furious with her and was sure to order
that she be beaten this time.

'Forgive me, my lord,' Karin said, hardly daring to
speak the words. 'Eleanor is lying down with the headache. She begged your pardon for not obeying your
summons, and asked that she be excused for the moment.'

Suleiman stared at her. She was clearly ill at ease
at bringing such a message, and he saw the reason for
her nervousness very plainly. Eleanor was not ill, she
was merely being stubborn.

'I trust she is not very ill?' he asked. 'Should I send
my physician to her do you think?'

'I—I do not think that necessary,' Karin said. 'I
believe it is merely a headache and will pass.'

'But I would leave nothing to chance,' Suleiman
replied, a little smile flickering across his mouth. 'Yes,
I believe I shall send the physician to her—I would
not have my lady languish for want of attention. Go
to her now and tell her the physician will see her immediately—for she may need to be bled or perhaps a
blister may be more helpful in this case…'

'Yes, my lord. I shall go at once.'

Suleiman nodded and turned away to glance at a
trinket he had recently purchased; it was a table clock
with pierced sides and fashioned of silver gilt. He had
it mind to present it as a gift to his intended bride, but
for the moment it would remain a secret since it
seemed that Eleanor was sulking.

Suleiman had little doubt of what had brought on
her sudden headache. She was angry because he had
broken his promise to her, and as he had not spoken

of what had occurred during the hunting trip to Karin, Eleanor would know nothing of it.

Her refusal to come to him would have made him angry had he not understood her better than she guessed. It amused him to play her little games, and he wondered what she would do when she received his message.

As it happened, he did not have long to wait. He was standing at the trestle table examining some manuscripts with the help of a long-handled glass when she came in softly. She made no sound nor did she speak but he knew she was there, for her perfume betrayed her. No other woman smelled quite as she did, for she used few of the heavy oils that were so popular in the harem and her scent was her own.

'I am glad your headache is better,' he said as he turned. 'It would have been a pity to apply the leeches. I think them most unpleasant, but I understand their use to be quite efficacious in the treatment of heated blood.'

'I had no need of leeches or blisters, my lord.'

'No, Eleanor, I did not think you did—your headache was a fit of temper, because I was forced to break my word to you.'

Her cheeks were hot as she looked at him, for he made her seem like a temperamental child. 'I would not have minded if you had told me yourself, my lord—but it seemed so careless to send word like that.'

'As if I did not know or care that you would be disappointed?' Suleiman nodded. 'Yes, I understand that, my lady—and I ask you to forgive me. I would have acted differently if I could. It was not my intention to slight you, believe me.'

Eleanor stared at him, torn between wanting to be-

lieve and trust him and the fear that if she gave her
heart to him he would abuse her love.

'I know that I am merely a woman and that women
are inferior in your eyes…'

'Why do you think that of me, Eleanor? Have I
given you cause to believe I consider you inferior?
Have I not shown that I respect and admire your intelligence and your bravery—for there are few who
would dare to defy the laws as you have, my lady.'

'No…' Eleanor was forced to be truthful as she
gazed into his eyes. What she saw there gave her a
jolt of surprise. There was such a haunted, unhappy
look that it made her want to reach out and comfort
him. 'No, you have not, my lord. It is my own fear
that makes me say such things to you—because I am
afraid of giving too much of myself.'

'Yes, I have realised this,' he said. 'Have you been
hurt, my lady?'

'No…not in the way you mean,' she said. 'But I
had a cousin I loved who was married against her will.
She wept in my arms the night before her wedding,
and I have never forgot it. But it was not only Mary's
unhappy marriage, my lord. I see women in your
harem who sigh and languish for one glance from
you—and I would not be like them.'

'If I took a wife I might grant freedom to the concubines,' Suleiman said, surprising her. 'I have come
to see that what you say concerning them is true. It is
unkind to force so many women to live useless, empty
lives when I shall never send for them.'

'You would set them free?' Eleanor's spine tingled.
'But it is your custom…would it not seem strange to
others if…?'

'Perhaps.' Suleiman shrugged. 'I care little for the

opinion of others, Eleanor. Would you think it a good thing if they were to be returned to their homes?'

'Some of the women have no home, my lord. If you send them away, they will only have to sell themselves back into slavery.'

'Perhaps marriages could be arranged for some of the women. I shall speak to Karin, to discover her thoughts concerning this—but some must remain, of course, as friends and ladies-in-waiting to my wife.'

'Yes, my lord. She would otherwise spend many hours alone.'

'Who should remain, Eleanor? Pray advise me in this matter—who amongst the women are most fitted to be my wife's attendants?'

Eleanor's heart was beating very fast, so fast that she found it difficult to answer immediately. 'Surely it should be for your wife to choose, my lord?' She dared not look at him lest she betray herself. He must not guess how much her heart had softened towards him.

'What—would you play games with me even yet, Eleanor?' He sounded stern, and yet she thought she detected a note of disappointment.

Her gaze lifted to his uncertainly. 'My lord spoke of—of such an honour, but I was not sure...I thought that perhaps I had made you angry? That you might have changed your mind as you did about the hunting trip.' Her head went up, challenging him.

'You have made me angry many times,' he agreed, his expression giving nothing away. 'However, I have decided that you are most fitted to become my wife. The mother of my sons must have both spirit and intelligence. I have overlooked your faults—and they are many—but I shall expect an improvement in your manners, my lady.'

'Indeed, sir?' Eleanor's head went up, her eyes sparking with indignation. 'In my country it is not the custom for a gentleman to summon the lady he is courting.'

'Courting?' Suleiman's mouth curved in gentle mockery. 'You expect the son of Caliph Bakhar to court you? What would you have me do, Eleanor? Must I go down on my knees and beg you to be my wife?'

'No—no, of course not. But it is the custom to ask rather than instruct in such matters, my lord. You might at least ask me if I would like to marry you.'

'If I asked, you might refuse.' His gaze narrowed as if he tried to read her mind.

'I should certainly refuse,' Eleanor replied, knowing that she lied. Her heart was thumping wildly and she could scarcely breathe.

'Then it is as well for both of us that I give you no choice,' Suleiman replied still inscrutable. 'Now, my lady, go into the bedchamber and change into the clothes you will find lying on the divan.'

Eleanor stared at him in alarm. 'Why? What are you—I mean, what kind of clothes?'

'Do you wish me to assist you to disrobe?'

Suleiman's eyes gleamed and she gave a little yelp and backed away, her face flushed as she saw his amusement. What was he up to now? Some mischief if she had judged that look correctly!

When she saw the robes lying on the silken covers of the divan, Eleanor was even more puzzled. She had expected to see thin, gauzy garments that would show every line of her body through the flimsy material.

Instead, she found the costume a youth or small man might wear for riding or working, plain and drab in colour. She glanced over her shoulder, still expecting some hidden meaning and half imagining that Suleiman would pounce on her when she was naked, but he did not come and she donned the trousers, tunic and caftan that a simple country youth might wear. She was trying to work out how to arrange the headdress, which was a plain white turban with a scarf that wrapped about the neck, when Suleiman entered.

He looked at her with approving eyes. 'You make a handsome boy, Eleanor. Let me help you with your headdress—we must make sure that your hair cannot escape and betray you.'

'Why are you dressing me as a youth, my lord?'

'You wished to ride with me, did you not? I thought we would take Scheherazade for a little hunting trip. Come, my lady. My most trusted men await us. We shall leave through my private gardens. No one will notice us go or see us return. This shall remain our secret.'

Eleanor saw his indulgent smile and her heart turned over. 'Oh, this is a wonderful surprise, my lord. Much better than the other hunting trip you promised me.'

'I am glad that you are pleased,' he said. 'Believe me when I tell you that it was as much a disappointment to me that you could not accompany us as it was to you.'

Eleanor wanted to ask him why he had changed his mind, for there was obviously some reason and it had not been a mere whim as she had imagined. However, there was no time; he was urging her on, his mood one of excitement as they slipped away into the gardens and out through a gate Suleiman unlocked to a small courtyard where three guards waited with horses.

Suleiman himself helped Eleanor to mount the pretty white mare provided for her use. Dressed as a youth, she was forced to ride astride, but fortunately her father's indulgence to her as a child meant that she was no stranger to this mode of travel, and Suleiman smiled as he saw how confidently she took her reins.

'Now we shall go,' he said, and mounted his own horse. A servant held up Scheherazade's cage, and the bird took its place on Suleiman's wrist. 'I believe we shall have good sport this afternoon, Eleanor, for my darling is restive. She has not been out of the gardens for some days and longs to try her wings.'

'As I do, my lord.'

Eleanor's eyes were bright with excitement as she looked at him. She had wrapped the two ends of the scarf about her face so that little but her eyes showed above it, but her feelings were plain for Suleiman to see and he smiled at her pleasure.

She had demanded that he court her in the manner of her own people. He could not go so far, but he could give her much that she desired and this hunting trip was only the beginning.

Eleanor watched as the hawk circled and then swooped, its wings closed as it dived upon its prey. Long, cruel talons extended as it clutched its quarry in flight, binding it and swooping lower as it bore the prey to the ground.

'Is she not a fine hunter?' Suleiman asked Eleanor as he recalled the falcon to his hand, holding the jesses securely with his fingers and replacing the leather ruf-

ter over Scheherazade's head. 'We have had fine sport with her this afternoon, have we not, my lady?'

'Yes, indeed, my lord,' Eleanor agreed, for the peregrine had successfully taken several birds. However, for Eleanor the pleasure had come as much from riding in the open air with the breeze in her face as from the sport—though it was a fine sight to watch the falcon. 'It is a lovely afternoon, and wonderful to be riding here with you, my lord. I feel so alive and free…'

Riding in the hills above the ancient Byzantine city, which had for so long been a Christian stronghold, the view of the Bosphorus Straits was magnificent, and the sense of almost being able to fly made Eleanor feel as if the past weeks had never happened. She had ridden out with her father often at home, and she had missed the exercise and the exhilaration of being on horseback.

'I am glad that you have enjoyed the outing,' Suleiman replied. 'We should return to the palace now, my lady, for it wants but an hour to sunset and there are still bandits roaming these hills.'

'Yes…yes, I suppose we must, my lord,' Eleanor replied with a stifled sigh. 'I wish we could just go on riding forever.'

Suleiman nodded, and there was a thoughtful, regretful expression in his eyes as though he too felt as she did—but surely that was merely her imagination? Yet Eleanor was beginning to know him, to sense his moods, and she knew that there were many facets to this man's character.

They rode back to the Caliph's palace side by side as the sun began to sink over the hills and darkness fell. It came quickly at this time of year and by the time they regained the safety of the palace gardens it was almost dark. Suleiman led the way back to his apartments.

'You must change now and return to the harem,' he told Eleanor. 'Say nothing of what we did this afternoon, my lady. We shall keep such outings a secret known only to a trusted few.'

'It shall be as you wish, my lord,' Eleanor replied. 'But may I ask my lord why? Surely you are free to do as you please?'

'I have enemies within the palace,' Suleiman replied gravely. 'It was because of one such that I was not able to take you on our hunting trip.'

'Will my lord not tell me more?' Eleanor had sensed a darkness in his mind all the time they were out with the hawk. He had enjoyed the outing, but she knew that something was troubling him. His dark eyes seemed to reflect pain—and a deeper distress as if he questioned his very existence. 'What has brought those shadows to your eyes?'

'I was forced to order the execution of my half-brother Hasan during the hunting trip,' Suleiman replied, his eyes intent on her face as if he wished to see her reaction. 'Abu and he plotted to kill both the Caliph and myself by stealth as we slept. Hasan planned to rule in my father's stead, but he was weak and Abu would have had the real power. I was warned of the plot only hours before we were due to leave the palace. I could not take you with me once I knew, Eleanor, for your presence would have made me more vulnerable—yet had I told you of my reasons for leaving you behind the traitors might have learned of it and taken flight.'

Eleanor understood how he was feeling; it was evident to her that he had found it difficult to order the

death of a brother. She knew that Abu must also have
been executed. Suleiman had spared Abu's life once,
but he could not do so a second time, because the
attack had been against his father and must be punished.

'I am sorry, my lord,' she said softly, and then without thinking she moved towards him, reaching up to
kiss his cheek. Her action was one of sympathy, but
when Suleiman caught her to him, he kissed her
fiercely with a hunger that stirred strange longings
deep within her.

His eyes sparked with mockery as he released her.
'You play with fire, Eleanor. Do not tempt me too far
or you may discover you have lit a flame that cannot
be controlled.'

Eleanor's cheeks flamed, for she had been foolish
to imagine he would want her sympathy or understanding. He desired her, but he did not love her—he
did not understand the quiet moments lovers shared,
or that she had meant only to comfort him.

'Forgive me, my lord. It was an impulse—and
kindly meant.'

His eyes glowed like hot coals. 'Do not offer me
kindness, my lady. I want much more than that from
you—and you should be prepared for your fate. This
evening I shall send for Karin and set the preparations
in train for our wedding. You shall be my wife,
Eleanor.'

She moved away from him, her heart racing wildly
as fear returned. 'Do not force me to this, my lord. I
pray you wait a while longer. Give me more time to
become accustomed to you.'

'No, there is to be no more time,' Suleiman replied,
his eyes sparking with anger. 'I have been patient with

you long enough, Eleanor. I will have no more of this nonsense. I have shown you that you need not fear your life here. You will be almost as free as I am myself, and that is all I can offer you.'

'Please, I beg you—do not...'

'Go before I lose my temper,' Suleiman said and now he was angry. 'I have given you more than any other woman, Eleanor. I would that you would give me a little in return—but if you are stubborn in your refusal you shall discover that I am not to be denied. If you will not give, I shall take. You are mine, and if you would but look into your foolish heart, you would glory in what you find there. Together we shall find that paradise known only to a few—but there is no escaping your destiny. It is bound with mine.'

Eleanor's cheeks burned as she turned away, and she knew that she was foolish to resist him still. He spoke only the truth when he said they were bound together, for she had cast her own chart as well as his and the stars showed that they were inextricably linked one to the other.

As she returned to the harem, Eleanor looked into her heart as Suleiman had bid her and discovered that it was no longer her own. She loved him despite herself; though a part of her still fought against the inevitable, it was already too late.

Eleanor shook her head in denial as she struggled to come to terms with her own thoughts. No, no, it was not possible! She respected Suleiman, liked him despite her resentment at being made his slave—but love? She could not love him! He was the very symbol of all that she had disliked in men of her own race: arrogance and the assumption that men should always rule, that women were somehow inferior. Yet

Suleiman never made her feel inferior, even when he was at his most lordly. Indeed, he seemed at times to treat her as though she was the most special of beings. Her mind raced as she tried to rationalise her feelings, but her heart told her there could be no other reason for the emotions that were raging through her.

She *was* in love with this fierce, strange man of contrasts, and she could find no happiness in anything that was not shared with him—so why had she not told him that? Why must she struggle and fight against her own desires and needs?

If it was a matter of religion and custom—she knew Suleiman well enough to know that they could reach some compromise. It would mean spending her life in this palace except for the times when her lord took her on some expedition, but something he had said to her had made her think that he was no freer than she.

Surely that was not the case? And yet she knew that he held his father in great respect, and the Caliph needed him—he needed Suleiman's strength and cleverness to outwit the enemies that surrounded them.

Chapter Nine

Eleanor spent what was left of the evening talking with her friends in the harem. She braided Elizabetta's hair, and Anastasia painted her toenails for her with a red dye. They laughed and talked together, but no one asked Eleanor what she had been doing, though Anastasia did mention that she had a fresh colour in her cheeks.

Fatima was holding court in another part of the hall, but she did not speak to them or they to her. Most of the other women still seemed to follow the favourite, though Suleiman had not sent for her since before his hunting trip.

No word of the plot to kill the Caliph and Suleiman, or of the subsequent executions, seemed to have filtered through to the harem, and Eleanor felt it best to keep her knowledge to herself. If Suleiman and the Caliph wished it known, Karin would be informed and she would tell the other women.

Karin did not come to the harem that evening, and Eleanor wondered if Suleiman had, after all, decided to wait before announcing his intention to take Eleanor as his wife. She was not sure whether she wanted the announcement to come or not, and spent a restless night going over all the reasons why she should not wish for this wedding.

She was a Christian and he was a Muslim, and she had a right to be free. As Suleiman's wife she would spend the rest of her life in this palace—but what was the alternative? There was no possibility of her being rescued, which meant that she was never going to leave the palace anyway. Surely it was better to live as the favoured wife than as one of the concubines?

She slept fitfully at last, having reached no sensible conclusion. It did not matter what she thought, for Suleiman had made up his mind and she had no choice in the matter of her future.

Yet there was no word from Karin, nor did Suleiman send for her that afternoon, though towards evening one of the eunuchs came to tell her she was needed. She followed him through the passages to a part of the palace she had never been before, and was ushered inside an apartment that she believed must belong to the Caliph's own harem.

Karin was lying on a bed, her face white and beaded with sweat. She looked terrible and as Eleanor came to her, she reached out her hand to her. Eleanor took her hand, holding it and looking at her anxiously.

'You are ill, Karin?'

'Yes. I have been very sick during the night, Eleanor. And the pain in my stomach has been terrible.'

'Has the physician been to see you?'

'Yes, several times. He says I must have eaten something that did not agree with me.' Karin gasped and bit her lip. 'I think someone has tried to poison me.'

'Oh, no, surely not! Who would want to do such a wicked thing?'

'I think…I think it may have been Fatima,' Karin replied. 'I spent some time in the harem when you were with Suleiman yesterday, Eleanor. Dinazade offered me fruit and I ate a little of a peach she gave me. Had I eaten all of it I might have been dead by now.'

'Oh, Karin, this is terrible. Have you told anyone what you suspect?'

'No…I wanted to warn you, because I believe I was meant to die first so that you could be killed without fear of discovery.'

'But why…?' Eleanor looked at her sadly. 'I am sorry that you have suffered, Karin. I can understand why Fatima wants me dead, but that you should have been harmed! I am distressed and angry that this has been done.'

'Fatima knew that I favoured you, and hoped to see you as Suleiman's wife. Perhaps I was wrong to think that…'

'No, you were not wrong,' Eleanor replied, and stroked the damp hair back from Karin's brow. 'This is my fault. Had I not resisted, Suleiman would have made his intentions known before this—and Fatima's anger would have turned against me, not you.'

'If this is true, you must be very careful,' Karin warned. 'She will stop at nothing to be rid of you and regain her lord's favour.'

'Fatima is a foolish woman, but I understand her fear,' Eleanor said. 'She will not be a danger to either of us for much longer, Karin. My lord wishes to know which women I would keep as my friends and attendants, and which I would have sent away. He was to have asked your opinion on whether marriages might be arranged for those who cannot return to their homes.'

Karin nodded weakly. 'Suleiman sent word that he would like to see me last evening, but I was already unwell, and when he knew that I was ill, he sent his own physicians to me. Had they not treated me I might have died.'

'I am very glad that you did not,' Eleanor said. 'Is there anything I may do for you, my friend?'

'No, nothing—except come to visit me again tomorrow. I shall send word to Suleiman and he will arrange it.'

'He has not sent for me today…'

'I think he is waiting to see what happens to me,' Karin replied. 'I have not told the lord Suleiman of my suspicions concerning Fatima, but he must have some inkling himself.'

'Why do you say that?'

'I have heard stories concerning Fatima,' Karin said. 'If they are true…any other master would have dealt with her by now, but he is waiting for her to betray herself.'

'Of what is she accused?'

'That I may not reveal, even to you,' Karin replied and sighed. 'She is a foolish woman, but I would have no ill come to her through me. I could have gone to Suleiman long ago, but had I done so she would have been severely punished. That is not my wish—merely that she is banished so that she can do no harm to others. I wish that I was not laid in my bed. I fear

what she may do while I am not there to restrain her.'
She gave a little moan of pain.

'May I not bathe your face and hands?' Eleanor
said, looking at her in concern. 'I would make you
more comfortable, Karin.'

'Thank you, Eleanor. My own women will attend
me. I am comfortable enough—but I cannot rest...'

'You must rest,' Eleanor replied. 'Fatima will not
harm anyone else but me. It is me she is jealous of—
and I am warned. Please do not worry for me, Karin.
I do not think she will dare to harm me once it is
known that I am to be my lord's wife.'

'But he has made no announcement...'

'He will once I have spoken to him,' Eleanor said
confidently. 'He waits to please me—but I shall ask
to see him, and I shall tell him that my doubts have
been put aside. I see what I must do now, Karin, and
I shall accept my duty.'

Karin took her hand and squeezed it gently. 'Ask
him to banish Fatima,' she advised. 'He must send her
away before she does more harm.'

'Yes,' Eleanor promised. 'As soon as I see the lord
Suleiman I shall ask that she be sent back to her homeland.'

'She will see to it that I am sent away!' Fatima
screamed in rage and struck the servant across the face
viciously. 'How dare she presume to think I can be
got rid of so easily?'

Dinazade stared at her resentfully. 'You bid me follow and listen, my lady. I can only tell you what I
heard. The lord Suleiman intends to take the
Englishwoman as his wife. She is to have her choice

of the women she desires about her—and she intends
to ask that you be sent away immediately.'

'Get out!' Fatima threw a cushion at the servant.
'Get out! I shall punish you for telling me lies. It
cannot be that my lord would send me away.'

After the servant had gone, Fatima began to pace
the floor of her apartment, her feet bare against the
coolness of the marble tiles. She was angry and frustrated that the poison she had rubbed into the skin of
the peach had merely made Karin sick and not killed
her. She had hoped that with the older woman out of
the way, she would have complete control over the
harem. While Suleiman continued to favour Eleanor
she would find it difficult to dispose of her—especially
now that Abu had been moved from his position in
the harem.

Fatima had sent word that she wished to speak with
him, but he had not answered her summons. She was
angry that he should ignore her, for she believed that
he still had access to the harem if he chose to come.
Had he done so, she would have asked him to smuggle
Eleanor out of the harem. He could then have disposed
of her as he wished, and Fatima believed she knew
what he would do to the upstart Englishwoman.

With her gone, Suleiman would send for Fatima
again. The last interview she'd had with him had been
very strange, for he had asked her curious questions,
which she had pretended not to understand—questions
about women who had disappeared and others who
had lain with two of the Janissaries. Since Suleiman
had neither accused nor punished her, merely sending
her back to the harem, she believed that he knew nothing of her treachery.

She had been told nothing of Abu having been condemned to the galleys, nor of his escape and subsequent treachery—nor of his death. Had Fatima been aware of these things, she might have feared for her own life, but on Suleiman's orders no one had told her. No whispers had reached her ears concerning these matters. In her vanity and ignorance, she still believed that she had only to be patient and her lord would turn to her again—once Eleanor had been disposed of.

But how was she to achieve this desirable end? Poisons were uncertain, and did not always bring death; besides, without Abu's help they were difficult to come by. Fatima wanted another way, one that would make certain Eleanor died.

She must act soon, while Karin was still tied to her bed. Karin suspected her; Fatima knew that the older woman had heard the inevitable whispers concerning her. She had no proof, of course. Had the proof been there, Karin would surely have taken her suspicions to Suleiman.

She must kill Eleanor herself. It was a risk because she would surely be put to death herself if her crime were discovered. Fatima would have hesitated to take such a step if Dinazade had not brought the news that Eleanor was to become the lord Suleiman's wife. Always before, she had watched as Abu punished the women who displeased her—and she had smiled at her own power. She had not needed to soil her own hands, but things had changed.

She did not know why Abu had not come to her in the gardens as she had asked. They had plotted the meeting between Eleanor and her brother together and their plan had failed, for the Englishwoman went unpunished. It was very odd that she had heard no word of Abu since then…a little tingle of fear went down Fatima's spine.

Had Abu been punished for the part he played in that masquerade—and had he betrayed Fatima? She knew that there were fearful tortures that might cause a man to reveal anything in his agony, but if that were so something would have happened before this. She would surely have been punished if Suleiman suspected her of betraying him.

She must make him want her again. He was bewitched by that golden-haired sorceress! Once she was dead, Suleiman would turn to her again. Fatima would wait no longer. Tonight, Eleanor must die!

Suleiman was studying his manuscripts when the eunuch approached. He turned to look at him, his gaze narrowed, his thoughts with the friend who now lay at death's door after a festering lump had been removed from his side by the surgeon's knife. It seemed that all their efforts to save him might be in vain, though the physicians, at first reluctant to try the poultice Eleanor had written of, were about to apply it that night. Suleiman prayed that this last might be effective.

'Yes?' he asked, brows raised at this intrusion by the eunuch. 'Does the Caliph send for me?'

'No, my lord. The Englishwoman asks if she might speak with you.'

'Eleanor?' Suleiman frowned. It was unusual for such a request to be brought to him by the eunuch. 'Ah, yes, I remember that Karin is ill. You may bring my lady to me.'

He turned back to his manuscripts as the eunuch left, and then he felt the touch of a hand on his arm and he swung round to look at Eleanor, his eyes going over her hungrily.

'Forgive me for the intrusion, my lord. I have been to visit Karin, and I asked if I might see you for a moment before returning to the harem.'

'Yes, I understand. You are worried for her. The physicians tell me she may have eaten something that was poisonous—but fortunately the dose was not lethal. They tell me she will live.'

'Yes, my lord, thanks to your prompt action in sending your physician to her.'

'Of course it was done. Karin is a good woman, I respect her and would not wish her to die from any neglect.'

'I realise that, my lord.' Eleanor took a deep breath. 'I wished to tell you…to tell you that I have come to realise many things.'

'Have you, my lady?' Suleiman took her hand and led her to one of the divans, indicating that she should sit beside him. 'And they are so important that they could not wait a few days?' His eyes reflected amusement. 'This interest me greatly, Eleanor. Pray continue.'

'My lord chooses to mock me,' Eleanor said and blushed. 'And perhaps I deserve that—for I have been foolish.'

'You admit your folly?'

Her blush deepened to a fiery red. 'It is difficult for me to admit, my lord, but I do. I was wrong to resist my destiny. We are bound together—the stars have foretold it and I know it in my heart. My lord told me to look into my heart and I have done so. I know that it is my destiny and my duty to be your wife.'

Suleiman frowned. 'Why your duty, Eleanor?'

'Karin told me she believed I could bring change to the harem, my lord. She said that it would be for good or evil and that it lay in my hands—and I fear that it may be because of me that—'

'You think that someone may deliberately have tried to kill her?'

Eleanor remembered Karin's warning and her eyes fell before his piercing gaze. 'I do not know how that may be, my lord. It may be that she ate something that she ought not by accident. I did not come here to accuse anyone.'

'But you came with some purpose in mind?'

'Yes, my lord.' Eleanor looked up, her eyes meeting his steadily. 'I came to beg your pardon for being so foolish when you told me of your intention to make me your wife. And to tell you that I should be honoured if that was still in your mind.'

'Did you think I had forgotten?' Suleiman's mouth curved in amusement. 'I could do nothing until Karin is better. She has charge of the women and it is for her to break the news and make the arrangements for the wedding. Customs must be observed, however impatient we may be, my lady. A wedding cannot be arranged overnight—there are many things needful to be done.'

'Yes, my lord.' Eleanor took a deep breath. 'I understand that we must talk of these things—matters of religion and custom. But my lord asked me which of the other women I would like to keep with me—and therefore who should be sent away. I shall consult with the others once the announcement is made as to who would be happy to stay—but I have a request...'

'You want one of the women sent away?' Suleiman raised his brows, guessing her intent.

'Yes, my lord. I bear her no ill will, nor do I want her to suffer—but I think it would be more comfortable for everyone if Fatima were to be sent to her home.'

'Fatima?' Suleiman looked at her, eyes narrowed. 'Will you tell me the reason for your request?'

'I have no reason, my lord—other than that she does not like me.'

Suleiman nodded. 'Yes, I see. It shall be done once the announcement has been made. Do you think you can be patient until then?'

Eleanor hesitated, but if she told Suleiman the whole truth he might punish Fatima, and neither she nor Karin wanted that.

'Yes, my lord. I am content that she should remain for the moment.'

'And is there any other request you would make of me, my lady?'

'None, my lord. I believe we must speak of other things—but I did not come to ask favours of you other than this.'

'And you are content that we are to be married—because you think it your duty to care for the women of the harem?'

She met the quizzing stare of his dark eyes and blushed. 'I—it is a part of my content, my lord.'

'And what of this, Eleanor?'

Suleiman reached out, drawing her to him, crushing her against him as his lips sought and found hers. She felt the heady sensations swirl within her and allowed herself to melt into the heat of his embrace, her lips parting in welcome of his mastery. She felt that she wanted to stay with him like this for always and keened for the loss as he released her.

'You tempt me, my little bird,' he said. 'But I have sworn to keep this night and two more in fasting for the sake of my friend who lies close to death. Since I hunger for you more than food, I should break my vow if I took you to my bed this night. Do not look for me to send for you for two days, Eleanor. I shall be keeping a vigil by his bed.'

'I am very sorry he is so ill,' Eleanor said. 'I wish that I might help him—but I have no skill in these things. I told you of a poultice I know from my studies, but I have never nursed anyone, though I believe Anastasia has. If my lord required her services for his friend, I am sure she would be glad to give them—or perhaps that is forbidden?'

'She shall be sent for,' Suleiman said. 'If she can save him, she shall be given her freedom—that is my promise to you and her.'

Eleanor nodded; she smiled at him as she left, and knew that he was watching her until the last. Her thoughts as she returned to the harem were a mixture of pleasure in the new understanding she had reached with her lord, and anxiety for her friend and his.

Several of the women came to her anxiously as she entered the communal hall. They had heard whispers of Karin's sickness, and they begged her to tell them what was the matter with their friend and comforter.

'She has been very sick,' Eleanor replied, careful to give nothing away. 'The physicians have given her something to make her easier and they say she will recover—but she may need to rest for several days. I shall visit her tomorrow and every day, and bring you news of her.'

'May we see her?' Anastasia asked. 'I might be able to help her—I have some skills with fevers.'

'You are wanted to nurse my lord's friend,' Eleanor told her. 'The eunuchs will take you to him—it is on the orders of the lord Suleiman, so you need not fear that you are to leave the harem quarters. You will not be punished whatever happens—but should your skills save my lord's friend, he will grant you your freedom.'

Anastasia stared at her. 'But I do not wish to leave the harem—or you, Eleanor.'

'Then you will not be forced to do so,' Eleanor replied and smiled at her. 'I shall request some other favour of my lord for you. Indeed, I should be sorry to part from you, Anastasia. I had hoped you might choose to remain with me.'

Anastasia stared at her, then she too began to smile. 'Then the rumours we have heard are true,' she said. 'You are to be the lord Suleiman's wife.'

'We must not speak of this yet,' Eleanor replied. 'Karin will make all clear when she returns to us. My lord has other things on his mind at the moment. He is sorely troubled by his friend's sickness, Anastasia. Please go at once and do what you can for him.'

'Yes, my lady.' Anastasia's manner had altered subtly. She bowed her head submissively, as if acknowledging Eleanor's superior standing in the harem, but Eleanor shook her head at her.

'No, Anastasia. We are friends—it shall always be so as long as you remain here.'

Eleanor noticed that some of the other ladies were staring at her a little oddly. As Anastasia went off to join the eunuch who was waiting to take her to the bedside of the sick Janissary, Eleanor took her customary seat on one of the divans. Immediately, one of the women brought her a dish of fruit, offering it respectfully.

'Would my lady care for something else?' she asked as Eleanor shook her head. 'May I send for food from the kitchens?'

'No, thank you. I am not hungry,' Eleanor said. 'We have not spoken much before—but I believe your name is Marisa. How long have you been here—and where did you live before you were captured?'

'I came from a Greek island called Kos,' the woman replied. 'My family lived close to the sea for they were fishermen. One day I was walking on the beach when the Corsairs took me. I did not see them until they fell upon me and carried me away with them.'

'How long have you been here, Marisa?'

'Three years, my lady. The lord Suleiman has never sent for me in all that time. I think I am not beautiful enough…'

'I think you are pretty,' Eleanor replied. 'And young. Tell me, Marisa—if you had the chance, would you marry or would you prefer to return to your family?'

Marisa blushed. 'It is forbidden to think of such things,' she said, glancing over her shoulder as if she feared that they would be heard and immediately punished. 'But I saw the lord Suleiman fighting with one of the Janissaries…a handsome young man who I think they call Ahmed… He saw me watching him, though I was veiled, of course—but our eyes met…'

Eleanor nodded. 'If Karin asks you this same question, you must answer truthfully, Marisa—will you promise to do that? I give you my word you will not be punished.'

'Yes, my lady.' Marisa hesitated, then, greatly daring, 'I know that sometimes when an important man takes a bride some of the concubines are returned to their homes or given in marriage to another man.'

'Yes, well, we shall see,' Eleanor said and smiled at her. 'I want everyone to have what they themselves want most…and I know that some will want to stay while others would prefer to leave. But we shall say no more of this until Karin is better and returns to us. I should not have spoken so openly. Please do not repeat what I have said, Marisa.'

'Oh, I give you my word, my lady,' Marisa replied. 'And I am sorry I have not spent more time talking to you—but I was afraid of offending Fatima.'

'Yes, I understand,' Eleanor replied. 'I have not taken offence—and you may repeat that to anyone who feels nervous of change in the harem.'

'Yes, my lady.' Marisa smiled and went off as Elizabetta brought the monkey to sit beside them. 'Thank you for your confidence.'

'What was all that about?' Elizabetta asked. She allowed the monkey to climb over her shoulder and investigate the bowl of fruit on the divan beside them. 'You should know that Marisa is one of Fatima's most intimate friends, Eleanor. Do not trust her.'

'Yes, I know that,' Eleanor replied. 'I am aware that I need to be careful…' She broke off as Elizabetta gave a little cry and looked at the monkey, who had keeled over and was obviously in pain. He had been eating a grape, and now his mouth was frothed with blood as he twitched horribly and then lay still. 'Oh, no…the poor little fellow. I think he is dead, Elizabetta. The grape…it must have been poisoned.' She stared at her friend in horror. 'Marisa brought the bowl to me…'

'It was meant for you,' Elizabetta said. 'You were meant to die…'

'Say nothing,' Eleanor warned as the other ladies began to gather round, their cries of distress shrill at the sudden death of their pet. 'Give this bowl to Morna and tell her to guard it well, but on no account to eat any of the fruit.'

Elizabetta took the bowl and left immediately. Marisa came hurrying back to see what all the commotion was about. She looked at Eleanor and her eyes were dark with fear.

'I was told to offer you the fruit,' she said, her voice a harsh whisper. 'Fatima made me bring it to you.'

'Would you repeat that to the lord Suleiman if you were asked?'

Marisa looked into Eleanor's eyes for a moment, and then nodded. 'Forgive me, my lady. I did not know that the fruit was…' She could not bring herself to say the word. 'I ate one of the grapes myself as we talked…' Her face was ashen. 'I might have died instead of that poor creature.'

'You should send to the lord Suleiman,' Elizabetta said. 'Fatima is evil, Eleanor, and she ought to be punished.'

'Yes, yes, she should be punished,' several voices were suddenly raised against the woman many of the others had feared and secretly hated. 'We should tell Karin.'

'Karin is ill,' Eleanor said. 'And my lord cannot be disturbed at this time. I shall deal with this myself.'

'Be careful,' Elizabetta warned. 'If you challenge her, she will turn on you like a wounded beast.'

'Yes, I know she may be dangerous,' Eleanor replied. 'But I cannot let this terrible thing she has done go unchallenged. Fatima must be brought to understand that her rule has ended.'

She got up and walked purposefully from the room, leaving the other women staring after her in dismay. Eleanor did not realise how cruel and ruthless Fatima could be. *She* had never been dragged from sleep by Abu and whipped until she begged for mercy.

'We should do something to help her,' Elizabetta said.

'But what can we do?' the others asked and looked at each other helplessly. None of them had ever dared to stand up to the favourite, and they were afraid of her. 'If only Karin were here to guide us.'

'That is why she was poisoned first,' Elizabetta said. 'Fatima is hoping that none of us will be brave enough to stand up to her—but we cannot let her kill Eleanor. She is our salvation.'

'Yes, yes, we must help her,' Marisa agreed, remembering the promise Eleanor had made her. 'We must all help her. Fatima cannot subdue us all if we are of one mind.'

Eleanor was unaware of the debate she had left behind her. She was not afraid of Fatima. She had guessed that poisoned fruit might be offered her by one of the women, and that the women would know nothing of what was planned. She had therefore warned Morna that she must prepare all their food herself, and let no one else touch anything. Yet the ploy had been so obvious that Eleanor suspected the plot went deeper.

Surely Fatima could not have hoped that Eleanor would eat the poisoned grape? Especially since she must know that Karin would have told her of her own suspicions concerning Fatima.

As she approached, she saw Dinazade about to leave her mistress's rooms. When the servant caught sight of Eleanor, she ran back inside to warn her mistress.

Fatima was waiting as Eleanor entered. Her dark eyes flashed with temper and her hatred was almost tangible.

'I did not send for you,' she said. 'How dare you come here without being sent for?'

'I need no invitation,' Eleanor replied quietly. 'We both know why I have come here, Fatima. You ordered Marisa to bring me that bowl of fruit. Why? Only some of the fruit was poisoned—how could you be sure I would eat it?'

'I do not know of what you speak,' Fatima said haughtily. 'I sent you no fruit. If Marisa says otherwise she lies.'

'I refused it,' Eleanor told her, her eyes never leaving the other woman's face for an instant. 'Marisa ate one of the grapes and the monkey ate another. That poor creature died horribly, but Marisa is alive and able to tell her story to the lord Suleiman.'

'He will not believe her,' Fatima said and smiled smugly. 'He knows that the other women are jealous and tell lies about me. Why should I try to kill you? He does not take you to his bed. You are merely his scribe.'

'I have used my skills with the Latin to assist my lord,' Eleanor agreed. 'But I am soon to be his wife—and when that happens you will be a long way from here, Fatima. You are to be sent back to Algiers.'

'You lie!' Fatima's lovely face was twisted and made ugly by anger. 'My lord will not send me away for your sake. You are merely a passing fancy. When he is tired of you, he will want me again.'

'If Karin were not ill it would already have been done.'

'No!' Fatima suddenly snatched up a knife she had been using to peel a peach and sprang at Eleanor with the blade. 'I shall kill you. When you are dead, my lord will send for me again.'

Eleanor ducked as the other woman stabbed at her viciously. She looked about for something with which to protect herself and caught up a plump cushion, holding it in front of her face. Fatima's knife tore through the silk, rendering it useless.

'Help me!' Fatima demanded of her servant as Eleanor continued to duck and weave, avoiding her slashing blade as the woman lunged at her again and again. 'Catch her and hold her while I teach her who is mistress here. I shall destroy her beauty. My lord will not want her then.'

'Do nothing, Dinazade,' Elizabetta commanded from the doorway. 'Put the knife down, Fatima. We have sent for the eunuchs and they will punish you if you injure…'

Eleanor had been momentarily distracted by the sound of Elizabetta's voice. She took her eyes from Fatima, and in that instant the other woman gave a cry of triumph as her knife struck home, slashing across Eleanor's upper arm. Eleanor gave a cry of pain, stumbled back and fell into Elizabetta's arms.

'You have killed her!' Marisa cried, helping Elizabetta to support Eleanor. 'You tried to poison her and now you have killed her!'

'She attacked me.' Fatima felt a flicker of fear as she saw accusation in the faces of the other women.

They had massed together in the doorway and were staring at her in anger and disgust. 'She was mad! She came here to kill me. You saw her, Dinazade! You saw her attack me. I wrested the knife from her to protect myself from her attack. Tell them! Tell them what you saw!'

Dinazade stared at her mistress in silence. She had hated and feared her for years; now at last she saw the way to be revenged for all the beatings she had suffered at Fatima's hands. Glancing over her shoulder, she saw that the eunuchs were pushing their way past the women.

'I saw you poison the grape,' she said clearly. 'I heard you order Marisa to take the bowl of fruit to the Englishwoman—and I saw you take up the knife. It was your intention to kill her. You wanted her dead because you knew that you had lost the lord Suleiman's favour. You knew that she would have you banished…'

'You traitor!' Fatima had lost all control as she screamed and flew at the servant. She stabbed her twice in the chest before Dinazade fell to the floor at her feet, the blood pouring from her wounds.

A silence had fallen over the women. The chief eunuch Hasar had been kneeling beside Eleanor. He glanced at two others who had followed him in and then pointed at Fatima.

'Take her,' he said harshly. 'She is to be imprisoned in the punishment cells and held there until the lord Suleiman decides her fate.'

'No!' Fatima screamed and struggled as the eunuchs approached her. Her eyes were wild and she still held the bloodied knife that had killed her servant and wounded Eleanor. 'Do not touch me or my lord will have you punished. He wants only me…only me…'

Even as she screamed the words, one of the eunuchs hit her at the base of the neck with the side of his hand, and she collapsed, not dead but rendered unconscious by the disabling blow. He hoisted her over his shoulder and the women parted to let him through, some of them spitting at Fatima's unconscious face as she was taken away. They had hated her with good reason, and not one of them was sorry for her. She deserved her punishment.

'Dinazade is dead,' one of the women said. 'Poor woman, Fatima killed her.'

'Eleanor is alive,' Elizabetta told them. 'She fainted from the pain, but she is alive.'

'I shall send the physician to her,' Hasar said. He bent down and lifted Eleanor in his arms, the other women fluttering behind him as he carried her to her room and laid her gently down on her divan. She was moaning slightly, barely conscious.

'Take care of her,' he instructed Elizabetta. 'The physician will come soon. But you may try to staunch the blood in the meantime.'

'She must not die,' Elizabetta said.

'Pray that Allah grants her life,' Hasar replied harshly. 'The lord Suleiman is at prayer and cannot be disturbed—but should this woman die, his anger will not be contained.'

'We shall care for her,' Elizabetta promised. 'She is our friend. It was only Fatima who hated her.'

'Others were present when this happened and did nothing to help her,' the eunuch replied severely. 'My master may choose to punish everyone if she dies. My own life is forfeit. I was told to protect her with my life, and I have failed.'

Elizabetta looked at Marisa and the others as he went out. 'We must pray that Eleanor lives—for we may all suffer if she dies.'

'If only Anastasia or Karin were here.'

'We must do what we can,' Marisa said, looking at her fearfully.

'Leave her to me,' Morna said, pushing them aside. 'Bring me clean water and cloths. I shall be the one to tend her, though you must all help to watch over her—but only I shall touch her. My life means little to me. If she dies, I shall take the blame.'

'I shall help you,' Elizabetta said.

'And I—only tell me what to do,' Marisa insisted. 'You cannot bear all the nursing alone, or all the blame.'

'I, too, shall help,' Rosamunde said, coming forward. 'I was in the garden while all this was going on and knew nothing until this moment. Why do you waste time in chatter? Eleanor will bleed to death if you do nothing to staunch the wound. Bring clean cloths and help me. I have seen such wounds before and know what must be done to stop the bleeding.'

Rosamunde's manner of calm authority brought instant response from the others. Elizabetta had been filling a basin with water, and Morna had produced a shift of clean white cloth, which she proceeded to tear into strips.

The other women stood just outside the door watching until Marisa shooed them away.

'She will sleep now,' the physician told Rosamunde as Eleanor's eyes closed and he laid her gently back against the cushions. He glanced at Rosamunde with approval. 'You did well to staunch the wound, lady. But she has lost too much blood and the wound is deep. She will need careful nursing if she is not to die of the putrid infection.'

'Tell me what I must do,' Rosamunde begged. 'She is my friend. I love her and would not have her die.'

The physician nodded. He had been robbed of his manhood long years ago, and no longer felt the desires of a natural man—but even he could appreciate the beauty of his patient. And he had been told that she was the intended bride of the Caliph's son.

'You must keep her drugged for at least two days,' he replied. 'Otherwise she will not bear the pain. Her bandages must be changed frequently. And if the fever strikes…' He shook his head sorrowfully. 'I shall bring you a mixture of herbs for her to drink, but in that case it will be as Allah wills it.'

Rosamunde nodded. She knew that the physician had done his best for Eleanor, repairing the deep slash in her arm skilfully. There was no doubt that his work would leave a scar, but that could not be helped. All that mattered now was that Eleanor should live.

Rosamunde wished that Anastasia was with them, for they sorely needed her skills, but somehow, she and the others must make Eleanor well. Rosamunde had not heard Hasar's warning herself, but Elizabetta and Marisa had told her that all their lives might be forfeit if Eleanor died.

Rosamunde had been sent for a few times by the lord Suleiman during her first year or two in the harem. She had found him a stern, passionate man, though he had asked her only to sing for him. She was

not sure what he might be capable of if his anger were
aroused.

Everyone said he loved Eleanor. If that were so, he
might go mad with grief if she should die of her
wound.

Rosamunde glanced at Elizabetta as she came to
take her turn at sitting beside their patient.

'Do you think he knows?' she asked. 'Do you suppose that anyone has told the lord Suleiman what has
happened to Eleanor?'

'I do not know,' Elizabetta replied. 'I believe he
keeps a vigil for his sick friend. I do not think anyone
would dare to approach him with such news at this
time.'

Rosamunde frowned. 'I have never said it—but I
find him intimidating. I thank God that I am not the
one who has to tell him.'

'Our lord can be fierce,' Elizabetta said thoughtfully. 'But he was always kind to me, though he sent
for me only a few times—and not at all once Fatima
came, for her dancing pleased him more than mine.
Yet I do not believe that he would punish us all for
something that was not our fault.'

'A man may do anything when half out of his mind
with grief,' Rosamunde replied. 'We must pray that
Eleanor recovers—for her sake and our own.

Chapter Ten

'I thank you for your care of my friend,' Suleiman said. 'Your nursing has done what all my wise physicians could not.' He smiled at Anastasia. 'I would grant you any boon that you ask—including your freedom and a pension to keep you from the need to return to slavery.'

'All I would ask is to be allowed to stay here, my lord. I would like to serve the lady Eleanor—and to be given freedom to nurse the sick. I believe there are many within the palace that would benefit from my help. If there could be a room somewhere within the palace grounds where I might tend any who need me...' She looked at him anxiously. 'And I must tell you, my lord, that the poultice the lady Eleanor recommended was a part of the cure. I have used it before and I know its healing properties.'

'You shall have all that you have asked and more,' Suleiman promised. 'I have been aware that too many die for lack of care—we shall see what can be done to remedy this, lady. From now on you are no longer bound by the rules of the harem. You may come and go as you please within the palace—and to the city with an escort to protect you.'

'You are generous, my lord.'

Suleiman shook his head. 'It is I who have much to thank you for, lady. You may return to the harem if you wish. I hope that the lady Karin will be well enough to resume her duties soon. I shall send her to you with news I believe you may already have guessed.'

Anastasia smiled and bowed her head as she left him. He was staring at his manuscripts through the long-handled glasses he had adopted for studying when the eunuch approached. At once, Suleiman realised that something was wrong—the man looked terrified!

'Yes, what is it, Hasar?'

The eunuch fell to his knees before him. 'Forgive me, my lord. I bring bad news...'

Suleiman felt chilled. He had spent two days fasting and praying, but since the remarkable recovery of the friend his physicians had given up as lost, his thoughts had been uneasy, though he did not know why.

'Tell me at once!'

'The concubine Fatima tried to poison the lady Eleanor,' Hasar said. 'The concubines' pet monkey ate the poisoned fruit and died—but Lady Eleanor challenged Fatima and the concubine attacked your lady and wounded her with a knife.'

'Eleanor has been wounded—badly?' Ice was creeping through Suleiman's veins as he saw the answer in the eunuch's eyes. 'What has been done for her—where is the wound?'

'In her upper arm,' Hasar replied. 'The physician

visits her every day and the women tend her—but she has a fever and…'

'Go on,' Suleiman said fiercely as the eunuch faltered. 'Has the wound become infected?'

'They say it is gathering putrid flesh…' Hasar gasped as he saw the flash of anger mixed with pain in his master's eyes. 'I know nothing of these things, my lord. I thought you should know…'

'When did this happen?'

'Two days ago…'

'For two days no one told me?'

'You were at prayer, my lord. We dared not intrude upon your vigil.'

Suleiman raised his clenched fist as if he would strike the eunuch, then turned away with a gasp of anguish and frustration. What good would it do to take his anger out on the unfortunate messenger? It could not change what had happened—and the man had done only as he had been told. Suleiman had left orders that he was not to be disturbed for anything—but he had not expected this!

Yet he should have done. What a blind, stupid fool he was! Eleanor had come to him straight from Karin's bedside with a request that Fatima should be sent away. He ought to have known that something lay behind such a request. Eleanor was not jealous of the other woman, she had no need to be. He should have realised that she was trying to protect herself and the others from Fatima's spite.

Had he not been so concerned for his friend, he might have realised her request was urgent. But his mind had been attuned to the vigil he had vowed to keep—and because he had done nothing, she was like to die of her wounds. His grief tore through him, striking him to the heart so that he was gripped with a terrible agony and hardly knew how to stand upright. Had he been alone, he might have given way to his grief, but pride kept him from shedding unmanly tears. Instead, his heart shed tears of blood.

'I shall come to her at once,' he said to Hasar. He glanced at the eunuch who was shivering, clearly expecting to be punished. 'You are not to blame. What has been done with Fatima?'

'She is in the punishment cells—awaiting your order, my lord.'

'Leave her for the moment,' Suleiman said. 'Give her only bread and water—and she is to see no one until I decide what to do with her.'

Fatima's punishment could wait—for the moment all he could think of was Eleanor. That she should have been harmed—and by a woman he ought to have sent away days ago—festered in Suleiman's mind like a poisoned thorn. It was his fault, his stupidity in being lenient towards the beautiful woman who had once pleased him, that had brought Eleanor to this!

If she should die! Suleiman hardly dared to allow the thought into his mind. She had been like a bright flame in the sky, bringing him closer to happiness than he had ever been in his life. He had thought to find content with her in this palace that had seemed like a prison before her coming; her smiles had soothed his restless nature; her anger had amused and sometimes burned him—and her spirit had delighted him.

As he walked towards the halls of the harem, a place that he had seldom visited, preferring to have his women brought to him, Suleiman's thoughts were gathering darkness. Until Eleanor's coming, he had sought a woman's company only for sensual pleasure—but she had changed him, teaching him the joy of companionship with a woman…something he had never expected to know after his mother's death.

To find such treasure only to lose it was to taste paradise only to be cast back into the fires of hell. He felt as if a thousand demons tore at his flesh, their talons piercing him until his agony was like to drive him mad. How could he bear it if she should die?

He heard the startled gasps as he strode into the harem unannounced, the women fluttering like jewel-bright birds as if a cat had got amongst them. He was annoyed that his presence should cause such a fluster, yet dismissed it in an instant. Why should they not fear him when they knew only that he was their master and could punish them for the slightest misdemeanour? He had never troubled himself to make them like or understand him, never spent time in discovering what made them happy. It had been enough that they were kept in comfort, awaiting his pleasure.

One of the women came to meet him. She seemed not to fear him, for she looked him in the eyes. 'You have come to see the lady Eleanor, my lord. Anastasia is with her now and is about to change her bandages. If you will wait but a moment…'

'And you are?'

'Elizabetta, my lord. I have danced and sung for you.'

'Yes, I remember,' Suleiman said. 'You have been nursing my lady?'

'Yes, with others—but we have not Anastasia's skill. She was angry when she came back and found Eleanor so ill. She is making changes and I am sure my lady will soon be much recovered.'

'Pray do not delay me,' Suleiman said. 'I must see her.'

He walked past Elizabetta, the other women watching him fearfully from a distance as he entered Eleanor's apartments.

Suleiman was shocked as he saw Eleanor's hair damp with sweat, her face flushed and heated from the fever that had her in its grip. Anastasia had just finished sponging her body with cool water, and, after covering her with a sheet, turned to look at him. He stood staring at Eleanor, his dark eyes tormented by fear.

'She will be more comfortable in a moment, my lord,' Anastasia comforted him. They have kept her too warm—but they did not know what they did was wrong. You must not punish them. We all love Eleanor, because she has been so kind to us. No one else would seek to harm her.'

'What makes any of you think I blame you for this?'

'We have been told that we may all be punished if she dies,' Rosamunde said from behind him. 'We have done our best for her, my lord—but none of us had any true skill in nursing.'

Suleiman nodded, eyes narrowing. This was yet another of his harem he hardly recognised. A lovely woman, but one that left him untouched—what was she doing here, wasting her youth?

'How is my lady?' he asked as he turned back to Anastasia. 'Can you save her? Will she die of her wounds?'

Anastasia smiled and shook her head. 'She is nowhere near as ill as the Janissary you summoned me to nurse—she has a fever and her wound must be lanced again to let out a little pus, but she will live, my lord. Had I been here sooner, she would not have been drugged—it is the drugs that have robbed her of her senses and frightened everyone else. Once they are no longer holding her mind prisoner, she will know us again.'

Suleiman controlled his desire to shout his relief aloud. 'Why have you so much knowledge when the physicians seem to have so little?'

Anastasia smiled and shook her head. 'That is not true, my lord. The physician has closed the wound more skilfully than I could—but he was not wise to keep her so heavily drugged. And the others did not understand the importance of making sure she was cool. Now that I am here we shall soon reduce the fever.'

'How can I repay you for all that you have done?'

'You have already repaid me by giving me the free-dom to serve others. I am a simple woman, my lord. I was born to serve and I have all that I need.'

'You have not been unhappy here?'

'Only a little, sometimes—when Fatima was unkind to one of us.'

'Yes, Fatima.' Suleiman nodded, his expression hardening as he recalled that she was responsible for Eleanor lying here injured. 'You will send me word of my lady—good or bad?'

'Do not fear, my lord. Eleanor will soon recover her health. She is young and strong and the fever will soon pass.'

Suleiman nodded, and then he walked to the bed and bent to kiss Eleanor's brow. She stirred, moaned a little and whispered something he could not quite catch.

'Rest, my darling,' he said in a voice so low that no one else could hear. 'I—I need you.'

Suleiman's shoulders squared as he left the bedside. He had work to do—things that had been neglected these past two days. As he emerged from Eleanor's apartment, the other women fell back and looked at him uncertainly. He lifted his hand to gain their attention, and then spoke to them in a voice devoid of emotion.

'You have none of you anything to fear from me,' he said. 'Only those who have harmed my lady shall be punished. Karin will come to you soon. She will ask you for the truth of this affair. When I have all the facts before me, the guilty shall be punished as the law demands. I shall take no petty revenge. Karin will discuss other things with you—you may speak to her freely without fear. That is my sworn word.'

The silence continued for several minutes after he had left, until curiosity at last forced them to ask, 'What did he mean? What must we confess to Karin?'

Only Marisa held her silence. She remembered what Eleanor had told her and kept her promise not to reveal anything until Karin was well enough to give them the news herself.

Eleanor's eyelids fluttered. She was aware of feeling very tired, and her arm was painful. She moaned and opened her eyes, looking up into Karin's anxious face.

'So at last you are come to yourself again. You foolish, foolish child,' Karin said, her tone sounding relieved rather than scolding. 'Did I not warn you to be careful?'

'Water...' Eleanor pleaded. She was becoming

more conscious of the pain in her arm and her mouth felt dry. 'What happened to me?'

'Fatima sent you poisoned fruit. You challenged her and she stabbed you in the arm. Thankfully, you must have taken her by surprise for the knife was not contaminated with poison—as it well might have been.'

'Oh, yes…' Eleanor sighed. She vaguely remembered something but her mind was still hazy. Rosamunde brought her water and she sipped it gratefully. 'Thank you. What time is it?'

'It is morning,' Karin replied. 'You have had a fever, Eleanor. It is five days now since this happened.'

'Five days…' She struggled to sit up, but found she was too weak and fell back against the pillows. 'What of my lord's friend…he was near to dying?'

'He is much better,' Anastasia said, bending over her to lay a hand on her forehead. 'Ah, so are you, my lady. The fever has gone and you will mend now.'

'You have been nursing me?'

'Since my return three days ago. My other patient does well; I have but this minute returned from seeing him.'

'Thank you…all of you.' Eleanor sighed and closed her eyes once more.

She woke again that evening, feeling better. Rosamunde was sitting with her now and smiled at her.

'Are you hungry, my lady? Anastasia said that we should give you a little nourishing broth if you woke. Morna will prepare it for you—though none here would seek to harm you now.'

'Fatima?' Eleanor whispered.

'Gone, my lady. We shall not see her again.'

Eleanor nodded, satisfied. Suleiman had sent her home as he'd promised. She need not concern herself further.

'Has Karin gone? She was here earlier. I meant to ask if she had recovered from her sickness?'

'Karin is well,' Rosamunde replied. 'She has spent the last few days talking to everyone. We have been promised nothing yet—but it seems we may be given our freedom should we wish it. Anastasia has already been granted hers, but she chooses to remain here—though she is allowed to go where she pleases within certain areas of the palace. She has not been out yet, but Karin said that a eunuch will take her to the city markets if she desires it.'

Eleanor nodded. It seemed that Suleiman was keeping all his promises. She was too tired to inquire further for the moment. She did not ask and was not told that her lord had come three times to visit her while she was in the grip of the fever.

Rosamunde went on, 'I think I shall stay—if you want me, my lady. I have nothing to return to now. My life is here…'

'Yes, yes, please stay,' Eleanor said and smiled at her. 'If Morna would fetch me something, I think I might try to eat a little…'

'You must eat,' Rosamunde agreed. 'We have all been so worried for you, my lady.'

Eleanor closed her eyes once more as Rosamunde went away to order the food. She still felt desperately tired, but the drugging heaviness was gradually fading. Soon she would begin to feel more like herself.

She ought to ask something, but she could not control her thoughts, could not remember what she wanted to know. All she desired was to rest and be well again and then... She was not sure what would happen then. Suleiman had said that they must observe the customs. Of course she could not expect him to visit her—why should he? A sigh of regret issued from her lips.

If he loved her he would have come—but he merely desired her. He was marrying her because he thought her best fitted from amongst the concubines to bear his sons. She had no choice. She must obey, because he was her master.

'Do you bring me news of my lady?' Suleiman asked eagerly as Karin came in answer to his request. 'You said that she had taken food and was able to sit up and talk to her friends—there has been no relapse?'

'Eleanor improves with every hour,' Karin replied, smiling at the way his eyes seemed to darken and glow at the mention of his intended bride. 'She insisted on getting out of bed, and with help has been sitting in the gardens this morning.'

'Is she well enough to be out of bed so soon? It is barely eight days since I saw her lying in a fever.'

'She is very strong, my lord.' Karin frowned, hesitated, then decided she must speak. 'Her arm is healing well and it seems she will be able to use it normally once the soreness has gone—but I fear there will be a scar.'

Suleiman's eyes narrowed. 'Why do you hesitate to tell me this? Do you imagine that I care for such details? My lady is alive. I thank Allah for her life—a scar means less than nothing.'

'I beg your pardon, my lord. I had not realised... quite what she means to you.'

'And you will keep your new-found knowledge to

yourself, Karin,' he replied with a rueful smile. 'I would not have Eleanor know—yet.'

'Ah…' Karin nodded, smiling now herself. 'I believe the lady Eleanor can sometimes be a little headstrong, my lord.'

'Yes.' His mouth quirked at the memory of various instances of her stubbornness. 'That is very true, Karin. Now, to other matters—you have questioned the concubines? They are all innocent of malice against my lady?'

'Most of them admire her for her bravery—some love her.'

'And you have consulted their feelings on the matter of returning to their homes?'

'Yes, my lord.' Karin took out a journal in which she had made notes. 'Ten of them have requested marriages be arranged here—with members of your own guard in most cases. It seems they have watched you at sport with your men—perhaps more often than we knew.' She waited for his reply but he made no comment, seeming indifferent. 'Five have asked to be returned to their families—they are mostly of our own faith and nationality. The others wish to remain here to serve the lady Eleanor, or in Anastasia's case to be allowed to nurse the sick.'

Suleiman nodded. 'Eleanor will make her choice. Those she does not wish to keep may have their wish.'

Karin knew that Eleanor would keep no one who did not wish to remain. Besides, there were more than enough ladies to wait on her, and her three particular friends had all chosen to stay.

'You wish me to speak to her—or shall you see her yourself?'

'My lady must receive instruction in the true religion before the marriage can take place. I believe this news would come best from you, Karin. You must make her aware of her duty—though I do not wish her instructed in the arts of pleasing her husband.'

'I understand, my lord.' Karin hesitated. 'The Caliph has granted me the favour of a visit to my daughters. May I ask when your marriage will take place—so that I may arrange the details of my journey?'

'If Eleanor is well enough—two weeks should suffice. She need only learn sufficient to confirm outwardly to custom.'

'Yes, my lord.' Karin was pleased at the prospect of seeing her daughters so soon. 'I shall convey your message to her—unless you have changed your mind and wish her to come to you?'

'No. I shall not see my bride until the wedding,' Suleiman replied. He did not inform Karin of his reasons, but he was afraid that if he was alone with Eleanor he would not be able to keep from confessing his love—or making love to her. 'Let it all be as we have discussed, Karin. My lady must make her choice, and receive instruction—but she must not tire herself. I do not wish her ill again.'

'Do not fear,' Karin said. 'For the moment she seems content to spend her time sitting quietly with the other ladies. I doubt this mood of tranquillity will last long, but for the moment she takes things easily. If you will excuse me, my lord, I shall go to her now.'

Suleiman nodded. He watched as she left, dark eyes brooding. Would Eleanor accept instruction in the Muslim religion without complaint? He had meant to speak to her himself, to explain that she need pay only lip service—to pacify the feelings of others. In accordance with the law, Suleiman could marry only a woman of his own faith—but he would have no personal objection if she held to her own beliefs in private, as his mother had.

It would have been better to have explained this himself, but she might have lost her temper, and he might have responded in kind—and she was not yet well enough to be thus distressed. She would listen to Karin more easily than to him. If they should both lose control…he could not vouch for what might happen.

He must control his own desires and needs until she was truly healed. He ached for her, longed to hold her in his arms and taste the sweetness of her lips—but he would behave as the civilised gentleman she would have for her husband. If she came to him now he might be tempted beyond bearing, unable to control this raging need inside him, so he would keep his distance until after the marriage ceremony had taken place.

'My lord says he wishes me to study enough of the Qur'an to understand and comply with custom?' Eleanor was aware of a little ache about her heart. Why had he not summoned her to talk of these things as he had promised? 'Please tell my lord that I have studied his religion before I came to this country. I already understand all that he wishes me to—and I shall give the proper responses if I am examined by religious instructors. However, that does not mean I shall believe in them.'

Karin looked at her stubborn face. No wonder Suleiman had left the task of telling Eleanor to her!

'We shall study together for an hour each day—is that so very much to ask?' Karin spoke persuasively.

'Think of the good fortune your…compliance will bring to others. You cannot be wed to the lord Suleiman unless you are believed to have converted to the true faith.'

Eleanor sighed. Karin was telling her it was her duty to marry the lord Suleiman for the sake of the others. She knew that all the women were excited about the wedding. For some it meant freedom, for others a chance to marry—and for those who had chosen to stay with her it meant a life of ease, free from the anxiety of wondering whether they would please their lord when he sent for them. They were to be her companions and friends, but no longer concubines.

Eleanor was already determined that once she was Suleiman's wife, she would ask to be allowed to go shopping in the souks and markets of Constantinople, and some of her ladies would accompany her each time. There would be more freedom for everyone if Eleanor had her way, though she knew that there was no avoiding the customs of the veil and casacche.

'Very well, we shall study together,' Eleanor replied. 'It is no hardship, Karin—and I may learn something new.' She laughed, a teasing look in her eyes. 'Did my lord send you to tell me of my duty lest I fly into a temper with him?'

Karin was tempted to tell her the truth, but held her tongue in check. Suleiman was being generous; there was no point in provoking his anger by betraying his trust.

She smiled. 'So I may tell him that you agree?'

'Yes—but I want something in return.'

'What is your request?'

'I have been told that my lord likes to wrestle and fight with the Janissaries. I would like to watch such a tournament—and the ladies who are to marry must be allowed to watch with me.'

'I shall ask my lord if he feels inclined to oblige you.'

'One more thing—we wish to come out into the courtyard to watch. We do not want to be hidden away out of sight.' Eleanor's eyes sparkled with mischief. 'Pray tell my lord that we shall wear the veil and the casacche as customs dictates.'

Karin frowned. 'You ask a great deal, Eleanor.'

'My lord would have much of me,' she said, her head going up proudly. 'Unless I have some kind of amusement to distract me, I may discover that I feel unwell again. Already my head begins to ache at the thought of all that study my lord would have me do.'

'Eleanor!' Karin shook her head warningly at her. 'If I were your lord I should have you beaten for wilfulness.'

'But you are not my lord,' Eleanor said and laughed huskily. 'My poor friend—are you afraid to carry my message to him?'

'Once I should not have dared...' Karin smiled. 'But I confess I am curious to hear what he will say when he hears your request.'

'The lady Eleanor says that she will study diligently to please you, my lord, but...' Karin hesitated. 'In return she makes a request of you.'

'Ah...' Suleiman's expression became wary. 'And what would my lady have of me? I thought I had granted all she had asked of me.'

'She—she wishes to watch you at sport with the Janissaries, my lord.' Karin saw that the idea pleased him and dared to go on. 'But not from a window overlooking the courtyard. She asks that she and ten of her ladies be allowed to come outside and watch.'

Suleiman stared at her for so long that Karin feared his anger, then his head went back and he laughed in delight. 'I had feared her illness might crush her spirit,' he murmured more to himself than Karin. 'They must be protected from prying eyes—I cannot have them exposed, but providing they wear the proper clothing, I agree.'

'I believe the lady Eleanor understands that, my lord. I shall make certain their modesty is protected— and I shall be with them.' She smiled in relief. 'I, too, would enjoy this spectacle.'

'Then it shall be arranged—the day after tomorrow. You may tell my lady that in return for her obedience I am pleased to grant her request.'

'Obedience?' Eleanor's eyes flashed. 'Ah yes, I see my lord still means to mock me. Well, we shall see…Go once more to the lord Suleiman, Karin. Ask that the ladies who wish to be returned to their homes should be allowed to leave at once.'

'Surely that can wait until after the wedding?' Karin looked at her suspiciously. 'What game are you playing, Eleanor? Are you trying to provoke the lord Suleiman? Remember that he is still your master. You could be beaten if you try him too far.'

'But then I should be too ill to marry him.'

'You play with fire,' Karin warned.

'I would tell him myself if he sent for me.'

Karin's gaze narrowed thoughtfully. 'Are you piqued because he does not send? Surely…' She was once again tempted to speak of Suleiman's feelings for Eleanor, but held true to her promise. 'Well, on your own head…'

'I have been thinking much the same,' Suleiman agreed when Karin presented Eleanor's latest request. 'Pray ask my lady if there is anything more I may do to please her. She asks so little…'

Karin saw the mocking glint in his eye and smiled inwardly. 'Why do you not send for her and tell her yourself, my lord?'

'Convey my message, Karin.' Suleiman waved her away. 'Tomorrow we shall have our tournament. Afterwards, I may decide to send for Eleanor. For the moment I am too busy. Please make sure she understands that I have important business and cannot make time to talk of trivial things.'

Karin nodded, wondering what game these two played with each other. Whatever it was, it certainly seemed to amuse the lord Suleiman, for she had seldom seen him in such good humour.

Eleanor fretted after Karin had brought the latest word from Suleiman. Why would he not send for her? She longed to see him, but it seemed he was determined not to speak to her until after the marriage ceremony. Why? It could only mean that he did not truly care for her.

He had granted all her requests, and she had no more outrageous demands to make of him—save one. And that she could not make through a third party.

She was beginning to be truly well again. Her arm was still a little sore, but the drugging weariness had gone. She was waited on hand and foot by the other women, who could not do enough to please her, and

spent most of her time talking to them and getting to
know those she had hardly spoken to before her illness. They were all willing and eager to be her friends,
though she still enjoyed most the company of those
she had known first. All three had chosen to stay with
her, and she had promised she would win favours for
them all.

'We shall ask my lord to let us go shopping one
day soon,' she said. 'But first the tournament.' She
smiled wickedly at the ladies who were to accompany
her into the courtyard. 'This time it will be for you to
do the choosing—and what better opportunity? I think
we shall have as good sport as the men.'

The ladies giggled and looked at her excitedly.
Several of them already knew which of the men they
would choose, and could not wait for the tournament
to begin.

Eleanor too was looking forward to the outing. She
had heard much about the lord Suleiman's skill and
now she wanted to see for herself.

Karin came to inspect them before they were conducted through the endless passages of the harem and
then a part of the palace that was normally forbidden
to them, unless special permission had been given. It
was quite a procession, and made Eleanor laugh at all
the fuss. Two eunuchs walked before them, thrusting
aside any servant who dared to glance at them, and
two behind.

She felt a shiver of excitement as they emerged into
the palace courtyard, remembering the night she had
been brought here and unceremoniously dumped while
the lord Suleiman rode back to help his men defeat
the bandits who had dared to attack them. So much
had changed since then that she felt as if she were

someone else and not the frightened girl who had been brought to this place against her will.

Screens had been placed at one end of the arena, and stools were placed beneath a silken awning to protect the ladies from the fierce heat of the afternoon sun. They were to see, but not be seen or approached by any who might wish to stare at them. The men taking part in the tournament could of course see them seated at the far end—but woe betide any man foolish enough to let his eyes stray from his opponent!

It was to be a contest of skill and strength, and no sacrifice of life would be demanded. Yet in the matched pairs the weapons were real and wounds could be inflicted, which might become infected—so the combatants would have no time to stare at the ladies!

The first contest was between a giant with coal-black skin and a man of equal size, but with fair skin and hair the colour of sunlight.

'The Nubian is called Mosra,' Marisa whispered in Eleanor's ear. 'And his opponent is Ahmed…'

Eleanor saw her smile and knew that this was the man she wished to marry. The contestants saluted the ladies, but their faces were expressionless. Did they know that they were performing to please their future brides?

The women were whispering to each other. Hidden behind their veils and enveloping cloaks, there was little to be seen of them except their eyes. But what messages might pass with a flash of sparkling eyes!

The contest was with the short sword, and fiercely fought. The two men pressed hard, seeming equally matched, but Ahmed eventually succeeded in overcoming his opponent. He came to salute the ladies as the victor, and Eleanor noted the way his eyes searched for and found Marisa's. It seemed that their future had been settled—though how he could know his bride in her casacche was difficult to say. Perhaps the ladies of the harem had had more opportunity to see what went on outside the harem than anyone supposed! Eleanor imagined there was always a way for those with the courage to seek it. It was as well that Suleiman chose not to notice.

After that, there was a succession of fierce fights. Eleanor heard the indrawn breath and little squeals of fright and knew that their chosen partners were not always winners. However, no one was injured apart from a few scratches and bruises, and so no harm was done.

The last contest was a wrestling match between Omar and the lord Suleiman. Eleanor's spine tingled as they came to salute the ladies, her eyes meeting Suleiman's—which seemed to gleam with mockery. He was stripped to the waist and wore only a loincloth to cover his lower body. She had known he was strong and lean when he pressed her in his arms, but she had not guessed how beautiful his body would look when he was all but naked.

His muscles rippled like those of a thoroughbred horse, and the sweat made his olive-toned skin glisten like silk. She swallowed hard as desire gripped her by the throat and she wanted— Oh, damn the wretch! She wanted him to love her.

'Omar is the captain of the palace guard,' Marisa whispered in her ear as the men walked to the centre of the arena. 'They say he is the strongest and most skilled of all—apart from your lord.'

Eleanor nodded but could not speak. Her chest was

tight with the mixed emotions raging inside her. She was conscious of an overwhelming excitement, but there was also fear. Supposing her lord was hurt? She had requested this contest, and it had proved entertaining—but now she was tingling from head to toe.

She watched breathlessly as the contest began. The men seemed evenly matched as they circled each other, waiting their time. Omar moved in first, his arms surrounding Suleiman in a huge bear hug, but Suleiman's strength broke that hold easily. Before Eleanor could draw breath, Omar had seized Suleiman's arm and had him flipped over and lying on his back on the ground beneath him.

She gave a little cry of alarm, but the next moment they were on their feet again. 'What is happening?' she asked Marisa.

'The first fall has gone to Omar—there are two more, for it is the best of three.'

Eleanor watched in apprehension. She suddenly wanted Suleiman to win. He must win! She could not bear to see him lose. He was her lord and her love and she wanted to see him triumph.

Seconds later, Suleiman brought Omar down and held him easily. He was laughing as they both regained their feet, and Omar was grinning as if he too enjoyed this test of skill between them. They were the best of friends, yet neither wanted to be bested and it was a true contest.

'One fall each,' Marisa said. 'All depends on the last!'

Eleanor could not speak. She could see that both men were relishing their fight, testing each other to the full. The third fall did not come easily, for both were skilled in the art and both seemed determined to win.

The tension was almost unbearable for Eleanor. Her nails curled into the palms of her hands as she watched, on the edge of her seat, breath catching as the advantage swayed one way and then the other—and then quite suddenly it was over. Suleiman had won!

Eleanor jumped to her feet to applaud, then, conscious of all eyes upon her, sat down again. Perhaps she was not supposed to show her approval so openly.

The two men were laughing and hugging each other, still jostling as though they would have liked to continue the contest.

'The tournament is over,' Karin announced and stood up, beckoning to the other ladies. 'We should return to the palace now. Come along, Eleanor. We must not linger. The lord Suleiman will send for you later if he wishes to see you.'

Eleanor was reluctant to leave. She glanced at Suleiman, wanting to catch his eye, but he was still laughing and jesting with his friend. She knew that she must do as Karin told her, for the ladies had become very excited and she had noticed that the men who had taken part and were still in the courtyard arena were looking their way rather too often. It was not seemly, and it would not do to flout the customs too much. Suleiman had been generous to give so much; his trust must not be abused.

'Yes, we shall come,' she said, taking Marisa's arm firmly. The other woman was clearly very reluctant to move and she gave her a little push. 'Be patient, Marisa. Karin will arrange the marriage if Ahmed is willing.'

'I wish that I could speak with him.' Marisa's tone

was petulant. The promise of a marriage with a man of her choice had made her impatient.

'I am sorry, but you cannot,' Eleanor said. 'Be grateful that you are to be allowed to marry.'

'Yes—yes, I am grateful to you and the lord Suleiman,' Marisa said with a last wistful look over her shoulder. 'I am so thankful that Fatima did not kill you, Eleanor. She deserved her punishment, awful though it was.'

They were back inside the palace now. Eleanor felt the chill strike her as she stopped walking and turned to look at her companion.

'What do you mean—her punishment? I thought she had been sent back to her home?'

'Oh, my foolish tongue! I am so sorry.' Marisa's eyes darkened with remorse. 'Karin told us we were not to say anything—in case it distressed you. I forgot after all the excitement. She will be so cross with me!'

'And I shall be angry if you do not tell me what happened to Fatima.'

'The lord Suleiman ordered that she be beaten and sent to the slave merchants. She will have been sold by now, but not to the harem of a noble lord. She— she was marked by the whip. Our master ordered it so, because she had misused her beauty and must never be able to do so again.'

'How cruel!' Eleanor cried. Her face was white with shock and she felt sick. 'How could he have done such a wicked thing? I cannot bear to think what will become of her.'

'I should not have told you,' Marisa said, looking guilty. 'It was no more than she deserved, my lady— truly.'

Eleanor did not speak again until they were back in

the harem. She went up to Karin as the other woman prepared to leave them.

'Why did you not tell me about Fatima?'

Karin stared at her in silence for a moment, and then sighed. 'Because I knew you would react this way. You do not understand, Eleanor. The lord Suleiman had to make an example of her. She could not simply be banished after all her wickedness. He might have had her put to death for her crimes had he wished.'

'Would not that have been kinder?' Eleanor asked angrily. 'She has been treated worse than a dog. To have her beaten in such a way that she could not hope to be sold into a harem! What will happen to her now? Is she to be sent to a brothel in the back streets of the city, to be used and abused by any man willing to pay a few coins for her? Cruel! Wicked! I cannot believe that my lord would do such a thing.'

Karin hesitated, but it was not for her to tell Eleanor the extent of Fatima's crimes, 'She tried to kill you,' she said. 'You should not blame Suleiman. He had little choice. Fatima knew what she did was punishable by death. She is fortunate to have escaped it.'

'Fortunate?' Eleanor stared at her in disbelief. 'I think what he has done is barbaric—despicable. Suleiman promised me she would be sent home. He promised!'

'That was before she tried to kill you.' Karin gave her a severe look. 'Remember where you are, Eleanor. I warned you that a beast lurks in all men. The lord Suleiman is no different from any other man, though I have always found him just. As he has been this time. He has acted according to the law.'

'A savage, cruel law!' Eleanor retorted.

'But the law by which we all live,' Karin reminded

her. 'You have been much indulged—perhaps too
much. Our laws are perhaps wiser than you think,
though they may seem harsh at times. You must learn
to accept that there are some things you cannot
change.'

'Never! I shall never accept such brutality.'

'Learn this, then,' Karin said and her tone was
harsh. 'You will gain nothing by defiance. The lord
Suleiman cares for you and you might make life easier
for many in this place—but only if you learn to bend
a little, to give as well as take. Tame the beast with
tenderness, make him weak with chains of love,
Eleanor, and you could bring happiness to many. Do
not seek to fight the beast—or it may turn and devour
you.'

'I want to see the lord Suleiman!'

Karin looked at her beautiful, tempestuous face,
then shook her head. 'No, I shall not request an audience for you. Not while you are in this mood.'

'Then I shall go without permission.' Eleanor cried
impetuously. 'I shall demand to see him.'

'You do not yet rule here.' Karin gave her a hard
look. 'If you persist in this folly I shall have you
locked in your room and place a guard over you—'
She broke off as Hasar approached. 'Yes? You wished
to speak with me?'

'The lord Suleiman has sent for the lady Eleanor.
He wishes to see her at once.'

'I shall come at once.' Eleanor's eyes were bright
with anger. 'I must not keep my lord waiting, Karin.'

Karin caught at her arm as she would have passed.
'Take care, Eleanor,' she warned. 'I am not your enemy. You know that I tried to protect Fatima from
herself. I would have had her banished if that were

possible—but Suleiman was angry. He came to you when we feared you might die, and he was half out of his mind with grief. I have never seen a man so close to breaking. I do not say that he was kind to have punished Fatima as he did—but he was within the law. He could have punished her a thousand times more harshly. Many men in his position have done far worse things for less reason.'

'But I do not wish to marry those other men,' Eleanor cried. 'I believed I had come to love Suleiman—but he is a barbarian. A cruel savage! And I do not wish to marry such a man.'

She tore herself from Karin's grasp and walked away. Karin stared after her with anxious eyes. Although it was not often allowed to rage out of control, Suleiman did have a fearful temper. And she was very much afraid that this time Eleanor would try his patience too far.

Chapter Eleven

The struggle with Omar had heated Suleiman's blood, leaving him with a sense of exhilaration and triumph. He had won fairly and Eleanor had been watching—that gave him a deep sense of satisfaction. Her request for the tournament had told him that she was far from being indifferent to him, as she had tried to pretend. Indeed, he had sensed the last time he'd held her in his arms that she was close to surrender. He could have taken her then, but he had controlled his desire and let her go.

Suleiman knew that he could possess Eleanor with or without her consent, but the act of possession without love was only a fleeting pleasure that he might have found with any of his concubines. There must be more! He had for some time past been aware of an emptiness within himself, but until he had begun to know and understand Eleanor he had not realised what was lacking in his life.

He loved her—not just with his body, but with his heart and mind. For the first time in his life he had met a woman who could touch the inner man. His loins burned with the need to lie with her, and sometimes at night he had lain restless, unable to sleep for the need inside him, but he had given her the time she had begged for because he wanted her to come to him in love.

'The hawk is made weak by the dove,' he murmured to himself, amused by the discovery within himself that he would once have termed folly in others. 'Yet I would have her come to me...'

His pulses quickened as he heard footsteps and knew that she had answered his call. It was for her sake that he had not sent for her before this, because she had been so ill and he had wanted her to be truly well again. But there must be no more play-acting. It was time that Eleanor understood the true nature of his feelings for her. He caught the scent of her perfume and turned eagerly. His smile faded as he saw the expression on her beautiful face. She had not looked at him this way since that first meeting in the gardens of the Corsair Mohamed Ali ben Ibn!

'Why are you angry?'

'You ask me why—after what you have done?' Her eyes narrowed, her look one of utter contempt. 'No one told me until after the contest. Karin ordered that it should be kept from me...'

'Of what do you speak?' Suleiman felt a sharp searing pain as he saw what he believed to be hatred in her eyes. 'What have I done that has so displeased you?'

'Was it so little to you that you cannot even remember?' Eleanor's eyes flashed in anger. 'You told me that Fatima would be sent back to her home. How could you have had her beaten so cruelly and then— to have condemned her to a life of true slavery! She had been treated almost as a queen in your household…' Her voice broke with emotion. 'I cannot believe that you could have been so savage, so unjust.'

'You think I was unjust?' Suleiman stared at her haughtily. That she should speak to him thus! It was unforgivable. How dare she criticise his judgement? He had allowed her much, but she went too far. A woman might not seek to dictate in such matters. 'Fatima was guilty of many crimes—more than you know. I might have ordered a painful death for her—or imprisonment—but I granted her life.'

'Life as a whore to be used and abused by any man who pays for her!'

'She tried to kill you—and she murdered the woman Dinazade.' His expression hardened. 'I was merciful because she had once pleased me—but such crimes must be punished. Even in your own country murder is punishable by death!'

'You are a barbarian!' Eleanor cried, too angry to recognise the justice in what he said. 'I had begun to believe that you were a man of wisdom and justice— but now I see I was wrong. You are as ruthless and cruel as those men who slew my father.'

Suleiman stared at her, his lips white with fury. 'Enough! You are insolent, woman. I have allowed you too much freedom, and now you seek to dictate what I may or may not do. I am the master here. You are a woman and my property.'

'I am well aware that a female slave is less than nothing in your eyes,' Eleanor retorted scornfully. 'I almost believed in you—but now I know you for what you are! Do with me as you please, my master. You are strong and I am weak—but punish me as you will, compel me to your bed, you shall never, never have me.'

'Be careful, Eleanor. You push me too far at your peril.'

'I care for nothing you do or say to me,' she cried. 'I thought I could be happy as your wife—that I could live here content to please you and leave behind all that I had known and loved—but now you make me hate you. You may force me to submit, but I shall never love you.'

She felt a flash of fear as she saw the silver flame leap up in his eyes and knew that she had indeed pushed him too far. He moved towards her purposefully, his intent stamped like a smouldering brand into the iron of his features.

'Then there is no point in waiting...' he muttered fiercely and there was something wild and primitive about him then as he reached out and caught her wrist. 'I had hoped you would come to accept your duty, Eleanor—but as you will not, I must teach you to know your master.'

'No!' Eleanor caught her breath as she gazed up into those dark eyes. 'Please...do not do this, my lord. I— I beg you. Let me go—send me away and let me be free.'

'I wanted your love,' he said in a voice that even in her distress she recognised as tormented. 'But if it is to be denied me even now, I shall glory in your hatred. You belong to me, Eleanor—and I will have you, willingly or no.'

She gave a cry of denial and pulled away as he began to draw her towards the inner chamber, struggling and fighting him every step of the way. He was much too strong for her. His fingers held her in a vice-like grip and she knew that she was helpless against the beast she had aroused in him. His grip bruised her, causing her to whimper with pain.

'Let me go!' she cried, fear sweeping her as she recognised the wisdom of Karin's warning too late. 'Let me go. If you do this I shall not forgive you.'

'You hate me anyway. Why should I not take that which is mine?'

She pulled back sharply and managed to break free of him, but he caught her before she could reach the outer hall, seizing her about the waist and sweeping off her feet. She beat against him with her fists as he carried her to the inner chamber and tossed her down on the silken softness of the divan. She lay gazing up at him as he untied the belt at his waist and threw off his caftan. His plain white tunic followed that to the floor, revealing the rippling muscles and bronzed skin she had found so exciting in the courtyard. He towered above her, magnificent, a pagan god in all his beauty, about to take a human sacrifice.

Eleanor caught her breath. Suleiman's hair was slightly damp as if he had bathed just before she came to him, and there was a clean, fresh scent exuding from his body that she found enticing. His dark eyes sought and held hers as he bent over her and unfastened the jeweled clasp at her waist. Beneath the heavy silk of her waistcoat, the flimsy gauze tunic did nothing to hide the perfection of her breasts, which were peaked by the sudden arousal of desire that had begun to sweep her body like a forest fire.

Suleiman's eyes seemed to devour her as he reached out and ripped away the fine material, exposing her soft, pale flesh to his burning gaze. His hand moved to her face, his fingers stroking her cheek and then down the arch of her slender throat, moving slowly down to caress the dark rose nipples, and then cupping the fullness of her breasts.

'Beautiful,' he murmured huskily. 'Beautiful... I have wanted to touch you this way since I first saw you bathing in that pool. I have burned for you, Eleanor.'

Her throat was tight with emotion; her anger drained away as she recognised the need in him and felt it answered deep within her. She could scarcely breathe for the churning excitement that now possessed her, spirals of desire curling up from the centre of her being. She should beg him to stop! She should fight him tooth and claw, but the will to resist was draining from her as she gazed into his dark eyes. He was savage and wild, an arrogant cruel man who would be her master...yet even as she formed the protest in her mind she denied it.

He could be capable of harshness, of that she had ample proof, but he was not wantonly cruel. The news of Fatima's punishment had shocked her, making her react angrily—but her accusations had not been entirely fair. She knew that Karin had spoken truly, and that many men in his position would have done much worse.

Why had she begun to defend him in her own mind? Why was her body betraying her, yearning to meld with his? Yet she knew all too well. It was because, despite his threats to show her he was the master, he was still hesitating, still careful not to hurt her. She might have expected rape after their fierce quarrel, but this was seduction. He was drawing her to him, coaxing her response with a tender care. His eyes held hers as his hand continued to stroke and explore the softness of her body, his touch beginning to make her flesh tingle with an exquisite pleasure.

'Do not fear me, my love,' he murmured, his voice husky with passion. 'The die is cast and I cannot draw back, but I shall not hurt you. I would never hurt you.'

'I do not fear you,' she whispered breathily. 'I have never feared you—only myself. I feared to give lest I was truly your slave.'

'You are my love,' he said. 'My only love.'

Eleanor moaned with pleasure as he bent his head to kiss her breasts, taking the rosy tips into his mouth one by one to taste and tease them with his tongue. Her breath quickened as he pushed the flimsy drawers down over her hips, tossing them away. Now he was kissing and tasting each inch of her, as if he found her as sweet as honey.

'I feel so strange,' she said, gazing up at him, her eyes wide with wonder. 'I have no will...no thought but you.'

Suleiman raised his head to smile at her. 'I am about to take you into paradise, my houri. We shall find our heaven on this earth, I promise you.'

The feelings his kisses and gentle stroking aroused in her were so unexpected and so sweet. Eleanor discovered that her body was no longer her own; it vibrated like the strings of a musical instrument beneath his hands as she arched and moaned beneath him.

'I think I shall die,' she whispered as his lips followed his stroking fingers to the centre of her femininity, making her gasp and writhe with the pleasure she could not hide. 'Oh...oh, my lord.'

She felt him move so that his body covered hers and knew that he was as naked as she. The heat of his loins burned her, and without needing instruction she opened to receive the sudden thrust of his throbbing manhood. A sharp pain made her cry out and draw back as the hugeness of him filled her, but his lips were on hers, teasing and coaxing her to acceptance once more. And then the pain was over and she could feel the rising tide of her own desire, swelling within her, driving her to meet his urgent thrusting, her hips grinding against him in her own need. Her lips parted in little mewing cries as he swept her on with him to that far place.

She was falling…falling through time and space into something that wrapped her about with warmth and pleasure. Indeed, it was as though she had died and gone to paradise. She moaned a little as she felt Suleiman move and tightened her arms about him, as if to hold her to him a little longer.

'Do not leave me,' she whispered.

'I shall never leave you or put you from me,' he vowed as he raised himself above her on one elbow so that he might look down at her. He wiped a tear from her cheek. 'Forgive me if I hurt you, my darling. It must always be so the first time.'

'You did not hurt me so very much,' she said, looking up at him shyly now as she marvelled in the sense of well being flooding through her. 'I think I cried because I am happy—and because I have been foolish to resist you. I did not know that I could feel like this…'

'You do not hate me now?' His gaze was thoughtful as it rested on her lovely face, flushed and smiling now. 'I meant to wait until you were my wife, Eleanor. I never intended to force you.'

'You did not,' she replied and blushed. 'At first, yes—but that was because I provoked you into losing your temper. I fear that I spoke harshly to you, my lord. I was distressed and hurt that you had punished Fatima—but I did not know that she had killed Dinazade. I thought it was because of what she did to me, that you had taken revenge out of anger.'

Suleiman straightened up. He reached for his robe and pulled it on, before sitting on the edge of the divan beside her. 'I did punish her the way I did because of how she attacked you, Eleanor. I am guilty of harshness towards her. I thought you would die and I hated her. She had committed many crimes, which were punishable by death, yet I stayed my hand against her these many weeks. I would have been content to banish her—until I thought she had robbed me of that which I treasure more than my life. Then indeed I acted with the savage anger my fear aroused. I warned you I was not perfect—though I have strived to be just. Love made me cruel—my love and need for you.'

'Oh, my lord…' Eleanor caught back a sob. 'I—I did know. I have held back, taunted you… Can you forgive me?'

'I shall no doubt think of some suitable punishment,' he said huskily. 'You must learn to know me, my dove.'

'Yes, my lord,' she replied demurely. 'I shall pay heed to your instruction most diligently.'

'So obedient!' Suleiman laughed. 'Why do I suspect you most when you are meek?'

'Perhaps because I have been wilful and impudent in the past?'

'Yes, that may have some bearing on the matter. But know that I would not have you change too much, my love. I think I gain much from battle with you— especially when I win!'

Eleanor's eyes sparked with mischief as she sat up and looked at him. 'You have shown me that I was foolish to fear love, my lord—but what makes you imagine you won the argument?'

'It is an argument neither of us can win,' he said, the laughter dying from his face. 'We do not live in a perfect world, Eleanor—nor am I without my faults.'

'Indeed, you are not, my lord!'

He smiled wryly. 'I have a feeling you will teach me to be more considerate of others, Eleanor. I have perhaps been too much indulged. Everything was always as I ordered it—until one woman refused to obey me when I told her I would dry her hair.'

Eleanor smiled. 'Why did you not drown me as you threatened—or have me beaten for my disobedience?'

'I could not bear to think of you in pain. When they told me you had been so ill…' He touched his fingers to the bandage on her arm. 'Does the wound still pain you?'

'Sometimes it is a little sore, but I do not regard it. I fear it will leave a scar—I am worth less than I was before.'

'You are beyond price to me,' he told her. He cursed suddenly, then stood up and began to pace about the room as if in agitation. She watched, sensing that he was fighting a battle within himself, and then he returned to her. 'I cannot hold you against your will. It would be a mockery of the love I bear you. I grant you your freedom, Eleanor. You may return to your family if that is your wish.'

For a moment Eleanor was stunned. Was he really offering her freedom? Once it had been all she wanted, a chance to return to her homeland and the life she had known…but now she knew deep in her heart that she could never leave him. Not because he was her master, but because she was bound to him by the ties of love. But supposing he did not truly want her?

She looked at him uncertainly. 'Do you want me to go?'

'You know that I do not. I would keep you with me always as my wife—my only wife, for I vow that I shall take no other.'

'Supposing I cannot give you a son?' She knew that it was very important to him to have a son, and that his religion made it possible for him to take another wife if she was unable to provide him with one.

He had been silent for several seconds now, and her heart caught. She could not expect him to renounce all that he had been born to for her sake, the culture that was so much a part of him, but when he spoke his words were so unexpected and so touching that they brought tears to her eyes.

'Then I shall have no son.'

'Do you love me so much, my lord?' she asked, misty-eyed.

'I have not the words to tell you—only time will show that I speak the truth.'

'Then I shall stay with you, my lord—for I love you. I tried to fight my feelings for you, but you were too strong for me.'

Suleiman sat beside her again. He reached out to trail his fingers down the curve of her cheek. 'If you left me I should be lost. I am trapped in this place, Eleanor. Caught by love and duty—and even my love for you cannot free me from the web that binds me. If you stay, you must live by our customs and religion, though I shall pretend not to notice if you cling to your own in private.'

'I know this, my lord. I have accepted it.'

'I would have you as free as my falcon when she flies, but you will never truly be free in this land. We protect our women from the harshness of a cruel world, Eleanor. I cannot let you go out without the eunuchs to guard you, because you would not be safe. A woman alone would not be considered worthy of respect and therefore vulnerable to abuse. Men are not to be trusted, my love. We are but base creatures, and only love may redeem us.'

'This also I know,' Eleanor assured him and smiled teasingly. 'Karin has done her work well, my lord. I know that I must conform in public, but in private…'

'Ah…in private you may command,' he said and laughed. 'I am your slave here, Eleanor.'

'My lord seeks to mock me,' she replied and shook her head at him, for there was a wildness in him that would never be quite tamed, though like his beloved hawk he could be coaxed. 'But I do have one request…'

'I imagined you might. Ask and it shall be granted—if it is possible.'

'Could you not buy Fatima back and send her home?'

Suleiman looked at her for some seconds in silence.

'It is already done,' he said at last. 'I have told no one in the palace—but the man who sold you to me held her for me at his house in the city. After she had been beaten, I regretted what I had done, Eleanor. Yet to have been seen to do less would have seemed weak. Fatima pleased me once, though she also betrayed me. I have given her into the charge of Mohamed, and he will take her back to Algiers. What she does then will be of her own choosing.'

Eleanor took his hand and held it. 'And I accused you of being unjust. Please forgive me. It is I who have wronged you, my lord.'

'What—am I no longer a savage?' His eyes gleamed with amusement.

'My lord is a most noble savage,' Eleanor replied. She put her hand out to pull his head down so that their lips touched, and then she kissed him…sweetly, slowly and with passion. 'I think that my master should continue my instruction…'

Suleiman's eyes glowed like hot coals, as he bent over her. 'My love…' he murmured. 'It will be my pleasure to meet this latest request of yours…'

They lay close together long into the night, whispering, sharing the secrets that neither had ever confessed to another, kissing, touching…loving as they came to know and enjoy each other's body.

'Should I not return to the harem?' Eleanor asked at one point. 'What will the others think?'

'They will know that their mistress has found her rightful place at last—and that place is here by my side, Eleanor.'

'I cannot stay forever in your bed. We are not yet married.'

'But we soon shall be,' he murmured, holding her fastened against him as if he would never release her. 'It must be soon. Tomorrow your brother shall be brought here to my apartments, Eleanor. I shall make arrangements for him to be returned to your family, but that will take time and until then you will want to see him as often as possible.'

'Yes, I should like to see Richard.' Eleanor kissed

his shoulder, tasting the salt of his sweat. 'When did you decide to give him his freedom?'

'When I realised that I loved you. I could not keep your brother against his will, but I needed to make you understand that we were meant for each other. Had I told you before this, you would have asked to go with him.'

'Yes, I should,' Eleanor admitted, snuggling against his hard chest with a sigh. 'I did not know myself. I think that I began to love you when you turned your back that day in the gardens...but it took me a long time to know my own heart.'

Suleiman's arms tightened about her and she felt the shudder run through him. 'Supposing Mohamed had not offered you to me—I cannot bear to think of what might have happened to you.'

'Or if I had managed to escape you!' She gazed up at him mischievously. 'How much I should have missed.'

'There was never any chance of you escaping me, woman!'

Eleanor laughed. He would always be the master of her heart, no matter what concessions he made to her—but he loved her and that was all she wanted of life.

'You look well, sister.' Richard seemed uncomfortable. He had been brought to the lord Suleiman's apartments wondering what to expect and was confused by what he found. Eleanor was richly dressed in cloth of gold and wearing jewels fit for a queen. 'Are you better? They told me you were ill for a while.'

'It was nothing much,' Eleanor replied carelessly. 'I

had a fever, but I have recovered. Are you content, Richard? They are treating you well at the school?'

'The discipline is harsh,' her brother replied. 'Most of the students are beaten for disobedience every now and then—but it is no more than a tutor would do at home. I enjoy it when they give us training in the courtyard. I saw you at the tournament.'

'I did not notice you. I am sorry.'

'You were watching the lord Suleiman.' Richard frowned at her. 'They say he is to take you as his wife in three days…'

'Yes, that is so…' She hesitated. 'Suleiman has told me that you will be given passage to Cyprus after our wedding. He has been arranging it.'

'So I am to be free…' Richard's eyes narrowed. 'What price have you paid for my freedom, sister? Are you his harlot? Yes, I see it is so—and it will never be any different. This marriage ceremony has no meaning. You are not of his faith. You will still be a whore in the eyes of the true church.'

'Richard…' Eleanor's face had gone white. Richard's scorn hurt her, all the more because she had always loved him dearly. 'You are unfair.'

'He has bewitched you…turned your head with fine gifts,' Richard said sourly. 'You have sold yourself to him, Eleanor. You are his property now—his thing to do with as he will.'

'You do not know of what you speak,' she replied, her lovely eyes mirroring her hurt. 'Suleiman loves me, and I love him. I want to be his wife.'

Richard stared at her, his manner hostile and disbelieving. 'Then you are a fool,' he said. 'He may promise many things now, but wait a while and he will put you aside as any man puts aside his whore when he tires of her.'

'Why do you want to hurt me?' Eleanor cried, tears slipping down her cheeks. 'Why do you say such terrible things to me? Do you hate me?'

Richard's face twisted with anger. 'I hate them, Eleanor. I hate the men who killed our father, and those who sold us—and I hate him. I hate and despise the man who will be your husband.'

'He has not harmed you.'

Richard gave a harsh laugh. 'He bought me as another man might buy a dog. I have been beaten and humiliated in his house, treated like dirt. Do you expect me to love him?'

'No...' Eleanor's heart contracted with pain. 'No, I do not expect you to love him—but you could try to understand his ways, as he does ours.'

Richard scowled. 'It is easy for him to understand. He made me his slave, now he will release me to please his whore. Should I grovel at his feet to thank him?'

'No—but you might respect what he has done. This is his country, Richard, and he lives by his customs. They may seem harsh to us sometimes, but he seeks always to be just.'

'I shall never respect him or his way of life. Nor you if you stay here willingly, Eleanor.'

'Then you must forget me,' she said sadly. 'Please leave, Richard. We have nothing more to say to each other.'

His eyes gleamed, then he turned and left without another word. Eleanor blinked away her tears as Suleiman came to her and opened his arms to receive her. He had been standing behind the screen, where he had retired to give her privacy with her brother.

'You heard?' She looked at him anxiously as he drew her close to comfort her. 'He is so bitter, my lord. He knows not what he says.'

'Richard hates me and my world,' Suleiman replied. 'He is not alone in this—many of his faith and ours have been sworn enemies for too long. I have often wished that we might begin to build a bridge towards a new understanding and peace, but I fear it may be too great a divide. Men like your brother will never try to understand us.'

'Yes, I know you are right' she said and sighed. 'It makes me sad for him, Suleiman.'

'I had hoped that he might have returned to visit you one day. I could have arranged for him to travel freely in our land and on the seas. It is not as difficult as you might imagine. I had thought it might be the start of understanding…'

'Perhaps he will relent one day,' Eleanor said. 'He is still raw from the grief of his father's death.'

'You have suffered as much as he in this.'

'Perhaps more. I was closer to my father. It may be that he resents that he was never given a chance to know Father better.'

Suleiman nodded agreement. 'Yes, perhaps. The relationship between father and son can be difficult. I have been blessed, but it was not thus for Hasan. Had my father shown him more favour, it might have prevented his treachery—and punishment.'

'That hurt you, my lord.' She moved towards him, reaching out to touch his cheek with the tips of her fingers. 'I saw it in your face when you told me what had happened…'

Suleiman pulled her close, his lips against her hair. 'We have both felt the sting of a brother's scorn, my love—but we have each other.'

'Yes, my lord. We are blessed indeed.'

As he drew her to him, Eleanor closed her eyes, shutting out the grief Richard's rejection had caused her. It would ease in time as did all such pain.

Eleanor sat with the other ladies. For this special occasion all the women had been allowed to mingle in the Caliph's own hall. Some of them were heavily veiled, but most wore a simple headdress with only gossamer of gauze to cover their faces if they so chose.

Several eunuchs were present, also the lord Suleiman, his younger brother Bayezid, who had been persuaded to leave the seclusion of his studies for the evening, and the Caliph himself.

It was the eve of Eleanor's wedding, and in what she believed was a departure from custom, she had been formally presented to her lord's father and brother. She herself wore only a pretty scarf over her hair, for the men present were family, and Suleiman had told her it was permissible to show her face to them if she chose.

'You show favour to those who are to be your family by not wearing the veil,' Suleiman had told her. 'And I am happy for you to do so at a private gathering.'

The Caliph had smiled on her, nodding and welcoming her to his family. 'My son has chosen well,' he told her. 'And though you are yet strange to our ways, I hear good things of you.'

In the strictest adherence to custom, Suleiman would probably not have met his bride or seen her face until the wedding ceremony was over, for often men of his standing married women who had been chosen for their own nobility. However, the Caliph himself had taken a concubine to wife and saw no reason to quarrel with his son's decision.

Caliph Bakhar had long been aware of Suleiman's restlessness, but could not bring himself to give him permission to leave. Perhaps now his son would find content at home.

That evening, Suleiman entertained the court with his singing, while one of the eunuchs accompanied him on a lute. Eleanor listened entranced, for the husky, sensual notes of her lord's song were deeply moving.

He sang of unrequited love and a young man dying of a broken heart because the woman he desired had been given to another man.

Eleanor's eyelashes were wet with tears as the last notes died away. She met his sultry gaze and knew that though he had sung at his father's request, his song had been for her. He was telling her that his heart would break if they were ever parted.

Since the unpleasant, hurtful meeting with Richard, Eleanor's mood had veered between happiness and near despair. She loved Suleiman, but her brother's cruel words had hurt her.

Would she truly be her lord's wife? They were to marry according to his religion, but in her heart she still believed in her own faith. Did that make her the whore her brother had named her?

After Suleiman's song, there was a display of dancing by beautiful girls who wore the scantiest of clothing, which revealed their charms. Then a little later, a eunuch juggled with balls and also ate fire. It was late in the evening when the ladies were escorted back to the harem.

Eleanor said goodnight to Suleiman, but they did not kiss or touch, because it would not be seemly before the court. She was to spend the night with her friends in accordance with custom, and would be heavily veiled when she went to her lord as a bride the next day.

She slept but little that night, wishing that she lay beside her lord so that he could hold her close and banish the doubts that plagued her throughout the dark hours.

Oh, she was foolish to doubt him! Eleanor had proof enough of his love, and he had been more than generous. She knew that she had only to ask for some boon and it would be granted.

She fell asleep just before dawn, but her dreams were unkind and she thought herself at sea again, witnessing the way her beloved father had been struck down.

Eleanor could not blame her brother for his bitterness. She too felt anger when she remembered the way they had been captured. Yet in her heart she knew that her destiny lay with the man she was to marry. And at last she was at peace.

The ceremony of the bath, and the sweet oils that were so gently massaged into her skin, were very soothing. Eleanor's hair was braided like a coronet around her head, and the rest left to fall in shining waves to the small of her back. Then a heavy silk veil was placed over her head; she was just able to see through it, but it would not be possible for others to see her face.

Her robes were of white silk heavily embroidered with gold thread and encrusted with jewels, and she had been told that Suleiman would wear much the same.

Eleanor was trembling inside as her ladies dressed her, fluttering about her like tiny humming birds. Their laughter and happiness for her was easing the knot of anxiety inside her. She laughed and blushed as they teased her, making her promise to have many children so that they could all enjoy looking after them.

Her fear and doubt had dissolved as though it had never been. This was a very different life to the one she had been born to, yet it was a good one. As long as Suleiman loved her she knew that she could be happy here.

The time for the ceremony had arrived, and Karin came to conduct the ladies to the Caliph's hall, where the marriage was to take place. Six eunuchs preceded them, all richly robed, and another six followed behind. The traditional music of the marriage dance sounded strange and slightly discordant to her ears, but also stirring.

Eleanor was showered with rose petals every step of the way, her ladies leading her as though she could not see—which was indeed difficult through the heavy veil. She held out her hand to Karin as they halted outside the hall, while her coming was heralded inside.

'You know your responses,' Karin whispered and smiled at her encouragingly. 'No one expects more of you.'

Eleanor's heart beat very fast as she saw how handsome Suleiman looked in his ceremonial robes. He usually preferred a simple mode of dress that any man might wear, but today he was clothed richly as befitted the Caliph's son on his wedding day.

The religious chanting had begun. Eleanor moved as if in a dream, following the words and ritual in her head. She had memorised them and was aware of all that was going around her, even though it had an un-real quality. She could scarcely breathe as she was led slowly towards her lord. The time had come for her responses; she made them flawlessly, bowing her head as a ceremonial garland of flowers was placed about her neck. She gave him a garland in return, and then she placed her hand in his as the words that would make them man and wife were intoned. It was as he was about to raise her veil that the interruption came.

'Stop! In the name of the Sultan Suleiman the Magnificent, I forbid this marriage. It is not legal, for the bride is a Christian and was brought here against her will.'

Eleanor was as startled as everyone else present. Surely she had misheard? How could this be? Who would dare to intrude on them at this time?

She peered through the thick veil, trying to discover what was happening and then, as she saw the men coming towards them, a gasp escaped her. The man who had commanded the ceremony to cease was Count Giovani Salvadore. But that was not possible! How could he be here? And how had he gained access to the palace?

'How dare you intrude?' Suleiman started forward angrily but even as he did so, several guards moved to surround him. Eleanor saw that they were wearing different colours to the Caliph's own men. 'Who gave you permission to enter here?'

'We are the Sultan's personal guard,' one of the

Janissaries replied harshly. 'It is at our master's command that we prevent this marriage. Suleiman Bakhar, you are under arrest for treachery—and Miss Eleanor Nash is to be taken to the Sultan's palace at once.'

'Suleiman!' Eleanor looked at him, her face white with shock beneath the veil. 'Can they do this?'

'It is a mistake,' Suleiman said. 'I shall speak to the Sultan myself. Do not be frightened, my dove. We shall be together again soon.'

The guards had laid hands on him and were hustling him away from her. Eleanor tried to follow him, but the count took hold of her arm, preventing her.

'There is no need to be afraid,' he said. 'I believe we were in time to halt the ceremony. It took some hours of negotiation or we should have been here yesterday. I have come to take you and Richard to Italy, Eleanor.'

'No! I shall not go with you. I am the lord Suleiman's wife.' She drew herself up haughtily. 'Pray take your hand from my arm, sir. It is forbidden that another man should touch me.'

'This ceremony will not stand,' he said, frowning at her. 'Your father did not consent.'

'My father?' She stared at him, eyes widening in shock. 'But my father is dead…'

'No, lady.' The count smiled. 'He was struck unconscious by those rogues who attacked your ship, but he was alive when the Spanish war galley reached him. Instead of continuing to Cyprus, he was brought back by them to Italy and now awaits you at my home.'

'My father is alive?' Eleanor stared at him. She was conscious of a feeling of joy that her father was not dead, but there was also pain. 'Does Richard know that our father lives?'

'He is being taken to the Sultan's palace under separate escort. We shall see him there. Come, we must go. I do not like the look of things here.'

Eleanor had been too stunned to realise what was going on around her. Now she saw that the eunuchs were muttering angrily amongst themselves at this intrusion—and the Caliph had disappeared. The women who had gathered to witness the ceremony were being quickly ushered from the hall. The atmosphere was tense and uneasy, for an insult had been offered to the Caliph's son and his wife.

She had no choice but to go with Count Salvadore. It was an order from the Sultan himself and must be obeyed. Besides, she needed to know what was happening to Suleiman. He had told her not to be frightened, but she could not help herself. Why had he been arrested? What crime had he committed?

She was surprised as Karin joined her just as they were leaving the hall. 'I have permission,' Karin whispered in the language of the harem. 'The Caliph has sent me to look after his son's wife.'

'I am his wife?'

'Yes, it is done. The Caliph fears for his son—but he will do what he can.'

'What is that woman saying to you?'

'She is my lady in waiting,' Eleanor replied. She did not wish the count to know that Karin was the Caliph's second wife lest they were separated. 'She comes with me. It is not seemly for me to travel without a female companion.'

'Very well,' the count replied. 'I have a litter waiting to convey you to the Seraglio. It will carry you both.'

Karin was wearing her casacche, and she had brought one for Eleanor, which she donned as she went out into the courtyard. They were just in time to witness a scuffle between some of the Caliph's guards and the Sultan's own elite Janissaries.

It was Suleiman himself who forbade his men to fight, warning them that they could be executed for treachery against their master.

'You must not resist. Fear not, my friends,' he told them. 'I shall return.'

Eleanor watched as he was told to mount a horse. He had not been bound, but he was clearly a prisoner. To resist an order from the Sultan was to invite a painful death.

Suleiman glanced towards Eleanor before he rode away. Since she was still wearing the heavy veil over her head, he could not see her anguished look—but she saw his and her heart wrenched with pain.

Supposing he could not reason with the Grand Turk? In the Ottoman Empire the Sultan's word was law. If he had decided that Eleanor must be returned to her father it would happen. But it must not be! It would break her heart if she were forced to leave Suleiman now.

Eleanor was happy to learn that her father lived, but her pleasure was clouded by the brutal end to her dreams of marrying the man she loved. She feared that she would be parted from Suleiman and never see him again.

'Do not despair,' Karin said when they were together in the litter and the escort had begun to move off. 'The Caliph has influence with the Sultan—and Suleiman has done nothing against the law.'

'Am I truly his wife?' Eleanor asked. 'Were they in time to halt the ceremony?'

'According to our laws, you are bound to him,' Karin assured her. 'As a true believer, you are his legal wife. It is up to you, Eleanor. If you deny your own faith and swear that you are a true convert, the Sultan may decide that you cannot now be returned to your father.'

'Then I shall do whatever I must,' Eleanor replied. 'Oh, Karin! I am so glad you made me study with you. If a religious teacher questions me, I shall be able to give the right responses.'

'It may be that you will be questioned by more than one such man,' Karin said. 'Is there anything that puzzles you? Any question you need to ask me?'

'Only why you chose to come with me? You were to have gone to your daughters tomorrow.'

'You are more important, my dearest Eleanor. Do you not know that you are as a daughter to me?'

Eleanor's eyes were moist with tears as she took the other woman's hand and held it. 'Thank you, Karin. I am not frightened as long as you are with me—not for myself.'

'You fear for your lord?'

'Yes. What will they do to him? Will he be beaten—or tortured?' A shiver ran through her as she thought of what could happen to Suleiman.

'I do not know,' Karin admitted. 'The Caliph and his son are sparing with punishments, but it is not always so. The law is harsh in this country, Eleanor. I do not understand why Suleiman has been arrested. They could have stopped the wedding—but there was no need for such harshness. Unless Suleiman has displeased the Sultan…'

'Why should he be displeased?' Eleanor asked. 'My lord bought me. I was his property and he chose to marry me. That is not against your laws. We did not flout the customs, Karin. Suleiman was careful to observe them.'

'That is what I do not understand,' Karin replied. 'We must be patient, Eleanor. It may be that the Sultan will send for you—and if he does you must be respectful. Do not imagine that you may speak boldly as you do with your lord. Be very careful. Answer when he questions you—but if you wish to say something more, ask permission to address his Magnificence.'

'Yes, I shall remember,' Eleanor replied. 'I have listened well to your teachings, Karin—though I have not always obeyed them in the past. This time my lord's life may depend on my behaving as you would have had me behave long ago.'

She looked out and saw the old walls of the city, which were remnants of the original settlement built in the year three hundred and twenty four by Constantine I of Rome, and then the building of the magnificent palace of the Ottoman sultans. An icy trickle went down her spine as she was carried towards it, and she remembered that Suleiman had intended her as a gift for the Sultan.

What would have been her fate if she had been brought here then?

'I shall be very careful. And I pray that the Sultan will give me the chance to tell him what I truly desire.'

'You wish to stay here—even though you father lives?'

'Yes, I have no choice,' Eleanor said. 'Suleiman is my husband. I love him, Karin. So much that I would rather die than be sent away from him...'

Chapter Twelve

Once within the palace, the women were led away by one of the Sultan's Kadins to a part of the harem reserved for visitors. She told them her name was Sonia, and welcomed them in the traditional way, offering refreshment before she left them alone.

'It seems that we are to be treated with respect,' Karin said. 'I wondered what might happen here, Eleanor—but for the moment it seems that we are to be welcomed as honoured guests.'

'How long do you think it will be before the Sultan sends for us?' Eleanor asked. 'How long before I am permitted to see my husband?'

Karin looked at her anxiously. 'You must be patient...' she began. 'These things take their course. There is nothing you can do until you are sent for, Eleanor. You have no power to command here and nor have I. The Caliph has some influence with his royal master. He will do all he can. We must leave the negotiations to him.'

Eleanor nodded. She glanced at the bowls of fruit and sweetmeats that had been provided for them. 'You should eat, Karin. I am sure you must be hungry.'

'Will you not try something yourself? I know that you have eaten little today.'

'I was too excited…' Eleanor caught back a sob. 'When I was first taken to the Caliph's palace I prayed that I might be returned to my family, but now…if they take me away from Suleiman, it will break my heart.'

'You can do nothing but wait,' Karin told her. 'You must accept what happens—it is Allah's will.'

Eleanor was about to deny her angrily, then, remembering all the warnings she had been given, she bent her head submissively. '*Insh'allah*—may it be as Allah wills.'

Karin smiled at her approvingly. 'Just so, Eleanor. Our master the Sultan will decide your fate in his wisdom and greatness. You must accept his judgement for he is just and good.'

'Yes, this I have been told by my husband,' Eleanor replied, following her lead. 'He has often told me how much he admires our overlord.'

'Sit and eat,' Karin bade her again. 'It may be some days before you are sent for.'

'Some days…' Eleanor was about to protest angrily when she remembered that everything they were saying was possibly being listened to by spies, who would carry tales to the Sultan. 'Then I must be patient—there is no more I can do.'

But how was she to be patient when she did not know what was going on elsewhere in the palace? How she wished there was some way she could discover what had happened to Suleiman—and whether the Count Salvadore had already persuaded the Grand Turk to let him take her back to Italy.

* * *

'I really must protest, your Magnificence,' Count Salvadore was saying. 'Why has Miss Nash been taken to the women's quarters? I have been refused permission to speak to her—and yet I believed you had given permission for me to take her home to her family?'

Suleiman the Magnificent, Sultan, Grand Turk, the giver of laws and absolute ruler of the powerful Ottoman Empire, met the impatient demands of his visitor with an inscrutable look. His face was thin and narrow, and he wore a slight beard and side-whiskers, his eyes piercing and cold. A huge jewel sparkled in the folds of his silken turban as he faced the pompous banking merchant in silence. Such men had their uses, and Suleiman was not called the Lawgiver for nothing. His victories in other lands had gained him a reputation as a ruthless destroyer, but in his own country he was revered because he had revised the legal system, bringing benefits to many of his subjects. Eleanor's father had told her that the Sultan was a clever, calculating man who would not hesitate to use others for his own purpose.

'Please be seated, noble lord,' the Sultan's Vizier replied for his master. 'His Magnificence wishes to question you on certain matters.'

'But we have talked,' Count Salvadore blustered. 'All day yesterday. I believed we had reached an understanding—Sir William's son and daughter are to be returned to him in return for trade and certain banking arrangements you have named.'

'But circumstances are altered,' the Vizier replied in a calm even tone. 'Forgive me, noble lord—but it may be that the woman in question is no longer the daughter of her father but the wife of Suleiman Bakhar, and belongs to him under the law.'

'How can this be? I was told that it is impossible for a Christian woman to become the wife of a Muslim.' Salvadore was on the point of losing his temper. All this had been gone through at length before permission to enter the Caliph's palace had been given.

'But it seems that the lady has become a Muslim…' the Vizier replied. 'My master requires to know why you wish to take Miss Nash away from her lawful husband.'

'It cannot be lawful to force a Christian woman to marry against her will.'

'Are you sure it was done against her will?'

'Of course. She could not want to live in a harem!'

The Vizier was about to continue with his questions, when the Sultan beckoned to him. He approached his master, bending to hear the whispered words, and then he nodded and turned to beckon one of the eunuchs.

'What is going on?' Count Salvadore demanded as the eunuch went away. 'What did his Magnificence say?'

'My master commanded that the woman be brought to answer for herself.'

'But…but…' the count faltered uncertainly. 'I do not see that this will serve. She will be afraid to speak her mind for fear of what may happen to her. Besides, only her father can consent to her marriage—and he does not. I have paid the ransom. A very generous ransom…'

The Vizier held up his hand to silence him. 'Your gift gained you an audience with the Sultan, nothing more. Be careful what you demand, infidel. It would not be wise to displease my master.'

Count Salvadore fumed inwardly. It was impossible

to treat with these people! They said one thing and did another. He distrusted them and wished that he might conclude his business quickly and leave. There was some mischief going on here—he felt it instinctively.

Yet surely Eleanor would tell them that she desired to be returned to her family? She could not wish to remain here as some kind of a harlot…unless…? He frowned as he recalled her haughty manner the previous day. Perhaps she had already become the Turk's mistress.

The seconds ticked by slowly, and Count Salvadore cursed inwardly. He had a ship waiting, and he wanted to catch the tide. The sooner he left this accursed place the better! He turned as he heard a slight commotion, and then saw that two women had returned with the eunuch. He started to rise, but a sharp gesture from the Vizier made him keep his seat.

Eleanor came forward, her heart beating very fast as she realised she had been brought into the presence of the Sultan and his court, who, Karin had told her, were gathered in the State Audience Chamber. It was here that the Grand Vizier held meetings with foreign ambassadors, and there was a window from which the Sultan could watch unobserved if he chose—but today he was seated on a magnificent throne on a raised dais.

Eleanor was still wearing her wedding veil, for no other had been given her, and she held tight to Karin's hand as they were told to approach the throne.

'Down on your knees, and keep your head bent until you are spoken to,' Karin whispered as they were told to halt their approach still some little distance from the throne. 'Remember all I have told you, Eleanor.'

Eleanor made no reply. She peered through her veil in an effort to see if Suleiman was also present, but

there was no sign of him. Where was he? What was
happening to him? She had lain awake most of the
night, her heart aching for a sight of him, but other
than the Kadin who had brought them more food that
evening, they had seen no one.

'You are Miss Eleanor Nash, daughter of the noble
lord Sir William?' a voice asked her. Eleanor looked
up and saw a man richly dressed in robes of purple
and gold. He was stout and his beard was grey, but
she looked into his eyes and saw that there was no
malice there. He smiled at her reassuringly as she hesitated. 'Speak to me—and then I will question you.
You must not speak to the Sultan unless he gives permission.'

'Yes, my lord Vizier,' Eleanor replied. 'I have been
taught what is proper by my lord's family.'

'Your lord?' The Vizier looked at her hard, his eyes
searching but unable to see through the veil that covered her face. 'Of whom do you speak, lady—your
master? The man who bought you from the Corsair
Mohamed Ali ben Ibn? Do you wish to remain with
him?'

'I have no master, sir. Suleiman Bakhar is my husband. I was married to him within the law yesterday,
and I am his true wife. It is both my duty and my wish
to remain with him. Under the law I can have no other
husband—and must retire from life if we are parted.
If I am sent back to Italy, I shall be desolate.'

'Are you then a believer?'

'Yes, my lord. I have studied the Qur'an.' Eleanor
lifted her veil, looking into the Vizier's face. 'Forgive
me for any immodesty, my lord Vizier, but I wish you
to be able to see that I do not lie to you. Long before
I came to this country, I knew of your faith and I had

studied the Qur'an. When my lord Suleiman did me the honour to ask me to become his wife, I studied diligently to become one of the Faithful. Karin, Caliph Bakhar's wife, taught me. She is with me now and will confirm this if asked.'

'This we have been told of already,' the Vizier replied. 'But if what you say is true about already being a believer before you came here, then there can be no accusations that you have been forced to convert to the true faith. Yet we would have the truth of this matter from you, lady.'

'If you will permit me, I can prove it is the truth, my lord.'

The Vizier's eyes narrowed. He glanced towards the Sultan, who beckoned him forward to whisper in his ear. After a few seconds, he nodded and came back to Eleanor.

'His Magnificence would hear more of this proof.'

'This was given to me by my father,' Eleanor said, reaching beneath her tunic for the treasure of the Far Cross. 'We were researching a legend when this came into our possession—and my father gave it to me to look after for him on our voyage. When we were at sea and our ship was tossed by the winds, it gave me courage—and I prayed to Allah to save me. I believe it was through his goodness that I was saved from the storm and delivered into the hands of a good and just man.'

'What is it?' the Vizier asked as he took the jewelled object from her, turning it over in his hand. 'I do not see the significance of this trinket.'

'If the lord Vizier would undo the stopper, he would see that it contains an ancient manuscript writ very small—and the words inscribed are a part of the

Qur'an. It is a part of the treasure of the Abbot of the Far Cross and was stolen many centuries ago by pirates.'

'Bring it to me!'

Eleanor looked at the man who had spoken. The Sultan was clearly interested in her treasure and she thought she saw a gleam of excitement in his eyes as he held out his hand imperiously. She handed the small vial to the Vizier who carried it to his master and offered it to him.

'Open it,' the Sultan commanded, and watched eagerly as his Vizier obeyed. 'Take out what is inside and tell me if she speaks the truth.'

The Vizier did as he was bid, then turned to his master and held it out once more. 'The woman speaks the truth, Magnificence.'

'Give it to me—the manuscript.' The Sultan studied it in silence for a moment, then his dark eyes returned it to his Vizier. 'Ask her why she wore it around her neck?'

Eleanor waited until the Vizier came back to her and asked the question of her before replying. It would be presumptuous of her to speak directly to the Sultan unless invited.

'My master wishes to know why you wear the trinket about your neck?'

'Because it has brought me good fortune,' Eleanor replied. 'I believe it protected me during the storm and afterwards when I was on the pirates' galley. I have not been treated ill—at least since I was brought to this country—and have known only kindness at the hands of Caliph Bakhar and my husband. Therefore, I kept it as a talisman even though my lord gave me finer jewels to wear.'

The Vizier glanced towards the Sultan once more, then back at Eleanor. 'His Magnificence has listened to your explanation. You may return to your apartments and await his judgement.' He did not return either the manuscript or its container to her.

'Thank you.' Eleanor let her veil fall forward to cover her face once more. 'I—I am grateful to you, my lord Vizier—and to his Magnificence for his patience.'

The Vizier waved her away, and she stood up, moving backwards from the hall until Karin touched her arm and told her they could now leave normally without giving offence.

She glanced at her friend when they were outside, but said nothing as they were conducted through the courtyard to the harem, which was a vast labyrinth of halls and rooms. The Royal Palace was the main residence of the Sultans of the Ottoman Empire and had been the headquarters of their seat of government from the year 1465. It was a huge complex of buildings, which was built on the Seraglio Point, overlooking the Mamara and the Bosphorus. The palace itself had been begun in 1459 by order of Sultan Muhammad II, who had conquered the city of Constantinople six years before that date.

It was here that the government and the elite units of the Janissaries lived, its various buildings separated by four large courtyards and many gardens. Karin had told Eleanor of the Divan in which the Grand Vizier and officials worked, and the school for the men who wished to learn about justice and government, besides the huge kitchens, the Imperial wardrobe—which was very large—and the harem baths.

'The Sultanas live in much grander state than we

do at home,' she had told Eleanor. 'I have been told that the baths here have a domed roof supported on many pillars and are very beautiful.'

Eleanor was able to see for herself that the palace was richly appointed, and there were many marvels on display. She thought she caught sight of the magnificent clock Suleiman had given to his overlord, but she could not be certain. There were so many treasures, which stood testament to the Sultan's love of beautiful things. Besides those on show, she understood that there were storerooms filled with rare objects, and the armoury contained suits of fabulous armour used by the Sultans for ceremonial occasions.

'What will happen now?' she asked when they were alone again. 'Why did no one say anything about what had been decided? My lord was not there—do you think he has been imprisoned?'

'Patience,' Karin counselled. 'You did well, Eleanor. I do not know what will happen—but you were very convincing. And that trinket you wore—I think the Sultan was very interested in the story you told about that.'

'He did not return it to me,' Eleanor said. 'But I do not care for such things. All I want is to be able to go home with Suleiman.'

'It was a mere trinket,' Karin replied. 'I do not suppose our master will wish to keep it—but it would be a small price to pay if he let you have your way.'

'He may have it and welcome,' Eleanor replied. 'Though it is more than just a trinket—and part of a far greater treasure, which may still exist somewhere. It was discovered on my father's land in Cyprus, and he had hoped he might find more in time.'

'Then it may please his Magnificence,' Karin said.

'We must hope so, Eleanor—for he will only grant your wish if he believes your story.'

Eleanor looked at her fearfully. She had hoped that Suleiman would be waiting for her when she was taken to the Sultan's halls, but there had been no sign of him. What had happened to him? She and Karin had been treated kindly enough, but it might not have been the same for her husband.

'How much longer do you think we shall be kept here?' Eleanor asked. 'Oh, how I wish I knew what was going on! Do you think the Sultan will send me back with Count Salvadore? I do not like him, Karin, and I fear what he may do. He wanted me for himself…'

'You must continue to be patient,' Karin warned. 'Remember that we can do nothing…we must await our master's judgement. As I have told you before, these things take time and diplomacy—they cannot be rushed.'

Eleanor turned away, her eyes dark with rebellion. She was angry at her own powerlessness, but there was nothing she could do. She had been granted an audience, which was more than might have been granted her—and now she must do as Karin bid her and wait patiently. But, oh, how hard that was, when her whole being cried out for the man she loved!

Supposing they had beaten him—or put him to death? What had Suleiman Bakhar done that had so angered the Sultan that he should be arrested?

Was it because he had kept her for himself? Had the Sultan learned that she was to have been a gift to him—but surely the fabulous clock Suleiman had given him would bring a man who loved beautiful things so much more pleasure than any woman? He must have so many women in his harem already!

The thoughts went round and round in Eleanor's mind, torturing her. Yet she knew that she could do nothing to hasten the decision; she could only pray that when it came it would be the right one.

Eleanor looked at Karin and sighed. How much longer could she bear this? They had now been in the Sultan's harem for three days. At some point clothes had been brought for them from the Caliph's palace, so that they had their own things about them, but no one had spoken to them or told them anything.

Eleanor had wondered if a religious teacher would question her, but no one came and she was not sent for again. She had begun to think that she might be kept here for ever, and spent much of the time pacing about the little courtyard garden to which they had been given free access.

It was halfway through the fourth day that the Kadin who had brought them here came to tell them they were wanted.

'Where are you taking us?' Eleanor asked as she beckoned them to follow. 'Are we to be taken to the Sultan again? What decision has been made?'

The Kadin smiled and shook her head. 'I do not know,' she said in her soft, husky voice. 'I have merely been told to show you the way.'

Eleanor's heart was pounding as they left the harem quarters under the escort of a eunuch. It was a different route to the one they had been taken previously and she thought they could not be going to the Sultan's halls this time. Where then were they being taken?

When at last they emerged into a large courtyard,

she saw that it housed most of the service buildings, including the bakery, hospital and what Karin whispered was the mint. It was opened to the public and not the private part of the palace to which she had been taken the first time. Eleanor's heart caught with fright as she saw that two litters were waiting—one with an escort that she recognized as wearing the Caliph's colours of red and gold, and the other with the Sultan's colours.

'You must say goodbye now,' the eunuch told them. 'The lady Karin returns to the Caliph's household— you do not.'

'Where am I going?' Eleanor stared at her friend in horror. 'Karin—where are they taking me?'

'I do not know,' the older woman replied. She reached out to take Eleanor's hand and squeezed it tightly. 'I love you, my dear. Have courage. It is useless to resist—for they will only punish you, and Suleiman. Do as you are told and he may escape further punishment.'

'But he has done nothing,' Eleanor cried, the tears starting to her eyes. 'Oh, Karin! I cannot bear to leave you. I love you as the mother I lost long ago. Forgive me for all the trouble I have caused you…'

'You were never a trouble to me, only a joy and a delight,' Karin said. 'Go in peace, my daughter. I pray that Allah will guide your footsteps and bring you happiness.'

'I shall never be happy without Suleiman,' Eleanor wept, clinging to her hand. 'Oh, why must I go? Why will they send me away when all I want is to stay here?'

'It is the Sultan's will,' Karin replied. 'And he is guided only by Allah.'

Eleanor nodded, but looked at her through tear-misted eyes as they were parted, the eunuch urging them to enter the litters that had been provided for their transport.

Karin let go her hand, and Eleanor was obliged to do as she was told. She looked for Count Salvadore but could not see him—her escort was made up entirely of the Sultan's guard. Glancing back at the palace, she tried to send a message of farewell to her love.

'God bless and keep you,' she whispered. 'They may rend us apart, my darling, but no other man but you shall be my husband. This I swear—to keep faith with our love for my life long.'

Once inside the litter, she could no longer hold back her tears, and wept as all hope left her. She knew that the litter was carrying her towards the harbour and that a ship awaited her. She was being taken back to Italy against her will, and silently she raged against the power of men. Women were mere possessions, at the mercy of their menfolk! It was wrong that she should be treated thus for the second time in her life.

But no one should force her to marry. She would take her own life first. All she could hope for now was that her father would allow her to spend the rest of her life in prayer and study.

Eleanor's heart caught with pain as she saw the ship in the harbour. If she had hoped that she might after all be returned to the Caliph's palace, that hope vanished. It was a merchant ship…but that flag! Had she not sailed beneath such a flag before? It was her uncle's vessel—Sir John Faversham, merchant of Cyprus. She had thought to travel on the count's ship. He had not mentioned that her uncle was also here—

though if truth were told she had not given him much
encouragement to tell her anything.

A tall gentleman with grey hair and a neat beard
was standing on deck, waiting to greet her. He was
dressed in the manner of a wealthy Englishman, and
was distinguished looking with faded blue eyes that
seemed to look at her with understanding. She was, of
course, still dressed as a woman of the harem, her face
half covered by a fine veil.

'Eleanor—you are Eleanor?' he asked as he came
to greet her, hands outstretched in greeting. 'My dear
child, how glad I am to meet you at last. There were
times when I feared I should never find you.'

'Sir John?' Eleanor looked at him uncertainly. 'You
are my uncle?'

'Yes, child. Your mother was my sister and I loved
her dearly. I have left no stone unturned to find you…'

'But I thought Count Salvadore… He said he was
taking me to Italy—' She halted as her uncle frowned.

'That fellow sought to steal a march on me. He
hoped to find you and also reach a trading agreement
with Suleiman the Magnificent. Fortunately, my own
agreement was settled some months ago and I was able
to reach the Sultan before him.'

'You were here before the count?' She stared at
him. 'But it was he who…came to the palace to stop
the marriage.'

'I could not prevent that, for he gave the Sultan a
magnificent gift and out of politeness had to be given
something in return…the customs here adhere to a
strict ritual, Eleanor—which was something the count
did not understand. He imagined that his gift would
buy your freedom. However, that is not the way the
Sultan does business—and your father's letter asks

that you be given into my care, Eleanor. Sir William was unwell for some weeks, but is better now and on his way to Cyprus. He will be waiting for you when we arrive. I do not think that he quite trusted Count Salvadore—though he was forced to accept his help until he could contact me.'

'Do you know that I am married, Uncle?' Eleanor looked at him anxiously. 'Will you help me? My husband has been arrested and is a prisoner at the Sultan's palace.'

'All in good time,' her uncle said, smiling at her. 'We are about to sail for Cyprus, my child. Go below to your cabin and change into something more suitable—my cabin boy will show you where to go and I shall be with you shortly.'

Eleanor sighed. Once again, it seemed that she must obey. It was no different here than it had been in the palace. Suleiman had been so indulgent towards her, so generous. But at least she would soon see her father, for that at least she must be grateful.

If only she could stop this ache in her chest from threatening to crush the life from her. She wished that she might run back to the Sultan's palace and beg for her husband's release, but such actions would merely cause more trouble. Perhaps when they were back in Cyprus, she might persuade her uncle to make inquires. She might even persuade him to let her return—if Suleiman still lived.

She nodded to the young boy who had stopped outside what was clearly the most important cabin on board ship. Her uncle must have given up his own accommodation for her sake, which was kind of him.

She went inside, and then stopped as she saw someone standing by the porthole, her heart catching as she saw the tall, broad-shouldered man with his back towards her. He was dressed in the simple, traditional style he liked to adopt when private—yet it could not be!

'Suleiman?' she breathed, walking towards him as if she were in a dream. 'Is it really you?'

He turned and smiled at her, opening his arms as she gave a scream of surprise and delight and ran to him. His arms closed about her, crushing her to him as their lips met in a hungry kiss that made her feel like swooning.

'I thought you were still a prisoner,' she cried, the tears running down her cheeks. 'I thought they were sending me away from you—that I should never see you again.'

'Would you have cared so much, my dove?'

'You know I would! I should not want to live if I could not be your wife. I *am* your wife, Suleiman—and can never marry any other man.'

'If you do, I shall kill him!' Suleiman said hoarsely. 'Did you really think I would let you go, Eleanor? I would have fought my way out of the palace if necessary rather than lose you. Better I died than let you go away from me.'

'But what are you doing here on my uncle's ship?' Eleanor looked up at him uncertainly. 'Did you not tell me that you could never leave your father?'

'I do so only on the Sultan's orders,' Suleiman replied, his expression serious. 'I have seen my father and he gave me his blessing—but he knows the time has come for me to leave him. I am to be our master's ambassador, Eleanor. The Sultan wishes for more trade with merchants like your uncle, and he also wishes me to seek out a way of building peace between our empire and its enemies—if one can be found that does not require him to make concessions.'

'Do you think that is possible?' Eleanor asked doubtfully.

'Perhaps there is a chance—I cannot tell,' Suleiman said. 'As you know, there is a wide divide between the Christian and Muslim way of life. Much blood has been spilled, and much hatred exists between our peoples—but the Sultan and I spoke much on this subject privately, and we are agreed that the empire will suffer in time if nothing is done.'

Eleanor stared at him. 'You spoke to the Sultan yourself—directly to him and not the Grand Vizier?'

'Yes.' Suleiman laughed. 'You, of course, were not permitted to address him yourself—but have you forgot, my love—you are merely a woman and I am a man. The case is entirely different.'

'You! You are a wicked tease,' she replied, her eyes flashing at him. 'I should punish you for your arrogance, my lord. Do not forget that we shall not be in your country for much longer!'

'And yet I am your husband—and a woman is the property of her husband wherever she may be in the world, Eleanor. I am sorry, my love, but it is the way of men to be superior.'

'You... Oh, I shall punish you,' she cried and beat against him with her fists until he caught her wrists. Then he drew her to him once more to kiss her lips. She stopped fighting him and clung to him, her body melting into his as the love flowed through her. 'I was so frightened when they arrested you,' she said when he released her lips at last. 'I do not know what I should have done if we had been parted, my lord.'

'Nor I, my darling,' he murmured and touched her

cheek with the tips of his fingers. 'I could not bear it any more than you. That is why I told the Sultan of my desire to serve him. It means that we must travel the world in search of treasures, Eleanor—and in doing trade perhaps we shall teach others that we Turks are not all as savage as they think us.'

'But what of your father? Shall you never see him again?'

'From time to time I shall return, to take back the treasures I have found—and to visit my home. My brother Bayezid will do his best to take my place, though I fear he would prefer to spend his time in study—but he will become my father's heir in my stead. It must be so or he would be exposed and vulnerable. Besides, Bayezid is worthy to take my father's place, more fitted for the honour of being Caliph than I could ever be.'

'Do you mind that, Suleiman?' she asked, looking at him anxiously.

'No—for I have used my privileges well, Eleanor. I am a wealthy man through my own endeavours, which is why the Sultan wanted me to become his ambassador. It was the clock I gave him that convinced him I was the man he sought for this task.'

'The clock you gave him instead of me?' Eleanor smiled up at him. 'I was sure he must be better pleased with such a gift than a mere woman.'

Suleiman laughed huskily. 'He told me that when he looked upon your face he was convinced that my taste in all things beautiful was not to be faulted. He said that a man who had the wisdom to choose such a woman over a clock was the man he desired as his representative in the capitals of the Western world.'

Eleanor blushed. 'I revealed my face so that the

Vizier would know I did not lie about the fact that I had studied the Qur'an before I ever came to your country. Forgive me, my lord. I know it was immodest of me.'

'It was done for my sake,' Suleiman said. 'Besides, that custom belongs in my father's house—in your father's house you will wear the clothes you were used to before your abduction.'

'Must I?' Eleanor sighed. 'The clothes you gave me were so much more becoming—and so comfortable. May I not at least wear them in private?'

Suleiman laughed down at her. 'So—you have become a convert to our way of life after all.'

'Yes, my lord—though I am not sure what I believe in the matter of religion.'

'In that you are not alone,' Suleiman said and sighed. 'I learned of your faith from my mother, Eleanor—and I have studied the Bible. I do not know where the truth may lie.'

'Perhaps there is only one God,' Eleanor replied, wrinkling her brow in thought. 'He may be called different names and worshipped in different ways—but He remains the same.'

'I think that perhaps to believe something of that sort is the only way we can be at peace within ourselves,' Suleiman said. 'We must live good lives, Eleanor, you and I—and in that way we may achieve the ideal that all the gods tell us is the true way.'

'If only others could be as tolerant as you,' Eleanor said and sighed as she gazed up at him with love in her eyes. 'I am so lucky to have found you, my dearest husband. I do love you so very much.'

'And I love you,' he replied. 'Now you must change into the clothes your uncle has provided, Eleanor.

Once we are at sea, he will come for you. For we are to be married by the captain of this ship.'

'Married?' Eleanor stared at him. 'But I am already your wife. Karin said the ceremony was complete.'

'According to Muslim law that is so, but your family will not be happy until we are married in their eyes—and that means under their law. Sir John explained to me that we could be married at sea by the captain of his ship and need not enter a Christian church—and I agreed that I would be happy to take part in such a ceremony for your sake.'

'You would do that for me?' She stared at him in wonder, her heart swelling with love for him.

'It is no more than you have already done for me.'

Suleiman came towards her, drawing her to him once more to kiss her on the lips tenderly. 'Had we never been married according to your law or mine, you would always have been my love—my life. You came to me as a slave, Eleanor—but you have become the queen of my heart. I know that I shall never love another woman.'

'And I shall never want more than your love,' she said. 'For you are all that I want and need…'

Epilogue

Eleanor stood looking out to sea as they left the shores of England far behind. She had thought never to return, but Suleiman had visited the English court as the Grand Turk's ambassador and she had gone with him. Afterwards, they had travelled to her old home in the west of England.

'It is just as you described it to me,' Suleiman had told her one night as they lay together in the huge four-poster bed after they had made love. 'Richard says that he will never return to England—but I think that we may choose to visit your home from time to time, my love.'

'Will my father sell the estate to you?'

Suleiman smiled down at her. Over the past three years he and Sir William had become firm friends, spending time examining many of the treasures Suleiman had discovered on his travels. Their return to Cyprus was always eagerly awaited—and it would be no different this time.

'Your father asked Richard his opinion first, my love—and he said that he had no objection.'

'I still cannot believe that you and my brother are friends.'

'I think that happened after our first child was born,' Suleiman replied. 'How could Richard hate me when he adores little Isabelle?'

Eleanor smiled and leaned against his shoulder as the shores of England faded into the distance. She had already given her lord a daughter and a son, Kasim, both of whom Suleiman spoiled dreadfully—but she was with child again.

They would teach their children to have open minds, to respect others and do what they could to unite the people of their two lands and cultures. And one day their children would live and flourish in the misty, beautiful countryside of her childhood home…

* * * * *

...

They would leave their children to have begun
... to prevent others could do, what they could to
...the people of taxing two lands... and culture, and
...she did their children would live, and that was in the
... beautiful community of the public interest.

Pearl Beyond Price
by
Claire Delacroix

New York Times bestselling author **Claire Delacroix** always wove stories in her mind. Since selling her first medieval romance in 1992, Claire has written more than twenty romances. Twice winner of the Colorado Romance Writers' Award of Excellence and nominee for *Romantic Times* Career Achievement in Medieval Romance, Claire has well over two million books in print. Claire lives in Canada with her husband.

For all my wonderful friends at RWA Ontario. Thanks.

> *"May you live in interesting times."*
> —*Ancient curse*

Prologue

Maragha—in modern Azerbaijan—February 1265

Chinkai's body was as cold as the dawn.

Thierry gritted his teeth at the volume of spilled blood, knowing that he would never grow used to the killing.

The wan fingers of light straining above the horizon did naught to warm the air, though their meager illumination showed Thierry the pallor of the old warrior's skin. Chinkai had been dead for some hours, mayhap since the previous eve. Too late, Thierry recalled that the grizzled warrior had left the khan's funeral celebrations and not returned.

That Chinkai's death was not a natural one was beyond doubt. No mistaking was there the viciousness of the slash across the throat that had ended his life, nor the copious quantity of dried blood staining his *kalat*. Indeed, it seemed the old warrior's eyes were still glazed with shock at the suddenness of his own demise.

Thierry swallowed carefully and forced himself to touch the older man's wizened flesh. 'Twas cold as stone.

Indeed, he had expected naught else, but still his bile rose. He lifted his gaze and scanned the silent camp, seeking some clue of what had transpired but knowing all the while he would find none. Just Chinkai, dead and alone on the grassy plain.

But one thing had Chinkai and Thierry in common and Thierry could not evict the thought from his mind. Thierry eyed the corpse as though willing it to confirm or deny his fears.

Both had aspired to be khan.

Had Chinkai died for his ambition?

The old khan was dead and opportunity was ripe for the selection of a new khan. But three candidates were there within the tribe. The third, Abaqa, was the son of the old khan. Though this assured him naught, Abaqa was known to be ambitious.

Now Chinkai drew breath no longer and Thierry could not help but wonder how ambitious Abaqa truly was.

Thierry jumped at the muffled sound of a footfall, only to meet the bright gaze of Abaqa. He stiffened warily despite himself and hoped naught of his thoughts showed in his expression.

Was he to join Chinkai this very morn?

"Too much drinking for our old comrade?" Abaqa inquired cheerfully. Thierry met the speculation in the other man's eyes and knew Abaqa saw more than his words revealed.

"Hardly that," Thierry replied tightly. "His throat has been slit."

"Ah." Abaqa jammed his thumbs into his belt as he paused beside the pair. Thierry was forced to look up from where he squatted to hold the other man's gaze. "Mayhap a squabble over a woman," Abaqa suggested with calm disinterest.

"I should think not," Thierry said dismissively. Abaqa's brows rose.

"Mayhap you *should* think so," he said silkily.

It seemed he had guessed aright. Thierry let his gaze drop to Chinkai and willed his heart to slow.

'Twas evident he was being threatened, though Thierry would know clearly how or why. Should Abaqa be behind Chinkai's death, Thierry would hear the threat fall in full from the man's lips. He straightened slowly and braced his own hands on his hips, savoring his height advantage over Abaqa.

"Indeed?" he asked stonily.

"Indeed," Abaqa affirmed. His dark eyes narrowed as he assessed Thierry. "'Twould seem to be unhealthy to not share my opinion these days."

"Your sire is but dead three days and no guarantee have you of the khanate," Thierry observed with forced calm. Abaqa's brows arched high.

"Nay?" he asked with feigned surprise. "Tell me not that you, too, believe the best-qualified man will hold the position."

"Always has it been thus," Thierry argued, but Abaqa laughed cynically.

"Nay," he whispered with evident delight. "Always has it been the *survivor* who became khan and none other." His eyes widened slightly as he watched Thierry absorb the assertion, then he stepped back and glanced to the fallen man with open disgust. "Fool," Abaqa muttered deprecatingly, the single word telling Thierry to be on his guard.

Thierry had best take to sleeping with an eye open.

Unexpectedly those bright eyes swiveled to lock with Thierry's regard once more, though this time the hint of a mocking smile played on Abaqa's lips. "No one else need see this but you," he whispered. A chill tripped down Thierry's spine but he refused to look away.

"Chinkai's absence is not likely to go unnoticed," he commented. Abaqa's smile broadened.

"My sire will be buried in the full Mongol tradition," Abaqa reminded him. "Who will know if one human sacrifice is a little more cold than the others?"

He would feign a sacrifice to cover his crime? Thierry was shocked that even Abaqa could be so callous. But one glimpse of the determination in the set of the other man's chin told him that he was a fool to even doubt the other man's intent.

"You cannot do this thing," Thierry protested, knowing the futility of his objection even as he made it.

"Nay, I can and will have it done. I, however, will be

occupied with becoming khan." Abaqa paused dramatically and eyed Thierry. "Which is why you will do this," he added quietly. "For your new khan. I trust you will make a good show."

"You cannot know that you will be khan," Thierry argued tightly. Abaqa leaned closer, his sharp scent invading Thierry's nostrils with a vengeance.

"I *will* be khan," Abaqa growled. "And you will kiss my boot, one way or the other. Just as Chinkai did. Do you understand our ways that much, outsider?" This last was delivered with an eloquent sneer.

Outsider. Despite all Thierry had done and all the years he had labored for the exaltation of the tribe. How many assaults had he led? How many successful forays had he planned? And all of it meant naught because of the taint of his mixed blood. Rage rose within Thierry that he should be so threatened at the very moment when all he had aspired to dangled within reach.

"Kubilai himself once told me that there could be no outsider with the legacy of Chinggis Khan's blood running in his veins," Thierry said. Abaqa laughed, and the brittle sound carried far in the chill morning air.

"That same lineage runs in my veins, as well you know," he argued. His lip curled before he continued. "But 'tis not thinned with western swill."

The two men's gazes locked and held for a charged moment. "Face the truth, Qaraq-Böke," Abaqa hissed. "The best man will be khan and that man will be me. You will kiss my boot or not live to tell the tale."

Clearly unless Thierry was willing to adopt Abaqa's tactics, the khanate would not be his. He dared not look to Chinkai, though the fallen warrior's image was crystal clear in his mind.

He was not willing to pay that price. He could not slaughter Abaqa to ensure his own ascendancy.

At the same instant that Thierry realized he was not prepared to commit murder, he saw in Abaqa's expression precisely the opposite. Abaqa would stop at naught to be khan. Thierry would be wise to mind his back, at least until Abaqa was certain of his ascendancy.

And until Thierry decided what path he would take from here.

"I will see to Chinkai," Thierry conceded gruffly. Abaqa grinned anew, displaying his array of yellowed teeth.

"Always did my sire consider you to be an intelligent man," he purred. "Mayhap he was right about something." He winked evilly, then turned and positively danced back to the camp. Thierry watched the older man go as he struggled to rein in his anger. Little option did he have, in truth. His own pride to the contrary, his only real choice was to do Abaqa's bidding.

At least for the time being.

He fought against the ground swell of disappointment that raged through him. So long he had labored for naught!

But Thierry had waited for his opportunity before and it seemed he would wait for it again. Time could only make his position stronger, and he was yet young. Even without his intervention, Abaqa could not live forever.

Thierry could afford to wait and work a little longer. He would continue. He would follow Abaqa's bidding. He would form another plan. And one day, the fate that he coveted would be his alone. It was his destiny.

But on this morning there was Chinkai. The camp was stirring to life and Thierry gritted his teeth as he bent to bear Chinkai away. Only too well did he understand that failure in any task Abaqa granted him would be seen as a sign of disloyalty to the new khan.

And no intention had Thierry of granting Abaqa such an easy victory.

Far across the plains of Asia, a man awakened in the night, haunted by ghostly visions of unicorns. Angry unicorns whose manes were snarled and whose feet tore impatiently at the ground, they set his heart to furious pounding.

He tossed and turned and tore himself from sleep. The sound

of his ragged breathing filled the room. He stared wide-eyed at the ceiling and fancied he still saw their blazing eyes.

He shivered despite himself. A dream. 'Twas no more than a dream. Dagobert clutched the coverlet as he fought to slow his breathing in the calm of the house. His palms were damp. To his astonishment he realized that 'twas heavy red samite that filled his hands, not the cotton coverlet he knew should be there.

He needed not to look to know 'twas the banner of his house, the one he knew to be safely stored away. 'Twas the one graced by the image of a single prancing unicorn that was inexplicably unfurled over the bed.

But look he did.

'Twas that very one. His heart missed a beat and an unfamiliar panic uncoiled in his veins. What did it mean? Why had the dream come to him?

The wan moonlight played tricks with his sight, for the embroidered gems encircling the beast's brow appeared as pearls in its otherworldly glow. Well did Dagobert know that Alienor had chosen the blood red floss of rubies for her work. He blinked, his heart raced, but the vision remained stubbornly unchanged.

He exhaled shakily and looked to his slumbering wife, noting how the moonlight traced the filigree of silver in her dark tresses cast across the pillows. The vestiges of his disturbing dream made him seek out the echo of his lost son's features in her peaceful visage. When he found what he sought, he closed his eyes against the pain of recollection.

But one thing had he promised the boy and that one thing he had not done. How he hated a task unfulfilled. Was this dream a reminder of that failure?

Dagobert looked to his sleeping wife once more. For a moment he feared that she was as insubstantial as the capricious moonlight, the ghostly pearls, his lost son. He tentatively touched one fingertip to her cheek, half-afraid of what he might feel.

The warm satin of Alienor's skin reassured him, as always it had. He released the breath trapped in his lungs and let his fingertips slide over her cheek in a slow caress as determination filled him anew.

So far they had come, so much they had lost, yet this one greatest treasure remained his. Dagobert smiled in relief and closed his eyes, willing his mind to supply the tang of salt air that had teased his nostrils in his dream.

That alone had been welcome. 'Twas the smell of home. 'Twas the smell of the wind vaulting over the high walls of his ancestral home of Montsalvat. Too long had he been without the bite of that wind against his skin.

Suddenly Dagobert knew with unerring conviction that his son yet lived and that he would find him at Montsalvat. That was, without doubt, the message his dream bore. His eyes flew open, though this time he saw naught but the ceiling itself arched above the bed.

There could he tell the boy of his heritage, he concluded with rising excitement. There alone could he complete the task that had been set before him. There alone could he happily pass from this world, should his time deign to come. Resolution flooded through him and he gathered Alienor close to his side, anticipation flickering to life within him.

Time 'twas to go home. And should the ghosts of the past demand to be confronted, Dagobert would meet them at Montsalvat.

Back in Languedoc, far west of both Thierry and Dagobert, the rising sun gilded the azure of the Mediterranean and burnished the ramparts of a fortress perched high in the hills. In the stables of that fortress, name of Montsalvat, an old knight urged yet another goat kid into the world.

A good spring it was proving to be and milk in ample quantities would they have this year, he thought with pride. He turned the new arrival, showing the young goatherd how to clean the mucus from the creature's nostrils before he noticed the deformity.

The beast had but one nub where a horn would grow.

Eustache's breath caught in his throat at the sign, for it could be naught else. He reached out and touched the creature's damp brow, ignoring the mother's protesting bleat.

'Twas time again. Twenty years had it been since a goat had been born thus at Montsalvat. Twenty years. He had almost begun to fear that he would not live to see the next attempt to regain the lost legacy.

But here was no mistaking the portent of this oddity. 'Twas rare that the beast who graced the standard of the Pereilles came to life, and when it did so, especially here at the family's home, all knew to be prepared.

Eustache let the thrill of anticipation ripple through him as he stroked the newborn's brow. Time again to stake the ancient claim that had long been denied. He would indeed see the day.

His mind raced with possibilities, his excitement rising that he might yet again lay eyes on his old comrade, Dagobert de Pereille. And the son! A mere babe he had been when they had left these walls behind, but that had been twenty years past. The babe must by now be a man.

Would this be his time? Would he gain the prize and vindicate his family?

Eustache straightened and stood suddenly, his mind filling with the responsibilities before him. Aid would be needed, arms and men and supplies. As temporary master of Montsalvat, the provision of all fell to Eustache.

All his knighted life had he served the Pereille clan and he would not fail in this task. A list began to form in his mind even as he left the stables, but Eustache smiled as he stepped out into the first blush of the dawn. They would be relying upon him to be prepared. And Eustache knew well what had to be done.

Optimism buoyed his step as he crossed the bailey. Mayhap this time the battle would be won. Mayhap this time all would be settled. He dared to hope for a moment, before his usual practicality settled in.

If naught else, 'twould be good to see what kind of son Alienor and Dagobert had wrought.

'Twas a day of beginnings and endings, a day on which all three men stepped onto the bright path of their destiny, though none of them knew where that path might lead. An old dream was there to pursue, a yet older score to settle, and none could foresee whether the demand for vengeance or the desire of ambition burned with the brighter flame.

Or mayhap a conquest of a gentler kind would win the day.

Chapter One

❧

*Tiflis—between the Black Sea and the Caspian Sea—
October 1265*

Thierry knew the pearls were counterfeit.

He rolled the pearls leisurely across his palm under his would-be ally's watchful eye. He wished he could either dismiss or justify his conviction. The gems looked real enough, but a glimmer in the other man's eye had triggered Thierry's suspicions.

And once active, his suspicion was not readily dismissed.

'Twas true that there were a goodly number of the gems in the velvet sack he had been offered as tribute, all of it summoned in but half a day. He eyed the ivory spheres speculatively, hoping the other man merely thought he was assessing the value of the offering.

In truth, he supposed he was.

No salve to his pride was it to be treated as Abaqa's runner, even after all these months, and he bit down on the increasingly familiar taste of annoyance. Still was he required to fetch tribute, to know all the while that each offering was considered a reflection of his own loyalty. Thierry gritted his teeth and let the gems play in his palm.

The pearls caught the light and indeed they gleamed with the luster of true pearls. This observation only served to give Thierry a grudging admiration of the counterfeiter's skill.

The other man made a nervous little laugh that drew the gaze of both Thierry and his old companion Nogai.

"Surely such an expensive gift is adequate," he said tentatively, the scholar's soft voice translating immediately after the man spoke. The four men virtually filled the small office, though the two townsmen managed to leave an eloquent space between themselves and the Mongols. The unexpected comment prompted Thierry to give the man a slow and thorough perusal.

He struggled to keep his lip from curling at the softness of the man the town revered as their leader. The flesh was loose around his middle, the pallor of his hands made him look almost feminine. Still worse, there was a light of fear in his darting eyes. This was a man? A leader? One entrusted to negotiate the town's safety? 'Twas almost too much to be believed.

Never did the kind of man these merchants and townsfolk chose as leaders cease to surprise Thierry. No blade could this man swing, no knowledge had he of summoning and dispatching troops, no ability had he to defend his town.

Which explained the presence of Abaqa's army camped just outside the town walls.

Thierry's eyes narrowed thoughtfully. He watched the man's flustered response to that move with interest before once more looking down to the gems cradled in his palm. Undoubtedly this was a shrewd man of business who could more than adequately govern his people under normal circumstances.

A man who likely thought he could outwit simple barbarians.

"Soon enough we shall see if the gift is adequate" was all he said, savoring the guttural sounds of the Mongol tongue. An admirable language it was for issuing threats, and that alone made him glad to have learned it.

The scholar Thierry had pressed into service translated his

words and the townsman blanched. Nogai chuckled and the other man recoiled slightly, though he tried to hide the gesture. His glance darted once more to the little velvet sack in trepidation. Thierry spared the man an intent look as he tucked the sack into his tunic, watching until he swallowed nervously.

Counterfeit beyond doubt.

Thierry toyed briefly with the idea of taking retribution now for the insult, his gaze steady on the other man while he reflected. But better 'twas to leave such a task to Abaqa, for he would relish it more than Thierry.

Revealing naught of his conclusion, Thierry held the man's gaze for a long moment. Fear grew in those eyes as the other man's imagination evidently conjured recollections of Mongol retaliation.

A reputation was not necessarily a liability in these matters.

Satisfied when the man's eyes flicked to Nogai as though he expected the pair of them to fall immediately upon him, Thierry turned silently on his heel. He strode back out into the sunlight, the scholar and Nogai in his wake. He sensed rather than saw Nogai leer with deliberation at the town leader before he followed.

Thierry considered the twisting street, carefully gazing in first one direction and then the other. The agitated man he had left behind was forgotten as he planned his next step. His own survival in Abaqa's camp had to be ensured, first and foremost.

"We should return to camp," Nogai suggested. Thierry only shot a sharp glance in his direction.

"Not yet."

Nogai frowned and folded his arms across his chest. "Why ever not? Surely you have not forgotten that we ride to battle tomorrow? This is but another whimsical test of Abaqa's, and already have we expended too much time upon it."

He waited with obvious anticipation, but Thierry merely shook his head again.

"We are not yet done" was all he said. He ignored the anticipation in the eyes of his *anda*.

A pearl merchant was what Thierry needed.

A tribute of false pearls would not be good for the town leader's health, nor indeed that of the town, should Abaqa discover the forgery. However, Thierry knew that it could also bode poorly for his own longevity and this interested him above all.

If he could expose a forgery before it created undue embarrassment, his usefulness would be assured.

For now. Thierry lifted his nose to the wind and determined that the souk was to the right. He gave no explanation to either of his companions before he strode determinedly in that direction, leaving them to scurry in his wake.

Kira frowned irritably at the bowl of pearls her father had left her to sort before his departure to Constantinople.

Naturally he had not granted her the task of sorting the pearls without a smug smile.

So my daughter fancies herself worthy of becoming a pearl merchant. Kira could hear his mocking tones as clearly as if he stood beside her, and she grimaced yet again at the memory.

She would not cry. She had not cried when he beat her and she would not do so now. Had she not the opportunity she had wanted?

Then prove yourself. Tell me where they are from. Still she could see him as he taunted her from the door. His condescending smile had told her that he had no doubt she would fail.

But she would not fail. Kira set her lips stubbornly. Here indeed was her chance to finally prove herself worthy of her father's love. As worthy as a son could she be to aid in his business, and succeeding in this test could only prove that fact.

She would succeed. Kira did not fool herself, for there was much she needed to learn. No advantage had her sire granted her in teaching her only his native Persian, insisting that that language alone be spoken in their home. She well knew that as a merchant, he conversed readily in half a dozen tongues. But even Persian, as universal as it was, was often not enough within Tiflis itself.

Despite that handicap, Kira would prove herself. She was determined to do so. And this was the first necessary step.

Sadly, the truth was that her father had included some pearls of ambiguous origins, no doubt deliberately. Indeed, 'twould not have been much of a test otherwise. She had already sorted out the obvious forgeries, but well enough she knew what her punishment would be should she make a single mistake.

Hundreds of gems there were. Kira squared her shoulders and took another handful of pearls. She slipped a half dozen of them into her mouth.

Salt. She spat the first one into the brimming bowl of pearls she had already determined to be from the Red Sea. Good sense did it make that there were more of them mixed into the batch, as they would fetch less at market. She nodded approvingly at her judgment.

Salt and salt again. Two more joined the bowl, then two less salty, but still saline.

The last pearl she rolled tentatively around with her tongue, wanting to be sure before she decided. Well could a pearl merchant's reputation be shattered by the selling of lesser pearls as better ones and she schooled herself to be cautious.

Definitely sweet, she concluded with conviction. Definitely from Oman. The pearl joined a mere handful reposing in the second dish of sorted pearls.

Mayhap she was getting better at this, she thought with a rush of pride. She had been quicker with that mouthful. Feeling more optimistic, she scooped up another half dozen pearls and popped them into her mouth.

A guttural declaration drew her startled gaze toward the sunlight flooding from the market. A man's tall frame blocked the light. Kira squinted at the man silhouetted in the alcove leading to her father's shop, unable to make out his features in the shadows yet curiously aware of the weight of his gaze upon her.

Evidently her silent reaction was not the expected one. Kira's heart tripped in trepidation. He repeated whatever he had said the first time, with a heavy emphasis more than adequately tinged with impatience.

No idea had Kira what he said and she knew not what to respond. She stood reluctantly, painfully aware of her short stature and wondering how on earth she would explain that she could not do business until her father returned.

"Where is your father?" another voice demanded breathlessly in familiar Persian. Kira looked past the massive man to find a well-known but markedly nervous face.

"Johannes," she said with mingled relief and pleasure to see the scholar.

The forgotten pearls beneath her tongue stumbled unexpectedly from her lips when she spoke. Kira gasped as they danced to the ground and scattered. They glimmered in the shadowed shop and rolled away to hide in the corners.

Half-wit, Kira cursed herself, bending hastily to retrieve the gems as her color rose.

In the same moment the tall man muttered something vehement that could have been a curse and took a hasty step backward.

Another male voice protested and Kira confirmed with a quick glance that there was a third man behind the tall one. He was considerably more agitated than his companion. He gesticulated to the fallen pearls, his hasty words similarly incomprehensible though he said much, much more.

Kira hastily gathered the errant gems before they were lost. She dropped them into her pocket and straightened, only to find all three men regarding her with utmost solemnity. The hairs pricked on the back of her neck. Kira looked instinctively to the tall man. His expression was tinged with a healthy measure of suspicion.

Suspicion of *her?* Why?

The tall man's retreat had taken him out of the shield of the shadows and Kira spared him a questioning glance, undeterred by his stern countenance. He was heavily tanned or else darker of skin than she, his expression hard and uncompromising. His shoulders were broad, his forearms heavily muscled, his strong legs planted against the dirt floor like veritable tree trunks.

Kira fancied he would be about as easy to move as a firmly rooted tree and had little doubt he earned his way as a mercenary of one kind or another. He was garbed in a rough manner unfamiliar to her, his blue tunic, although as dirty as his dark blue trousers and heavy boots, unexpectedly trimmed with lavish gold embroidery.

Fear flickered within her but she refused to indulge it. Who were these men and what did they want? She met the steely glint of suspicion in his eyes, something about his very stillness making her wish he had stayed in the shadows. He apparently had a similar effect on the normally garrulous Johannes, who spared a quick glance to the tall man in much the same manner as one would regard an unfamiliar and potentially vicious dog.

Kira looked to the third man, his Asiatic features making her heart still. He sported a pointed goatee and thin mustache, unlike his companion, who was clean shaven. Both men wore their hair tied back tightly and bound into a braid, but the very sight of the shorter man's distinctively narrow eyes fed Kira's fear.

It could not be, she told herself wildly, even as she watched Johannes eye the two foreigners. Kira shivered at the possibility she could not even voice within her own mind and willed herself not to take a step backward. Never had she shown her sire her fear. She would show none to these strangers. Kira swallowed carefully and deliberately squared her shoulders.

"My father has gone to Constantinople, so the stall is not open for business," she explained formally to the scholar. The expression of raw fear that transformed the older man's features startled her and she flicked a glance to the impassive warrior.

"Nay, nay, nay," Johannes fussed, literally wringing his slim hands before himself. "This is not good, not good at all."

The tall man barked something short but incoherent that was clearly a demand. Kira's trepidation rose as Johannes responded quickly in kind, the third man's dark eyes bright in the shadows as he watched.

"What is this about?" she demanded, her uncertainty making her speak more sharply than was her custom.

The tall man's eyes narrowed speculatively and he spoke tersely to Johannes. The way his gaze wandered over Kira sent reluctant color rising over her cheeks.

She was *not* that sort of woman.

Kira lifted her chin indignantly and boldly held his gaze. She knew that her heavy, draped and hooded djellaba thrown over her high-necked *kurta* was demure beyond even the current mode, and that her full *chalwar* trousers hid all but her ankles from view. No need had she to tempt the glances of men in town, for that, too, bore the price of her father's lash.

Was that amusement briefly flickering in the warrior's eyes? Kira dismissed her whimsical thought out of hand, knowing intuitively that a sense of humor would not be an attribute of this rough warrior. Indeed, she had not found it an attribute of men in general, unless they mocked at another's expense.

"He wants to know when your father will return," Johannes translated. Kira shrugged in response.

"Just last week 'twas that he left," she confessed, incapable of tearing her gaze away from those scrutinizing eyes even though she felt that they bored into her very soul. "No less than a month could his journey require."

The warrior nodded curtly, apparently having understood the gist of her response from her gesture, and barked an order to Johannes. The scholar raised imploring eyes to Kira.

"Some pearls he needs valued immediately for the Mongol khan," he whispered. Kira felt her eyes widen in surprise despite her determination to keep her thoughts hidden.

Mongols. 'Twas true, then. Her gaze flicked reluctantly back to the third man with his characteristically Eastern features as though to verify her original suspicions.

When the Asiatic man grinned wickedly, Kira inhaled

sharply. Her gaze danced back to the tall man seemingly of its own accord. He was watching her with that unnervingly silent scrutiny. Kira took a slow breath as she came to terms with Johannes' revelation.

No need had she to look into either pair of cold eyes again to know that these men would slaughter anyone who did not do their bidding. 'Twas all part of their daily business, she had little doubt.

No wonder Johannes was terrified.

But she would not give them the satisfaction of seeing her fear.

Kira drew herself up straighter and endeavored to look confident of her own abilities. No heart had she for abandoning Johannes to this forbidding man's disapproval.

"A rough value can I give him of the gems," she offered, the strength of her voice surprising her. Johannes translated her words and Kira took a deep breath, willing her heartbeat to slow. Truly she hoped that she could fulfill this task.

And her father thought that *he* had left her a test of her abilities. Kira licked her lips nervously as the warrior slowly slid a small pouch from his tunic. Could she do this? In truth there was little choice now. The warrior said something directly to her and Kira was forced to meet his compelling gaze once more though she did not understand his words.

"He says that the way pearls drop from your lips when you speak is a sign you can be trusted," Johannes supplied.

Kira swallowed with difficulty, knowing that she dare not reveal the truth of what he had obviously misinterpreted. She reached for the bulging velvet pouch, startled at the jolt that tripped over her skin when the warrior's rough fingertips brushed hers.

His skin was warm.

Suddenly Kira was aware of him in a much more intimate sense than she would have preferred. The unexpected contact and the faint waft of his musky scent awakened something within Kira that would have been better left slumbering.

She snatched the bag and backed hastily away, hating the knowing expression that lit his eyes at her move. Curse him for presuming to guess her thoughts. For no flattering thoughts had she of a barbarian warrior, regardless of his own interpretation of her response. Kira lifted her chin defiantly and glared at the tall man.

"Time will this take," she managed to say, forcing herself to continue even when that jaw hardened with displeasure. "Mayhap you could return later."

Impossible 'twould be to work under this merciless scrutiny. Irrational 'twas and she knew it, but Kira wanted this man out of her father's shop. Now. She felt agitated as she never had before and told herself 'twas the man's very stillness that unnerved her. And the way he watched every move so impassively. 'Twas unnatural.

Her heart sank when Johannes' voice faded, his translation not even complete before the warrior shook his head with certainty. He bit out something that Kira had no trouble recognizing as a recrimination or a threat or both and she felt her cheeks heat again. Too much 'twas to have him question her honesty.

"No intention have I of cheating him and you had best make that clear," she told Johannes tersely. She felt the heat of an indignant flush staining her cheeks but did not care. "An honest house is this. 'Twas only my suspicion that 'twould be easier for me to concentrate on the task without supervision that prompted my suggestion."

A flurry of Mongol followed her words and again the warrior shook his head, deliberately settling himself onto an inverted oil vessel that her father had abandoned in his packing. He braced his elbows on his knees, looking even more immobile than he had before, and growled one last comment.

"He says you will have to get used to him," Johannes supplied in a small voice. Though his words came as no surprise to Kira, her heart took an unsteady lurch as she met the warrior's resolute gaze.

Fine. She dropped the sack of pearls deliberately on her worktable. The sooner the pearls were assessed, the sooner he would be gone. And a good riddance 'twould be.

She was annoyed, of that there was little doubt. Thierry found the unexpectedness of her response curiously amusing. Fear he was used to, but disgruntled cooperation was a response that was entirely novel.

Evidently the woman was a witch.

Those full lips had tightened, and the teeth that had flashed when she smiled earlier were gritted together in a clear bid for self-control. The soft gold of her complexion was now tinged with a more ruddy hue. She cleared her work space brusquely of other gems, the expression in those wide dark eyes mutinous at a minimum.

For all of that, though, she did his bidding. Thierry supposed another less perceptive than he might have been fooled, but he saw every minute sign of her displeasure. That such a small and feminine creature would even consider defying him was as fascinating as it was unprecedented. Thierry could not help but watch her tiny hands as she worked.

Though she refused to glance in his direction, Thierry knew she was completely aware of his regard. He leaned back against the wall, fingering the hilt of his blade speculatively. What manner of woman spewed pearls from her mouth when she spoke?

A puzzle that was, but no less of one than her response to him. Why was she not terrified? Certainly the thin scholar had made it clear that he was Mongol. Fear had flashed through her eyes, telling Thierry that she was well familiar with their reputation. But she had not recoiled in the manner of most soft urban women who had seen naught of life.

What kind of woman would have the audacity to act thus? A Mongol woman, surely, but this woman's delicate features hinted naught at Eastern blood.

A witch she must truly be. Indeed, 'twas well Thierry had

guessed her game, for he would need to guard himself against her sorcery. No other explanation could there be. Convinced of his own logic, Thierry watched the woman with grim determination.

Incredibly, his suggestion that she might cheat him if left alone seemed to have struck a nerve. That aroused Thierry's curiosity. Surely these town people did not expect foreigners to trust them?

Or mayhap she simply disliked that he had guessed her game so early.

"Mayhap you should have the pearls assessed back at camp," Nogai suggested.

Thierry stiffened, hearing the leer in his old companion's voice. He did not have to look to know full well the path his *anda*'s thoughts had taken. Though the woman's garb was cut full, 'twas clear enough that she would be small and shapely. He stifled an uncharacteristic surge of annoyance at his old companion's appetites.

"They will be assessed here," he said flatly, hating Nogai's knowing chuckle. Thierry felt the other man lean closer, fully anticipating that his next words would be for his ears alone.

"Tempted, are you not?" Nogai whispered mischievously. Thierry did not acknowledge the taunt, staring resolutely forward. He was *not* tempted. Women did not tempt him. "Well should you be, for she is a tasty morsel, indeed." When his words still garnered no response, Nogai dropped his voice yet further. Thierry struggled not to bristle.

"Mayhap should you not be interested, I should sample her myself."

"Nay!" Thierry bit out the denial more harshly than he intended.

The woman glanced up like a frightened doe, her startled expression making him consider apologizing.

Apologizing? Khanbaliq loomed in Thierry's mind and he straightened his shoulders deliberately. 'Twas only the soft folk of Khanbaliq and other courts who apologized to women.

Urban folk. He tried unsuccessfully to summon a sneer. A Mongol would not apologize. Thierry held the woman's startled gaze for a charged moment, then her color rose and she turned abruptly away.

A Mongol he was these days and he had best recall that fact. This woman he owed naught. Thierry felt his eyes narrow as he recalled the way the pearls had spewed from her lips. And the tingle she had launched over his skin when their hands had accidentally brushed.

"A witch is she," he pronounced, as much to remind himself as anything else. To his completely unwarranted relief, Nogai's manner cooled immediately.

"Touch her not," Thierry added testily.

"Nay," Nogai concurred. He even took a wary step backward, unconsciously granting the woman more space. "No telling is there what price she would extract for that."

The scholar drew himself up taller as though he personally took insult for the charge. One cold glance from Thierry silenced any protest he might have made.

The woman's gaze flicked between the three of them uncomprehendingly. Clearly she sensed that they discussed her. All three men remained stubbornly silent, even the scholar refusing to clarify the charges for her. The woman's lips thinned in annoyance and Thierry almost smiled.

Smiled? First apologizing, then smiling. Surely his wits were addled this day. Thierry scowled. 'Twas the witch and her sorcery that did this to him. She spun with a defiant flick of her chin and carried a broad vessel back into the shadows.

Where was she going? Thierry panicked and jumped to his feet.

For his obvious suspicions he earned a scathing glance from the lady in question that effectively checked his pursuit. Thierry almost smiled at her indignation, but the ripe curve of her buttocks outlined when she bent to scoop water from an urn halted that rare impulse before it had truly begun.

Nogai made an admiring sound under his breath that Thierry

alone seemed to note. She was yet more shapely than he had guessed and Thierry's mouth went unexpectedly dry. How long *had* he been chaste? He could not cease fingering the hilt of his blade, though he told himself the gesture was merely a habit.

She propped the brimming clay bowl on her hip as she returned. The further evidence of the slender curves hidden beneath the full cotton garment fed Thierry's awareness of both her and his own increasingly agitated state. Abruptly and uncharacteristically he wished he had been able to completely adopt his tribesmen's penchant for simply taking whatever they wanted.

The value of the pearls was all he was here for, he reminded himself sternly. Once he had that information, he would return to the khan's camp. With Nogai alone. Abaqa would have his tribute from Tiflis, such as it was, and they would ride to battle on the morrow.

He watched the woman settle the brimming bowl on her worktable. Her hands were long fingered and graceful for all their delicate size, though Thierry knew not why he noted such a thing.

'Twould be ridiculous to undermine any of his aspirations for what could amount to no more than base desire. Abaqa might not thrive as long as his sire, and Thierry might yet have the opportunity to vie for his ambition. No woman was worth jeopardizing all of that.

The woman moved quickly, her sudden gesture as she cast the pearls into the vessel catching Thierry's eye. He leaped forward in alarm, too late to intervene, as the contents of the velvet pouch spilled into the water.

A trick 'twas! And too absorbed had he been in his own troubles to anticipate her move!

Nogai swore. He lunged forward in the same moment as Thierry. The two of them towered over the woman as she glanced up in alarm. Thierry peered into the depth of the water, his anger flaring when he realized he could not see the pearls.

They were gone! He had failed!

The vessel had some sort of false bottom, Thierry concluded

in dismay. He cursed his own stupidity in letting his baser instincts cloud his normal caution.

He would not grant Abaqa such an easy victory.

The woman's eyes widened when Thierry hauled his blade purposefully out of his belt. He silently applauded how well she played her role for she looked confused, then perfectly incredulous to find the unsheathed blade right beneath her nose. She met his gaze, her beautiful dark eyes startled. Thierry hated himself for his inexplicable urge to reassure her.

Was she not bent on deceiving him? Did such intent not grant him the right to take her life? Why then did he have this inexplicable urge to stroke the furrows from her brow?

"Tell him that this is the best way to find forgeries."

She spoke hastily to Johannes, the translation making Thierry frown. He watched with amazement as she gestured to bobbing orbs on the surface of the water. She murmured something else, and the scholar's quick translation sparked Thierry's interest.

"You have been tricked."

He dared to wonder in that moment if his own assessment of the gems had been correct. The woman quickly plucked the "pearls" that floated off the surface of the water as Thierry watched. Before he could intervene, she offered them to him with a dismissive gesture that told Thierry more than eloquently their authenticity. They *were* counterfeit. He grudgingly acknowledged her skill as he looked at the "gems," lowering his blade but not yet ready to put it away.

"Counterfeit," Nogai breathed. Thierry felt his friend's regard upon him. "You suspected as much before we even came here, then?" he demanded admiringly. Thierry merely nodded, watching the woman carefully to see what she would do next. "City dwellers," Nogai sneered as he shook his head. "Surely they cannot think we are such fools as to let such an insult pass?"

"The matter is best left to Abaqa," Thierry said calmly, a newfound admiration in his gaze as he watched the witch.

Mayhap he had misjudged her. She flicked a self-conscious

glance to him and flushed in a most fetching way. Thierry's gaze dropped to her lips. She licked them and something raged to life within him.

Thierry frowned and tore his gaze away. He filed the false gems carefully in one of his pockets that Abaqa might be shown the fullness of the insult. He peered into the depths of the bowl with curiosity, all too aware of her sweet scent. The water had cleared and Thierry counted ten pearls nestled together in the bottom.

'Twas obviously a magic trick of hers to be able to so easily sort the wheat from the chaff. Though he knew not the means of her sorcery, Thierry respected the result. She pushed up a sleeve to reveal a slim and honey-hued forearm and scooped the remaining pearls from the base of the bowl. Was her skin the same shade everywhere? The question was more intriguing than it ought to have been. Thierry abruptly held out his hand to claim the meager spoils, uncomfortable with the direction of his thoughts.

To his complete astonishment the woman plopped the gems into her mouth.

Nay! She meant to swallow the only part of the tribute that was valuable!

Rage filled Thierry, rage with himself for being so foolish as to trust a stranger. He dove across the narrow table separating them. The vessel of water toppled precariously. The woman cried out and stepped back in surprise, but Thierry was quicker.

His hands locked around the slim length of her throat with practiced ease. The water splashed over their feet. The scholar shouted in dismay, Nogai swore yet again, but Thierry had no time for qualms.

He could not let her swallow them.

That one thought filled his mind even as he noted the softness of her skin beneath his hands. The woman's eyes opened even wider as his grip tightened purposefully. He noted with some satisfaction that fear had finally claimed her.

He flexed his fingers so they would not slide over her silky skin of their own accord. She had tricked him!

The witch choked unevenly and spat a half dozen pearls to the floor, tears filling her dark eyes as still she coughed. Out of the corner of his eye Thierry noted that Nogai retrieved the gems.

There had been ten pearls in the water, Thierry was certain of it.

Four there were still unaccounted for and well he intended to wait them out.

He gave the woman a little shake and she made a gurgling sound deep in her throat. Furious that she had so deceived him and was showing a perverse inclination to expire at this most inopportune time, Thierry released her throat and slapped her back hard.

Another pearl leaped to the floor.

Three more! He smacked her shoulder blades once more when she still choked, ignoring the older man's fervent and useless prayers. A second gem made the jump, rolling across the dirt. Finally a third gleamed as it fell from her lips. The woman drew a shuddering breath and cleared her throat slowly, wiping her tears as Thierry glared at her impatiently.

One more there was.

When she spoke, he would have the last pearl, he resolved grimly. His eyes narrowed at the look of outright hostility she shot at him. Traitorous witch! He gripped her shoulders that she might not bolt and waited patiently.

"You stupid fool!"

She spat an insult he had no interest in understanding. Thierry watched her full lips with growing disbelief when no gem dropped from them. He frowned at her tirade even as the older man translated, the indisputably angry words flowing over him unattended. There could be little doubting her meaning, those brown eyes flashing with fury as she wagged an admonishing finger beneath his nose.

"Look what you have done with your meddling!" she charged

angrily. *She* was angry? Thierry inhaled slowly when the scholar's words made clear her accusation that he was at fault.

Mayhap she was annoyed that he had foiled her plan, he speculated thoughtfully. Otherwise she might have had nine more pearls. His lips set grimly.

No right had she to the khan's tribute. To think he had thought her insulted by his earlier charge that she meant to cheat him. She had simply been annoyed that he had so accurately anticipated her intent. A fool he had been to trust her at all. Thierry regarded her coldly, then held out his palm between them in a silent but eloquent gesture.

The woman shook her head firmly and pointed to her stomach once more.

"Ways there are to retrieve something swallowed," Nogai asserted calmly as he unsheathed his blade. The woman took a hasty step backward, evidently needing no translation of the other man's intent.

"Aye," Thierry agreed and headed purposefully for her.

The gem would be his. She darted to the back of the shop in a futile effort to evade him. When he cornered her, her breath was coming in quick gasps, her eyes and the hasty flutter of the pulse in her throat revealing that she was finally truly afraid. She said something that was obviously an entreaty, but Thierry had no intention of following Nogai's suggestion.

He would not question why. He pressed down on her shoulders until she dropped to her knees, unable to help noticing how tiny she was as he closed one hand around her jaw. The other slipped into the thick silk of the hair at her nape.

Soft, he marveled, hesitating for an instant. Years had it been since he had felt anything so soft as this woman's hair. She spared him a terrified glance that recalled him fully to his senses. Thierry pushed his finger into her mouth and down her throat.

She clutched at his hand, her grip surprisingly strong as she coughed and gagged. Thierry knelt over her as she dropped to all fours, sensing that the pearl would shortly be his.

Her offering, though, was completely devoid of gems.

A witch she was, indeed. He glanced to her speculatively, finding her looking thoroughly human with those tears of exertion streaming over her cheeks. Despite her state, she managed to glare at him indignantly. Thierry once more stifled that unfamiliar urge to smile.

Instead he frowned and held out his hand once more.

"Gone 'tis," she insisted, the scholar's rapid translation filling Thierry's ears. He refused to look away and she pointed emphatically to her stomach. "None have you to thank for that but yourself," she chided, her chin tilting up defiantly.

Something about her indignant response niggled at Thierry, even as her lack of fear intrigued him. He looked quickly to the scholar, wondering if he had misunderstood her intent.

"What does she mean?" he demanded impatiently, still not relinquishing his grip on her shoulders.

His fingers curled around her and without thinking, he drew her closer. The spice of her skin was intoxicating and he forced himself to look away as he gathered his jumbled thoughts. Thierry felt rather than saw her look to the scholar in turn. Her breathing quickened when he simply responded without translating.

"The flavor of a pearl reveals its origin and hence its value," the older man supplied quietly. Thierry glanced back to the woman in time to see her flick a glance filled with trepidation up to him. She demanded something of the scholar, presumably an explanation, and he noted that her voice had risen.

"She should have told me her intent," he growled, staring at her so hard that she seemed compelled to look to him anew. When she did, he savored his threat, relishing the sound of the Mongol tripping off his tongue as she shivered beneath the weight of his hands. "Now she will have to pay the price."

Chapter Two

The warrior released his grip on her so abruptly that Kira nearly fell back on the floor; Johannes' translation of his last words no reassurance at all. What did he mean? Her mouth went dry as he retrieved the pearls from his companion and jammed them back into the velvet sack. He shoved it into his tunic as he turned slowly and regarded her.

She would not cower.

Her heart began to gallop, however, her mind filling with a thousand possibilities. Would they kill her now to retrieve the gem? Kira had barely the chance to note a newly decisive gleam in his eye and panic before the warrior had closed the space between them and tossed her over his shoulder.

She struggled instinctively against him, earning herself a stinging slap on the buttocks and a tightened grip on the back of her knees. In truth, the blow hurt little but her pride. The other Mongol laughed, his lecherous grin right before her, and Kira cringed in anticipation of her fate. The time of reckoning had come and there was naught she could do to turn the tide. The warrior turned abruptly, the echo of his low voice rumbling against her thighs in a most disconcerting way.

'Twas intimate beyond compare to be pressed against him thus. Kira desperately tried to put some distance between the warrior's warm flesh and her own. His heat rose through his garments to taunt her breasts, her thighs, even her palms pressed against his shoulders. 'Twas futile she knew to struggle, but Kira could do naught else.

"He says to tell you he means to have the pearl," Johannes offered as he appeared abruptly before her eyes. His own dark eyes filled with sympathy before he continued. "One way or the other."

Kira's mind recoiled in shock at the promise in those words, but the warrior was ducking back out into the sunlight. His long strides took them across the market square and away from the only home she had known in record time.

"Johannes!" Kira cried out. She noted suddenly that the busy market had fallen silent as all simply watched her being carted away. "Johannes! You must help me!" Although Johannes had trotted into the market behind them, the warrior's determined pace was quickly leaving him behind.

Much to Kira's chagrin, Johannes seemed to be making no efforts to close the gaping distance. Would she be abandoned by her neighbors to the Mongols' whim? What would her father have to say of this? Worse yet, she was leaving the shop untended in his absence. Kira cursed her own sorry hide for failing in yet another of her sire's tasks. Never would she prove herself worthy of his love this way.

"Johannes!" The other warrior strode behind her captor with equally long steps. When Kira made the mistake of meeting his eyes, he very deliberately licked his lips. She recoiled, but he laughed harshly. Only too readily could she imagine what this one had in store for her. Truly she had fallen into the hands of the devil's own spawn.

Mayhap it would have been a mercy if they had her killed quickly.

"None can help you but yourself, child," Johannes called from far behind them. Kira heard the thread of fear in his voice. She looked desperately to the old neighbors in the market, dismayed to find them clearing out of the Mongols' path, as well. They stood silently aside with terrified expressions.

But when had they ever helped her? Indeed, she was a fool to be surprised. Kira gritted her teeth and lifted her chin. How many times must they have heard her cry out during the night? How many times had they heard the bite of her father's lash finding its mark and done naught for her? How often had she greeted her fate alone before?

How often, indeed.

No one to help her but herself. Truly, naught had changed.

Kira's breath abandoned her lungs in one sharp move when the Mongol unexpectedly tossed her across the back of a horse. At least he touched her no more, though her skin still tingled from the imprint of his hands.

The beast wore a high red saddle, caparisons rich with embroidery hanging over its sides. Though the trappings were dirty and showing signs of wear, the horse's chestnut coat was glossy as though it were well tended. It pranced impatiently beneath her weight, yet more evidence that it suffered naught beneath this man's hand.

Mayhap another tended his beast, she told herself stubbornly. It could not be that a Mongol showed concern for any other than himself. Kira slanted a glance at her captor and confirmed her own silent judgment. Certainly no kindness ever passed from the hand of this stern man. Had he not slapped her own buttocks? Truly, men were all the same.

The horse took another nervous step and the ground moved dizzyingly beneath Kira's gaze. She inhaled sharply at the promise of her first horseback ride and fought against the bile rising in her throat. Too unsteady a perch was this for her taste, and the journey had yet to begin.

She found the weight of an uncompromising hand in the small of her back and the warrior's knees nudging her shoulder and thigh before she could collect her thoughts. Warmth

flooded through her garments and across her skin from that outstretched palm, and Kira panicked.

He muttered something impatiently when Kira struggled to
right herself. She glared up at him through the tangle of her hair.

"I will not ride like a sack of grain," she informed him
frostily, taking refuge from the barrage of unfamiliar feelings
in anger once again.

He seemed somehow to understand, for one hand gripped
her hair and hauled her upright painfully to sit before him in
the saddle. Kira voiced no complaint, merely gritted her teeth.
She would show no weakness. She felt the other Mongol
watching them, painfully aware of his poorly concealed amusement. She stubbornly ignored him as she fought against her
rising fear. What did they intend to do with her? Her imagination was only too ready to supply the obvious alternative. Her
warrior made a demand, an imperious point of his finger
making it clear that he intended her to ride astride.

Like a common whore. Never. Kira shook her head immediately at the inappropriateness of that, watching his lips thin
to a grim line. 'Twas bad enough to guess her fate without
having to agree to the deed. Without preamble the warrior
pushed her head resolutely back down toward his knee.

Well, if that was her choice, she would ride astride, Kira
resolved. Anything would be better than the indignity of riding
like a sack of grain. Not to mention that she would likely
become ill in such a posture. She impatiently pushed aside his
hand and sat up once more, gripping the horse's mane as she
struggled against her full djellaba to lift her leg over the
creature's back.

The Mongol muttered what was surely an oath. Kira flushed
as his hands closed firmly around her waist as he lifted her high.
Only too aware was Kira that his hands fully encompassed her
waist and she felt claimed by him in some inexplicably new and
disorienting way.

Nonsense. Kira's cheeks flamed yet ruddier beneath the

other Mongol's interested eye. Full *chalwar* trousers she wore and naught was there for him to see. And well they both knew that she was no whore.

Even if he might mean to change that fact. Kira felt her hands begin to tremble as though they were not a part of her.

Kira leaned forward but evidently 'twas not the warrior's intent that they be separated, for one muscled arm locked around her waist. He imprisoned her easily against his chest, her arms pinned to her side beneath his relentless grip.

She struggled indignantly, the recent wounds on her back stinging with friction from her efforts as she roundly cursed his familiarity with her. The unmistakable feel of something hardening against her buttocks brought her to a flustered halt.

Kira panicked silently, for no doubt had she what that something was. A virgin she might be, but she was not a fool. A woman need not be a whore to know what was what in this world.

Would he possess her here and now if she vexed him? No good could come of this, to be sure. At this very real indication of what might be in store for her, fear threatened to overwhelm Kira. How often had her father threatened her with the beating of her life if a man laid a hand upon her? 'Twould be her fault alone, she had been made to understand, and the lash a necessary punishment. A fine match did her father intend to make for her one day, a marriage that would financially assure the leisure of his days.

Only an ungrateful wretch of a daughter would steal the promise of that away from her sire.

Surely her maidenhead could not be the price he would compel her to pay her for swallowing the pearl?

Kira's heart chilled and she felt herself begin to tremble as the possibilities became more clear. No doubt had she that a Mongol would take what he wanted, regardless of her entreaties. She felt the blood drain from her face at the realization that no explanation would suffice for her father.

His future would be destroyed and 'twould be all her doing.

The warrior's fingers fanned to close more resolutely around her elbow, eliminating any option Kira might have had to move farther away. She stiffened at the restriction and he grunted, though it seemed that she could no longer feel his arousal.

No time had Kira to reflect upon the matter, for his stirrups jingled and he dug his heels into the horse's side in that same moment. The creature seemed to have been waiting only for such a sign to flee the town at a recklessly wild pace.

She shrank instinctively back against the warrior's strength as the horse ran, certain she would be bounced loose and shattered like a doll on the ground. She clutched at the sinewy forearm wrapped around her, knowing her nails were digging into his flesh but unable to check her fear.

Her loose hair flailed around them, its binding long gone and her hood fallen away. The man behind her cursed again as Kira clung to him. He dropped the reins and she thought her heart might stop in terror. The beast ran unchecked! They would be thrown to the ground and their bones broken in a hundred places! Had this warrior not a scrap of mercy in his soul?

His freed hand swept savagely around Kira's head, his rough thumb brushing her nape and sending an unexpected shiver down her spine as he gathered her hair and twisted its length. 'Twas long enough that he could grip the ends in the hand clasped over her elbow. No reassurance did she take from the ease with which he accomplished his objective and nonchalantly picked up the reins again. Kira tugged against this new restraint, feeling hopelessly tethered even as she bounced precariously on her unsteady perch.

She would be jostled until everything within her was shaken loose. That was to be her fate. Powerless would she be to even stand when this wild ride was completed. Indeed, she could fairly feel the bruises rising on her buttocks already.

Her father would have much to say to her about such inappropriate behavior.

The Mongol said something to her, but she shook her head

uncomprehendingly until his free hand curved firmly about her knee. No time was this for further familiarities. Kira recoiled from his touch. He repeated his command more slowly and did not release her knee, pressing the joint firmly into the horse's side and holding it there.

He gripped the horse with his knees, she realized suddenly, glancing down to find his knees clamped against the beast's ribs. Kira tentatively followed suit, imagining that his muttered response as he released her knee was approving.

'Twas better! Kira fancied she had a steadier perch. Her panicked breathing slowed with the realization that she was not likely to topple to her death.

Not until she returned home to her father, at least. Her heart sank.

If indeed she lived long enough to do that. Kira sighed and stubbornly blinked back her tears.

She would not think upon her fate. She would not even speculate on this barbarian's plans for her. Kira lifted her chin and surveyed the grassland sweeping beneath the horse's feet.

As her heartbeat slowed, she forced herself to concede that riding a horse was not so terrifying at all. Indeed, she felt warm and secure, though certainly such feelings were completely unwarranted. 'Twas only the fact that she could no longer see the warrior's cold expression that allowed her to relax, sitting as she was, virtually in his lap.

Kira became suddenly aware of the strength of his thighs behind hers. That recently awakened tingle struck again with new vigor. Though his grip around her waist was uncompromising and she knew there was no escape, the warrior did not hurt her. Could he truly be as brutal as she feared? Kira looked down to his fingers wrapped so proprietarily around her elbow, hating herself for liking their tanned strength.

Who knew what those hands had done? The man was a Mongol. A barbarian.

Mayhap she was losing her mind. Certainly the jumble of

emotions churning within her this day could not be sorted into any order. Mayhap the warrior was saving her hide for some other fate. Kira chilled at the thought and refused to reflect on it further.

In the distance a dark smudge grew more distinct. Kira gradually picked out the forms of horses grazing all around an apparent settlement. Gradually it became clear that the smudge across the landscape was composed of thousands of round homes. Kira had little doubt what sort of settlement they approached.

'Twas the Mongol camp. A cold trickle of dread meandered into her stomach at the sight. What gruesome fate awaited her here?

Thierry rode directly to his own yurt, liking its welcome familiarity. The round felt tent gave him a sense as close to homecoming as he found these days.

But he would not indulge himself in another recollection of Khanbaliq. Truly he could not recall when those images had last haunted him as they did this day. But no time had he for such poignant and pointless reminiscing.

The woman had clenched up before him as the camp came into sight. Once again he stifled the urge to reassure her. Had she not tried to trick him once already? Indeed, there was no way of telling what sort of treachery was filtering through her mind even now.

A witch she was. He should know better than to trust such a lovely face.

Undoubtedly she was used to turning her beauty to her advantage. 'Twould not work this time, Thierry reminded himself determinedly. He halted the horse with a barely audible sound and nudged his knee beneath hers. She apparently understood his intent, letting him lift her knee over the horse's back with his.

At least she was not a fool, he concluded with an unwarranted rush of pride. He savored the pleasant feel of her cradled in his lap before he slid to the ground. Was the rest of her as soft as her hair? She gained her footing less gracefully than he had expected. That as much as anything was an indication of her unfamiliarity with horses.

That could well be changed. Thierry was amused when the witch immediately tried to pull away from him. Where did she think she might find safer haven than with him in this camp? Nogai would offer her company, 'twas true, but somehow he doubted that kind of companionship would please her.

Thierry kept a firm grip on the end of her hair that had her shortly spinning to a stop, her eyes flashing angrily when they met his. Nogai laughed at her predicament and she spared him a hostile glance before she confronted Thierry once more.

She spat something, but the translator had been left in Tiflis. Mayhap not the best conceived plan, but then, Thierry needed no more from her than the pearl. Her anger was fascinating though, and Thierry watched her, unable to help being intrigued.

"Mayhap you will find out firsthand the cost of coupling with a witch," Nogai taunted. The woman flicked him a venomous look, though she could not have understood the comment. Thierry chose to ignore the gibe.

She demanded something breathlessly, her tug on her hair communicating her request. Thierry almost smiled at her foolishness as he shook his head slowly. Her lips set mutinously and she crossed her arms under her breasts. Bewitching she was indeed, with those dark eyes shooting sparks. Thierry resolved in that moment to show both her and Nogai that he was unaffected by her charm.

He coiled her long hair once more around his hand, compelling her to come closer to him as he watched her silently. Her eyes widened in trepidation when he very deliberately repeated the gesture. She swallowed but took the requisite step closer. He wound her hair around his hand over and over again until his fingers were almost touching her throat. Thierry allowed himself a moment to flex his fingers in the thick mass, marveling at that softness, noting her discomfiture as she stared up at him helplessly.

Her skin was so golden a hue, he mused, recalling only too well the delicacy of her throat beneath his hands, the ripe press of her buttocks against his groin. He should not have teased her with his arousal, he knew, but she was so tempting, he had done so before he thought.

And now, he concluded as he looked into those wide brown eyes, she was certain that he intended to ravish her. He saw fear in those dark depths now where none had lurked in the shop. Her fear struck a nerve within him, as had her fearful response on the horse, dissolving his lust before it could truly take possession of him.

Dismissing his recurring urge to reassure her, Thierry nudged her impatiently forward. He felt his brows pull together in a frown of displeasure, even as he reminded himself that 'twould be much easier if she remained afraid of him.

Women were a liability, an indulgence that made a man soft. And softness made a man vulnerable to his enemies.

Like Abaqa. Thierry's blood ran cold as he noted again the woman's delicacy.

This woman in particular was not to be trusted. Thierry had only to keep the witch close until the pearl reappeared. A day, mayhap two, depending on what she ate. Mayhap he would even return her to Tiflis unscathed if she granted him the gem quickly enough.

Making him soft already she was, he concluded angrily to himself. No Mongol would have considered setting her free. Did the blood of the great Khan not course through his veins? He opened the flap to his yurt with a savage sweep and shoved the woman inside, leaving a chuckling Nogai outside.

A day might well be all he could afford of her company.

Kira had not expected the interior of the brown tent to be so luxuriously appointed. She gaped openly at the thick, patterned rugs covering the ground. Embroidered cushions were scattered in one corner, a small unlit stove in the other with various cooking implements and small vessels. A brass lamp hung from the central pole that supported the roof, though it, too, was unlit and her captor showed no inclination to light it. He left the flap open behind them, his grip unrelenting in her hair as he bent and hauled cushions into a pile around the pole.

One tug on her hair had Kira on her knees and she protested, earning a hostile glare. The warrior broke into a spate of Mongol longer than anything he had said to date, angrily gesturing to their surroundings with a broad sweep of his free hand.

"No idea have I what you mean," she countered irritably. "If you think that I will hold my tongue simply because you bid me do so, then you are indeed sorely mistaken—"

Kira got no further before the warrior scooped up a thick scarf and shoved it uncompromisingly into her mouth. She struggled against him as he tried to tie the gag. Kira managed to bite him hard enough that he cursed and released her hair to better finish the job. 'Twas all the encouragement Kira needed to make a run for the open flap. She got no more than two steps before the warrior grimly swept her off her feet.

He was coldly angry, that much was readily apparent when he cast her onto her back on the cushions. Kira squirmed but he dropped one knee onto her belly, lowering just enough weight onto her to keep her captive but not crush her. His eyes flashed as he lashed her wrists to the pole with crisp efficiency. Another scarf served to bind her ankles. The ends of the one filling her mouth were knotted behind her head so that she had no hope of breaking free.

She was trapped!

The warrior glared down at her for a long moment, and Kira feared her heart would stop in terror when he bent toward her. Kira's mouth went dry as her mind flooded with the certainty that he would surely rape her.

He merely tugged on the scarf knotted around her ankles so that her knees were forced between her elbows and tied it to the post, as well. He cast a blanket over her in evident disgust.

Then he braced his hands on either side of her shoulders and
barked out several terse, incomprehensible commands.

She had to break free somehow. Kira wriggled defiantly
against her bonds, her movements setting the pole wobbling
unsteadily. They both glanced up as the tent swayed. Kira
stilled, then he glared down at her once more. A short lecture
was undoubtedly what he was delivering, his hand signs
making it more than evident to Kira that her fighting could haul
down the tent.

Precisely, she thought victoriously. The warrior must have
guessed the direction of her thoughts, for he shook his head
with that maddening slowness. He moved out of her line of
sight, then returned with a thick scrap of wool felt that looked
much like the fiber of the tent itself. The warrior stood over her,
mimicking the sway of the tent before dropping to his knees
and pressing the piece of felt over Kira's nose.

The wool itched for an instant, then she realized she could
not breathe. Her eyes widened in horror at his meaning. He
would sit by and let her suffocate? Surely not! she thought
wildly. His untroubled expression shocked her, answering her
doubts more eloquently than words.

They were barbarians, one and all, these Mongols.

The warrior stood slowly and cast the piece of cloth aside,
satisfaction gleaming in his eyes that she had understood his
meaning. He lifted the lantern from the pole where it dangled
over her head and set it beside the stove. Kira frowned at him,
unable to believe even a Mongol could be so callous.

Barbarian.

The final piece of the puzzle dropped into place when the
warrior strode purposefully out of the tent, dropping the flap
in his wake.

The tent fell into darkness in the same moment that Kira
realized that he was leaving her alone. The muffled sound of
his horse's footfalls made her feel more abandoned than she had
in all her life.

Indeed, she knew not even whether he would return. And that possibility troubled Kira more than she knew it should.

"The others will well enjoy this news," Nogai commented wryly.

Thierry gritted his teeth as he dismounted, wishing there was some way he could keep the tale of his deed from spreading through the camp. But Nogai was not known for holding his tongue, especially once he had some *qumis* under his belt. The fermented mare's milk was intoxicating beyond anything else Thierry had ever sampled and enough to loosen the most reluctant tongue.

That Nogai's tongue was willing made the liquor's effect all the worse.

"The tribute will be well received," he restrained himself to commenting, knowing full well that this was not the news Nogai meant. His companion laughed and clapped him on the shoulder.

"But naught compared to the news that the Qaraq-Böke has taken a woman," he teased in a low voice. Thierry spared Nogai a scathing glance.

"I take no woman," he insisted. Nogai laughed again and Thierry was dismayed to feel the back of his neck heating.

"Good news that is, for should you not claim her, there will surely be others willing to take on the burden of the task," Nogai remarked lightly. Thierry stopped dead on the path, waiting until Nogai did likewise and turned to meet his eyes. The horses nickered in the darkness behind them. The revelry from the yurt ahead beckoned them onward.

"The woman will surrender naught but the pearl," he growled. Nogai lifted his brows eloquently, evidently not convinced.

"And then?"

"She will return to Tiflis," Thierry insisted, disliking the slow grin that spread over Nogai's features.

"Surely you jest," he charged. "No time had you to ride to Tiflis on this day and even less time have you to return there.

Do you forget already that we engage the Golden Horde tomorrow?" Nogai rubbed his goatee with an affected gesture of recollection. "'Tis a battle of some import, as I recall. Mayhap I err, but 'twould seem that might distract your interest from one, admittedly small, woman." Nogai paused, darting a sidelong glance in Thierry's direction before he turned to swagger confidently to Abaqa's tent.

How Thierry loathed it when Nogai insisted on seeing matters as they were not.

"Unless, of course, your interest in the woman is more than passing." Nogai cast the taunt insouciantly over his shoulder as he walked away. Thierry stalked in pursuit, his expression turning grim. No time had he for this nonsense and already was he regretting this excursion into Tiflis.

"My interest is solely in regaining the pearl," he reiterated doggedly.

"Aye, one pearl is well worth this trouble when already you have nine," Nogai remarked with the innocent air of a child. Thierry did not trouble himself to respond to that comment. He was not in the least surprised that Nogai could not leave the matter alone. "Mayhap if you are not interested in her charms, you might indulge an old friend's fancy?" Nogai suggested impishly. Thierry's gut went cold.

"Naught but the pearl," he repeated stonily. He hated the way Nogai shook his head and clucked his tongue.

"And the good people of Tiflis will believe that?" he scoffed. "The woman will be outcast on her return, regardless of what tale she tells. And well enough we both know how outcast women earn their keep throughout the world." Nogai's voice dropped confidentially and as he leaned closer, Thierry struggled to bolster his resolve against the appeal of the inevitable suggestion.

"Should she be fated to be condemned, should you not at least avail yourself of the pleasure of her companionship?" he whispered temptingly.

Thierry did not even dare to imagine such a thing. Already was he far too aware of the woman's allure. And the reminder that her reputation had already been destroyed by his capturing her was less than welcome.

He thought of the way her eyes flashed in anger and something clenched within him.

Naught had this to do with retrieving the pearl that was rightfully part of the khan's tribute, he reminded himself savagely. The woman would have to come to terms with her own fate when she returned to town. Had she not swallowed the gem, he would not have been compelled to bring her along.

His had been a perfectly logical choice under the circumstances and certain was Thierry that the khan would feel the same way. He shot a hostile glance in Nogai's direction by way of answer and stalked ahead to the well-lit tent, leaving his companion to trail behind.

"And who will be sifting through her leavings, I wonder?" Nogai taunted unrepentantly, though Thierry resolutely ignored him. "Well would I like to see you on your hands and knees at that task," he jested. His laughter did little to ease Thierry's own doubts about the situation he had wrought.

"Mayhap you should find somewhere else to sleep tonight," Thierry found himself saying. 'Twas unreasonable how he hated the thought of his companions looking upon the softness of the witch as she slept.

Nogai laughed. "Then none will know if you keep your word," he taunted. Thierry ignored him though the accusation made his ears burn.

The pair of *keshik* guards at the opening of Abaqa's yurt stood aside when they recognized Thierry and Nogai. Thierry hesitated on the threshold, disliking that the sound of revelry was so high this early in the evening. In no shape would these men be for battle on the morrow, he thought with disgust, knowing that Nogai had oft proved that very same prediction wrong.

Mayhap if he had more Mongol blood within him, he might have similarly been able to fight well after a night of drinking.

Odd 'twas that of late all seemed to remind him of the deficiency flowing through his veins.

The khan made a beckoning gesture to Thierry that struck him as slightly mocking. He stonily refused to take offense. Abaqa had made his position clear and Thierry knew well the alternative to doing the khan's will. No matter if this subservient role increasingly chafed at him.

No matter if he was a better warrior than his khan. No matter at all.

"Come tell me of the results of your labors," Abaqa invited, no evidence in his tone of how much he had imbibed.

"Tribute from Tiflis, as you requested," Thierry offered matter-of-factly, pulling the small pouch of genuine pearls from his tunic. The khan riffled through the meager offering skeptically.

"'Tis not much," he commented, as though the insufficiency pleased him in some way. A victorious sense flooded through Thierry at the knowledge that he had not failed as anticipated. He dug the remainder of the pearls from his pocket with satisfaction.

"This part of the tribute are frauds," he added. The other man's eyes lit with a predictable gleam.

"Frauds? They dare offer frauds as tribute? Mayhap we should visit Tiflis," Abaqa suggested. A rousing cheer filled the tent. "Berke and his Golden Horde first," he shouted over the enthusiastic response of his men and turned a smug smile on Thierry. "An old score have I to settle there," he added in an undertone. "Those around me know that I do not soon forget a slight."

Thierry met Abaqa's gaze as toasts were raised by the assembled commanders at the idea of two battles in short order. He saw the animosity reflected there as their gazes locked, but refused to look away as another round of raucous music broke out. The shaman pounded his horse-headed staff on the ground and the men stamped their feet in time, until their laughter broke the rhythm.

Abaqa smiled and the tension was broken. He glanced over his military elite indulgently as he quaffed his own draught. Thierry followed his gaze and was caught short by the knowing expression etched on the features of the shaman. That man was avidly watching his discussion with Abaqa from the other side of the yurt.

The shaman's gaze brightened as he noted Thierry's regard. Thierry stifled his inevitable sense of dislike when the man threaded his way across the yurt to stand just behind the khan. He nodded to the religious man. The shaman smiled archly and responded in kind.

Had the man divined something of this battle already? Did he know anything of the woman captive in Thierry's own yurt? A sense of vulnerability assailed Thierry and he suddenly wished the woman was not there, whether she was his own or not. Better 'twould be for both of them if she was safely back in Tiflis.

The hair on the back of Thierry's neck prickled, even as he knew the very idea was nonsense. Naught could anyone see of the future. The shaman knew naught.

Abaqa rolled the pearls across his palm, much as Thierry had done earlier, and shot the younger man a sharp glance. "Clever you were indeed to suspect the value of the gems," he asserted quietly. His eyes narrowed slightly as he held Thierry's regard.

His tone was not approving. Thierry's pulse leaped in dismay. Something was wrong.

"Mayhap *too* clever," Abaqa added deliberately.

His unexpected words hung in the smoke-filled air as the other three men waited for him to continue. The pearls rolled across the khan's callused palm and gleamed in the flickering lantern light. The four men barely seemed to breathe, the flickering lamplight illuminating the curious stillness of their tanned features as the revelry continued unabated around them.

Had Thierry been too audacious? Had Abaqa's tolerance for his presence in the camp expired?

Would he share the same fate as Chinkai?

Abaqa poured the pearls into his empty chalice and considered them in the bottom thoughtfully for a long moment. He looked up suddenly, his bright gaze revealing that he enjoyed the air of anticipation surrounding him. He tapped the chalice methodically with one finger and held it up to Thierry's view.

"I once heard tell of another commander having a chalice made of the skull of an opponent who rode unsuccessfully against him," he mused. He held Thierry's gaze for a long moment. Were his words meant to be a personal threat? Thierry's pulse accelerated. Abaqa leaned forward with a confidential air that fully captured the attention of all three men.

"I would have Berke's skull bear my *qumis*," Abaqa concluded slowly.

He had named the khan of the Golden Horde, their opponents on the morrow. Thierry exhaled in silent relief.

Abaqa smiled a dangerous smile, making Thierry suspect that every nuance of his response had been detected. He struggled not to fidget with the knowledge that Abaqa was enjoying toying with him.

"'Tis time we saw what legacy you bear in your veins," Abaqa suggested with seeming indifference. His lids dropped as he watched his own fingertip slide around the rim of his chalice. Thierry wished he could see the expression in the older man's eyes. "You should have no qualms leading the right wing on the morrow," the khan added flatly and his lip curled condescendingly before he continued. "We shall see soon enough whether you are truly as stealthy as the black wind itself."

Thierry's heart skipped a beat at the risk and the opportunity, though he carefully schooled his features as he nodded.

Was this the opportunity he had been waiting for? Was this the chance that would prove his ability as a leader? A single *tümen* of ten thousand men riding under his command on the morrow. Should Thierry manage to prove his loyalty and survive this test, it could be the first step to establishing his own foundation of support within the tribe.

"May the Golden One's blood bring you luck," Abaqa concluded, his tone revealing that he expected exactly the opposite to occur.

And should Thierry fail? The expression in the other man's eyes told him that any failure on the field would be interpreted as disloyalty to the new khan. Abaqa held Thierry's gaze that he might see the fullness of the threat before snapping his fingers impatiently for more *qumis*.

"I thank you for your salute," Thierry said politely. He did not need to look to know that Nogai had detected the same skepticism in Abaqa's eyes.

Thierry's gaze sought the shaman's regard seemingly of its own accord. The shaman quirked a knowing brow and smiled a secretive smile. Thierry's resolve to ride successfully from the field redoubled in that one long moment.

He would show them all of what he was made on the morrow.

Chapter Three

Thierry was surprised to find the shaman behind them when he and Nogai finally abandoned the khan's yurt and gained the relative silence of the night. The man moved more silently than Thierry could fathom and he felt a twinge of annoyance at his presence. The shaman smiled anew as though he had detected the path of Thierry's thoughts.

"An assumption you make that you will succeed on the field tomorrow," he purred silkily. Thierry shot a glance to Nogai. His companion said naught, but 'twas easy to detect his nervousness at the unexpected comment.

"Not unreasonable would such an expectation seem to be," Thierry observed, hating that he was beginning to question the matter himself. No power had this man in truth, he reminded himself. Political aspirations of his own had the shaman and the truth was clear to all who dared to see. Indeed, how could he manage to divine the future before it occurred? Illogical 'twas.

The shaman's eyes glittered in the shadows and the moonlight gleamed on the polished wood of his staff. Beneath such light, the horse's head seemed to take on a life of its own and Thierry fancied that the hoof at the base of the staff stamped impatiently in the dirt of its own accord.

Suddenly the sounds of celebrating in the khan's yurt

seemed much, much farther away. They were alone under the moonlight, just the three of them. The sounds of merrymaking were more muted than Thierry knew them to be in truth. Was this some sorcery of the shaman's? He looked into the ancient eyes of the shaman and felt as though they had been magically shifted to some other world.

Indeed, the world he knew seemed too far away in this moment.

Nonsense 'twas. But the shaman's smile widened despite Thierry's conviction.

"Naught have I to fear from you and your ambitious dreams," the shaman intoned as he leaned closer to Thierry. Nogai took a tentative step back, but Thierry refused to follow suit. He would not let this man intimidate him, no matter how close his words struck.

"Shown to me 'twas," the shaman hissed when Thierry said naught. He rattled the bag of sacred sheep bones he carried for making his predictions and his eyes narrowed as he leaned yet closer.

Thierry did not dare recoil or break the man's regard.

"The gods showed me their hand in your fate and 'twas not a pretty sight, Qaraq-Böke. Aspirations have you, 'tis evident to all, but all your ambitions will amount to naught. Tiflis was but the beginning." The shaman arched his brows high and sneered. Thierry knew a moment of dread but he stifled his fear, hoping it did not show in his eyes.

"Naught," the shaman repeated. He smiled with relish as he cast a scornful glance over Thierry. "A failure will you make of your life and, worse, 'twill be by your own hand that you fail."

That last proved the fallacy of the tale. Success did Thierry want and well enough did he know himself to understand that he would never forsake his own ambitions.

"Naught do you know of this," Thierry argued skeptically. The shaman's eyes widened at his disrespectful tone.

"Do I not?" he mused, his arching brow eloquently conveying his skepticism. "Mayhap you know better than I. Mayhap you can divine the future better than I. Mayhap you have garnered the support of more powerful spirits than I in your short life." His lip curled as he paused to glance over Thierry.

"Mayhap," the shaman sneered. "But I think not." He spun on his heel and his white cloak swirled out behind him, the colorful strips that hung from it dancing in his wake. "Mayhap we shall see on the morrow who knows best." He cast the words over his shoulder with a carefree air and they hung ominously in the night.

Thierry refused to respond. Nogai shivered openly when the shaman turned away, but Thierry resolutely held his ground as he watched the man go.

Threatened he had been before and he would not take this taunt any more seriously than the others. 'Twas but a game to disarm him and undermine his confidence.

Victory would be theirs on the morrow and Thierry knew the fact well. And when ultimately his own success was rewarded, as Thierry had no doubt it would be, the shaman's error would be clear for all to see.

Thierry let his horse run with the others for the night so that it might graze. For a long moment he let the harness swing from his hand, his gaze tracing the beast's path. What had he wrought of his life this day? Naught but trouble, as far as he could see.

And yet more trouble, of an entirely different nature, awaited him at his own hearth. He turned with a frown and stalked back to his yurt in poor humor. 'Twas humiliating enough for Nogai to joke about who would sift the woman's leavings, but 'twas doubly unnerving to find himself resenting the other men's delight in discovering that the woman was not his whore.

Never mind his rising anticipation at the knowledge that she awaited him just steps ahead. He should not have returned to Abaqa's yurt. Even if Nogai had insisted on a fortifying shot of *qumis* in the wake of the shaman's warning.

Thierry would ignore the woman. No use had he, after all,

for women or the vulnerability they created. Thierry wondered if he had imagined the glint in the khan's eye when he had confessed to taking her. Foul luck it had been indeed that a flushed Nogai had spilled the entire story. Thierry had been asked for naught but affirmation, which he could not deny.

Witch. Already had she turned his life on end. Was she at the root of this new uncertainty stalking him? Had Abaqa changed his mind about Thierry in truth, or did he simply continue to toy with Thierry? And if Abaqa *had* changed his mind, had the witch somehow contrived the change? Did she take retribution for her captivity?

The thought was more than unsettling. Witchcraft or not, her very presence had undermined the security of his position within the tribe, just as he had feared. Women meant vulnerability in a culture where all pursued their own interests alone. 'Twas as simple as that.

Mayhap 'twas time enough he gave up this vagabond life. After all, the Mongol strain was but a quarter of what coursed through his veins.

The unexpected thought caught Thierry completely off guard. He actually considered the possibility for the barest instant before discarding it with disgust.

What nonsense was this? No other life had he. Khanbaliq tempted him, but he resolutely pushed that recollection aside, as well. Naught was there for him in Khanbaliq, even if he chose to ride across the width of Asia to return to that town.

This was his life. *This* was the path he had chosen. And the labor of his years was destined to bear fruit, sooner or later. Thierry could feel it. Mayhap it had been too soon when the old khan died, but he was young enough to wait out Abaqa's reign. And continue to consolidate his support while he waited. Leading a *tümen* on the morrow was but the first step. No interest had Thierry in casting all aside now for what amounted to no more than whimsy.

More nervous must he be about this battle than he had thought.

Thierry shoved open the tent flap in poor humor. The wan
moonlight was enough to show that the woman was not only
awake but watching him warily. What did she expect of him?
he thought irritably. He trudged into the yurt and squatted down
to light the brass lamp. Had she not tried to deceive him? Was
she responsible for his woes? When the flame flickered to his
satisfaction, Thierry swiveled without standing and silently
returned her regard.

Was that relief he had briefly glimpsed in those dark eyes?

It helped his resolve not a bit that the golden lamplight
seemed to heighten her soft femininity. The position her bonds
had forced her to take showed the ripe curve of her hips to advantage from where he crouched. Her skirts had pulled up
almost to her knees, leaving her feet and calves temptingly
bare. Thierry fancied he could discern a hint of more private
treasures in the shadows of her skirt. Her hair was cast loose
over the cushions, dark and thick. He well recalled the smoothness of it between his fingers, and he shoved to his feet with a
determined grunt.

Not for him was this.

He bent and untied her ankles with swift gestures, ensuring
that he did not touch her flesh. Was it truly as soft as it appeared?
His curiosity tempted him but he would not indulge himself.

She immediately straightened her legs, stretching with a
wince. Thierry refused to acknowledge a nudge of guilt at the
marks on her skin. She would not play on his sympathy so
readily, he told himself, knowing without doubt that looser
bonds would only ensure that she escaped.

Her movement revealed that she did wear *chalwar,* and he
cursed his mind for the tempting images it had contrived.
Naught could he have seen of anything. Clearly the woman's
very presence was addling his wits.

Witch.

He untied her hands and she rubbed her wrists but once
before she rolled and sat up. The motion brought her in such

close proximity that Thierry could smell the sweetness of her skin. The teasing scent fairly undid all of his resolve to leave her alone. Her hands leaped to the knot in the scarf that gagged her when he did not immediately untie the knot.

She hesitated, her eyes lifting reluctantly to his. Well could a man drown in the fathomless appeal of those dark orbs. And those lashes. Had ever he seen such lavishly thick eyelashes? Like some forbidden princess she was and he wondered if she deliberately flaunted her appeal.

Thierry nodded once and shoved to his feet, having no interest in getting closer to her that he might loosen the knot himself. She sighed with relief when that scarf, too, was discarded. Thierry could not help but covertly watch the rise and fall of her full breasts at the gesture.

How well would she fit beneath his hand? Too easily he recalled the delicacy of her shoulders under his grip. Everything tightened within him and Thierry realized how long he had been alone.

Because he had no space in his life for the vulnerability women brought.

Somehow the reminder carried less conviction as he regarded the woman in the soft light. She watched him warily, as though she knew not what he might do, and Thierry collected his thoughts hastily. He leaned over to grasp her slender wrist and haul her to her feet.

She was so much tinier than he. For an instant Thierry appreciated anew the difference in their relative sizes. He liked the delicacy of her features, the fact that the top of her head did not even reach his shoulder, the fragility of the wrist within his grip.

She tipped her head back to meet his gaze questioningly. Her lips were full and soft. Thierry wondered how she tasted before the flicker of trepidation in her eyes hauled his thoughts back to matters at hand.

'Twas best he ensured that she feared him. Her fear alone could eliminate his desire, and business there was to attend to.

The sooner she surrendered the pearl, the sooner Thierry could see temptation out of the way.

The latrine pits were behind the camp and open to the four winds. The emptiness of the plains surrounding them gave Thierry no qualms at letting the woman have some measure of privacy. He turned his back on her and scanned the distant hills with disinterest, forcing himself to breathe evenly. Even if she ran from here, he would catch her before she got far.

And 'twas far easier for her to search her own leavings.

When he heard her footsteps approaching, he glanced down at her, resolutely holding her gaze as he extended his hand once more between them. She shook her head firmly and he nodded.

A good draught of *qumis* was what she needed to set things on their way, he concluded. And the liquor would make her sleep soundly this night, as well, which was no small advantage, either. If he rode to battle on the morrow, Thierry certainly had need of his own rest. Little desire had he to spend his night awake and worrying about his fetching captive's escape.

Qumis it would be.

Kira shot her captor a glance of scathing suspicion when he offered her a battered tin cup. When she hesitated, he lifted his dark brows once, then drained half the cup's contents in one swallow. He offered the remainder to her once more.

Clearly she was supposed to drink it. Kira accepted the cup, sniffed tentatively and winced at its content's foul odor. Swill! She glanced to the warrior dubiously. He nodded once, firmly, and let his fingertips stray suggestively to the hilt of his knife.

Drink or die. 'Twas not much of a choice, but there was a possibility that this vile substance would not kill her.

A very small possibility.

But how would she ever force it down? Kira flicked a glance to the warrior, realizing in the same moment that there was no chance he might look away. She would have to drink it. She eyed the evil brew, took a deep breath and drained the cup in one swallow.

The liquor burned a path to her belly. Kira coughed at its unexpected heat and felt tears come to her eyes. The warrior swore under his breath. She took a shaky breath when she recovered herself and glared at him reproachfully through her tears.

He might have warned her that it was a concoction to be sipped.

The warrior said naught, merely refilled her cup. Kira almost rolled her eyes. Surely he did not expect her to drink more?

Although, to her surprise, the fire in her belly had diminished to a rather comforting glow. He hesitated before he handed her the refilled cup, lifting it toward his lips and making a series of sipping gestures.

Did he think her completely witless? That much she had deduced already. Kira knew her lips twisted scornfully before she could stop the expression. She nodded hastily and took the cup, dropping her gaze so she would not have to see his response.

Their fingers brushed inadvertently in the exchange, making Kira inordinately aware once more of the quiet intimacy of their surroundings. The drink unfolded a heat in her veins, making her uncomfortably aware of her companion's allure.

But this warrior had no use for her. Had he wanted her favor, he would already have taken it, when she was bound and unable to fight him.

Unless this liquor was part of a greater scheme. There was an unsettling thought. Kira's gaze slipped of its own accord to his full *chalwar* trousers. Her eyes widened at what she found and her gaze flicked immediately to his.

The warrior arched a brow, seemingly tempting her with the possibility.

Kira caught her breath. She was trapped in truth. No one would help her here, even if she screamed. Kira was suddenly, and mayhap tardily, well aware of the precariousness of her position. She inched backward, hoping he might not guess her intent.

His gaze hardened, making her heart skip a beat, then he

pointed one finger at her. This was the moment Kira had dreaded, she was certain of it. She swallowed and nodded once in acknowledgement, powerless to look away from him. He quickly flicked his finger at the cushions on the side of the yurt farthest from the flap. Kira frowned uncomprehendingly and he growled in annoyance, repeating the gestures with the addition of closing his eyes and dropping his cheek to rest on one hand.

He said something to her in Mongol. He pointed to himself and gestured in the direction of the door, then said something else.

Was he telling her that they were sleeping separately? Impossible. Truly she was finding only the meaning she sought in his utterance. It could not be.

Kira carefully put down the cup and repeated his gestures rapidly. "I will sleep here and you will sleep there?" she asked doubtfully. It could not be so. The warrior watched her avidly. He nodded once when she finished and looked up at him inquiringly.

This was beyond belief. Surely she had misunderstood. Mayhap he meant *after*…

Kira had to ask the embarrassing question. There was no other way to be certain.

"Do you mean to couple with me?" she asked, feeling the heat of a flush stain her cheeks. The warrior's expression remained impassive and Kira knew he had not understood. She scowled. How…? But of course.

Not having the audacity to look directly to him, Kira made a fist and inserted her other index finger into the space. She pumped the finger up and down in the space, certain there could be no doubting her meaning.

The warrior immediately shook his head quickly in denial.

He said something that Kira did not understand and she did not dare to be relieved too soon. With a grunt of frustration, he held out his hand between them. Kira stared at his outstretched palm for just a moment before she understood.

The pearl! He wanted only the pearl!

"No more do you desire of me than the pearl?" she demanded breathlessly, barely able to believe her luck.

The warrior said something and tapped his outspread hand with one fingertip.

Only the pearl. Praise be that her allure was so meager. Kira tucked up her feet and sipped at the contents of her cup with satisfaction, barely noticing how the warrior glowered at her change of mood.

He turned away and when his face was averted, Kira watched him with interest. It could be naught but this glow that had been sparked within her, but she noted for the first time his rugged appeal. If naught else, her warrior was well-wrought. Kira smiled to herself at the whimsy of the thought, her interest captured when he produced some flat bread and what looked to be cheese.

Indeed she was hungry. The warrior crouched down and made easy progress through the food. It seemed he had forgotten Kira's presence. She cleared her throat pointedly, raising her brows when she caught his eye.

The warrior shook his head firmly.

So she was to be starved! Fine! It seemed she had counted her blessings too soon. Kira drew herself up proudly at his refusal and defiantly took a great draught of the liquor as she held his regard. If naught else, she would drink!

The woman made it through another cup before she fell asleep. Thierry grudgingly admired her stamina as he sat motionless and watched the gentle rhythm of her breathing. She had slid down on the cushions and lay on her back with the confidence in sleep shown only by children and drunkards.

He cautiously moved forward but she did not stir, her breathing unaltered by his approach. Thierry knew she slept in truth. He crouched beside her, fascinated by the way her rosy lips had parted, the dark crescents of her long lashes splayed against her cheeks. He cast a glance over the length of her and wondered if townsfolk truly slept in their clothing.

He most assuredly did not. It took but an instant for the idea to trickle into Thierry's mind before he leaned over and carefully unfastened her djellaba. She stirred slightly and mumbled something in her sleep beneath his fingers.

Thierry froze, fearing he had awakened her.

But the woman fell silent once more and slumbered on. Thierry returned to his task, anticipation rising in his chest.

It was only the *qumis* that did this to him, he told himself resolutely. 'Twas the liquor alone that fed his fascination with her. He caught his breath despite his assertion when he peeled her *kurta* away, its removal revealing the drape of her trousers. Thierry's fingers trembled slightly as he divested her of the *chalwar.*

She was perfectly golden from head to toe, her skin as unblemished as the finest silk. Little doubt had he that she would be as soft, but now that opportunity beckoned, Thierry could not bring himself to touch her.

Her breasts were full, the nipples rosily dark, her waist temptingly small, her hips gently flaring. Her skin was so smooth that he almost could not believe it was real, even though the whisper of her breathing filled the tent. Thierry took an unsteady breath and reached out one hand tentatively to caress her flesh, just to be sure.

Vulnerability.

The word shot through his mind and brought his hand to a halt. The heat from her skin rose to tease his palm held less than a handspan above her. He swallowed with difficulty and pulled his hand back, knowing she was not his to touch.

But he could not tear his gaze away and he retreated just a short distance. He sat on the cushions, his bread forgotten as he watched her sleep. Thierry found himself memorizing every curve, noting every mole, every dimple, fascinated by the differences between the two of them.

Impossible 'twas that even a woman could be so small and perfectly formed.

She murmured once more much later and he feared anew

that she would discover him, her incomprehensible words making those full lips stir in the most intriguing ways. Then she turned toward him. Thierry's heart fairly stopped, so certain was he that those dark eyes would fly open and instantly be filled with accusation.

But he could not move, watching transfixed as she rolled gracefully onto her stomach. Her hair spilled leisurely over her shoulder in a dark cascade that covered her back from shoulders to waist and spread over the cushions. She pointed her toes and he followed the gesture hungrily. She sighed as she nuzzled the cushion, the sound drawing his gaze back in time to see her slim fingers stretch to span the embroidered cloth. She murmured and rubbed her cheek on the cushion, sending her hair sliding into a glossy puddle on the carpet.

Leaving an angry network of scars on her back bare to his view.

Thierry frowned and blinked, but the marks remained. Did these townspeople flog witches? What else could have been her crime?

He dared to creep forward to peer at her marred flesh. Fresh red welts there were, signs of a recent lashing, for they could be naught else. Thierry leaned closer, inhaling deeply of her sleepy scent as he noted the healed marks below the new ones. He looked to the woman's features in repose and his scowl deepened. Habitual this had been, unless he missed his guess, and the matter did not sit well with him.

Who could willfully abuse such a small and perfect creature?

And what business was it of his to be angered by that fact?

Thierry hastily retreated across the yurt, fairly tripping over the unlit stove in his haste to put space between them. He crouched down, his gaze returning of its own accord to thoughtfully trace the network of scars.

What could she have done to merit such punishment? 'Twas a puzzle he was unlikely to solve. He sat, only half aware of the silence gradually descending over the camp as he watched her sleep and teased his mind with the search for an explanation.

'Twas only much later when his own exhaustion threatened to claim him that Thierry could turn away. He retrieved the scarves from the center of the yurt and stared down at her for a long moment. He heaved a sigh before he bent to tie her ankles once more.

'Twould be foolhardy to trust her, he knew, but still he did not like his task. And was the task any less effectively done if he wound the cloth between her ankles that they did not chafe? Or what did it matter if the bond was less tight than it could be? She was drunk and fully asleep and he would bar the only exit himself.

Thierry tied her wrists together in the same manner, stunned when the woman rolled to her back. She stretched her bound hands high over her head even before he had knotted the scarf. The sight of her stretching right beneath him, her back arched and nipples straining high fed his imagination only too well. The idea of her beneath him in truth fairly undid his resolve not to touch her, and his hands shook slightly as he hastily tied the knot.

He promised her. Panic flooded through Thierry and he retrieved the blanket he usually slept in, hastily tossing it over her that temptation might be at least hidden from view. No consolation was her murmur of pleasure. He glanced down to find her smiling slightly in her sleep as she snuggled into the covering.

Considerably more disgruntled than he felt he ought to be, Thierry turned abruptly away. He shed his own clothes impatiently and rolled himself in a blanket with unconcealed annoyance, convinced that it was particularly cold this night.

Kira awoke with the sense that something had gone foul in her mouth. Her stomach rolled and her eyes flew open with the certainty that she had need of the outdoor facilities.

The shadowed interior of the tent drifted into focus and Kira frowned in recollection, not having any explanation at all for the soft warmth that caressed her skin. She put one hand down that she might sit up on the cushions, discovering that her wrists were bound in that same instant. Her feet were similarly tied and she scowled irritably, swinging her shoulders so that she abruptly sat up.

The blanket covering her midriff fell away. Kira gasped to find herself nude. Her breasts were bared to both the chilly morning air and the inscrutable gaze of the man crouched on the opposite side of the tent.

He neither moved nor spoke, but Kira was past expecting anything different from this warrior. She was mortified when he did not look away, though, and clutched the blanket with both hands, hauling it over her breasts. Barbarian. Kira hoped he had not noted the way her nipples had beaded under his perusal, knowing all the while how unlikely 'twas that he would fail to observe anything at all.

He stood, his movements as economical as always. Kira started when she saw that he wore naught at all, her gaze stopping stubbornly at the thick pelt of hair on his chest. As he moved closer and she stared at his chest, she noted despite the poor light that a mark stretched across his skin from beneath the wiry dark hair. The mark extended toward his shoulder and Kira discerned that 'twas in the shape of a cross.

Could he be Christian? Well she knew that the sect used the cross as the symbol of their faith but never had she seen a believer mark his own flesh. When he paused before her, she could see the distinctive port-wine color of a birthmark and frowned in confusion. He had been born with such a distinctive mark upon his skin?

Reluctantly, Kira looked up to meet his eyes and more immediate questions filled her mind. What had happened the night before? So little did she remember after his promise—if indeed he had promised what Kira thought he had. She panicked slightly at that acknowledgment, scooting backward when he took another step toward her. He paused, his eyes narrowing slightly, and she dared not drop her gaze for fear of what she might see. Too close he was, for she felt that she could feel the heat from his skin.

Worse, she could smell him, and the scent did naught to bolster her resolve. He smelled warm and spicy, and that unfamiliar warmth, which she could no longer blame on the drink, coiled once again in the depths of her belly. Kira clutched the blanket as she felt her color rise and knew she could no longer hold his regard.

"Well I thought that you did not intend to take advantage," she charged breathlessly, holding the blanket before her like a barrier as he regarded her silently. "Where are my clothes? Why am I naked? What happened?"

He grimaced and used the same sign language he had used the night before, speaking as he did so in that incomprehensible tongue. He pointed to her, bending to scoop up the cup he had offered her the night before and making a sipping motion. Kira nodded quickly.

That part she recalled well enough, she thought irritably, wishing he would hasten to the heart of the matter. He pointed to her once more, closed his eyes and dropped his cheek to one palm.

Kira nodded impatiently once more. "Aye, that I well enough understand, but I would know what *you* did last night," she insisted. When he did not immediately respond, she pointed imperiously to him and lifted her brows in silent query.

The warrior nodded, speaking quickly as he indicated himself and pointed to a discarded blanket by the tent flap. So he had done as he had said. Kira expelled a sigh of relief, the gesture bringing her bare nipples in contact with the soft wool once more.

"But what about my clothes?" she demanded with newfound dismay. He looked blank and she glanced pointedly down behind the blanket at her nakedness. He frowned and swept a hand before himself in a gesture that compelled Kira to note his nudity, dropping his cheek to his palm once more.

So, he slept naked. Kira shook her head resolutely when he gestured to her and lifted his brows. "Nay, I do not sleep naked," she affirmed, spotting her *kurta* with relief. She stretched to reach it with some difficulty and when she managed to grasp it, shook it in his direction. "I sleep with this."

He shrugged, as if disinterested, turning away to haul on his *chalwar* and his boots.

Kira stifled a very feminine surge of irritation that he had so little interest in her nudity. Not easy for her pride was it that he so readily admitted to finding her unattractive, and she struggled to her knees, letting the blanket drop away. Little point was there in shielding herself from him, for he undoubtedly had more interest in his horse.

Men, she thought with disgust, surprised to find his hand heavy on her shoulder when she tried to rise. How had he moved across the space so quietly and quickly? He frowned and shook his head, leaning over her to untie the scarf that bound her wrists.

That dark thicket of hair on his chest brushed against her shoulder and Kira took the opportunity to study him through her lashes at such close quarters. Though he was bigger than she, there was not an ounce of spare flesh on his body, all of it lean strength and muscle.

His eyes were gray, she noted with amazement, wondering at his heritage, for his eyes were not as narrow as the Mongols', either. She felt that increasingly familiar tingle of awareness when his fingers brushed her skin, knowing all the while that 'twas futile and foolish to feel anything at all for a bloodthirsty warrior like this.

But he had not abused her, she was forced to concede. Fixed on his task, he dropped to one knee to undo the binding at her ankles with surprisingly gentle fingers. Lucky for her 'twas that rape was not among his objectives, Kira concluded as she noted the disparity in their sizes once more. Little enough was there she might have done to defend herself against one so much larger and stronger.

Mayhap 'twas a blessing that he liked her not, she reflected, watching his strong fingers make short work of the tie at her ankles.

Her father might be pleased.

Surprisingly enough, Kira found that neither the warrior's apparent disinterest nor the promise of her sire's grudging satisfaction sat well with her. Clearly, her irrational thinking of the night before still plagued her.

Her stomach rumbled once more and the warrior spoke brusquely, indicating her garments with an imperious finger. Kira hastily donned her *kurta, chalwar* and djellaba, grateful that he seemed to understand her haste when he immediately opened the tent flap and hastened her to the latrine.

The most savage expulsion of her life left Kira weak-kneed with relief when 'twas over. She inhaled shakily, passing one hand over her sweat-beaded brow. Knowing she had no choice, she turned to look, gasping aloud at the sight of the creamy pearl reposing amidst the dirt.

Kira glanced to her warrior, but he was scanning the horizon, frowning thoughtfully at the dawn with his arms folded impatiently across his chest. Her heart pounding erratically, she flicked the pearl into the grass with her toe and rolled it around under her foot.

Convinced he was distracted, she finally picked up the pearl and slipped it surreptitiously into her pocket. She looked guiltily to him again, but he evidently had not noticed her furtive move and she willed her heart to slow.

For no intention had Kira of surrendering the gem as yet. At least, not until she knew his plans for her.

Kira knew only too much about broken promises. He might not have abused her so far, but Kira would be sure of his intent before surrendering her only asset. Well might the warrior be biding his time, only to strike a more telling blow once he had what he wanted from her.

Kira strolled toward him as nonchalantly as she could manage, rubbing her troubled stomach to ease its aching. He turned that sharp gaze upon her and frowned, extending his hand between them in silent demand. Kira jumped at the abruptness of the gesture, then shook her head. She hoped against hope that she looked as convincing as she had the day before. His scowl deepened as he glanced back to the space she had used, offering his hand once more insistently.

"Nay, I did not pass it yet," Kira lied. She shrugged as though she did not understand the matter.

The warrior's brow darkened thunderously before he abruptly strode back to the spot where she had crouched. The precision with which he went to the exact location sent Kira's heart plummeting. Much more had he observed than she had suspected and she feared suddenly that he might have seen her covert retrieval of the gem.

Had she left some mark in the dirt when she pushed it to the grass? She knew not and her heart pounded as she watched. He peered into the dirt, then strode back to her impatiently a moment later and grasped her elbow as he hastened her back to the tent.

Kira hesitated just inside the opening, not at all trusting his grim expression as he hauled on a short *kurta* with long sleeves that gleamed with the luster of silk. He left the *kurta* untucked and pulled a coat of mail over it, followed by a leather cuirass that laced over his chest. He looked as though he were dressing for battle, though Kira was an uneducated judge of such matters, and she could not help but wonder where he was going.

And what he was going to do with her.

Finally the gold-trimmed tunic he had worn the day before was pulled over the laced leather. He buckled on a scimitar, lashed a knife to the inside of his left forearm and scooped up an iron helmet lined with leather, jamming it on his head. His gaze fell on Kira as he fastened the strap under his chin and she fairly fidgeted beneath that steady regard.

He could not know that she had lied to him. Kira dropped her gaze that he might not see the truth in her eyes. Mayhap, with luck, he would merely think her uncommonly modest.

The warrior grunted to himself, undoubtedly making a comment on her response, and Kira dared to peek between her lashes as he retrieved his weapons. Had she not seen the evidence herself, she would not have imagined that he could look more forbidding than he had already. This sight, though, made her fold her hands cautiously together before herself.

For what battle did he gird himself? And what was going to happen to her?

She was only too well aware of the weight of his regard upon her, although she did not dare meet his gaze. Neither would she cower, and so the two stood silently for a long moment, Kira feeling each heartbeat pass with agonizingly slow speed.

The warrior remained silent, not a clue to be gleaned from his stony features when Kira glanced between her lashes yet again.

Mayhap he knew what she had done. Mayhap he had seen. Mayhap he was granting her one last opportunity to confess.

Mayhap she should have given him the pearl, she thought wildly.

No further time was she allowed to reflect upon the matter. A round shield, a bow and pair of quivers were the last items the warrior took. Then Kira found herself being hustled outside and through the rows of round tents, trepidation making her heart race.

Chapter Four

"**P**ersian, are you?"

Kira started at the sound of that achingly familiar language and almost turned before she caught herself. She frowned and scrubbed the filthy garment she had been commanded to wash, wishing any would-be companions would leave her alone.

The warrior had left her to wash clothes under the direction of an ancient harridan, and wash clothes she would. At worst, the task occupied her hands, if not her mind.

Although there was absolutely no need to make idle conversation with any of the other women standing knee-deep in the stream. None whatsoever.

Why would any of these women talk to Kira? Grist for the gossip mill, no more than that. Surprisingly, her relief to understand anything anybody said had nearly overpowered her usual caution. Long ago Kira had learned that her business was naught but hers alone.

"Indeed, you well look Persian. Certain am I that I have not seen you in the camp before, so you must be newly arrived."

Unfortunately Kira's lack of response did not seem to be affecting the woman's friendliness. The woman dunked a garment alongside Kira and Kira noticed the dark gold hue of the woman's skin. Persian skin. Slender fingers had she, much like Kira's, though Kira could see that the nails had been broken, and graceful hands that moved as though they had once been pampered now bore hard calluses.

Kira's gaze dropped stubbornly to her own hands and the similarity was inescapable. Would her hands soon be so abused? And what of the rest of her? She plunged the dirty garment into the river up to her elbows so that her hands were lost in the murky water.

The woman sighed. "I had so hoped you would be Persian," she said softly. There was no missing the subtle recrimination in her tone, and the familiarity of the language rolled around Kira's heart, entreating her to respond. "'Tis tedious to have none to talk with in one's own tongue."

Curiosity got the better of Kira with that comment. Too close 'twas to her own thoughts that she could not at least look to this woman. Kira schooled her expression carefully before she glanced up.

Her companion could not have been more than a few years older than Kira, for there was a youthfulness to her complexion that could not be subdued. She was slim and a full head taller than Kira, her hands moving with the fluid grace of a woman of station. Her dark hair was long but coiled back behind her head, several threads of silver catching the sunlight.

She smiled and though the gesture was welcoming, it revealed the unexpected hardness that dwelled in her dark eyes. Bitter she was, for all her solicitude, and Kira wondered what she had endured in the Mongol camp.

Did Kira dare ask?

"I am Persian," Kira confessed in as noncommittal a tone as she could manage. The woman's smile broadened.

"And recently arrived?" she prompted.

"Aye," Kira admitted unencouragingly. No interest had she in sharing her entire sordid tale with this stranger. The woman waited expectantly, but Kira ignored her and returned studiously to her labor.

"Ha! Right on both counts I was, then." The woman picked

up her own work with satisfaction, but Kira let the remark pass without comment.

The silence between them was an uneasy one and Kira fancied the other woman was waiting for a confession of sorts. Kira scrubbed the dirty cloth determinedly, well aware the watchful eye of the old one on the riverbank was missing naught of this exchange.

"Persian I was once, as well," the woman continued conversationally.

Kira gritted her teeth. Naught had she to confide in this woman.

More pressing matters had Kira to consider on this morning. Where had her warrior gone? Had he abandoned her for good or simply for the day? When would he return?

What would she do if he did *not* return? Not a backward glance had he cast in her direction when he had left her with the old one. Though it should not have surprised Kira, the matter bothered her more than she thought it should have. Nervous she was amidst these people, much more nervous than she had been before in his presence. Well enough she knew that the only change was the warrior's absence, but Kira stubbornly refused to think any further along those lines.

"The *kalat* of your man is that?" the persistent Persian woman inquired. Kira looked to her uncomprehendingly, not knowing the term. "His tunic," she whispered in explanation. Kira glanced down to find a blue garment similar to the one her warrior wore in her hands. Indeed, she had not taken the trouble to study the garment she worked on.

"Nay," she said flatly, surprised when the woman exhaled with a hiss. Her friendly manner disappeared so abruptly and completely that Kira could only watch the transformation in astonishment. What had Kira said to so dismay the woman?

"And you would wash the *kalat* of another so openly?" she demanded in obvious shock. Kira knew she looked blank, but she gestured with one hand to the old woman who had given her the work.

"She bade me wash it," she explained tersely. And little enough choice had Kira had in the matter. The Persian woman took a small step away from Kira's side as though fearing to associate with her.

"Then Black Wind is not your man?" she asked sharply.

Kira knew her lack of understanding showed and the other woman shook her head irritably. "The tall one who brought you here. He is called Black Wind," she said impatiently. Kira could not help but wonder at the import of his name. "Is he not your man?"

Kira shook her head. The woman glanced hastily from side to side before she leaned closer to whisper conspiratorially. "Have you not a man?" she demanded incredulously. Kira could but shake her head again. The woman looked surprised, then her eyes narrowed dangerously.

"Truly you cannot know the way of things here to speak to me without telling me your status," she informed Kira frostily.

"'Twas you who spoke to me," Kira observed with a grimace. Clearly the woman was mad. She plunged the garment into the brown water swirling around her knees to rinse it out, deliberately ignoring the anger emanating from the other woman.

"No matter who began the talk. 'Twas your place to tell me your lowly status," the woman maintained. Kira's interest was piqued by the reference. Lowly? "Claimed by one of the *keshik* am I," the woman continued in a lofty tone, "and of considerably higher rank than a common whore like yourself."

Whore? Kira dropped the garment into the water in her indignation. "No whore am I!" she asserted, and the woman laughed in disbelief.

"No secrets are there between we women," she said with a malicious smile. "All within the camp know there are but three kinds of women here." Kira knew her lack of comprehension showed and the woman continued scornfully. "Jest not with me. Openly claimed women like myself are there and whores who welcome any between their thighs."

Kira drew herself up taller. "Chaste am I," she stated proudly. "Clearly that makes me of the third type." To her surprise, the other woman laughed harshly once more.

"Aye, mayhap it does, though you may well regret your status soon enough."

"What mean you?" Kira demanded.

The woman smothered a smile and deliberately returned to her work. "War fodder are they," she supplied with evident enjoyment. "Like children and prisoners of war, women like yourself lead the army into battle."

"I do not understand."

"They are slaughtered first by the opposing army," Kira was informed with no small measure of relish. The woman smiled and turned deliberately back to her work. "Aye, more than one way is there to rid an army of extra and useless mouths," she commented, examining a tear in the garment as though they discussed nothing more alarming than the weather. "Mayhap if you had a whit of sense, you would part your precious thighs."

"Well you said yourself that there is no honor in that life," Kira snapped, disliking the woman's self-satisfied air.

"At least 'tis a *life*," she observed pointedly. "And should you not learn quickly the value of that, 'twill be of little import at all." The woman's eyes narrowed and she leaned closer to Kira to continue in a confidential tone that Kira did not trust. "Mayhap there are but two kinds of women in the Mongol camp," she murmured. "Those who choose to live, and those who die." Kira exhaled her breath slowly, feeling her stomach churn sickeningly as she looked in the direction her warrior had disappeared.

"Did they not ride to battle this day?" she asked, and was not relieved when her companion nodded amiably.

"Aye, that they did and a big battle 'twas to be indeed." The woman glanced up with bright eyes, a knowing smile playing over her lips as she regarded Kira assessingly. "And yet you are here, not before the troops," she observed coyly. "A pretty enough creature are you—mayhap Black Wind has hopes for you yet."

Nay, Kira thought wildly to herself. It could not be so. The warrior wanted only the pearl before he consigned her to her fate, for clear enough had he made his disinterest in her form.

Suddenly Kira was very grateful for her impulse to keep the gem and she stifled the urge to finger it where 'twas secreted within her pocket. Flatly refusing to reflect further upon her meager chances for the future, she carefully retrieved the garment from the muddy water and began to scrub once more.

The field was empty.

Birds wheeled overhead and called to each other, the dried grass of summer past waved in the wind and made a slight whispering noise as the wind slipped through it. The sky was a flawless cerulean blue and there was a faint hint of spring in the morning air.

The pastoral scene was markedly different than the one Thierry had expected. He stopped his horse in disbelief and eyed the view with skepticism. He squinted at the distant smudge of horizon but not a hint could he discern of the Golden Horde.

There was no enemy to engage.

"Where is Berke? Where are his troops?" Nogai demanded impatiently as he pulled up alongside Thierry. Thierry could only shake his head.

"I know not," Thierry admitted calmly. Nogai snorted and surveyed the empty field arrayed before them with open disgust.

"But our spies said they were here but two nights past," he protested. "With no less than two *tümen* of men. Promise of a great battle there was. Where could they have gone?"

That Nogai was disappointed, there was little doubt. Far to his left, Thierry spotted a movement, but did not bother to look closely. 'Twas the other flank, the left wing of Abaqa's own troops. Still unwilling to believe the evidence of his eyes, he scanned the horizon yet again.

Naught.

"Mayhap 'tis a trap," he suggested, unable to conceive how

Berke could have concealed his men in the dead grass. No valley was there where Abaqa's troops could be drawn unsuspectingly and encircled. No hills, no river gully, no trees. Naught but flat, unrippled plain confronted him as far as the eye could see.

"One could only hope," Nogai commented in a disgruntled tone. "Never did I expect that we would have all but an opponent this morn." Thierry glanced to his old friend in surprise.

"Well it seems that you are disappointed," he said. Nogai grinned outright.

"I had thought to collect Abaqa's new chalice," he added wickedly. "Unsporting 'tis of Berke to deprive us of the game, especially when I have oft heard how skilled the Golden Horde is in battle. Well had I been looking forward to the chance to empty my quiver into the ranks of a worthy opponent." Thierry shook his head indulgently and frowned at the empty plain once again.

"'Tis most odd that they should be gone," he mused, almost to himself. "Well must it be a trap of sorts." He looked to Nogai to find his own speculative thoughts reflected there. "Could your bloodthirstiness be sated by pursuit alone?" he asked with a quirk of one brow. Nogai laughed.

"But one way is there to discover the truth," he said and gave Thierry a bold wink before he spurred his horse. "And mayhap there is still a chalice to be retrieved this day. If not, one might hope for some game, at least."

"Then we ride in pursuit." Thierry raised one hand to his troops and beckoned them onward with a shout as he spurred his horse. A glance to his left confirmed that the commander of that *tümen* had made much the same conclusion as Thierry, for those troops were also thundering onto the plain.

Thierry's lips thinned with determination. Even should Berke be laying a trap, he would be hard-pressed to deal with the full press of Abaqa's forces. Though if Berke truly traveled with two *tümen*, the match might be closer than Thierry would have liked.

Though the stakes were high, as well. The two hordes battled for dominion over these very grasslands, extensive and fertile lands imperative to the grazing needs of both nomadic groups. Without these lands, the sheep and horse stocks would have to diminish and Abaqa's tribe would suffer less wealthy circumstances, if not outright hardship.

Abaqa's sire had held these plains long, but his demise had opened the question again for his rival, Berke, who wished to expand. 'Twas Abaqa's first test as khan and one that he could not afford to lose.

And should matters go awry, Thierry well knew that the field commanders would pay the price for that loss.

Little doubt had he that Berke's logic was much the same, and he puzzled anew over the Golden Horde's absence. They could not have simply ridden away from a battle of import like this. Indeed, if Berke bested Abaqa here, he might well be able to absorb all of Abaqa's dominion by continuing to sweep south. A new khan was at his most vulnerable in the first year of his dominion.

It made no sense. Thierry's scowl deepened and he decided that Berke must have set a trap. A particularly devious trap that Thierry had best discern before 'twas too late. Indeed, he saw in this moment the fullness of the risk he had taken in assuming the command of the right wing. Much was at stake. Too much, mayhap.

Mayhap Nogai would indeed see enough battle this day to satisfy even his taste.

Far behind the departing troops the shaman sat motionless on his white horse and watched the dust rise in the riders' wake. He lifted his nose to the wind and listened to the voices of the spirits whispering in his ears, trying to discern more than they chose to tell him this day.

Death there was in the air, for naught else could that pervasive scent that tickled his nostrils be. Well the shaman knew that 'twas no normal smell he caught in the wind, but a precognitive one that he alone of the tribe could discern.

But 'twas there nonetheless, even if only to him, and the shaman knew not its source or meaning. He frowned and asked the elusive spirits, but they confided naught new to him. Their whispers assured him only that Death had passed and done his work already.

At least the Dark One came not for him this time.

Which gave the shaman pause to think. His eyes narrowed as Qaraq-Böke's horse was lost in the distance, and he tapped his staff thoughtfully. The Dark One evidently had not come for that warrior, either.

Unfortunately. Far easier would life be without the threat of a nonbeliever becoming khan, even in the distant future. Despite the shaman's efforts to undermine him, Qaraq-Böke continued to prove himself an able warrior. Indeed, should all continue thus, the shaman might well lose credibility with Abaqa, who was a believer. Only too willing had Abaqa been to believe his rival a poor warrior at first, but a few well-won battles might easily sway his mind.

And the shaman would have to ensure that he was not on the losing edge of that transition. He clicked his tongue against his teeth with dissatisfaction, wishing the spirits would be more forthcoming on this day. Something had gone amiss, for Berke's troops were inexplicably gone. And should there be no battle, Qaraq-Böke could not be "accidentally" lost in the fray.

The shaman pursed his lips and hoped the men he had commissioned had more sense than he expected they did.

He recalled Abaqa's unruly drinking and frowned. Unless he missed his guess, made even without the sheep bones, Abaqa would not boast the longevity of his sire. Nay, something had to be done about Qaraq-Böke before 'twas too late. Annoying 'twas that the man revealed no vulnerability, no weak spot that might be turned against him and that the shaman might use for his own advantage.

Even the shaman's threats and premonitions of the previous night had apparently not affected the impassive warrior. And genuine they had been, as well. The shaman shook his head, disliking even further that Qaraq-Böke did not listen to the warnings of the spirits. One thing 'twas to be a nonbeliever who would take little guidance from a shaman once empowered, quite another 'twas to be a fool.

Aye, Qaraq-Böke could not be khan, under any circumstances. And since the shaman alone saw the threat, then he alone must correct the situation.

If only there was some weakness he could exploit. If only…

But of course. The shaman's gaze drifted down the river to where the women were washing clothes. But of course. Too quick had Qaraq-Böke been to deny his interest in the Persian woman he had captured. That he had even bothered to capture her was of note in itself, when the man had not been known to ever take a woman.

The shaman smiled to himself, pleased with his own cleverness. Perfect 'twas. For who, other than a shaman, could coax a reluctant pearl from the woman's gullet without causing her harm?

The old crone who guarded the women would not dare to defy him.

This Kira did not trust.

The white-cloaked man who had claimed her from the river hauled her through the deserted camp, dodging between rows of tents with unexpected agility. His carved staff pounded regularly into the dirt as he walked, his other hand latched around her wrist with a will that brooked no argument. His long nails bit into her skin and Kira cringed at their yellow color, but made not a sound.

Kira liked not that the old harridan had made no protest. She liked not that she had never seen this man. She liked not that he dressed differently than the others. And she liked even less that her warrior was not here to witness the transaction.

Had the warrior passed her to another? Kira knew not and her heart pounded unevenly as her mind filled with ugly possibilities. That this man was not a warrior was evident by his dress, his staff making Kira wonder if he was some sort of religious man. He selected a tent that was white, not dark like the others, and impatiently tugged Kira inside. Her mouth went dry.

'Twas shadowed inside despite the light-colored fleece and her eyes took a moment to adjust from the bright sunlight, though her companion hesitated naught. He lashed her wrists to the center pole with frightening efficiency, much as the warrior had done the night before, but this time the rope gnawed into Kira's skin. She did not dare protest, but eyed him warily, wondering what lay in store for her.

The man pushed back his hood and smiled. Kira did not trust the sight.

She could not fathom a guess as to his age, which did little to reassure her.

Though his darkly tanned skin was smooth as a child's, something lurked in his eyes that spoke of knowledge beyond what could be gleaned in one lifetime alone. His smile was toothless, the braid of his gray hair thick and luxuriantly long. His hands were as strong as a young warrior's, as she had already experienced, yet his nails were as yellowed and long as a hermit's. A drum hung at his side and his carved staff was fashioned into a horse's head instead of a crook at its top. A trio of white animal tails dangled from the staff where the horse's mane might have been.

His smile made everything within her go cold.

He said something in that vulgar guttural language they all used. Kira did not understand, but she boldly held his gaze in her determination not to show her fear. He spoke again, and though she could have been mistaken, Kira fancied that the language he used had changed. Still she did not comprehend the words, however.

"Well do I understand that you possess one of the khan's

pearls," he said next, his Persian so impeccable that Kira was taken completely by surprise.

To her own disgust she answered before she thought to do otherwise.

"Aye," she admitted. The man's eyes gleamed and Kira cursed her own stupidity. Thanks to her own loose tongue, he knew not only that she had understood but that she still had the pearl. A plague on herself for not being more circumspect.

"Aye," he repeated, clearly pleased with her response. "Then well should you know that I have been charged with its retrieval."

"By whom?" Kira demanded as though she had every right to ask. If her warrior had abandoned her, then she would know the truth of it.

The man turned slightly aside. "It matters not," he said smoothly. "All that is relevant is that you will surrender the gem to me."

"Unwilling 'tis to make its reappearance," Kira lied audaciously. The older man slanted her a glance that did naught to assuage her fears.

"Ways have I to convert reluctance to willingness," he purred as he abruptly pulled back a dark curtain on the far side of the tent.

Kira gasped when all manner of brass containers and small vials were revealed, their contents almost indiscernible in the shadows of the tent. Above the array, a carving of a man with blue skin hung, his cheeks puffed as though he blew out a flame. Beneath him was a figure of a woman, plump beyond compare and nude in her fullness. The mouths of both figures were smudged, as though offerings had been pressed against their carved lips. Kira shivered and struggled against the rope that bound her.

This she definitely did not like.

The man evidently forgot her presence as he made his preparations. As to what he prepared, Kira would rather not have known, but as she twisted futilely against the rope she realized that she might have little option. He began to hum to himself as he selected several vials from the collection. He lit a fire in the brass stove on the floor and mixed a concoction beneath Kira's horrified gaze.

Surely he would not expect her to consume this? Somehow Kira imagined its effect would be stronger than the foul liquor she had already imbibed in this camp. Wordlessly, the man lit an array of candles before the two figures. When he lit a cone and she smelled the perfumed smoke of incense, Kira had no doubt that his arrangement of vials served as an altar of sorts.

Nay, she liked this not a bit. He began to chant, his arms rising beside him as though he would embrace the sky. The candle flames seemed to leap higher, the sun brightened the white walls and roof of the tent, the faces of the carved deities glowed. His voice rose, the words incomprehensible to Kira. His foot stamped and the very ground vibrated.

He lifted the bowl containing his preparation high, then smeared some of it across the mouth of each carved figure.

He pivoted with an abruptness that took Kira's breath away. His eyes were closed, but he walked straight toward her. Kira panicked. She writhed and twisted, desperately trying to loosen the rope, but it remained resolutely knotted around her wrists as though 'twere charmed. He dipped his fingers into the lumpy mixture when he stopped beside her, and the smell was fit to make Kira retch. She jerked her head away when 'twas evident he intended to feed her the mixture.

Undeterred and without opening his eyes, he cast aside the bowl with a flick of his wrist. He grasped the back of her neck with one mercilessly strong hand without dropping any of the mixture from the other. He squeezed her throat threateningly, his other hand held before her stubbornly locked lips. Kira made an unwilling sound of protest.

The man's eyes flew open abruptly. His gaze bored into hers and Kira could not look away. He blinked naught and his gaze seemed focused deep within her soul. She felt suddenly certain that he was not of this world, though she could not have said where the thought came from.

"Open your mouth."

Kira heard the command echo in her own mind, though she knew the man had uttered not a sound. The candles he had lit sputtered, and fragrant smoke wended its way toward the ceiling as the carved deities watched avidly. Kira shook her head mutely, already feeling the man's will wind its way into her thinking.

His eyes widened and he leaned closer. His fingertips, covered with the foul-smelling concoction, touched her lips. Kira shuddered from head to toe and, against the silent protest of every fiber of her being, slowly opened her mouth.

The last thing she felt was the mealy texture of the substance forced into her mouth. Kira felt it slip traitorously down her throat, as though it had a will of its own, just before her surroundings faded to naught.

The women were not at the river when Thierry and his men returned.

For an instant Thierry feared the woman had come to some harm and his heart skipped a beat before he chided his own foolishness.

"Woho!" Nogai taunted. "Mayhap she had a better offer this night than yours!" Thierry fired an annoyed glance at his companion but Nogai only winked.

"I expect she is with the old one," Thierry said flatly. Nogai laughed, which did naught to improve Thierry's temper.

"That an old woman makes a better offer says little of your persuasive skills, my friend," Nogai teased. Thierry felt his ears redden and his irritation grew.

"Well I told you that she would surrender naught but the pearl," he growled, wishing he knew the source of his annoyance. Naught did it mean that she was not where he had left her. And certainly there was no reason for that twinge of disappointment he had felt when he had spied the empty river.

No reason at all. And there could have been no anticipation lightening his heart in returning to camp this night, especially after the complete lack of a battle this day.

Exhausted Thierry was from a fruitless day's ride in pursuit of men who were not there. 'Twas no more than that that made him leap to conclusions. The sun was sinking low and 'twas not unreasonable that the women had ceased their labor for the day.

It meant naught that she was not here. And his twinge of disappointment had been for no more than the delay. Now before he could retire, he would have to fetch her from the old one.

"Abaqa will be awaiting our report," he reminded Nogai tersely, not missing the way his *anda*'s brows rose.

"Mayhap he has had some news this day that will explain things," Nogai agreed. Thierry almost thought the other matter closed until the two dismounted and matched steps.

"And of course, the more haste is made to report to Abaqa, the sooner you might retrieve your fetching baggage," Nogai whispered mischievously.

"Clearly you have forgotten that the woman is a witch," Thierry snapped.

"Me? Nay, I have not forgotten," Nogai retorted confidently. "But 'twas not I who was so anxious to return to camp this night."

Thierry slanted Nogai a hostile glance and earned a merry grin for his trouble.

"I shall ensure the khan is quick," Nogai assured him. Thierry stifled a healthy urge to kick his friend and strode to Abaqa's yurt in poor temper.

Clear 'twas that he would have no peace until the woman was gone. Indeed, he hoped she had passed the cursed pearl this very day, that he might send her home. The thought sent a curious pang through Thierry that prompted yet another unwelcome recollection of Khanbaliq. He gritted his teeth and told himself that Abaqa's distrust was wearing down his resolve.

The sooner the woman was gone, the better.

* * *

The *keshik* guards at the khan's yurt stood aside when Thierry approached, Nogai in his immediate wake. Inside, Abaqa glanced up and grinned.

"Little enough chance had you to prove yourself this day," he commented, clearly in a jovial mood. Mercifully the shaman was nowhere in sight.

"What happened?" Thierry demanded tersely.

"Still you have not heard?" Abaqa's brows rose. "Berke died yesterday."

Thierry's heart leaped in his astonishment. "Of what did he die?" he asked.

Abaqa snorted. "Avarice," he retorted sharply. "Mayhap ambition beyond his station." He traced the design on his chair with one fingertip before glancing up sharply. "'Tis poor judgment to covet something that is mine," he said consideringly. Thierry went cold but refused to let Abaqa see that his barb had struck home.

"What did he covet of yours?" he inquired instead, knowing the answer all the while but unable to think of another alternative quickly enough. Abaqa shook his head indulgently.

"My territories," he said. He glanced away and his lips thinned dangerously. "My armies, my gold, my wives. All that is mine did he covet, for why else would he have invaded this territory as soon as my sire died?"

"I suspected as much but did not know for certain," Thierry said hastily. Abaqa leisurely looked him over, then snorted again.

"Indeed, you should understand the fact of the matter," he said. His voice dropped to a threateningly low timbre as his gaze locked with Thierry's. "'Tis not healthy for a man to crave what is mine."

"Who succeeds Berke?" Thierry dared to ask.

Abaqa smiled. "Why am I not surprised that you, of all men, would ask that question?" he mused. He tapped his fingers on the arm of his chair and regarded Thierry for a long moment before shaking his head, as if to clear it. "I know not. No clear successor is there."

"Then that is why they left the field," Nogai guessed. Abaqa flicked a glance to Thierry's companion.

"I would expect as much," he said quietly. "Undoubtedly, they have returned north to burn their Khan in a fitting manner. For the time being, it would seem there is no threat to me." Abaqa's gaze meandered back to Thierry and he raised one brow thoughtfully. "At least, not from *outside* the tribe," he added.

With that, the khan snapped his fingers and summoned a drink for himself, effectively dismissing the two warriors from his company.

An enraged roar woke Kira abruptly from her slumber.

Her father had discovered her crime. She cringed in anticipation of the lash's bite, and when none came, dared to take a breath. Kira opened her eyes with difficulty to find herself huddled on the damp ground, her wrists still bound to the tent pole, and recollection came flooding back.

She blinked to clear her foggy vision and the roar erupted again. Kira cringed at the proximity of the sound and her gaze flew across the tent.

The man in white stood before her warrior, his manner calm as he gestured toward her. The warrior was markedly less calm. Kira could virtually feel the heat of the anger emanating from him. His eyes glittered and his jaw was set. His companion with the goatee lounged in the opening to the outside. Kira met his gaze and he winked broadly. Her gaze skittered uncertainly back to the warrior.

What had angered him? And what price would his fury bear? Only too similar was this to her father's frequent tempers and she could only fear for the worst. Would he beat her? Rape her? No help was her addled mind in this matter, for it seemed to Kira that she could barely put two thoughts in order. Curse the white one and his mixture.

Should she surrender the pearl or was it already too late to save her own hide? She struggled against her bonds, able to think of naught but escape. To her dismay, her body did not readily follow her bidding and her clumsy movements were futile.

Her warrior barked a short question and the man in white shrugged. The warrior looked fit to explode when he jabbed one finger at the other man, his tight words evidently a threat of some kind. The white-robed man drew himself up taller at the apparent insult, but the warrior had already turned away.

To Kira's chagrin, the warrior turned his attention on her. She scurried backward but could not move far because of her bindings. Incapable was she of hiding her fear in this state, with her body fighting every move and the warrior's anger clearly beyond anything her father had ever let her see.

He squatted purposefully beside Kira. She cringed and his scowl deepened with displeasure as he untied her wrists. Fearing his anger was directed at her, Kira instinctively shrank away, only to have him glance to her in surprise. He touched the chafe marks on her skin with one gentle fingertip. She shivered, not knowing what to expect, certainly not expecting to look up and find him watching her with what might have been concern.

Not here. Not from this man. He cared only that she live long enough to return his property. Kira's heart skittered unsteadily, then lurched when he folded one heavy hand around hers. Naught could this mean, she told herself wildly, even as that increasingly familiar tingle of awareness launched over her flesh. The warrior snarled something at the man in white. That man shrugged indifference and the warrior's lips thinned.

He grasped Kira's elbows when she might have pulled away again, confusion puckering his brow when she gasped in response. He stood slowly and virtually lifted her to her feet, arching one brow in silent query. Kira nodded hastily, wanting no more than to be free of his unsettling touch.

When he released his grip on her, no one was more surprised

than Kira that her knees gave out beneath her. She gave a little cry as she crumpled toward the ground again and heard the white one's knowing chuckle.

The warrior swore and scooped her up before she collapsed. The tent danced around them and Kira closed her eyes weakly, despising the single tear that crept out from between her lashes.

Weakness. How she hated weakness. Especially in herself.

The warrior said something and the white one answered with apparent reluctance. Kira squeezed her eyes tightly as the warrior carried her outside, the motion of his step making her stomach roll uncertainly. She leaned closer to his warmth despite herself and found his heartbeat beneath her fingertips. Its echo was curiously reassuring and she dared to release the breath she had been holding and relax ever so slightly against him.

Just for a moment. Until she could be strong again.

She was safe, Kira thought, feeling the fog in her mind advancing to claim her once again. Nonsense, she corrected sharply, knowing the first thought was naught but whimsy.

Curiously, Kira's conviction in that fact did naught to halt her fingers from spreading across his chest. Well it seemed she would grip the beat of the warrior's heart within her very hand as all faded to naught.

Chapter Five

When Kira awakened in the familiarity of the warrior's tent, 'twas nearly dark. She rolled over and found him watching her silently. Kira's breath caught in her throat. Their gazes locked and he moved not a muscle, as though he was waiting for her to collect her thoughts.

Disconcerting it had been, to say the least, to find herself relieved to see the stern warrior in the white tent. Kira could make little sense of her response. Certainly the man had done little to endear himself to her, though she had to admit that he had not been as cruel as she had anticipated.

At least, not as yet. 'Twas a particularly heinous tactic he had in mind, she surmised, for evidently he meant to gain her trust before abusing her.

Although she was forced to concede that she could scarcely have imagined that her maidenhead would be intact after an entire night in the Mongol camp.

He rose abruptly to his feet and closed the distance between them. When he bent over her, Kira refused to show her trepidation. Her mind was clearer for the sleep and she boldly held his gaze.

Had she not known better, she might have thought that he smothered a smile at that.

He urged Kira to her feet and her guts writhed. She gasped and he seemed to understand, for he hastened her immediately outside and toward the latrine pits.

Well it seemed that matters had changed. Though Kira knew that she had never been so thoroughly voided in her life as she had been in this camp, the warrior demanded naught of her when she had finished at the pits. To her astonishment he led her purposefully in the opposite direction from that of his tent. His silence seemed particularly ominous and Kira could not help but speculate whether she had been grateful too soon.

Mayhap the time of her reckoning had come.

He led her away from the camp. Kira hoped they made but a roundabout return, but when they stepped outside a cluster of tents, her heart began to pound. His pace continued relentlessly into the open fields on the far side of the camp and Kira knew she would not stride away from this place. Naught but the grasses weaving in the wind was here and her heart almost ceased to beat when he stopped abruptly.

Was it here he intended to take her? Or did he mean to retrieve the gem with his knife? The grass rippled around them and the uncanny silence of the plain filled Kira's ears. Indeed, none would hear her scream in these remote pastures. Her heart took off at a gallop at the realization, for 'twas quickly followed by the certainty that there was naught she could do about it. He was larger than her, stronger, undoubtedly more cruel. She could fight, but the battle would not last long.

Well it seemed that she could not draw enough air into her lungs and Kira feared she might faint. She felt the utter stillness of her companion and dreaded his intent before he raised his fingers to his lips and let out a long, low whistle.

Then he stood perfectly still, waiting it seemed, his grip relentless on her arm. Kira scanned the horizon in confusion, fancying she heard a faint sound stirring above the silence. The warrior squeezed her arm once and lifted a heavy finger to point into the middle distance, never uttering a word. Kira suddenly saw the dark shapes approaching.

What was this? Beasts he needed for his diabolical plan? She could not even imagine what wickedness he planned to wreak upon her.

Four horses became discernible as they drew closer, their manes blowing loose, their hoofbeats becoming more and more distinct. Kira glanced up and fancied that the warrior's features softened as he watched the creatures run. She could not be sure and looked back to the beasts in confusion.

They ran directly toward them. Kira was certain they meant to run right over them. There was a death she would expect to be painful, though it made no sense that the man beside her held his ground. When the creatures bore directly upon them and Kira thought she could see their eyes, she bolted.

The warrior impassively tightened his grip on her arm before she could take a second step. Well it seemed he had anticipated her move, but as the horses drew yet nearer, Kira could not even summon surprise.

They whinnied and she covered her ears with her hands, knowing they were too close to turn. Kira cringed and turned toward the warrior, his grip on her arm allowing her precious little movement, indeed. Her heart pounded and she cowered against him, but the horses veered off unexpectedly.

Kira glanced up in astonishment. Her fear transformed magically to delight when the horses cantered around them in an ever-tightening circle to slow their pace. He had summoned them. And they had come. Kira looked to her warrior with newfound respect. Never had she known anyone who had a way with beasts. The creatures walked the last few paces between them, one nuzzling the warrior's other hand with its nose.

They had not been trampled to death. Kira watched in amazement as the warrior scratched the beast behind its ears with what might have been affection. When the one with cream markings on its brown coat nudged its nose against her knee, she dared to stretch out a hand and mimic the warrior's gesture.

To her surprise the wild creature tolerated her tentative caress. Its coat was thicker and softer than she might have anticipated and Kira reached to touch the furry curve of its ear. The horse abruptly snorted and proudly tossed its head, backing away to fix her with an assessing eye.

She feared it would run away and the warrior would be angry with her, but the horse stood his ground and regarded her cautiously. Kira remained as still as she could, sensing this was part of the warrior's strategy with the creatures. She barely dared to breathe as the beast eyed her warily.

A long moment later, the horse stepped toward her again. It ducked its muzzle under her hand demandingly this time and Kira could not help but smile.

It liked her. She rubbed its ears, daring to press her fingers a little more firmly into the fur, and the horse amazingly leaned into her caress.

The warrior released her elbow abruptly, moving with a speed that startled her. In the blink of an eye he had cast a harness over the head of the horse before her. The creature tossed its head indignantly and pranced for a few paces. Her warrior did not relinquish his grip on the reins and the horse soon settled.

Could it be that the horse had been harnessed before? Kira could not imagine that a wild creature would take so readily to the restraint otherwise. But no time had she to reflect upon the matter. Suddenly the warrior dropped the reins to the ground and stepped on them, simultaneously gripping her waist and lifting her. Kira panicked.

He would not put her on this horse alone!

She struggled against him and the horse nervously danced sideways. The warrior dropped her to her feet once more though he did not release his grip on her waist. He said something quickly to her, but Kira could not understand him. She shook her head desperately, unable to think beyond her terror of being on the horse.

His voice dropped when he spoke again and she fancied he spoke more slowly. Despite that, Kira looked stubbornly at the ground, unwilling to aid him in any way with whatever foul plans he had for her. The warrior muttered something and gripped her chin, relentlessly forcing her to meet his eyes. Once again she was startled by their silvery tone, that momentary surprise long enough for him to snare her attention.

"Tiflis," he said slowly, his accent making it difficult for Kira to immediately understand his meaning. "Tiflis," he repeated. She nodded quickly. Tiflis. What about Tiflis? He pointed to her and the horse, turning to gesture toward the horizon past the Mongol camp. "Tiflis," he said again, and Kira understood.

He was sending her home.

Her heart fluttered but she did not dare to hope until she knew the fullness of his plan. Too good to be true this was and a catch there must be. Kira pointed tentatively to the warrior, not daring to touch him with her fingertip.

"Tiflis?" she asked. Uncertain she was whether he meant to accompany her, but he shook his head firmly. He repeated his assertion and Kira nodded once more.

She was going home alone. Was it possible that she had misunderstood him? One glance to the resolute gleam in the warrior's eyes destroyed that illusion. Relief flooded through her and she dared not think too much about the matter. No understanding had she of his reasoning, but she would grasp the unexpected gift with both hands and flee directly home.

But she had to ride this horse to get there. She turned a wary eye on the horse, knowing full well that the creature was her only possible means of transport. Mayhap to go home, she could conquer this fear.

When the warrior lifted her once more, Kira did not struggle and the horse did not stir as her weight was settled on its back. The warrior flicked an imperious finger at Kira's knee and she obediently lifted it over the horse's back, her color rising with the awareness that the warrior was seeing far more of her *chalwar* than was truly appropriate.

But well enough had he shown that he was not tempted by her, she reminded herself fiercely, accepting the reins from him as her nervousness rose.

Could she really ride this creature all the way home?

The warrior stayed her with one hand and she watched as he unlashed the sheath on the inside of his left forearm. A dagger obviously reposed within it and Kira's fear rose once again. What did he intend to do? Was this all a ruse to raise her hopes before he killed her? Did he mean to retrieve the pearl once and for all in this secluded spot where none might help her?

Kira recoiled when he reached for her arm. He frowned impatiently, the fact that he seemed puzzled by her response dissipating some of Kira's doubts. He tucked her hand firmly under her arm and pressed it against his side, leaving the soft flesh of her forearm turned up. Kira shivered, but he simply laid the sheath over her arm and lashed it there with his characteristic efficiency of movement.

When he released her arm and handed her the reins, Kira understood that he was giving her a means of protecting herself. When last had anyone given her anything? When last had anyone done anything for her at all? Kira looked to him in amazement, but he merely propped his hands on his hips and jerked his head in the direction she was to ride.

"Tiflis," he repeated yet again, sparing a pointed glance to the sinking sun.

Kira touched the hilt of the knife tentatively, struggling to accept what he was doing for her. A gift he had granted her that could save her life.

Impulsively she reached into her pocket and retrieved the pearl she had passed. She thrust her hand out between them and held the gem out to him at arm's length. 'Twas only fair, after all, that she give him the pearl.

He frowned as he held out his hand, then understanding dawned in his eyes as he realized what she offered. His gaze rose slowly to lock with hers and Kira fought the tremor that danced over her flesh when he deliberately took the gem from her fingers.

"Thank you," Kira said simply. She willed him to understand what she meant, touching the knife once more and laying a hand on the horse's neck.

The warrior's eyes gleamed and he rolled the lustrous pearl between his rough thumb and forefinger as he silently held her gaze. Something changed in his expression, though Kira could not have named that tentative softening in his eyes. Precious little chance had she to do so, for he half turned away and scowled when she did not urge the horse onward.

"Tiflis," he insisted flatly.

When Kira did not yet move, uncertain what kept her from doing so, the warrior raised a hand and gave the creature's rump a resounding smack. Kira yelped in surprise and desperately tried to grip the beast's round belly with her knees as it ran at breakneck speed toward home.

When she had gained her balance, she risked one glance over her shoulder to find the warrior far behind her, his hands propped on his hips as he watched her flight. The grasses waved about him but he stood completely motionless, silhouetted against the distant hills, the other three horses grazing nonchalantly about him.

Thierry found the yurt unnaturally quiet when he returned. He prowled around its interior restlessly, unaccountably annoyed that naught had appeared to change, when in fact so much had.

The shaman had moved openly against Thierry for the first time. No idle threat had he made this time, for in taking the woman, the shaman had challenged Thierry's prior claim. No doubt had Thierry that all within the camp already knew the tale. This could not bode well for Thierry's future.

Vulnerability he had feared, and vulnerability she had brought. Never had he been challenged like this; never had another dared. Although the woman was gone, Thierry wondered what fruit this incident would bear. Would his authority be questioned? His command over the *tümen* revoked? He knew not and liked not the uncertainty.

'Twas clear already that Abaqa was losing patience with him, though whether the two incidents were linked, Thierry could not say. Abaqa's threats were openly made this day and 'twas clear Thierry had gained naught of credit on the field. Berke's retreat had stolen his sole opportunity to redeem himself.

Would Abaqa cast him out? Or would he suffer the same fate as Chinkai?

Thierry scuffed at the carpets and scowled across the shadows of his yurt, startled to find his vision of the sleeping woman sprawled across his cushions as clear as if she were really there.

He turned away from the haunting image, dismayed to find his anger rising. She was gone. Headed home to her family where he should have left her. Thierry's gut clenched at the thought but he forced himself to face reality. Destined she was to spend her life sorting pearls. Mayhap she would wed one of those soft urban men. Bear him robust sons and delicate daughters.

Thierry strode out into the growing darkness, biting down on the bile that rose in his throat. She had not been his to touch. Though he tried to forget its presence, the pearl he had shoved into his pocket seemed to burn a mark in his thigh. Only too well did he understand that it was the pearl he had demanded. Thierry resolutely ignored the press of the gem as he decided to seek out some *qumis*.

He would not reflect upon the irony of the fact that she was gone just when he had naught left to lose.

No solution was it and well he knew it, but he would dismiss the woman from his thoughts this night one way or the other. And well might the *qumis* dispel some of the anger still simmering within him.

Thierry's blood heated at the realization that the woman could easily have been hurt. A fool he had been to take her from Tiflis for the sake of a pearl. Yet Thierry knew, in the same circumstance, he would make the same choice again. His fingers clenched in recollection of the incredible softness of her hair.

Mercifully, the shaman had sought the pearl first.

And the witch had tricked him. Thierry bit down his urge to smile once again and scuffed his toe in the dirt appreciatively. How she had managed to conceal the pearl from the shaman, he did not know. Mayhap her sorcery was stronger than his.

It mattered not the means. Yet again, Thierry could but appreciate the result. His gaze wandered over the tents as though he might see the distant town of Tiflis despite the obstacles and the darkness.

Stubborn witch, he corrected himself, and shook his head.

She was safer in Tiflis. Thierry forced himself to face the truth of that and sighed.

How he wished he could dismiss this niggling sense that all was not right. He had done his best for the woman. He had kept his word and she had surrendered the pearl. Their business was completed and he would do best to forget the entire matter.

Her own fate had the woman to meet. She had surrendered the gem and he had kept his promise. Now their ways must part. Despite his determined reminder, the thought did not ring as true as Thierry thought that it should.

And 'twas less easy than it should have been to turn his footsteps toward the khan's yurt and the promise of *qumis*.

'Twas dark when Kira first spotted the protective white walls of Tiflis. The sight of those walls suddenly made her consider the wisdom of her return.

How could she simply go home? How could she tell her father that she had abandoned his shop? How could she not tell him, when all the neighbors were certain to delight in sharing the tale?

What if some of the gems had been stolen in her absence?

What if everything had been stolen? How would she ever explain? How would she ever repay the loss? Kira licked her lips nervously. An ungrateful wretch of a daughter she was, in truth.

But it had not been her fault.

The assertion rang boldly in Kira's mind and she was shocked by the audacity of her own thoughts. For the first time, Kira was not willing to immediately cede to the argument she knew her father would make. How could she make her father understand that she had been powerless against the warrior's will? Indeed, he had carried her bodily from the town, despite her protest.

It had not been her fault.

A dangerous thought that was and Kira instinctively shrank away from it. Better she knew than that. And even if it was true that the blame lay elsewhere, Kira knew well that her explanation would fall on deaf ears. She blinked back stubborn tears and forced herself to face the truth.

No excuse could there be for what she had done, especially if her father's shop had sustained damage. Kira eyed the approaching walls of Tiflis and could not imagine that the jeweler's premises could have remained untended all this time without consequence. She inhaled sharply, knowing she would taste the lash yet again on her father's return.

Still, the stubborn thought that this whipping would be undeserved could not be wiped from her mind.

Impudent. Good-for-naught. Lazy ingrate. Kira called herself a string of her father's favorite insults to no effect. No choice had she made in this, and though she had been left responsible for the shop, naught else could she have done. The warrior had carried her away, despite her protests, and her neighbors had helped naught.

A dutiful daughter would have contrived somehow to stay and protect the shop, she reminded herself fiercely to no avail. Well enough she knew the argument, but hearing it echo in her mind only angered Kira. She squirmed in anticipation of the new wounds she would sport for her own unreliability and tentatively glanced back where she knew the Mongol camp to be.

Without warning she recalled the weight of a man's fingertip on the reddened chafe mark on her wrist. A gentle and warm fingertip. Kira shivered in the chill of the evening air.

Would any in Tiflis believe that she had survived a night in the Mongol camp unscathed? Still more unlikely, would they believe that she had retained her maidenhead?

Well could she hear her father's accusations ring out. A faithful daughter would never have permitted herself to be in such circumstances. A worthy daughter would not cast her chastity into doubt. A loyal daughter would not selfishly jeopardize her sire's hopes for a secure future.

The charges rang false in Kira's ears, for well she knew that she could not have effected any difference in her situation. But nay. Unfair she was being to her sire. Wise he was and always right. Kira had the scars to testify to that. Her chin set stubbornly and she pulled the horse to a halt.

She need not go home.

The mutinous thought excited and terrified Kira simultaneously. Did she dare? Did she want to dare? Or would she meekly return to the shop and await her father's return, that he might beat her for something she had been powerless to change?

'Twas more than an unearned beating at stake, though. Well enough Kira knew that no honorable man would have her after this. Not with such a taint on her name as having spent a night within the Mongol camp. Suspicions would fester in whatever remained of Tiflis despite her claims of innocence, and her sire's dream of buying his leisure with Kira's hand would fade to naught.

Kira needed not long to see where that path led. Her life would become less than it had been, for there would no longer be any promise of reward. Kira frowned in confusion as once again she compared how the warrior had treated her with her father's treatment.

No sense did it make that a barbarian who cared naught

would show her greater kindness than her own sire. Well did Kira know that her father loved her, but her frown deepened as she struggled to make sense of it all.

Mayhap love was an overrated commodity.

The thought made Kira feel guilty as soon as it formed. How could she think thus of her own sire? How could she even conceive of such a thing when he had cared for her and raised her all these years? Truly her father's cry of "ingrate" was a proper one.

Kira hung her head in shame. Mayhap her father was best left without an ungrateful daughter such as herself. Mayhap her absence alone would make him happy. Kira bit her lip and considered her plight as the horse nibbled disinterestedly on the grass.

She could not shame her sire by coming home after this.

But if she did not return to Tiflis, where could she go? Kira glanced reluctantly again over her shoulder to the horizon.

War fodder, whores and claimed women. Was there a role that she was worthy of in that? Mayhap 'twas the sole choice that would do honor to her sire.

Kira could not imagine that she deserved any better for so failing her father and she inexpertly urged the horse to turn around before she had time to question her choice.

The moon was setting when Kira fancied she caught the scent of roasting meat on the wind. She shook her head, knowing that her mind was teasing her achingly empty stomach. Surely the Mongols had already retired, as she would dearly love to do.

She rested her cheek against the horse's sleek coat as it closed the last increment of distance to the camp, liking the way the creature's warmth penetrated her skin when she closed her eyes. The creature's pace had slowed, but Kira cared naught, for well she knew it must be tired, as well. She closed her eyes and let the scent of the horse's fur fill her nostrils.

Indeed, riding was not such an ordeal as she had once

believed. And had Kira not had the gift of a horse, how might she have returned so rapidly to the camp?

Who would have guessed that something she so feared could have become her ally?

The horse nickered and Kira reluctantly sat up as the camp came into sight. Fires there were burning despite the fullness of the night, their golden light flickering between the tents, much to Kira's surprise. Laughter rose to her ears, that tempting scent of roasted meat making her belly growl anew.

The Mongols were awake.

Her warrior might still be here. Only now, Kira realized that she had been concerned that the Mongols might have left. Were they not nomads, in truth? Incredible 'twas that such knowledge could send relief flooding through her, and Kira wondered what had happened to her once clear thinking.

But in truth, the warrior was the only soul who had ever shown her any consideration. Kira looked to the blade lashed to her arm in confusion and not for the first time marveled at his deed.

Mayhap he had simply not had time to take his hand to her.

But nay. Unfair that was, for had she not slept in his tent unescorted? Kira frowned, still unable to understand the man, yet wishing she could check her anticipation at the possibility of seeing him once more. Though he might not be as enchanted to see her. Kira frowned.

What sort of reflection on her life was it that a Mongol warrior had shown her the greatest kindness she had known?

A traitorous thought that was, and Kira would not indulge it further. Had her father not fed her all these years? Kept a roof over her head? Clothed her after a fashion? Surely she was the most ungrateful child ever born to man, as he had been so fond of reminding her, if she could not value such luxuries that many others did not know.

What was she going to do now that she had found the Mongols? How would she find her warrior? The tents looked much the same and continued endlessly one after the other. And well she knew that she could not ask after him, for she spoke no Mongol.

Kira hesitated on the fringe of the camp, filled with uncertainty. Mayhap she should have left some message for her father. Guilt consumed her and she sat and inventoried her shortcomings by rote. Ungrateful, lazy, stupid, slow, scrawny, weak, female...

The laughter of women startled Kira abruptly out of her thoughts. Her glance darted from side to side as she sought some place to hide, but the cursed horse whinnied just as the women came out of the shelter of the clustered tents. Their voices stilled and Kira froze, any explanation dying on her lips. Her mouth went dry, her heart ceased to beat while the women eyed her silently.

Finally one of the women stepped forward and held a flickering lantern high. Kira could not speak, even when she recognized the nosy Persian woman from the stream. The woman smiled and Kira's heart went cold.

"You came looking for Black Wind," the woman commented with a measure of amusement. Kira shook her head in immediate denial, her heart recovering to run at an erratic pace.

"Nay, I...I..." Kira stammered, then swallowed resolutely and held up her head proudly. No gracious explanation was there for her behavior and little point could she see in not being direct after she had come so far.

"I cannot go home," she stated flatly. The woman's eyes sobered as she held Kira's regard, then she shook her head disparagingly and smiled a fleeting sad smile.

"Nay, none of us can," she said quietly, a thread of understanding in her tone. Much to Kira's surprise, the woman stretched out one hand welcomingly. "Come with us," she invited. Kira could not believe her ears.

What did this woman expect in exchange for her aid? Kira regarded the woman's hand with suspicion, knowing full well that no one offered assistance to another without another objective in mind.

"What do you want from me?" she demanded coldly, disliking this false pretense of friendship. The woman's expression became surprised.

"Naught," she said quietly, but Kira shook her head.

"Too much have I seen of the world to believe that," she retorted. The woman's gaze flicked assessingly over Kira once more and she nodded deliberately before she took a decisive step closer.

"I have been abandoned and turned out of home," she confided in a harsh whisper, her eyes gleaming in the shadows. "So well I know that 'tis easier to face this with others than alone."

Kira said naught, certain her face showed that she was unconvinced.

"Are you not hungry?" the woman asked. Kira was forced to acknowledge at least to herself that she was. "What will you eat on your own? A huntress are you, then?" The woman smiled and half turned back to the camp. "Lift your nose and smell the meat we eat this night. And tired are you after your ride? Blankets aplenty are there here to sleep under and felt tents to take shelter within."

"And what price must I pay to so indulge myself?" Kira demanded suspiciously.

The woman's voice dropped another increment. "You must trust me," she said slowly. "As I must trust you."

"A high price, indeed," Kira scoffed, though her skepticism was fading quickly.

"Aye, we both have much to lose," the woman agreed.

The silence stretched between them as they regarded each other solemnly, then the woman extended her hand once more.

"What choice do you imagine you have?" she whispered. Kira was forced to face the truth. As war fodder, she had none too long to live, anyway.

"None," she admitted heavily, hesitating for a moment before she slipped her hand into the other woman's warm grip.

The woman's fingers tightened over hers and Kira was surprised to find herself reassured by the gesture. She slipped from the horse's back and held fast to the creature's reins. Her nerves settled a little more when the beast she had grown to rely upon showed no reservations in following the Persian woman into the cluster of tents.

When Kira awoke, sunlight was shining brightly through the partially opened flap of the tent and she could smell it heating the wool felt overhead. She frowned, thinking herself in her warrior's tent once more, and wondered whether the ride to Tiflis and back had been a vivid dream.

She rolled over, fully expecting to find him watching her with that inscrutable expression on his face, but instead she met the sharp gaze of the Persian woman. Events of the previous night came back to her in a flash and she dropped her chin to the cushion, unable to deny her disappointment.

"Good morning," the woman said. Kira halfheartedly returned the greeting. How many more mornings would she see now that she had committed herself to becoming war fodder? How many days until the Mongols rode to battle once more? Kira sighed and rolled over.

"More enthusiasm will you need to show should you wish to snare a man," the woman commented dryly. "Mayhap a smile would be in order once in a while." Kira spared the woman a dark look.

"I do not expect to be claimed," she informed her tersely, not liking having false possibilities dangled before her.

"Too pretty are you to become a whore," the woman observed matter-of-factly. She dug out some flat bread and offered it to Kira, smearing some white cheese across the top of it. Kira accepted the offering gratefully, surprised to find it quite flavorful. The woman's eyes narrowed speculatively. "Unless you are not as chaste as you would maintain."

Kira grimaced at that. "Never have I known a man," she clarified flatly, secretly amazed to find herself discussing such personal matters with a relative stranger. But something there was about this life-style, something more earthbound than town living that made such conversation seem natural. And what matter if the woman thought her common? Kira would not live long enough to be troubled by such a judgment.

The woman leaned forward purposefully. "Surely you cannot believe yourself destined to walk in front of the armies," she charged. Kira glanced up from her meal in surprise.

"Aye."

The woman shook her head in unconcealed disgust and shoved to her feet. "Fool!" she snapped, leaning over to clutch a handful of Kira's hair and let it run through her fingers. "Have you never seen yourself in a glass? Truly you could aspire to being claimed, should you only trouble yourself to make the effort."

"Do not jest with me," Kira insisted through the tightness of her throat. "Well enough do I know my shortcomings."

"Believe what you like," the woman declared with a wave of her hand. She propped her hands on her hips as she regarded Kira. "But well enough did I see the look in Black Wind's eye when he brought you to the stream. That man was not aware of whatever shortcomings you imagine yourself to have."

Kira's heart leaped but she refused to indulge herself in any such hopeful whimsy.

"He is in the camp, you know," the woman confided and Kira looked to her in shock. "Aye, they all are. All of the *ba'atur* remain." At Kira's evident confusion, she grimaced and explained. "The blooded ones, the 'nobility' one might call them for lack of a better name. Drinking and celebrating Berke's army's retreat they were in the khan's tent all last night. Likely all of this day and night, as well." She folded her arms across her chest and held Kira's gaze. "Well enough do I know that 'tis simple to tempt my man when he stumbles home after one of these binges. Would you not tempt Black Wind?"

Kira drew herself up proudly. "I would not become a whore."

"'Twas not what I suggested," the woman countered irritably. "A claimed woman is as close to a wife as one may be here. A ceremony have they, but 'tis neither Zoroastrian nor Moslem, so I feel not wed in my match."

"But they claim to be wed?"

"Aye, in their own terms," the woman agreed with a world-weary shrug.

"Your man is faithful to you alone?"

The woman laughed. "Aye, to me and his four other women should the mood to claim another not take him."

Kira shuddered. "I could not do this thing."

The woman leaned over her and there was no denying the intelligence that sparkled in her eyes. "You would be alive," she reminded Kira in a low voice. "And you would be protected should you be claimed by a blooded one like Black Wind."

Kira nibbled her lip, barely daring to be tempted by the possibility. "Why is he called that?" she demanded abruptly. The woman shrugged.

"His name he would not give when he rode in, so one was given to him. Few questions are asked of any who would join, especially one who fights as well as he. Claimed to have the great one's blood in his veins, though none believed him until he began to show the signs."

"The signs?"

"Luck," the woman supplied flatly. "'Tis clear the gods and the elements smile upon him, for little he takes on fails. He is a blessed one, despite the stigma of his mark." She leaned closer and her voice dropped to a confidential whisper. "'Tis said he bears the mark of some dark god on his chest and that it cannot be removed. Those who ride into battle with him say it glows so that it can be seen through his *kalat* and that the enemies fall back in fear from the sight."

Kira did not dare to let her skepticism show, but merely held the woman's gaze with what she hoped might pass for amazement. Superstitious nonsense. 'Twas a birthmark alone her warrior sported, liken to many others Kira had seen except for its distinctive shape.

"But his name?" she prompted.

The woman shrugged. "Rode in from the north, he did, and so stealthily did he pass that none heard him afore he stood before the khan's own tent. Directions they call by colors here, and 'north' to you and me is 'black' to them. 'Tis said he passes as silently and appears as unexpectedly as the north wind itself, hence the name Black Wind."

And was about as warm. Kira regarded her bread with disinterest, unable to reconcile herself to the woman's suggestion despite the quiver of excitement fluttering within her stomach.

"I do not believe he can be tempted," she protested, then glanced up when the woman laughed again.

"*All* men can well be tempted," she assured Kira confidently. "Come and I will show you. A little *qumis* and a few hours of dancing and you will be ready to show the man your charms."

"But—" Kira protested halfheartedly, her words silenced with a cutting glance from the other woman.

"Would you rather live than die?" the woman demanded flatly. Kira found herself nodding.

"Aye," she admitted, knowing it to be the truth.

"Then surely coupling with a man cannot be too high a price to pay," the woman observed. Seeing Kira's doubt, she gave her a maternal pat on the shoulder. "I would not see you die, child, especially when one such as Black Wind desires you."

"He does not," Kira argued, but the woman only smiled.

"Naught do you know of men if you believe that," she chided, and Kira dared to hope. The woman extended her hand again. This time Kira let herself be pulled to her feet, her own tentative smile matching the woman's confident one. "Well do I think dancing will suit you," the woman mused. "What is your name, child?"

"Kira."

"Kira," she repeated carefully as her gaze ran over her.

"Named for the sun, are you. Does the sun not choose life every day?" The woman leaned closer and her voice dropped to a whisper. "Would you not choose life, little Kira?"

"Aye," Kira said after a moment's pause, her voice growing firmer with her burgeoning conviction. Optimism burned brightly within her now that she gave it rein and she dared to hope that her warrior could indeed be tempted to claim her for his own. "Aye," she said again. "I will choose life. Teach me what I need to know."

Chapter Six

Thierry could not believe his eyes when he saw her in the khan's own tent two nights after he had sent her home.

Surely 'twas a trick of the light, or the copious amount of *qumis* he had imbibed, for his woman appeared to be among the dancers. Serfs and whores they were, by and large, women who ensured their own survival by the granting of their ample favors.

No place had his witch with them. Surely his eyes erred.

"Time enough 'tis that you showed interest in the fair sex," Nogai jested beside him.

Thierry acknowledged that he was probably not as circumspect about his intrigue as usually he was. Indeed, it mattered little now. Invincibility was of import only for those who had power, those with something worth stealing. A battle that had not been meant quite simply that Thierry had had no opportunity to prove himself. And unproven, he had no power within the tribe.

The smoke was thick from incense in the khan's tent and the cloying sweetness stung Thierry's eyes as he dared to peer once more at the dancers. His eye fell immediately on the same tiny figure and he shook his head stubbornly. In Tiflis she was, but his fogged mind refused to relinquish its certainty. 'Twas a trick of the flickering lamplight alone.

Indeed, she heavily favored his witch, but her movements

were more languid. A drum was struck, bells shaken and the women took to a cleared space on the floor, their hips undulating in time to the music. A confusing swirl of scarves temporarily obscured his vision as the women ran in a tight circle amidst the sound of applause. When they stopped, he glimpsed a trim ankle before the flowing cloth drifted down to hide it from view once more. Thierry looked up to find his woman not two arm's lengths before him.

There was no disputing his impression now. 'Twas her, though her gaze was less sharp than he recalled.

His heart skipped a beat. He saw that the slowness of her movement was probably *qumis*-induced and stifled an indulgent smile. Her large eyes appeared yet wider and darker with the sweep of dark kohl accenting them. Her lips seemed ruddier and fuller and he had no doubt they had been painted, as well. She met his eyes and smiled timidly before she rolled one shoulder in an amateurish parody of the more experienced dancers.

Thierry licked his lips and glanced away, unable to account for the sudden dampness of his palms. How had she come to be here? No explanation could he find for her presence, especially dancing as she was, though Thierry cared little for that fact. In truth, he was pleased to see her again, though he would not have admitted as much to another living soul. Could he have missed her? Impossible, but he definitely felt better than he had just moments before.

He could not help but turn his gaze upon her once more.

'Twas endearing how she tried to dance like the other women, her innocence as obvious as the nose on her face. Thierry felt an unexpected glow of affection swell within him as he settled back to sip his *qumis*. Yet again in this woman's presence, he was tempted to smile.

"Witch." Nogai reminded Thierry of the danger she posed with the terse word, but Thierry silenced him with a glance.

No interest had he in any superstitious nonsense, though little indeed did it please him to know that Nogai had discerned the direction of his thoughts so readily. Naught did he need to spoil the sweetness of this moment. Even if she should be gone by the morrow, Thierry would savor this chance to see her again.

And he had naught to lose by making his interest clear. The very thought sent a heated spark of anticipation running through him. Thierry told himself 'twas naught but the *qumis,* though indeed he knew better.

The men hollered and hooted at the dancers in typical fashion, several of the women blowing kisses and making beckoning gestures as they danced. The witch looked only to him and only briefly before her gaze dropped to the floor. Thierry saw that she nibbled her bottom lip occasionally, her nervousness more than readily apparent, her color unnaturally high.

The gracefulness of her every gesture recalled the sight of her gloriously nude all too readily to Thierry's mind. He licked his lips, feeling the spark kindled within grow to a flame. The yurt was suddenly much warmer than it had been, to Thierry, at least, but still he could not look away from the unexpected sight of her dancing.

'Twas when she glanced at the other dancers and mimicked their gesture, tossing aside the large emerald scarf wrapped around her fully, that Thierry realized this could not be some harmless indulgence. Though she threw the silk aside with less practiced aplomb than her companions, her grace was made evident by the gesture.

As was much of the rest of her, he acknowledged with some discomfort. Thierry straightened slowly at the sight of her bare midriff, knowing full well that there was a mole to the left of her navel and liking it not that everyone else in the khan's tent knew it, as well.

The thought of touching that mole tempted him, but he ignored it.

A crisscrossed red scarf bound her breasts, another in brilliant blue girded her hips. An array of other scarves in bright hues hung from or around the blue one, the moving gaps between them affording tempting glimpses of her shapely legs. The men's hooting troubled Thierry now as it had not before and he wondered how many were gazing upon the soft flesh of his woman. The very thought made him cringe, illogical though that was. No claim had he here.

This time when she rolled her hips, it garnered more of a response from him than a cringe, though Thierry dared show naught of his feelings. Nogai whistled loudly but Thierry remained stock-still. The woman looked to him and smiled tentatively once more when she met his eyes. He refused to show any sign of her effect upon him. She must have discerned something in his expression, though, for she raised her hands over her head as the tempo of the music increased. She rocked her hips in time, the very provocativeness of the gesture shocking Thierry, though his companions seemed to have another response.

The woman smiled slowly and Thierry knew she had guessed that he was not unaffected. But what was her objective? Surely she could not mean to tempt him? Not after her relieved response the other night to his stated intention to leave her be?

The very possibility was provocative, but Thierry refused to let himself indulge in such whimsy. She could not be tempting him. She took a step closer to him, seemingly oblivious to the other men in the tent. She spun on one toe and unraveled another scarf from her hips. As yellow as the sun it was. Thierry wondered how he could ever have thought her dancing amateurish when she deliberately cast it to him.

Mayhap he had misinterpreted. The invitation was blatantly unmistakable. He snatched the scarf from the air, schooling his features to remain impassive. Deliberately he sipped his *qumis* and held her gaze. Well it seemed that she intended to tease him this night, but he would know her desire with resounding certainty before he did anything in response.

Her ankles and calves could be seen more clearly since the yellow scarf had been removed. Thierry admired the view, even as the lewd calls of his companions fairly made his ears burn. Fortunate 'twas that she could not understand the Mongol tongue. He followed one leg upward, devouring the sight of her golden curves until finally he met her eyes once more.

Still she regarded him as though he were the only man in the tent. The realization fed the heat already burning within him. When her slender hands fell to another knot on her hip, Thierry's heart leaped. No desire had he for more of her to be displayed to common view lest another be tempted to make her his own.

'Twas time. He tapped his index finger on the floor of the tent directly before him. Something flickered in the woman's eyes. Her color blossomed anew but she took the steps needed to bring her directly before him.

And resumed her dancing.

Thierry immediately regretted his impulse. He was inundated by her sweet scent and clenched one hand around his cup in a bid for self-control. Too tempting 'twas to have her swaying so seductively directly before him. Should he care to look straight ahead from his seat on the floor, he could fairly stare right into the most fragrant part of her. Thierry resolutely avoided the option.

Instead he made the mistake of looking up to her face.

Vulnerability he saw in those dark eyes. And fear. What had brought her to this camp? He wondered what she had found in Tiflis. Had the marks on her back anything to do with her return? She spun on her toe again and he caught a glimpse of her back, relieved to see that she sported no fresh wounds. What then? Had she come back for his protection? Deliberately was she tempting him and Thierry could only assume that she wanted him to claim her.

His woman. Bewitched he must be, for the idea held no small measure of appeal.

But two days past, he would have declined, regardless of the spell she cast over him. Even this day, he would decline the offer from any other without regret. But in truth, this witch provoked him even when she sought no such end. This night he knew not how he might resist her allure. Naught had he to lose indeed by the softness of a woman, for he was powerless in a society that held only power in esteem.

He could do as she asked.

Thierry's heart leaped at the very possibility but he forced himself to consider the realities. She was a virgin, unless he knew absolutely naught of the world. Was this truly the price she was prepared to pay? No merchant would have her for certain after this.

Mayhap Nogai had been right and none would have her now.

If only he could be certain 'twas what she wanted. Thierry tapped the floor closer to his knee and she instantly took the requisite step. The smell of her engulfed him and he blinked disconcertedly, his gaze dropping abruptly from the swaying silk to her feet.

Her delightfully small and well-formed feet.

A red mark there was, mayhap a callus, that had not been there before. Thierry reached to touch the spot on her instep without thinking, startled at the contrast between his rough hands and her smooth skin. She laughed unexpectedly at his touch, her foot wriggling away as she shivered. Thierry glanced up at the unexpected sound in time to see her eyes glimmer with mischief. An amethyst scarf was unknotted from her hips, those tiny feet playfully dancing a hand's span away.

Thierry looked up in confusion, surprised to find a flurry of soft purple enfolding his senses. He pulled the silk from obscuring his vision and held fast to the end. She danced at the other end of the scarf, undulating with the increased tempo of the drum. Thierry saw naught but her golden loveliness.

She could be his.

When her eyes met his again, he held her gaze and deliberately put his cup aside. She licked her lips nervously but neither broke his regard nor ceased her dancing. With an abrupt flick of his wrist, the amethyst cloth danced out of her grip and fluttered through the air to Thierry.

She looked confused, but little time did he give her to reflect upon the matter. No sooner had he the scarf within his grip than he snapped it again, sending a furl of silk to encircle her hips. He snatched the loose end out of the air and, much to the approval of his companions, pulled her resolutely closer.

She smiled openly at him and danced within the circle of silk, stretching her arms high in that pose that so enflamed him. Thierry gripped the scarf in one hand and reached out to touch the softness of her ankle once more. Instantly she planted her feet on the floor, the music becoming a frenzied beating at that same point. She shimmied her hips in a timeless move, the vibration fueling Thierry's desire.

Unable to help himself, he let his fingertip trail leisurely up her leg. To his surprise, she shivered but did not move away. Thierry looked up to meet her eyes, seeing his own desire reflected there. Deliberately did she tempt him, he was certain of it, the light in her eyes making him believe she wanted their mating as much as he did.

As smooth as satin was her skin. Thierry swallowed as that fingertip dared ever higher. Not only did she not move away but she slipped one foot farther away from the other. Thierry's heart pounded at the promise of that, and he allowed his finger to relentlessly continue.

The drumbeat slowed to a repetitive pounding, a pulse that was taken up by dancers and crowd alike. The golden light of the lamps flickered restlessly. The tent resonated, the women pumped their hips, the men stamped their feet and Thierry looked into the acquiescent eyes of his woman.

When he encountered the dampness at the juncture of her thighs, all else was forgotten.

She wanted him. Her eyes widened at his bold touch, but she neither ceased dancing nor looked away. Indeed, it seemed to Thierry that there were none but the two of them within the smoke-filled tent.

But there were more than the two of them. And if she was

to be Thierry's woman, she would be his alone. Not a private society was this one and well enough he knew that only a deed witnessed by many was believed to be the truth. The evidence of one's own eyes alone could not be disputed.

If she was to be his woman and none were to have any doubt of her status, his possession would have to be a public one. Only that would leave no doubt. Thierry arched one brow, hoping she understood the import of what he asked when she nodded quick agreement without breaking his gaze.

So be it. She would be his for this night and all others. His path resolved, he willfully forgot the others in the yurt once more.

This moment was between the two of them, in truth.

Thierry gave the amethyst scarf the slightest tug, loving the way she tumbled trustingly into his arms. Had he spared the time to think, he might have thought her relieved, but other matters were there to attend. Her small hands were on his shoulders, her breath in his ear, her scent filling his nostrils fit to drown him, her softness filling his hands.

His woman.

She was on her back beside him in a flash, her gleaming hair spread over the bright carpets layered on the tent floor. Thierry was atop her in a heartbeat, his *chalwar* torn open. Incense and her scent mingled in his nostrils, the *qumis* burned hot in his veins, the pulse in his ears echoed the beating drums. He hauled the scarves out of his path and buried himself within her in one move, deaf to the cries of the men around him.

Her gasp he heard alone. He whispered some reassurance in the Frankish tongue he had not dared to let pass his lips in years before her sweetness overwhelmed him. Too tight was she for him to last, but mayhap 'twas better for this to be concluded quickly. He thrust within her and felt the bite of her nails in his shoulders. He managed to thrust only once more before he arched back and spilled his seed.

Witch.

His witch. Thierry collapsed atop her, knowing he had never

been so completely claimed. It seemed her softness invited him closer and he was sorely tempted to fall asleep thus. No one would lay an abusing hand upon her again, he thought fiercely, daring to whisper once more within the soft curve of her ear. She was his and his alone.

She was silent beneath him, her breath coming in anxious spurts, and Thierry reluctantly acknowledged the press of men around them. No place was this for such a sweet union. The deed had been done and now he would have his temptress to himself.

Her eyes were closed when Thierry dared to look and he knew a moment's doubt, but he resolutely shoved to his elbows. Business was there at hand. The deed was done, but he must ensure that none doubted the evidence of their eyes. Ample time would there be in privacy for the slow loving he longed to savor with her. The night was yet young and his anticipation at the promise of that thought rose much more quickly than he could have expected.

Flooded with a protectiveness he dared not explore, he pulled his cloak to cover her as he withdrew, leaving himself exposed to draw the men's attention from her. His. A murmur went through the tent as Thierry stood slowly over his woman, his feet braced on either side of her draped and prone form. Slowly he met the gaze of every man in the yurt, daring each to acknowledge the evidence of her broken maidenhead smeared upon his flesh.

No doubt would there be on the morrow that he had done this thing. No question would there be to whom this woman belonged. She had curled up at his feet beneath the cloak, yet again reminding him of a small cat, though her hands concealed her face from view.

One of the other men reached for the cloak with a mumbled joke, but Thierry drew his blade in a flash. The point at the man's throat halted his gesture before he could unveil the woman. He swallowed carefully and straightened beneath Thierry's gaze, though none moved to aid him. The tent fell yet more silent as the others awaited the outcome of the challenge.

"None shall look upon what is mine," Thierry growled.

The stillness in the tent was so complete that he had not a doubt all had heard his claim. Once again he met the gaze of each in turn, waiting until the challenge faded from each pair of dark eyes before moving on. Satisfied, he deliberately sheathed his blade, adjusted his *chalwar* and crouched down to pick up his woman.

She recoiled from his touch, the accusation in her wide eyes when she pulled her hands away fairly sickening him.

But no time was this for dissent. Thierry hoped she saw the warning in his eyes before she buried her face again in the folds of the cloak. He reached for her anew, hoping none had witnessed her response other than him. He only dared to exhale when she did not fight him and he stood with her cradled in his arms.

Lighter even than he had expected was she and he marveled once more at her delicacy, letting his hand spread to span the slenderness of her waist. He felt the tension coiled within her and understood suddenly the shock their coupling must have been. No easy task had it been for her to allow his touch this soon, he was certain. Deciding on this path had taken courage and Thierry's admiration surged for his woman. Soon enough would he show her that the reality of coupling had not to be such a hasty deed.

Impossible 'twas to check his pride that she was his in truth, that he had been the first and that there would be no others as long as he drew breath. Thierry resolutely held her closer, determined to sweeten her recollection of their first mating before the night was through.

Ways there were of pleasing a woman and though he had long been chaste, he was well enough acquainted with such techniques. Indeed, the very thought of touching her in more private circumstances lent purpose to his step as he left the khan's yurt.

'Twas only when he gained the outside air that Thierry discerned her quiet sobbing. His lips thinned at the muted sound, his elaborate rationalizations forgotten as he roundly cursed the barbarian he had become.

She would not cry.

Kira willed her tears to stop, certain the warrior would think her a complete fool for such behavior. Though little enough did she care what he thought after what he had done to her.

Like animals had they coupled. Before an audience of yet baser animals. What kind of people dared to watch such intimacy? Certainly Kira had expected that their mating would be an inevitable result of her dancing, should she be successful, but never had she imagined 'twould take place in public.

Indeed, she could scarce believe it now.

And why had this made her cry when her father's frequent beatings had never drawn a tear? Although there had been a twinge of pain and certainly some discomfort, what had happened this night could not compare to the painful bite of the lash she knew so well.

'Twas the shock alone that fed her tears, Kira told herself stubbornly, even as they refused to halt. Naught could her response have to do with this man. It could not, for she knew naught of him. And no credence would she give to the ache between her thighs. Little enough excuse was that for tears.

The night air was cold but Kira flatly refused to huddle any closer to the uncompromising man who carried her. What had she done? No gratitude had she anymore for the *qumis* that had fed her resolve and loosed her inhibitions, for its heat had completely abandoned her. Kira shivered, hating the filmy veils that clung silkily to her flesh.

Cold and alone she was with the man who had claimed her. Kira dared not look up to his face and stayed huddled within his cloak as she struggled to come to terms with what had happened.

Had this not been what she wanted?

Her traitorous body was too aware of the lean strength of his chest as the warrior carried her away from the scene of the spectacle they had made. She heard his solid footfalls in the beaten-down grass and felt the determination in the arms that held her against him.

No doubt his expression was as stonily impassive as ever. She despised him suddenly for granting her what she had asked of him, wishing too late that the loss of her maidenhead might have been a sweet mating. His fault it was that she had been forced to make such a choice, for had he not stolen her from Tiflis and the life she knew? Had he not taken her to the Mongol camp from which she could never return home?

Truly, it seemed she had plenty for which to blame this man, and her silent tears rolled unchecked over her cheeks.

But 'twas she who had chosen him of all the men assembled there, and indeed Kira could make little sense of her choice. Surely she could not have any regard for a man with whom she had never spoken? Surely she could not feel anything but disgust for a man who had done what he had just done?

Kira's feelings on the matter were more confused than she would have liked them to have been. Too comforting was his warmth for her taste, too easy would it be to subside against him and let him gather her yet closer.

Or worse, to let him touch her with such familiarity again. The scent of his skin reminded her that her own desire had not been quenched in her shock and she fidgeted as she struggled to dispel such inappropriate thoughts. She should loathe him. This warrior deserved no more than that.

He ducked into the enveloping shadow of the tent they had already shared and Kira's pulse quickened. Did he mean to mate again? And yet more troubling, why did the thought prompt anticipation to mingle with her fear?

She gasped when he crouched without striking a flint, cradling her yet closer in his lap. Too aware was Kira of the darkness pressing around them and the distant sound of merrymaking. Indeed, the shadows made her yet more aware of the warrior's proximity, his scent filling her lungs and heightening the intimacy of this setting. Mayhap 'twas better to be in public after all, she thought wildly, trying desperately to scurry away from him.

His arms tightened around her, checking her retreat as he kept her resolutely in his lap, and he muttered something under his breath as he sat down. Kira froze, startled that his tone did not sound angry, and listened attentively for some abrupt change in his manner.

When none came, she dared to glance up through her tears even as her heart thudded in her ears, cringing at the shadow of his hand rising above her. His hand paused for a moment and she knew he had noted her fear before he gently pushed the hood back from her damp face.

He had left the tent flap open and Kira could discern his features in the half-light. His eyes were gleaming in the shadows and she fancied she saw concern in his expression, though she hastily dropped her gaze and refused to indulge her whimsy.

If only she could stop the flow of these cursed tears.

To Kira's surprise, a rough thumb slid slowly across her cheek, collecting her tears in a single gesture. She watched transfixed as the warrior raised his hand and carefully licked the salty drops from his own flesh. Kira dared to meet his gaze, her mouth going dry at the intensity of his expression.

Slowly, as though he feared to startle her, he repeated the gesture and wiped the tears from her other cheek. Never did he even blink, let alone break her regard, and Kira's chest clenched as his tongue languidly collected his new harvest of tears from his thumb. Something awakened within her again but she refused to indulge it, forcing herself to recall the kind of man she confronted.

A Mongol. A barbarian. A ruthless warrior. Kira swallowed carefully, not daring to believe the thought that immediately crossed her mind when he reached for the new tears on her cheek.

He simply could not be apologizing. What could a man such as this know about such social niceties? His very tenderness fed her tears and they flowed with new vigor despite her efforts, leaving Kira powerless within the maelstrom of her conflicting emotions. How could this man confuse her so? And why did he do so?

He leaned slowly toward her and Kira's breath caught in her lungs, his move reminding her suddenly that she was cradled in his lap. His other hand was curled surely around her waist, his fingers gripping her pelvis with a gentle firmness. The strength of his thighs was bunched beneath her and when his free hand curled under her chin, Kira was stunned to hear a faint sigh escape her own lips.

When the tip of his tongue touched her cheek ever so gently and lifted away another tear, Kira shivered. He pulled her closer within the circle of his embrace as though he thought her cold and her fingers spread of their own accord to fan out on his shoulders. His careful removal of her tears was eroding any thought that he was to blame for her horrendous fate and she could not fight her instincts on this matter.

He *was* apologizing.

Kira's heart melted at the realization, his touch igniting her desire once more. Indeed, she was only too aware beneath his gentle assault that the unfamiliar tension within her when she had danced for him had not been released. She was agitated deep inside and though she knew not what to do about it, she imagined her warrior did.

When his lips closed firmly over hers, Kira could think of naught but gaining that release. He nudged open her lips with his tongue and the world spun giddily at the warm spice of his kiss. Kira closed her eyes as she submitted and clasped her warrior's neck, liking the feel of his corded strength beneath her hands.

She trembled when his fingers gripped the hair at the nape of her neck, her back arching high when his other hand explored the fullness of her breast. He teased her nipple with work-roughened fingers and Kira nearly cried out at the pleasure that coursed through her from that point.

Emboldened by his sure touch, she dared to run her hands

over the breadth of his shoulders. Without breaking his languor-
ous kiss, he guided her hands to the front of his *kalat,* his own
hands roving to curve around her buttocks. Kira's heart leaped
to her throat and her fingers trembled, but she unfastened the
ties nonetheless.

She hesitated for a moment, then slipped her hands beneath
both the fur-lined tunic and the silk shirt beneath. His skin was
as warm and smooth as heavy satin left in the sun, the wiry hair
on his chest tickling her fingers. Kira recalled only too well the
sight of his nudity the other morning, and her pulse accelerated.

She found his nipple and gave it an impudent pinch, liking
the way he jumped in surprise. Before Kira could savor the unexpected moment, he shifted her weight in his lap and she was
startled by the press of his hardness against her buttocks. The
warmth of his hand landed flat on her bare stomach and Kira
froze, suddenly certain that she knew what he was about.

This was no apology, she thought wildly. He meant only to earn
her complaisance that he might take her again this night. What a
fool she had been! This man had no regard for her feelings! And
she had virtually begged him to make her his whore.

Kira squirmed in panic, but the way the warrior's strong
fingers slipped purposefully beneath the scarf wound about
her hips brought her struggles to an abrupt halt. The warm
span of his fingers speared through the tangle of hair at her
crotch, the very possessiveness of the gesture making her
suddenly afraid.

Mayhap her feelings about another coupling this night truly
would carry no weight.

Kira met the warrior's gaze tentatively, feeling completely
captured beneath his grip. He was watching her, though she
should have anticipated that, just as she should have expected
his stony expression. He did not move and she had the sense
he was waiting for her reaction.

Much as she was waiting to see what he would do next.

The two regarded each other silently for a long moment,

Kira only too aware of the sound of her agitated breathing filling the tent.

Then the warrior's finger slipped decisively lower. Kira caught her breath, knowing his destination without a doubt yet powerless to stop him. A jolt tripped through her when he touched that spot again, the one he had teased briefly in the other tent.

Kira panicked. She would not couple with him again this night. She was sore, she was confused, she was tired and rather less than herself thanks to the effect of the *qumis*.

And he was teasing her, breaking down her resistance with single-minded resolve just so they could mate again. No regard did he truly have for her, for had she not seen his lack of response to her nudity the other morning? Indeed, he had only partaken of what was offered. No remorse did he feel for his deed, and at her telling response to the gentle pressure of his fingertip, Kira thrashed in an almost certainly futile attempt to gain her freedom.

To her astonishment the warrior let her go.

Chapter Seven

Kira gained her footing in a flurry of tangled silk, and felt an utter fool when the warrior did not move at all in pursuit. She gulped unsteadily to regulate her breathing, finding herself snared once more by his assessing regard.

Again they watched each other warily.

Kira began to wonder if he had turned to stone in truth, then his eyes narrowed suddenly and he abruptly stood. She darted out of his range and he spared her a glance that could have been indulgent had it come from any other man.

With smooth gestures he lit a lamp and hung it from the central pole. He carried a flame from the lamp to a small stove reposing in one corner, his intensity in focusing on his task leaving Kira feeling as though she had overreacted. Indeed, it seemed unlikely that this supremely unconcerned man even knew she was with him, let alone that he expected her to couple with him. Kira shifted her weight uncertainly from one foot to the other, not knowing what she should do next.

Should she run?

But where else would she find haven on this night and in this camp? Had she not wanted him to claim her? Evidently he had done so and it seemed that her place was here.

Even if her companion was markedly disinterested in that particular fact.

He filled a large pot with water and set it on the small stove. Kira nibbled her lip, wondering what was his intent. To her surprise he began to peel off his clothes and methodically fold them before laying them neatly aside.

He meant to couple again! Kira panicked anew. She scurried to the farthest side of the tent. Full well did she know that she would be able to do little to fend him off, but Kira kept her distance. No reason was there to make his conquest an easy one.

The warrior continued disrobing, clearly undeterred by her actions. Not a glance did he spare in her direction, even when he stood splendidly nude, and Kira acknowledged a niggle of doubt as to his objective. Could she have misread him? The pot of water steamed and he squatted before the short stove to pour the water into a bowl. He rummaged in his saddlebags, producing a length of cloth, from which he tore a shorter piece, and a brown block that fit easily into his hand.

Only now did he turn to Kira, and she was disconcerted at how readily he looked directly to her. Indeed, the man fairly had eyes in the back of his head. He offered the trio to her, but she hastily shook her head. Kira scurried backward, not trusting him enough to close the distance between them. The warrior shrugged and plunged the block into the water.

Only when it began to lather on his skin did Kira realize that it was soap. Considerably coarser and darker soap than she knew, certainly, but still she licked her lips carefully at the very promise of a bath. Filthy she felt after these past few days. How long had it been since she had indulged in the luxury of bathing twice daily? Indeed, that ritual of her life in Tiflis seemed but a distant memory.

Of course, she would have to disrobe to wash properly and that was out of the question.

Kira stubbornly turned her back on the sight of her warrior's nudity and folded her arms across her chest. She could well enough go without a bath this night.

Although, she conceded as she spared a glance down to the filmy array of garish scarves beneath his heavy cloak, the man could not see much more of her than he already had. And had she not been nude in his presence before?

She flicked a glance over her shoulder to find him scrubbing his body with evident relish. He ran the wet cloth over his skin with a flourish, closing his eyes as the warm water ran over his skin.

Curse him. Had she any idea that the man had a sense of humor, she might have thought him deliberately teasing her. But not this man. He glanced up and their gazes locked for a long moment, Kira fancying she spied a glimmer of something in those silver depths before he abruptly returned to his task.

She turned and stared resolutely at the cavorting shadows thrown on the tent wall. Had she not been in the river but two days past? How dirty indeed could she be? Her belly itched at the thought. The warrior made some low sound of satisfaction in his throat and splashed in the water with obvious pleasure.

Well it seemed to Kira that her very skin crawled at that unwelcome reminder. The river water had been filthy and brown. And that *had* been two days past. She noted the dark line beneath her nails as the splash of his bathing taunted her anew.

Enough.

The man had seen and indeed sampled all she had. Foolish pride would not keep her from being clean. Kira dropped his cloak from her shoulders and bent to untie the knotted scarves with shaking fingers before she could change her mind.

Her nipples beaded as she turned to confront him in her nudity and she could not have met his eyes to save her life. She tossed her hair over her shoulder as though untroubled and resolutely crossed the tent to demand the soap with one outstretched hand.

The warrior did not surrender the soap.

Kira gritted her teeth before she looked up to meet his eyes, only to find him shaking his head with that maddening slowness. He said something that was evidently an explanation and she was certain he was denying her a bath.

Of all the wicked ways to tempt her! Anger shot through Kira. She heartily wished that she could tell him in no uncertain terms what she thought of such churlish behavior.

Indeed, it might be worth telling him, whether he could understand her words or not.

Kira propped her hands on her hips and opened her mouth to do just that, only to find the warrior's heavy finger firm against her lips.

It was wet, and a trickle of warm water ran over her chin from his hand, but Kira could not move to stop it. Her eyes widened in surprise.

Kira reluctantly met his gaze as she fell silent, unable to deny the twinkle she found there. The very sight disconcerted her with its unexpectedness so that she lost the thread of her argument. Instead she found herself nodding dumbly when he held up one cautionary finger and cocked a brow.

His wet skin glistened as he tossed his water out the tent flap and she could not help but notice the play of the muscles across his back. Kira set her lips stubbornly, mentally granting him but an instant more of tolerance before she made her thoughts most clear.

To her surprise he filled the bowl with the remainder of the hot water and offered her the bowl. Indeed, it seemed he had divided the water in half as if he fully expected her to bathe despite her original refusal.

It irked Kira that he found her so predictable, the reappearance of that twinkle in his silver eyes doing little to improve her temper. A new length of cloth did he tear, offering it and the block of soap with all the gallantry of a foreign courtier.

Curse him.

Kira snatched the soap and cloth in ill humor, momentarily grateful that he did not seem determined to aid her in this task at least.

Although, the way he casually turned aside and ignored her nudity left something to be desired, as well. He laid out a pair of blankets nonchalantly near his folded garments, evidently completely oblivious of her nakedness or even her presence. At least he could glance in her direction once in a while, Kira thought irritably as she scrubbed her skin. The man could make a pretense of being attracted to her, if truly he had claimed her.

Unless he thought her merely a whore. Kira's eyes widened at the possibility and her fingers fumbled so that she nearly dropped the soap. Could she have sacrificed her virginity for naught but a night?

'Twas unthinkable, but not so easy to dismiss as Kira might have liked. She looked to the warrior to find him squatting atop the blanket, apparently at ease with his own nudity and watching her carefully. Kira had the uncanny sense that he had sensed her distress over that last thought, though truly there was no way he could know what was in her mind. He cocked one dark brow, as though inviting her to explain. Kira wished she could.

Somehow she sensed that he might reassure her, irrational though that thought was. What *had* she done? Tears blurred her vision once more but Kira refused to let them fall, stubbornly reminding herself that she was yet alive. Had that not been the point of surrendering her virginity? To ensure her very survival?

But had that truly been achieved? Kira wished she had some assurance as to the security of her role, whether she be whore or claimed woman.

She frowned and scrubbed the remainder of the soap from her skin, surprised to find the warrior looming in her peripheral vision. His brows tightened together as though he, too, was frustrated by their lack of common language, then he began pointing around the tent. Each time he pointed, he said something terse, a word or mayhap a phrase, but Kira knew not what was going on.

When he pointed to his tunic and stated *"kalat,"* she suddenly understood.

He was naming objects in Mongolian. Kira nodded quickly, glancing around for some way to indicate that she understood him. Her gaze fell on a tin cup and she pointed inside it.

"Qumis," she said hopefully. The warrior nodded once with evident satisfaction. He held her gaze and pointed to the middle of his chest.

"Thierry," he said firmly. Kira felt her eyes narrow, for the word did not sound Mongolian to even her untrained ears. He repeated it, though, and she realized he was telling her his name.

Thierry. Kira almost said his name herself, having an inexplicable urge to feel the word roll over her tongue, but checked her response just in time.

She would *not* say his name. She would not forgive him so readily. Not until she understood whether she was his woman for good or his whore for this night alone.

And neither would she couple with him again, should she have any choice in the matter.

The warrior watched her expectantly, but Kira stubbornly said naught as she lifted her chin high. She certainly would not tell him her name, for that would be worse than saying his. That silver gaze bored into hers, as though willing her to understand, but Kira resolutely made no acknowledgment of his demand.

Finally he gestured to her and cocked one brow questioningly, but Kira shook her head adamantly. She would not tell him. His lips thinned and he turned away, indicating with one hand the blankets he had unfolded and beckoning to Kira. She shook her head again, pointing determinedly to the other side of the tent.

She would not sleep with him.

There was no doubt that she had displeased him with that. The warrior folded his arms across his chest and shook his head just as determinedly. Kira straightened her shoulders, knowing that she had no intention of acquiescing to share a bed with him this night. Had he not let her sleep in privacy before?

A male voice raised in song outside the tent drew Kira's attention away from their contest of wills. Two women giggled before the man outside began to laugh raucously, as well. No doubt there were some indulging themselves this night. They were close, though, and she wondered fleetingly, as their voices drew yet nearer, if they intended to come right into the tent.

Kira looked back to the warrior in trepidation. He counted off three fingers and gestured outside with those fingers, then pointed to the side of the tent where Kira had intended to sleep. She shook her head quickly, certain he was just trying to frighten her, but he nodded confidently and repeated the gesture. They could not be coming here. Had she and the warrior not been alone here before?

The voices grew yet louder. The warrior watched her silently and Kira wondered if that night had been an exception. Certainly the tent was much too large for one man alone. Kira licked her lips nervously as the laughter grew nearer.

Well it seemed that their privacy was to be short-lived.

Still Kira hesitated as the voices outside grew in volume, jumping when the warrior unexpectedly scooped up his silk *kurta* with uncharacteristic impatience and strode across the space between them. He planted himself between Kira and the tent flap, shooting her a murderous look when she might have stepped away. He shook out the folded shirt with a snap of his wrist.

An instant later her vision was clouded by the undyed silk as he hauled it over her head. The lustrous fabric slid over her face, releasing the warm scent of his skin. Kira closed her eyes for a moment, opening them to find the singing man and two women staggering into the tent. Only just in time had the warrior covered her nudity and she was astonished to find gratitude flooding through her.

Surely she was confused this night to feel gratitude for the warrior who had taken her so publicly. Truly the *qumis* had addled her mind.

The newly arrived man whistled appreciatively and made a

drunken grab in Kira's direction. The warrior moved quickly to kick out the other man's ankle, sending him sprawling on his face, much to his women's giggling delight. The fallen man laughed and shook a finger at the warrior as he rolled to his back and made some jest, though indeed the warrior did not seem to see the humor in the situation.

Kira barely had time to note that the man was the same who had been the warrior's companion earlier before she was scooped off her feet. Her breath caught and she was unexpectedly deposited in the middle of the unfolded blanket.

The warrior had dropped down beside her before she could voice her complaint, one arm clamped around her waist while the other swept the blanket over them in a savage gesture. She glanced up to find a dangerous gleam in his eye and a stern set to his mouth that effectively checked any impulse to make any protest clear.

Indeed, he seemed quite agitated that his companion had reached for her, his relentless grip on Kira naught if not possessive. His very response seemed to make his ownership clear, and Kira could not help but wonder at the cause.

Could she have been claimed after all? If so, for how long and on what terms? She glanced up at the warrior's stern countenance and he seemed to sense her doubt, for he caught her eye even as his fingers spread to span her waist. He tucked her slightly closer to his side and, knowing she had little choice in the matter, Kira settled against his hard warmth to sleep.

She supposed the morning would show more clearly her role. Kira bit down on her frustration, knowing there was naught she could do to make the matter clear sooner.

But tired she was and he was wonderfully warm. Mayhap 'twould not be so bad to sleep here. Indeed, what had she to fear from this man now? The warrior spoke to his friend, his voice rumbling beneath her ear in a most pleasant manner, and Kira dared to settle more thoroughly against him.

Thierry, she thought dreamily, saying his name in her mind despite her resolve not to do so as sleep crept up on her.

* * *

She was afraid of him.

Why else would she refuse to tell him her name? Thierry knew she had understood his request, for there was no lack of intelligence in those dark eyes. She had simply denied him, and though her refusal had stung at the time, he could well understand her uncertainty.

The shaman says a curse comes to a man who takes a witch. Indeed, I could not help but ask him the way of it. You should know that he was most *interested in the matter.*

Nogai's taunting words burned in Thierry's mind yet again and he gritted his teeth. Ironic 'twas that she seemed afraid of him, for the shaman had evidently made it more than clear that he would be the one to pay the price for this night's mating.

The curse? Aye, that will interest you, I should imagine, for 'tis an ugly fate. 'Tis said 'twill shrivel and fall off once it has been buried in a witch. 'Tis thus the shaman says and well you know he has seen much in his day.

A lie. A whimsy. It simply could not be that this sweet creature could extract such a toll from his body. Despite his doubts, Thierry could not help sparing a glance beneath the blanket to check.

Indeed, it seemed this witch made him larger, not smaller. He swallowed a smug smile at the thought.

And what did Nogai know of such matters? Superstitious he was, even beyond the inclination of the others within the tribe. Apt he was to believe every tale from abroad and see signs in the most mundane occurrences.

The shaman predicted your lack of success at Tiflis, did he not?

Nogai's closing taunt echoed relentlessly within Thierry's mind. Had the shaman truly said as much? Thierry did not know, Nogai's manner indicating that the prediction had been well-known. Had he had a downfall? Certainly Thierry had lost an opportunity to prove himself, but his conviction that his time of ascendancy was upon him had diminished naught. He was not quite ready to concede that he had failed.

Although Abaqa's manner lately had been less than encouraging. Thierry shifted restlessly, unable to dismiss the veracity of that last thought, his own wishes to the contrary.

Mayhap the shaman was right about taking witches.

Thierry looked down as the woman sighed, hearing evidence in the change of her breathing that she was truly asleep now. He shook his head mutely, unable or unwilling to condemn her so readily as a witch. Intrigued him in a most unnatural way she did, but that alone did not provide the proof he desired. Indeed, the pearls had fallen from her lips but once and once alone.

He recalled the scholar's assertion that the taste of a pearl revealed its source, and wondered. Could she have been assessing pearls when they came upon her? A most practical solution to the puzzle was that and Thierry tried to assess it independently of its allure.

She could be naught but a woman stolen from her home. A fetching and frightened woman who had deliberately tempted him this night to ensure her own survival.

Or mayhap a witch.

But claimed she was. By him. And together they must find their path from this night onward. Somehow he had to earn this tiny creature's trust without the ability to simply talk to her.

Thierry lay on his back and stared at the roof of the yurt, ignoring the giggling that accompanied Nogai's sport as he puzzled over what to do. His thumb stroked the softness of her shoulder blade absently, the soft puff of her breath against his skin and the tentative press of her fingertips on his chest filling him with an unusual contentment.

How much did she understand of what had happened this night? Thierry knew not and suspected that only time would reveal the truth to her. No way had he of telling her that he intended to keep her by his side without fetching the annoying scholar from Tiflis. Soon they would be on the move again and it would be unreasonable—not to mention unpleasant—to be permanently blessed with that man's company. Nay, this was an obstacle he and his witch had to conquer alone.

He could only make his intent clear by keeping her at his side, and that would take time.

In the interim, he would set himself to the task of earning her trust.

No intention had Thierry of partaking of her charms without her explicit consent again. Not only did the very recollection of his deed make him cringe inwardly, even knowing the necessity of it, but 'twas clear that she intended to extract a toll from him for it, as well. Beside the risk of the shaman's threats coming true, there was the unquestionable fact of her newfound distrust of him. The price was clearly too high all around.

He would have her come to him when next they mated.

Thierry frowned thoughtfully, knowing well that this night must have been less than a pleasant experience for her. Would she even *want* to come to him after such a mating? Doubt grew within him as he stared down at her, as peaceful in sleep as a child.

Impulsively, he bent and brushed his lips across her smooth brow, liking the way her silky hair caressed his nose. The very softness of her triggered his arousal once more and Thierry wondered in that moment how he would keep himself from her, mayhap indefinitely.

Wither and fall off. Truly the shaman knew naught of what he spoke and Thierry was tempted to show him the evidence of that himself. This witch would keep him engorged when even she ignored him, let alone when she turned her will upon him.

But what if she never came to him again?

As Thierry stared down at her, an idea formed in his mind, tempting him with the possibility so that it could not be denied. Mayhap if he showed her the pleasure that could be hers from this pastime, she would eventually come to him of her own volition.

Mayhap 'twas worth a try.

* * *

Kira was having the most wonderful dream.

Her mind was repainting the memory of the loss of her maidenhead and well she knew it, but she granted her imagination free reign, knowing that a dream could hurt naught. She was floating in a warm sea of silk, drifting languidly while a school of little fishes nibbled at her thighs. Kira sighed and stretched amidst the soft swirl of silk, smiling to herself when the teasing fishes ventured higher.

They were nudging at the apex of her thighs where that sensitive spot was concealed. Kira spared not a thought before she parted her legs to grant them access. They dived gleefully through her nest of curls and she imagined the sight of them disappearing into the secretive darkness before their nibbles stole her breath away.

She twisted away from temptation but the persistent fishes followed her diligently, their feather-light teasing sending a tide of warmth coursing through her. The sea of silk grew warmer, or else her skin became more sensitive, for it seemed every fiber of her being had come alive.

Kira dared to part her thighs yet farther, gasping aloud when yet more fishes attacked her breasts with their seductive touch. She felt her nipples bead beneath the warm assault and arched high, stretching her hands above her to encounter a broad pair of shoulders that were decidedly not fishy.

Kira's eyes flew open. Her heart fairly stopped at the silhouette of her warrior bent over her, his mouth gently tugging her nipple to an impertinent point. She watched in amazement as he lifted his head an increment and pursed his lips. The warm breath that fanned over her skin launched an army of goose pimples across her flesh. Kira shivered and he spared her a fathomless silver glance.

Their gazes locked for a long moment in the night shadows, the sounds of the others sleeping filling Kira's ears as she silently regarded him. Then the warrior's fingers moved expertly within the warm shelter of her dampness and all thought fled her mind. He leaned toward her purposefully and Kira closed her eyes as his lips found hers, knowing she was too aroused to deny his touch now.

Her senses were filled with the smell and the taste of him, his warmth, his strength. He coaxed and cajoled her flesh and, as surely as if she had willed it herself, Kira felt the fires kindled beneath her skin once again. Her legs shifted restlessly beneath the blanket as he ran an intoxicating row of kisses under her chin. She thought her heart would burst when he nuzzled her earlobe, his breath tickling the tender flesh there before he boldly licked behind it. Kira shuddered but her response gained her no respite from his fiery touch.

Those fingers between her thighs caressed and kneaded incessantly, demanding yet more of her even when she knew not what to do. She felt a moan rise to her lips but her warrior was quick to swallow the faint sound, his firm lips locking over hers once more. The move brought his bare chest into aching proximity with hers and Kira arched high at the persuasive brush of those wiry hairs against her aching nipples.

Suddenly a frenzy was loosed beneath her skin and she writhed against it. Her fingernails dug into his shoulders when his fingers continued to demand. It was too close, too much, too overwhelming and nameless, this tension that would not be denied.

With an abruptness that took her breath away, everything clenched within Kira. She made a cry into the warrior's kiss as the convulsions swept through her. For an instant her heart stopped, her lungs clenched and her womb contracted with a strength that astounded her. She saw a blinding light behind her eyelids and felt a frisson of heat fit to fry her skin.

Then there was naught.

Naught but the darkness, the sound of her breathing and the gleaming silver of her warrior's eyes. A seductive warmth flooded leisurely through her and she snuggled deeper into the embrace of the blanket. Kira barely had time to spare him a smile before she slipped back into that silky sea of dreams once more.

The summons from the khan came before the dawn.

Thierry was awake and heard the messenger's pace on the grass before the man even reached the yurt. Instinctively he knew that he was the one being summoned. 'Twas the time of reckoning, unless he missed his guess.

'Twas a relief in a way to know that Abaqa would finally make his move, and Thierry found himself unnervingly calm. The *keshik* guard ducked his head into the yurt without preamble, his uniform revealing his regiment as the khan's private guard. He nodded once when he met Thierry's gaze, then ducked back outside.

Thierry extricated himself slowly from the delightful tangle of silk and softness that was his woman. He did not want to wake her so early and moved carefully, bending to tuck the blanket carefully back around her. She nestled down into the wool, rubbing her cheek against the spot where he had rested. His heart leaped, but Thierry refused to permit himself any romantic whimsy.

She had sought him out for his protection. He had granted her request in exchange for the pleasures she could grant him. 'Twas best to keep matters simple between them. He would keep his end of the bargain and that was all there was of import here.

Well it seemed that the light of morning had restored his reason.

He could not halt his quick visual check before donning his *chalwar,* grunting with skeptical satisfaction that all was as it should be. As though it could be any other way. Shrivel and fall away. Naught did the shaman know, that much was clear. Was he not a warrior trained to believe solely the evidence of his own eyes? Rationale alone would govern his thoughts. Thierry could not completely quell an unexpected surge of scorn that these Mongols should be so gullible.

But was he not part Mongol? And what precisely was the other part that of late had made him think himself separate from them? Thierry dressed hastily, as though running from his traitorous thoughts.

As he made to join the messenger outside, he found himself unable to subdue the urge to look back on his woman one last time. She would be safe here with Nogai and well he knew it. Not wanting to look like a complete fool, Thierry made a pretense of adjusting his scabbard as he surreptitiously slanted a glance in her direction.

She slept, as before, with all the innocence of a child.

He wished suddenly that she would not awaken before he returned.

Nonsense. Foolish whimsy. The khan was summoning him this morn and well he should know that this interview would require his full attention. Changes were afoot. Thierry snapped the buckle on his belt and strode out into the waning darkness. The men exchanged another terse nod and the messenger set a quick pace for the khan's yurt.

Chapter Eight

Abaqa was eating dates, or more accurately, was having dates fed to him by one of his wives. He smiled a predatory smile at Thierry's appearance and Thierry noted that 'twas his western wife draped by his side. From Constantinople had this one come, to forge an alliance, although Thierry had seen precious little evidence of such a truce.

Though truly, with the current state of affairs in the Byzantine Empire, it seemed there was little enough to be gained from a link with the Byzantine royals. Undoubtedly the woman was better out of her homeland. The men exchanged greetings politely, the guard stepped back and Thierry waited patiently. The khan chewed thoughtfully for a long moment.

"Had Berke not died in so timely a fashion, you might have had expectations," he said finally, emphasizing the last word in a most pronounced way.

Aye, Thierry conceded to himself, he had had expectations when he had ridden from the camp. The retreat of the Golden Horde had stolen away the promise of the fulfillment of his ambitions, but still he could hope 'twas but a temporary setback.

Even if the shaman's actions and Abaqa's words told him clearly otherwise.

"Mayhap," he agreed carefully. "'Tis of little import now."

"Mayhap not," the khan said enigmatically. He waved away his wife with an impatient gesture, fixing his gaze on Thierry. He smiled slowly, evidently realizing that he had captured the younger man's attention, and carefully folded his hands together before he spoke.

"As the commander I know you to be, you must realize that this battle was our last chance to expand to the north." Thierry nodded, unable to divine the path of this discussion. Such matters were well-known, even within the ranks.

"Constrained on every side are we now, even with the Golden Horde's retreat. No interest have I in their lands north of the plains that are clearly ours once more, for the land is useless for grazing. Clear enough 'tis, as well, that the lands north of Tiflis have already been raided so extensively that there is little enough remaining to take from them. The size and value of the tribute you collected from Tiflis can only be taken as a sign that 'tis time to find greener pastures." Abaqa spoke quietly, studying his fingernails with more interest than seemed appropriate. "The time has come that we must explore our final option."

Thierry's mind readily supplied dozens of equally drastic possibilities. He intuitively disliked that the khan was telling him about this, not at all comfortable that his destiny was apparently entwined with this option.

Not a good sign for his own fate could this be, for he was not usually among Abaqa's confidants.

"We must make an alliance with the Franks," Abaqa concluded, raising his dark eyes to meet Thierry's. Thierry knew his surprise showed, for he had not the chance to check it.

"The Franks?" he asked when it seemed he was expected to say something.

"Aye," Abaqa grunted, and frowned. "Palestine do they hold and many a time over the years have they contacted us about combining our forces against the Mamluk dogs. Now they have lost Jerusalem, a matter of much import to them, though 'tis truly a hopeless town to hold. A question of religion is it undoubtedly. Well do we know that their emissaries are oft filled with this unreasonable desire to see us baptized." He plucked another date from the bowl his wife had abandoned and plopped it into his mouth.

"In truth, 'tis why my sire refused to trouble himself with them. Who indeed can imagine a man of such faith at war?" He made a vague gesture, and truly, Thierry could not imagine the Buddhist monks he was familiar with wielding a sword. Not even the shaman in the camp picked up a blade, though that man was filled with enough threats and dire warnings to suffice.

"My wife, though, knows of these Franks," the khan confided, leaning forward to prop one elbow on his knee. "Ravaged Constantinople they did once in their religious lust and left most of the city for dead." He met Thierry's gaze and Thierry noted the spark in the man's eyes.

"Such information leaves me pondering this Frankish alliance," Abaqa continued, nibbling the clinging bits of date from his fingers with affected nonchalance. "I would know what kind of men they are." His voice dropped slightly and Thierry stiffened. "I would have a military man provide me an assessment." That dark gaze swiveled back to pin Thierry to the spot. "I would have *you* find out."

"What do you mean?" Thierry asked pointedly. 'Twas evident what Abaqa meant but he wanted to hear the matter stated clearly.

"I would have you ride to this Paris of theirs as an emissary. My greetings will you carry and mayhap my encouragement of a treaty, depending on the evidence before your own eyes."

Thierry swallowed carefully, knowing full well the impertinence of the question he would ask but having no choice. He had to know.

"Why me?"

The khan smiled a predatory smile that told Thierry that he was not expected to succeed. "Well it seems to me that I recall hearing a tale that you speak the Frankish tongue," Abaqa commented idly. Though this was true, Thierry suspected 'twas not the fullness of the tale. The shaman's silhouette separated from the shadows behind the khan. The man's eyes gleamed and Thierry knew a moment of dread to have his suspicions so readily confirmed.

Was he being sent on a futile mission in the hope he might not return?

Truly it seemed that his fate was not to be markedly different from that of Chinkai. But at least Thierry had a chance of surviving. And survive he would, despite the conviction of these two men.

"Aye, I have spoken the Frankish tongue," he agreed carefully. "Though it has been many years."

"The road is long," Abaqa said offhandedly. "Much time will you have to practice." His eyes brightened and he leaned forward once more. "There *is* another reason," he confided in a low voice. Thierry's heart began to pound.

"Aye?"

"Aye. Show me your mark."

Thierry frowned in confusion, then reluctantly unfastened his *kalat*. Only too well did he know the suspicion the Mongols had of his birthmark, though he gave it little heed. Had his father not sported one much like it? And what had it to do with this mission? He bared the port-wine stain to view, surprised to hear a woman's gasp.

"'Tis the mark of the Christ," the khan's Byzantine wife declared breathlessly. The shaman's eyes glittered triumphantly and the khan's smile widened.

Thierry watched in stunned amazement as she darted forward to gingerly trace the outline of the mark with a quivering fingertip, though she did not touch his flesh. Her hand paused and hovered before him as her gaze flicked audaciously to his, then danced away, her head bowing as she dropped to her knees before him.

Thierry glanced up in surprise to meet the knowing smile of the khan. He felt the woman's lips brush across his boot.

"They will believe you," Abaqa growled with satisfaction, his gaze sweeping scornfully over his wife.

Thierry's head reeled but he took a step back from the kneeling woman and cleared his throat deliberately. "When shall I leave?" he asked hoarsely.

"This very day," the khan asserted curtly, snapping his fingers impatiently at his wife. "No need is there for you to ride all the way back to Tabriz with us. The way is shorter from here."

His wife stood hastily and scurried back to his side, her eyes downcast once she noted her spouse's dissatisfied frown. Gravely had she erred in dropping to her knees before any other but the khan himself. Thierry hoped he would not have to pay for her insolence.

"The message will be ready shortly." The khan tented his fingers together and smiled yet again as he met Thierry's gaze. "Mayhap that rebel Nogai would be well advised to accompany you," Abaqa added in a dangerously low tone. Thierry's heart clenched that his fall from grace should implicate his friend as well, but there was little he could do about the matter now.

"After all," Abaqa commented under his breath as he selected another plump date, his easy manner apparently restored, "I have no space in my camp for ambitious men." The men's gazes met and held once more. The glint in the khan's eye told Thierry that 'twas not Nogai's ambition that troubled him.

Indeed, he was being cast out of the camp, Nogai condemned to accompany him because of their long and openly acknowledged friendship. Thierry flicked a glance around the yurt and met the satisfied gleam in the shaman's eye once more.

The other man tapped his staff on the ground with satisfaction, the tails attached to the horse's head carved at its top dancing in the fitful light. No doubt had Thierry that his influence was responsible for this discussion. As their gazes held, the other man smiled slowly, his gaze dropping pointedly to Thierry's crotch.

"I would assume," Abaqa commented with feigned disinterest, "that I would have no reason to concern myself about witches in the camp on the morrow."

"Witches?" Thierry asked mildly, refusing to be goaded. He held the shaman's gaze until the man's smile faded before looking back to the khan.

"Aye, *witches*."

"Naught do I know of witches," Thierry commented, watching the khan's brows rise.

"You coupled with one before us all last night!" the shaman charged abruptly as he strode forward. All within the yurt looked up with interest, but Thierry maintained his calm.

"Claimed a woman, I did, in the usual manner," he declared softly.

The shaman's eyes gleamed and he shook his head. "Nay, she is a witch, for Nogai told me so and well do you know it, as well." The shaman leaned forward confidently and Abaqa watched him avidly. "'Twas her sorcery alone that gave her the strength to refuse my elixir," he whispered ominously.

Thierry saw the truth flicker in the old one's eyes and knew that his woman's refusal to surrender the pearl to the shaman had not been taken well. Yet again, he wondered how she had contrived to hide it, though it mattered naught now. His disagreement with the shaman had precipitated Abaqa's move and naught could change the matter.

All the same, he could not suppress a flicker of pride that she had bested the shaman.

Thierry shrugged with mock complacency. "Witches, shaman, holy men. Are you not all the same in truth?"

"Nay!" the shaman claimed wildly. "Evil are witches, for they twist the hearts and minds of men and destroy their form." Again that glance dropped and Thierry noted the khan's interest in the same part of his anatomy.

"Well it seems that you have erred in this prediction," Thierry stated quietly. "Indeed, the reverse seems true."

"He lies," the shaman whispered to the khan.

"Mayhap you would like to see for yourself," Thierry suggested silkily. Both men's eyes widened and the shaman's voice dropped to a hiss.

"Best he leaves the camp with his witch immediately, for no good can come of his presence. Have you not seen how the gods have turned against him? His golden luck is gone and with it, any need for us to shelter his kind."

"I shall be gone as soon as the message is prepared," Thierry interjected flatly. No interest had he in hearing any more of the man's nonsense.

Threatened the shaman was undoubtedly by the promise of another within the camp who might lay claim to his influential role. Women and men both could be shaman within the Mongol tribes, and Thierry was sorely tempted to make some brash claim of his woman's influence. The khan looked as though he would ask a question but Thierry spoke quickly first, knowing all the while the impertinence of the deed.

"My woman and *anda* will accompany me," he concluded, backing away before both men's relief.

Good 'twould be to put this life behind him, for thoroughly tired was he of the suspicions and superstitions that traveled with it. A relief 'twould be indeed not to be looking over his shoulder at every turn in anticipation of a betrayal. The matter was settled with Abaqa finally, and though Thierry hated to admit his ambitions thwarted, in a sense he was relieved. No more would he bow and scrape under the implied threat of his own demise.

A simple man he was again. A warrior, a mercenary, a blade for hire once the khan's message was delivered. No future had the Mongols in these parts, penned in as they were, and Thierry lifted his nose to the wind.

His mind filled with possibilities of adventure and fortune to be gained in other foreign lands just over the horizon. Had he not always had the certainty that he was destined for greatness? Mayhap his destiny was with others than the Mongols.

So close he had come here to gaining ascendancy, only to have victory stolen away by foolish errors. It seemed the fates did not see success for him here. But still he had learned much these years and such experience would come readily to his hand when he had need of it again.

The land of the Franks beckoned. It could not be coincidence that sent him to the land where he had been born, the land that he had never known. A new spring was there in Thierry's step when he gained the outside and he thought he saw promise even in the rain. Always had he lived in the East and he wondered for the first time what had compelled his parents to leave their homeland so soon after his birth.

But no option had he of asking that question, with angry words and the width of Asia between himself and his father. And no need had he of an answer, in truth, for he was heading to his native land this very day.

Did Dame Fortune await him there?

Kira awoke to the drone of rain on the tent. She snuggled deeper into the warmth of the blanket, not knowing whether to be disappointed or relieved to find her warrior gone.

Had she dreamed that magical interval in the night or had he truly touched her? An exploring finger revealed the slick dampness between her thighs and she smelled her own scent heavy beneath the blankets. Kira's color rose and her certainty grew that the warrior would certainly think her no better than a whore for her shockingly loose behavior.

Indeed, she could scarce believe she had acted thus herself.

A woman groaned and a masculine voice raised in sleepy complaint. Kira closed her eyes again to feign sleep and rolled over to covertly seek out the source of the sound. The warrior's companion sat up with a scowl and scratched his bare skin, sparing a terse comment to one of the women who slept beside him. She argued briefly but he cocked his head uncompromisingly toward the tent flap. Kira slid farther under the protection of the blanket as the woman roused her companion with irritable resignation. The two of them, their kohl eyeliner smeared and hair bedraggled, made their way out of the tent.

Was this the way of whores in the camp? Kira hunkered down under the blanket and wondered what her warrior would expect when he returned. Would he similarly send her on her way? And where exactly did these women go?

The sound of breathing filled the tent again in the women's wake, the warrior's companion sprawling on his back and snoring with his mouth open as though he had not even awakened a moment past. Kira dared to peek around. She decided immediately that she liked the look of this one even less when he slept. Rougher he appeared than her warrior, more poorly groomed, dirtier and evidently of lower rank.

Well it seemed that she might have done worse the previous night. Kira shivered. But what had she gained? Would her warrior return to similarly oust her?

It seemed forever had come and gone in the time she lay there and fretted over her status, though indeed the tent had only become incrementally lighter when the warrior made his appearance once more. Kira's heart jumped at the decisive opening of the tent flap, no doubt in her mind who would stand framed against the morning's grayness should she dare to look.

But she could not. She squeezed her eyes shut and pretended to sleep as her heart pounded in her ears. Mayhap then, he would not have the heart to awaken her and cast her out, though well enough did Kira know that she was hoping thus in vain.

The tent was silent except for the other man's snores, the very air charged with expectancy. Well did Kira know that she was being watched again, but she resolutely kept her eyes closed.

If only she could slow her breathing or unclench her fingers beneath the blanket.

The warrior took a barely audible step and Kira heard whatever he carried drop to the ground. She tensed when she felt him stretch his length out alongside her, bracing herself for the worst.

Naught happened. Kira fancied she could feel his breath fan her skin, his breathing annoyingly more regular and slower of pace than her own. She panicked, knowing that she would do well to fool him at such close range, and desperately hoped that he merely intended to fall asleep once more like his brethren.

A sharp tap on the end of her nose made her jump. Kira's eyes flew open to confront the knowing expression in the disconcerting gray gaze so close to her own. Was that amusement that almost tugged at the corner of his lips? Indeed, it could not be and she stared back at him fearfully, uncertain what he intended to do now that he had discovered her ruse.

To her surprise he merely coaxed her to sit up before him. Kira shivered and clutched the blanket to her chest, not entirely convinced that his intentions were good ones. The way he moved to sit directly behind her fed her trepidation and she felt herself stiffen at his proximity.

Then his fingers were in her hair. Kira almost leaped skyward in alarm until she realized that he was finger-combing its length. She twisted slightly to look at him, only to earn a quick condemnation and a gentle finger beneath her chin urging her to face forward once more.

No desire had he that she witness whatever vile deed he had in mind, Kira thought bitterly. She jabbed her chin into the air stubbornly, certain she would see that he had not an easy way of whatever he intended to do.

There was no mistaking the rhythmic tug of having her hair braided, though Kira fought the evidence for a more rational explanation. He was grooming her? How could this be? It defied reason that he would do such a thing. She twisted around, not knowing what to do in the face of this unexpected development, and her gaze fell upon the burden he had dropped.

Clothing. Similar to his in style it looked, but smaller of cut.

Was she to have these clothes? And was this a sign of possession? Kira glanced over her shoulder uncertainly. The warrior had finished her braid and was tying the end with a short length of rawhide. He met her gaze, one end of the rawhide in his teeth, and raised his brows expressively.

Kira fought the urge to smile at his unexpectedly playful expression and quickly turned away from him. Her heart pounded erratically and she told herself not to be a fool. The man had no interest in her. Likely he knew she had no garments and would see her garbed before tossing her out.

The assertion did not ring as true as Kira thought it should have, for surely a man who cared naught for her would not worry whether she was soaked in this rain. But then, surely a man who cared naught for her would not have pleasured her in the night as he had.

Mayhap she merely knew too little about men who cared naught. Well did her father care for her, this she knew without doubt, and that alone should have told her that affection was a demanding burden. Mayhap a lack of regard was a less painful obligation.

Kira frowned, knowing herself to be more thoroughly confused than ever she had been. She closed her eyes and let the scent of the warrior's skin fill her nostrils, acknowledging that his very presence calmed her fears. Mayhap that was enough.

Mayhap that would have to be enough.

The warrior urged her to her feet with a hand beneath her elbow. He indicated with an imperious finger the deep blue *kurta, kalat* and *chalwar* he had brought, and Kira reached for the loose shirt. A solid finger on her shoulder brought her up short and she cursed herself for making the mistake of meeting his eyes. Too aware of him was she in the humid warmth of the tent with the beat of the rain filling her ears and the memory of his intoxicating touch heating her cheeks.

He pointed to the silk *kurta* she wore and said something, his gesture indicating that she should remove it. Kira's face flamed but he remained resolute.

'Twas his shirt, after all, she supposed. Kira dropped her gaze miserably, uncertain she could cavalierly disrobe before him this morning. His flat palm intruded on her peripheral vision, that signal of demand that he knew she understood. Kira nodded quickly. He would have his *kurta* but she would grant him no view of what was beneath. 'Twas irrational and well she knew it but still she could not do it.

She squared her shoulders to brace herself before meeting his gaze once more. With a swirl of one finger, she tried to show him that she wanted him to turn around. His features remained impassive and he showed no signs of moving. Kira sighed, gritting her teeth as she resolutely gripped his arm and tried to turn him. Well enough she knew that he had no interest in her form, but still her modesty compelled her to maintain some dignity.

At least she would not be forced to confront the disinterest in his eyes. She gave his elbow a resolute shove and, to her surprise, he complied.

No need had there been to be so readily complaisant, she thought irritably. At least the man could pretend to having some interest. Unreasonable she was being, and Kira was fully aware of her erratic mood, though this uncertainty over her fate did her temper few favors.

She desperately wished there was some way to know her status once and for all.

Kira spared a glance to the other occupant of the tent to ensure that he was sleeping, then hastily peeled off his silk *kurta*. Having no idea how much time the warrior would grant her to change, she quickly donned the garments he had brought. Kira frowned at the padding in the hips of the loose *chalwar* trousers, certain it would make her look hugely round. With a muttered sound of disgust she removed the pads and cast them aside, then hauled the fur-lined tunic over her head just as the warrior turned around.

He nodded with what might have been approval and pointed to a pair of boots Kira had not noticed before. She jammed her foot into one, lacing the open front up to the knee similar to the way the warrior wore his. Kira picked up the other boot, seeing out of the corner of her eye that he had dropped to a crouch and was quickly rolling up the blankets she had just abandoned.

He said something to his companion, who snorted in his sleep but continued to snore more or less undisturbed. A frown briefly darkened the warrior's brow as he put the blankets aside, then he stepped over to shake the other man.

His companion sat up with alarm, his gaze focusing reluctantly on the tent around him. He blinked and frowned, the pair exchanging a quick volley of comments as Kira watched. The other man looked perplexed and made a demand, which the warrior answered with a single terse word.

He straightened abruptly, leaving his companion with a moderately dazed expression. The warrior collected a pair of leather saddlebags and matter-of-factly packed the blankets away. He removed a pair of heavy cloaks, casting the shorter one about Kira's shoulders before he donned the other. His companion seemed to take that as a sign of some kind, for he stood so quickly that Kira had no chance to avoid a glimpse of his nudity.

She stared stubbornly at her freshly booted toe, not knowing what was happening and uncertain she even wanted to know. Then the warrior loomed in her peripheral vision and she glanced up to find him tossing one of the saddlebags over his shoulder. He handed her the other one and gestured her toward the tent flap, his companion hauling on his boots as he hastened to follow them out into the rain.

The surrounding tents looked dejected in the gray morning light, their heavy felt sagging with the weight of the rain. Misty 'twas and damp, and Kira shivered within the warm embrace of her new clothes. She glanced back to find her warrior hefting onto his shoulders a saddle that he had left just inside the tent.

Her pulse leaped when his companion followed suit. She needed little imagination to see that they were leaving the camp. Her warrior's gaze met hers and Kira's heart gave an unsteady lurch, the sensation leaving her unsure whether to be pleased or not that he had not so far cast her aside.

Would he take her with him, wherever he was going? Or would she be consigned to the ranks of the whores servicing the camp? Kira licked her lips carefully, trudging in the direction he indicated with trepidation weighing heavily on her heart.

The realization that the price for taking a witch was evidently quite low pleased Thierry more than he would have preferred. Touching her had reassured him yet again that the shaman had evidently misunderstood the inclination of her powers, if indeed she was a witch at all.

Simple 'twould have been to be able to blame this small woman for the khan's decision of this morn, but Thierry knew 'twas not the case. Only too aware was he that his becoming an outcast had been in the wind afore he knew she was in the camp.

Thierry's optimism about visiting his native land dismissed any such worries out of hand. A new future had he in the land of the Franks and Thierry was assailed by a sense that his would be a noble destiny there. In fact, he was feeling remarkably hale this morn, despite the khan's choice. His woman walked before him, her hips swaying temptingly, and he acknowledged himself to be feeling healthy, indeed.

But a few hours since they had coupled and already he was anxiously wondering how long 'twould take her to come to him. Truly he had denied himself too long.

The shaman was a fool.

He watched his woman's shapely buttocks and recalled the flutter of her heart beneath his hand. Something clenched within him at the memory and he vowed silently that she would come to him again. Had he not pleased her in the night?

Unless she had no recollection of his touch. Thierry searched his mind for some minute sign she had made this morn of her newfound awareness of him. Not a gesture, not a glance, not a flush could he recall that might signify that she, too, had needs. Indeed, she seemed yet more supremely unaware of him than before.

Could it be that witches truly had no need of men? Could this be the price of taking one? To be enchanted and have no hope of possessing her again? The very possibility of that being true made Thierry itch to make her taste her need once more.

But nay. He had vowed to himself that he would wait for her. Khanbaliq invaded his thinking yet again and for the first time, he felt a wave of ingratitude toward his sire.

Curse the man for teaching him to hold the sanctity of a vow above all else.

Chapter Nine

"Congratulations," the Persian woman purred into Kira's ear.

Kira turned away from the latrines, astonished to find anyone else awake in the silent camp. The Persian woman smiled knowingly. "Well did I tell you that you were too pretty for war fodder. And no doubt was there left that Black Wind chose you as his woman."

Kira felt her brows rise skeptically. "Indeed, the deed could scarcely be missed," she commented sourly as she adjusted her *chalwar*. The other woman gripped her arm, and Kira glanced up in surprise.

"Know you not what he did?"

"Aye." Kira winced in wry recollection. "I know well enough what he did."

The woman smothered a smile. "Nay, Kira, not that. You do understand that 'tis their way to stake a claim publicly?" she added in a lower tone. Kira felt her eyes widen.

"I do not understand," she said carefully, not daring to believe what the woman seemed intent on telling her. Surely 'twas not a custom to possess a woman before all the others?

The Persian woman nodded slowly as she saw comprehension dawn in Kira's eyes. "'Tis evident he wanted to leave no doubt that you are his," she hissed. "Possessiveness in a man is good sign, indeed."

Kira's heart leaped and she flicked a quick glance to the warrior standing at the far side of the latrine. He was facing toward the open fields behind as though completely unconcerned with her actions, but well enough she knew by now that he was fully aware of what she did and precisely where she stood.

In a way, such an awareness was strangely comforting. Had it been someone who threatened her this morn, instead of merely the chat of this woman, Kira knew that little could go amiss before her warrior was at hand.

She rather liked that. The other woman chuckled and patted Kira companionably on the shoulder, jarring her out of her thoughts.

"Aye, little Kira. Well do you know what I mean. Make no mistake, for Black Wind has claimed you for his woman."

Black Wind. Was that what "Thierry" meant? Kira turned to the other woman and looked right into her eyes. "How do the Mongols say 'Black Wind'?" she asked.

The woman looked surprised, then smiled confidentially. "Qaraq-Böke," she said, much to Kira's confusion. Naught at all did that sound like "Thierry." So harsh was the word in contrast to the name that the warrior had given her that Kira's heart began to pound.

Surely he could not have told her the name he would confide in no other here?

"No other way is there to say it?" she demanded breathlessly. The woman shook her head quickly, confusion lighting her eyes.

"Nay, Kira. 'Tis Qaraq-Böke he is called. Would you not say it to me first?" she asked helpfully. "Well you should know that but a slight inflection changes the meaning of a word in their tongue. I would not have you insult him when all seems to be progressing so well."

Kira smiled and glanced to her warrior as the surety of her conclusion flooded through her. "I will not insult him," she murmured with growing confidence. She gave the other woman an impulsive hug before she spun away, filled with an uncharacteristic optimism.

"I fear we are leaving and would wish you good luck," she said gaily. The other woman looked mildly surprised, but Kira waved and danced away. "Thank you!" she called before turning to her warrior triumphantly and granting him the same sunny smile.

For Kira had no doubt that her warrior had confided in her his real name. And that was more a sign that he had claimed her for his own than anything the Persian woman might have told her.

He turned to watch her approach, his sight landing unerringly on her as though he knew exactly where she was the entire time. Kira's pulse echoed in her ears and she stifled her jubilant smile as she fairly skipped across the grass to him.

He had told *her* his name after but a few days. And these people had known him years without learning his true name. Indeed, that could only be a good portent of things to come.

Something had changed in her assessment of him, though Thierry could not guess what 'twas. He puzzled over it as he saddled his horse in the misty rain, well aware of her complacency as she stood beside him. Calmer she seemed and he risked a covert glance in her direction to find her expression uncharacteristically patient.

Surely a woman would fuss over the foul weather? But nay, she merely stood and watched him work as though she would learn the task. Aye, he thought sourly, a woman afraid of horses well needed to know how to saddle a beast.

What game did she play with him now? Did she mean to steal a horse and escape him in the night? The idea that she might never come to him had unnerved Thierry more than he was certain it should have. Well he knew his current mood was the result. He spared her a glance and she met his gaze pertly.

Thierry spun back to his task, his fingers fumbling with the horse's trap. Indeed, the woman would make him skittish with her incessant changes of mood. Well it seemed that he could not foresee what she might do. 'Twas a new sensation and not one that Thierry was finding enjoyable.

Predictable had her response been when he had awakened her in the night, though he could not have expected her passion. And truly, had he troubled to reflect upon the matter, he might have anticipated the way she had recoiled after their mating.

But how or why had she ended up in Abaqa's camp again? Sent her directly to Tiflis he had and he wondered what had changed her path. There was a puzzle. And what had originally given her the audacity to openly defy him, a Mongol, in her father's shop?

Witch, he concluded readily, sparing her another covert glance. Naught did it help matters that the garb he had obtained for her accented her petite figure. Even without the padding in her *chalwar,* her hips were delightfully rounded and her waist small enough that he longed to fold his hands around her.

She smiled at him and Thierry's heart fairly stopped.

He felt the scowl darken his brow as he abruptly turned back to the horse's harness. Glad he was that she had not done *that* sooner, for the sight was fetching, indeed. Too readily did he recall her laughter when he had tickled her foot in the khan's yurt. That delicate foot with its high arch and tiny red callus. Thierry swallowed carefully and fastened the last strap on the harness.

Suddenly Thierry was markedly less certain of his ability to keep his vow.

He gestured to another of his horses and then to her, making a mock riding movement. Her eyes widened and she looked from the saddled horse to the unbridled one in momentary confusion. She pointed to him with one slim finger, her blank expression all the question Thierry needed.

He pointed to himself and laid one hand on the saddle. The horse stepped sideways, anxious to be on the run. His woman pointed to herself tentatively and Thierry pointed to his horse, then the other and shrugged.

"Tiflis?" she asked. Thierry shook his head firmly, surprised that she did not seem disappointed by the news. Had she not family in Tiflis?

"Paris," he informed her, but her expression changed not. Mayhap she had not heard tell of the Frankish city.

"Constantinople," he said flatly, hoping she knew the name of that city.

Her expression revealed that she was familiar with the town, the way she hastily laid one hand on his saddle beside his, showing at least an awareness of the distance. Aye, well he could imagine that she did not want to ride all that way alone with her uncertainty of horses, but he had had to offer the choice. For the sake of his vow, if naught else.

Thierry glanced down and was struck again by the difference in size between their hands lying so close together on the red leather saddle. He deliberately tore his glance away from her small hand and met her eyes.

"Constantinople?" she asked, pointing to him, then herself.

Any fear she had shown of him seemed to have dissipated rapidly, Thierry thought irritably, not in the least pleased that any sexual interest in him had seemed to depart along with it. Had he not ensured she was pleased? How long would she force him to endure the haunting scent of her skin?

How long could he endure her proximity without the barbarian within him bursting forth once more?

When Thierry forced himself to nod in response to her question, she pointed inquiringly to Nogai, then to all the horses, and he nodded once more. She chewed her lip for an instant, firing his desire to taste her anew. Evidently unaware of her impact on him, she patted the embroidered saddle once more and indicated herself.

"Constantinople," she said with a decisive nod.

So be it. Thierry nodded and swung up into his saddle. He gave in to his impulse and gripped her around the waist when he leaned down, savoring the fact that his hands virtually encompassed her as he lifted her into the high saddle behind him.

The cursed witch smiled at him again before he managed to turn away.

Had the other women told her something? Thierry knew he called more hastily to Nogai than was his custom, the proximity of his woman troubling him as they rode out of the sleeping camp.

The ride did naught to improve his mood.

Their lack of a common tongue irked Thierry more than it ever had and he found frustration chafing at him as they rode west. Too tempting indeed was it to have her ride behind him, every step of the horse sending her breasts pressing against his back. Well it seemed to Thierry that he could feel the imprint of her nipples, though 'twas impossible through all the layers of clothes between them.

He refused to ride at a slower pace in deference to her unfamiliarity in the saddle or the weather. A mission had he from the khan and no woman would hinder his path. The assertion sounded like an excuse even to Thierry's ears, but he rode on determinedly, even as the rain soaked them to the skin. This was his life, a mercenary's life, he thought stubbornly. Well enough had she chosen to be with him—now she would see the fullness of the path she had taken.

They stopped but once to let the horses drink from a river. To Thierry's astonishment the woman complained naught. She merely offered a slightly more tired version of her smile when he climbed into the saddle again. Impossible that she was not uncomfortable. Indeed, his own wet garments were chafing.

But nay. She simply brushed her wet hair out of her eyes and slipped her arms cautiously around Thierry's neck when he lifted her high. It helped his frustration not one iota that she was apparently perfectly content with both her choice and his denial of his own needs. The wave of possessiveness that shot through him had him placing her before him in the saddle before he dare to think. Nogai smothered a smile, but Thierry flatly refused to indulge his friend's humor.

They stopped finally when the moon was high overhead. The rain had slowed to a fitful drizzle and the woman stirred sleepily when Thierry dismounted. The gently rolling land extended as far as the eye could see in every direction and he frowned at the thought that they would have to stop in such an open place. At least the horses could readily graze.

Her eyes opened blearily and she met his gaze with less than her usual clarity of vision. Thierry folded his hands together and dropped his cheek to rest on one as he had once before. She smiled yet again, a softly seductive and sleepy smile that sent a startling pang directly through him. She slipped from the saddle like a woman in a dream, folding her arms about herself and shivering slightly as she glanced around.

"Mayhap we should kindle a fire," Thierry suggested.

Nogai laughed. "Oh, aye, well do I recall that always do we kindle one," he jested. Thierry felt his neck heat at the reminder that they seldom kindled a fire except on nights of dire cold. Which this one was not. Already was he more than fully aware himself that 'twas the woman's presence that had prompted his suggestion. Still, he did not appreciate Nogai reminding him of that fact.

Civilized 'twould be to warm themselves on such a damp night. Indeed, 'twas only sensible to ensure none of them sickened on the long path to Paris, lest the khan's message go undelivered.

"'Tis a cold enough night to merit one," he snapped, only too aware of her gaze upon him.

"Certainly," Nogai agreed with mocking deference. "I would not have you catch a chill at your sport this night." The shorter man turned to dig his tinderbox from his saddlebag, shooting a bright glance over his shoulder. "That is, unless the shaman spoke aright and you have naught with which to make your sport."

Thierry bit back a sharp retort, gritting his teeth as he resolutely unfastened his horse's saddle. Such a comment deserved no response. Nogai chuckled to himself and Thierry felt his ears burn, so certain was he that the woman looked between the two of them in confusion.

He lifted the saddle to the ground, dropping the saddlebags alongside. With a quick gesture he unfolded a blanket from one pack and cast it over the saddle, beckoning to the woman without meeting her eyes and patting its seat. She immediately did his bidding, a fact that pleased him more than he thought it should have. He folded the blanket around her with a brusque gesture, not waiting to see whether she smiled or not.

"Oho, surely the place of a woman has changed now that you have taken one," Nogai taunted. "Should she not be tending to our needs, instead of the other way around?" Thierry remained stubbornly silent while he removed the rest of the horse's harness, setting the beast free to run with its companions.

"She is tired," Thierry argued, knowing that Nogai would not leave the matter alone.

"And we are not?" the other man demanded archly. Despite his protest, he dropped to his knees and began to rummage in his tinderbox. "Should you spoil her now, no chance will you have of having her do your bidding later," Nogai advised. "Soon enough will you weary of her charms and wish she was doing all, as other women do." Thierry's lips thinned as he passed his friend a pair of fagots from his pack.

"'Tis not the way of my kin to leave the women do all," he muttered. Nogai looked to him in astonishment.

"Your kin?" he demanded with interest. "Naught have I ever heard you say of your kin afore."

"And now you have," Thierry retorted curtly.

What had prompted him to speak of personal matters with Nogai? Never had he even mentioned his family; indeed, none of the Mongols even knew his true name. The woman he had told already. Thierry slanted a wary glance in her direction, not in the least reassured by that realization. Why had he confided in her? He frowned and gestured pointedly to the unlit tinder.

"Are we to have a blaze this night or not?"

Nogai's brows rose, but he said naught else as he struck the flint. An awkward silence settled between the pair of them, a silence curiously unfamiliar for all the times they had sat together wordlessly on the plain.

Hot tea did they make to accompany the yogurt and flat bread they carried, though the meal was consumed wordlessly. The rain made the fire fizzle fitfully, and though Thierry knew his friend was curious, he could not speak of Khanbaliq and what he had left behind.

This woman was reminding him of matters best forgotten. Mayhap that was the root of her sorcery.

"Mayhap the fire was not such a good idea," he conceded finally when it fizzled to smoke yet again. Nogai's grin flashed opposite him before he sobered.

"The wood will do us for another night," he agreed quietly. Thierry smiled in turn, reassured that his reticence had not offended his friend. Nogai winked unexpectedly and jerked his head toward the woman. "Should you wish your sport this night, you had best be quick about it. She looks on the verge of sleep."

Thierry glanced to his woman in time to see her stifle a yawn, and barely checked an affectionate smile from spreading across his features. No sport would he have this night, nor indeed any other, he reminded himself firmly, without her express consent.

But no need was there for Nogai to know that. Thierry agreed and kicked out the fire, spreading his second blanket on the damp ground before coaxing the woman to lie down. She curled up immediately within the wool, looking very feline before she spared him an inquiring glance. Thierry knew not how to tell her 'twas up to her whether he joined her or not, so he simply stood and held her gaze.

Finally she shivered with exaggerated tremors and reached

out one hand to pat the expanse of blanket behind her. Thierry needed no second invitation, his anticipation firing as he dropped behind her. He thanked his lucky stars that he had not had to endure the waiting much longer, astonished when she did not unfurl her blanket to welcome him against her warmth.

To his surprise, his woman cuddled up against him and made a sound of satisfaction much like a contented purr before she closed her eyes. Thierry regarded her in amazement, knowing she could not be feigning the way her breathing slowed in sleep.

Nogai's smothered chuckle did little to ease his annoyance. Thierry hauled his cloak and the end of the blanket over himself in dissatisfaction, telling himself that 'twas his imagination alone that she smiled against his shoulder in her sleep.

The woman grew increasingly more comfortable in Thierry's presence as they drew ever nearer to Constantinople, though indeed she did not show any signs of planning to invite him between her thighs once more. Indeed, she cuddled against him on the third night as though his presence was no more threatening than that of an indulged family pet.

Tempted he was to not sleep with her at all, but he could not deny her his warmth. The nights were growing colder and she was small. When he felt her shiver, something nameless within him prompted him to ensure she did not fall ill.

A far cry indeed were these feelings from those he expected from the independent barbarian he knew he had become. Was it possible she was awakening all that was not Mongol within him? The return of such tender feelings did not sit well with Thierry, especially when the woman granted him naught with which to assuage his own needs.

For truly the shaman knew naught of what he spoke, the proof of that fact keeping Thierry from sleep. Except that mayhap this desire without release kept him snared within her web, be it a trap of sorcery or simply her soft femininity.

His vow irked him, but he would not break it now. Only the

certainty that the woman rode with him because of her fear of
the horses kept him from touching her again in the night. Clear
'twas that she had not the nerve to ride alone, should she be
given a choice.

Mayhap for the sake of his vow he should give her a choice,
Thierry concluded savagely. As though she sensed the direction of his thoughts, she wriggled closer and sighed with contentment. Thierry gritted his teeth at the invitingly ripe curve
of her buttock pressed against his thigh.

Like some cursed lapdog did she treat him, not a Mongol
warrior.

For a tempting moment he half considered doing something
dramatic to show her the error of her ways, but the soft sound of
her breathing brought him up short. Asleep she was already and
he had not the heart to awaken her. Thierry folded his arms behind
his head and stared into the fathomless indigo of the night sky.

Lapdog. He fairly snorted at the thought. Had she not been
shocked when they had coupled before the others? Mayhap he
should shock her again. Nogai was not much of an audience,
but he would do. She was small enough that she would not be
able to keep him from his goal, were he truly set upon it, he
reasoned savagely.

She rolled over and the feather-light fall of her delicate
fingers on his tunic brought all such thought to an abrupt halt.

Thierry stared at her relaxed fingers, unable to quell his satisfaction that she was showing signs of trusting him. And there
was the matter of his vow. Not to mention his own desire to love
her tenderly and gently when next they mated.

Even if it killed him, he must grant her the opportunity to
come to him.

And well it might kill him if she persisted in smiling at him
with such maddening sweetness, but going no further.

The muted sounds of the night reached his ears and Nogai
began to snore with characteristic relish as they lay once again
on the open plains. The woman burrowed into the warmth of

Thierry's shoulder and he stared unseeingly up at the stars, wishing she might come to him soon.

Very soon.

The warrior was sleeping when Kira awoke. She remained nestled against him as she watched the sky tinge pink to greet their fourth morning of travel. Her buttocks ached from their ceaseless riding and she felt filthy beyond compare, but at least she was warm. And mercifully the rain had stopped. Kira was relieved that her clothes were finally drying and vowed she would never take such simple comforts for granted again.

How long until they reached Constantinople? Indeed, she had little idea how far the great city was, even from Tiflis, let alone what kind of pace they made. And why were they going there? What would happen when they arrived? No clue had Kira and she stifled anew her impatience. She wished she could remember what her warrior had said first, before he had said "Constantinople." Had it been the name of another town? Was Constantinople simply en route or was it in the vicinity of this other place? Had that been the name of a place at all?

Annoying 'twas beyond compare that Kira did not know and yet more so that she could not ask. She would simply have to wait and see.

The warrior's arm flexed, shifting the weight cast across her waist, and Kira watched him sleep. No less threatening did he look in peaceful repose, the line of his mouth as uncompromising as ever it was. She squinted and tried to imagine his lips curved in a smile, without success. At least he had claimed her for his woman and she had the certainty that she would not be cast before the advancing army as war fodder.

Though still it irked her that he obviously had no desire for her form. Why then had he claimed her? Impossible 'twas that he might have felt some responsibility for tearing her from her home, for he was a mercenary. That much was clear to even

Kira's inexperienced eye. No feelings had this man, though truly she had expected that he might be more lustful.

It must be that her inadequacies did not tempt him.

What would happen if another crossed their path who did tempt him? Indeed, what fate did he plan for her, if not as his woman? Surely even a Mongol man took his pleasure with his woman more frequently than this? Kira knew not and wished that she knew more of men and their ways.

Or even that she was capable of asking him for the truth.

Could the Persian woman have been mistaken? Could he be taking her to Constantinople to meet some other, even less attractive fate? Kira considered the uncompromising lines of her warrior's sleeping visage and could not imagine that 'twas so. For all his stern manner, he had shown her a manner of kindness she had not known before and she would not condemn him out of hand.

Nor would she reflect upon her fate should one who did tempt him cross their path. Naught could she do if he chose to cast her aside, and she could not worry about troubles before they came. This was her life. For now, she would take life, such as it was, and be grateful for each day.

Indeed, she had little choice.

Kira rolled out of the warrior's grasp and listened, fancying she heard the sound of running water. How enticing 'twould be to have a bath and scrub this mire from her skin! And should she be quick about it, the men need never know.

She slipped carefully from the warm clutch of the blanket, holding her breath as she watched the warrior. He did not awaken, or else he feigned sleep so well that she could not discern the difference. He did not appear to notice her departure from his side, a fact that did little to bolster Kira's pride. The other one snored undisturbed.

Soundlessly, Kira unfastened the warrior's saddlebag, surprised to find its contents meticulously well organized. She found the soap and the length of cloth, sparing a covert glance over her shoulder before she hastily pursued the sound of running water.

Thierry knew something was amiss as soon as he awakened.

She was gone. At the realization that the woman was not beside him, his eyes flew open to scan the camp. Nogai snored comfortably but not a sign of her was there. His heart missed a beat.

Had another stolen her away? Or had she run from him?

Thierry was on his feet in a flash, the sight of his opened saddlebag bringing a frown to his brow. He squatted and checked the contents, surprised to find his soap missing.

Then he heard the running water. His mind put the pieces together and he breathed a shaky sigh of relief.

Bathing she was again. He shook his head tolerantly at the fancies of urban women and shoved to his feet. His gaze scanned the horizon as he listened and he picked out the change of vegetation at the edge of a rise. The river was there. Too readily did he recall the bronzed perfection of her skin, the realization that it had been long since he had gazed upon his woman following quickly in the memory's wake.

She would be bathing nude, he was certain of it. Thierry licked his lips and stared resolutely at the ground. No business had he watching her. Had he not made a vow? Had he not pledged to leave her be? How would he deny himself with her loveliness arrayed before him again?

Water splashed and he turned immediately at the sound. She might have slipped. Indeed, another could have come upon her at her leisure. Unable to check his steps, Thierry followed the sound of the water. After all, he told himself self-righteously, 'twas unsafe for her to bathe unescorted. Who knew what manner of bandits and vagabonds frequented these hills?

Though at the sight of his woman thigh-deep in the river and gloriously nude, all thought of anyone else was dismissed from Thierry's mind.

She was more beautiful than he recalled, her skin that even golden tone, every facet of her figure delicately wrought. His desire fired with an intensity that astounded him as she bathed, completely unaware of his presence. Thierry could not move from where he stood, everything within him captured by the sight of her.

She turned and he fairly heard her gasp when she saw him.

They both froze in place, eyeing each other warily. She vainly tried to cover her bare breasts with the small bar of soap and her tiny hands. Thierry could think of naught but covering them with his own hands, the thought thickening him in a denial of the shaman's dire prediction.

An instant later he was striding down the bank purposefully, abandoning his clothes as he splashed into the water. He noted with amazement that she held her ground, but even that observation did not slow his pace. The river swirled about her hips, its water icily green, its chill sending her nipples into pert peaks. Thierry knew he had never desired a woman more, but he finally stopped a pace away from her with uncertainty.

He did not want to frighten her again. And he had vowed to let her come to him.

Thierry looked into the dark glory of her eyes, the sight of her hesitancy renewing the hold of his vow over his desire. He held out his hand for the soap with matter-of-fact ease and she immediately surrendered it, as though glad to abandon its burden. Their fingers brushed accidentally in the transaction, sending a jolt through him. He glanced to her eyes again, surprised to find a scarlet flush burning her cheeks.

Thierry cocked one eyebrow inquiringly and his woman became truly agitated. Her color rose impossibly higher and she gestured hastily to his arousal, her gaze dancing nervously to meet his before she averted her face with a jerk.

Surely this could not be. Could his temptress doubt her own charms? Thierry lifted her chin with one finger that she would be compelled to meet his gaze. The way she swallowed awk-wardly beneath his touch fed the tenderness flooding within him.

So, she did not understand the reason for his state. He glanced down to himself, then looked to her, willing her to understand that 'twas the sight of her that enflamed him. She hastily shook her head and looked away nervously once more.

Nay, sweet witch, Thierry thought affectionately. The fault was indeed hers and he impulsively decided to make the matter most clear. Well should she understand the power she held over him. He tipped her chin once more and held her gaze for a long moment, letting his fingertip slide slowly down to her collar-bone and trace its shape. Thierry let his gaze follow his finger-tip, knowing all his hunger for her must be blazing in his eyes.

She shivered beneath his perusal, but did not move away.

His fingertip lovingly slipped over the full curve of her breast, outlining the dark circle of one areola with what he hoped was evident admiration. The nipple tightened, the woman gasped and Thierry marveled anew at the softness of her skin. Well could he lose himself in her softness and warmth, the feel of her beneath one finger loosening his resolution to keep his pledge.

His finger slid tantalizingly lower, tracing a lazy pattern back and forth over the silhouette of each rib. Thierry leisurely encircled her navel with that feather-light touch, pausing to tap that enchanting mole but once. His gaze fell to the dark tangle of curls and he knew his stamina could not bear the test.

Should he touch her there, he would be lost.

Thierry flattened his hand instead and caressed the silky curve of her hips with his palm. He nearly closed his eyes in pleasure as his fingertips rolled over the smooth indent of her waist. He exhaled unsteadily, never having anticipated that such a slow and simple gesture could ignite him so fully, and dared to meet her eyes once more.

Disbelief shone in those dark depths and Thierry could not understand the sight. Could she truly doubt that she aroused him beyond compare? But one other way was there to make the matter most clear.

His fingers slid over her and abruptly speared into the hair held tight by her braid, his thumb tipping up her chin as he possessively kissed her. Thierry poured all of his passion into his kiss, willing her to understand her effect on him. Magnificent she was; indeed, he had never seen another who fired his desire so. He wished he knew the words to tell her so, hoped that his urgency would be communicated by his kiss.

Thierry's heart pounded when his woman tentatively placed her hands on his shoulders and leaned against him to taste him more fully. The casual brush of her nipples against his chest was enough to drive him to distraction, but he willed himself to keep a slow pace. He pulled her yet closer, cradling her head in his palms as he deepened his kiss. To his complete astonishment her tongue mimicked the gesture of his and nudged against his teeth.

The tentative flicking of her tongue made Thierry doubt he could control himself. He felt himself press against the softness of her stomach and heard himself groan aloud.

'Twas too much that she should kiss him thus when he had made such a vow. No more could he stand without the assurance that she would come to him fully. Indeed, he only fed his own madness by touching her thus. The embrace had to stop.

Determined to keep his word, Thierry tore his lips from hers and turned to stalk out of the water, blind to everything before him. Only the weight of her gaze upon him did he sense until he crested the small rise alongside the bank and scooped up his clothes.

He was back in the camp, agitatedly listening to Nogai's contented snores, before he realized he still held the soap.

Chapter Ten

Kira's fingertips rose to her lips in wonder as the warrior disappeared from sight.

'Twas not possible. She quivered inside with that same tension he had roused in her before. But the evidence he had given her was undeniable.

The man desired her. Her. Kira of Tiflis with her scarred back and ridiculously childlike body. With her breasts her father had called too small to nurse a babe. Had her sire not oft told her that she looked much like a poorly fed orphan? How often had she been reminded that he would be hard-pressed indeed to find her a spouse? Ingratitude it had been surely that had made her grow up in such an unattractive fashion to challenge her father's objectives.

But this man seemed to desire her. 'Twas too much to be believed. Kira straightened her posture with an unfamiliar measure of pride.

Mayhap she was simply the only female hereabouts. That thought eliminated her pleasure. Well enough had Kira heard that men needed a woman regularly to satisfy their desires. 'Twas evident that she alone was female of the three of them and that no other women had crossed their path these past days.

She nibbled her lip thoughtfully, unable to suppress the argument that came immediately to mind.

No denial could she make of the heat burning in the warrior's eyes when he looked at her. Nor could she deny that he had claimed her in the camp, over all the other more amply endowed and more graceful women. Kira the warrior had chosen alone. Kira of Tiflis, over all the other women there. And clearly, he wanted her to know that that had not been an impulse regretted. The warrior still desired her. Kira allowed herself a brief flicker of pride and stifled a triumphant smile.

She was his woman, Black Wind's woman to the exclusion of all others.

Thierry's woman. Her pulse filled her ears at the heady reminder of his confidence.

Mayhap he had claimed her that she might have protection alone, she reasoned, still unable to accept what her heart told her was the truth. Mayhap he had thought himself responsible for her plight and aimed only to right the wrong.

Mayhap. But that argument's power was naught in the face of the incendiary kiss he had just granted her. Kira touched her lips wonderingly once more and permitted another thrill to trip along her veins. Indeed, she well enough understood what he was trying to tell her when he pressed against her.

Her warrior wanted to bed her again. Should she have had any doubt of that fact, the red flush rising on the back of his neck as he stalked away would remove all doubt.

But why had he left? Was it not the Mongol way to simply take what one wanted? Kira shook her head and rinsed her skin, reasoning that had the warrior wanted her, he might have taken her many times by now. She must have misunderstood him.

But he had simply pleasured her that last time he had touched her. She halted and considered that. No sense did it make that he could desire her and not take her again. Kira frowned and strode to the bank in his wake, absently picked up her clothes and began to dress.

Suddenly Kira recalled his manner with the wild horses on the plain and froze mid-gesture. She saw him again, standing silently and waiting for the skittish horses to approach him.

'Twas immediately clear to her. The warrior was waiting for Kira to make a sign that she wanted him. The conclusion was inescapable and Kira smiled in delight. No move would he make without her encouragement.

No barbarian way was that and her heart warmed at his consideration. Could he have understood her dismay after that first mating? Could he have shown her pleasure that she might understand 'twas not all pain?

Could he truly be waiting for her to indicate that she wanted him?

The very thought was both dizzying and intoxicating. Kira knew not what she would do. *Did* she want him? She scarcely knew, though when he touched her as he just had, she could think of naught but having more. She recalled the weight of his hands upon her skin and the fullness of him within her and shivered in anticipation.

Could she be so bold as to choose to mate with him again?

But how would she tell him what she wanted, if indeed another mating was what she wanted? Could she be audacious enough to show him without the fortifying strength of the *qumis?*

Clearly, touching his lips with her tongue was not enough, for she had done that moments past and he had left. Kira bit her lip, certain she had been bold beyond belief in making that gesture, but it had not sufficed. She knew not whether she could summon the nerve to do more; indeed, she was not certain she wanted more, but her heart was pounding when she climbed the rise and made her way back to camp.

Surely if he did desire her, mating with him again would better ensure that he not cast her aside. Kira frowned as she considered the wisdom of that and wondered if she was making all of this out of whole cloth. Could she have read more into his behavior than was warranted?

She crested the rise to find him watching a pot on the fire with a decidedly disgruntled air, and could not dismiss the thought that she had read him aright. A lightness buoyed Kira's heart and she acknowledged a sense of relief that he would leave her alone while she considered her options.

Consider them she would, for time aplenty had she to think while they rode. And should she decide that a coupling was what she truly desired, some way would Kira find to tell her warrior.

To tell Thierry, she corrected herself, and found herself smiling once again as she stepped toward the makeshift camp.

The setting sun turned the domes and spires of Constantinople to burnished gold, making the city look yet more exotic than even its reputation. Beyond the walls of the city the Bosphoros shone like indigo silk, reflecting the golden light of the setting sun. Lights gleamed from the windows of homes within the town, the bright pinpoints echoing the stars just becoming clear overhead.

Thierry sighed with satisfaction that they had made it this far before nightfall. They would reach the city gates with adequate time to enter the city before they were locked for the night. A hot bath, a hot meal, a firm straw pallet before the fire were all he wanted this night.

And the softness of his woman curled before him. She sat silently now, but he felt her awe and wondered if she found the size of the city as overwhelming as he did. Well would she appreciate the small luxuries to be found within the city walls and he found himself spurring his horse onward that they might find an inn yet sooner.

"Did I not know better, I would think you rode to the very gates of the city," Nogai commented. Thierry shot his companion a telling glance.

"What would be wrong with that?" he asked.

Nogai snorted. "Well you know that these town folk will not

tolerate our camping right outside the gates," he scoffed. He lifted his nose to the wind and gestured off to their right. "A fine rise is there to shelter our camp from the wind this night."

"I make no camp this night," Thierry said calmly. Nogai's startled expression made Thierry writhe inside. Was it so unthinkable that he should desire some comfort this night?

"Surely you cannot mean to enter the city?" Nogai demanded skeptically.

Thierry could but nod. "Aye."

"And stay there?" Nogai dropped his voice to an incredulous whisper. Thierry nodded again. Nogai swore in eloquent disbelief and Thierry felt his lips thin in irritation.

No crime was it to not want to sleep on the cold ground again.

"'Tis the woman making you soft," Nogai accused unexpectedly. Thierry swiveled and glared at his friend.

"Well you know that she cannot tell me her desires," he retorted.

Nogai sniffed. "From Tiflis is she," he said with a sneer. "No soothsayer does it take to guess that she would prefer to stay at some foul inn in town."

"I intend to take no foul accommodations," Thierry argued, but Nogai simply laughed deprecatingly.

"*All* inns are foul, by their very nature," he scoffed. "Filled with vermin of all orders and ripe with the mingled scent of many men. Disgusting 'tis to sleep in such close proximity with others, without the bite of the wind in your nostrils and the sound of the waving grasses in your ears."

"Warmer 'tis there," Thierry interjected, having little interest in Nogai's ode to nomadic life. Often enough had he heard this particular piece of poetry to be warned of its charms.

"Warmer?" Nogai demanded archly. "Mayhap, but at what price? Filled with scent is the air, such that a man might fall dizzy in confusion. Meat and smoke and skin and incense and dozens of unnamed smells wrought from the decadence of living such entangled lives."

"No worse than a full yurt does an inn smell," Thierry argued.

Nogai raised one brow. "But amidst strangers," he hissed. "'Tis unthinkable to mingle thus with those who share no blood."

Thierry returned his friend's skeptical expression. "No kin are you and I," he felt obliged to point out, but Nogai simply smiled.

"To be *anda* is no small link," he argued. "Sword brothers we are sworn to be, and well you know that 'tis as strong a link betwixt us as blood."

"Then no trouble should you have sharing a room in an inn with me," Thierry countered reasonably.

Nogai recoiled in horror. "You cannot mean to sleep within the walls of the town?" he demanded again. Thierry nodded and Nogai's lips thinned as the argument grew more serious for him. "Why would you do this thing?" he asked scornfully. "Never have I known you to turn your back on the plain when there was a choice."

That assertion rang annoyingly true in Thierry's ears but he drew himself up taller. "A warm bath would I have this night and a hot meal in my belly."

Nogai's eyes narrowed. "Hot tea have we had almost every night," he observed in a low voice. "And the ground is soft enough to service a man's needs."

This last pricked Thierry's pride and his response sounded colder than he had intended. "What mean you by that?" he asked coldly.

Nogai snorted. "Methinks the woman makes another woman of you," he charged. The air was silent between the two of them for a long moment, then Thierry spurred his horse onward.

"Sleep on the plains like a dog if you will." He cast the comment over his shoulder. "I would sleep soundly this night."

Nogai muttered something deprecating under his breath before he spoke clearly enough for Thierry to hear. "And how would you sleep soundly amidst whores and thieves?" he challenged.

"Better than I would on the ground with the bite of winter in the air," Thierry retorted hotly. Nogai's horse galloped up beside him and Thierry glanced to that side to find his friend's features distorted in scorn.

"Next will you be wanting a bath more than once a year," he taunted. Thierry felt his eyes blaze in anger.

"Mayhap you should consider the same," he snapped. Nogai drew himself up with affront.

"Thinking more like that of townsfolk than tribesman is that," he declared savagely.

"And no less valid for all of that," Thierry retorted coldly. Nogai's lip curled in a sneer.

"Well it seems that you are other than the man I have ridden with all these years," Nogai accused. "Man and Mongol both was he, but you show signs of becoming soft. No doubt 'tis the result of cosseting a woman better left to clear the paths for the army."

Something clenched within Thierry's gut at that and his tone was harsher than any he had used with Nogai before. "Mayhap 'tis but the greater part of my heritage asserting itself," he concluded fiercely. "And well it seems time for it to take precedence. Have I not become a barbarian in putting it aside all these years?"

"You have become a Mongol," Nogai stated flatly. Thierry shot him a cold glance.

"Aye. 'Tis exactly that of which I speak," he said quietly. "Sleep in the grass if you will. I would seek the warmth of shelter from the elements this night."

"Expect me not to seek you out within the town," Nogai called after him stubbornly, but Thierry did not grace him with a reply. With the length of time that had passed since Nogai had last bathed, Thierry was certain he could find his *anda* by smell alone no matter how far afield he made his camp.

Kira knew not what to think when the warrior's companion veered his horse away from them and galloped into the low hills outside the city walls. His terse whistle had the other horses running in pursuit of him, leaving Kira and her warrior with naught but the horse they rode. Where was he going? Never did

he look back, and though Kira understood the two men had exchanged angry words, she could not help but wonder what had
come to pass.

And of what import was it that they had reached Constantinople? Why had they come here? What did the warrior intend
to do now that they had?

More importantly, what did he intend to do with her? Too
late, Kira regretted not granting him access between her thighs
again, for it seemed she had not guarded her value to him well
by making that choice. No reassurance did a covert glance to
his set features grant her and she could not help but fret about
her fate. Too easy would it be for him to abandon her here. She
fidgeted restlessly before him as they passed under the shadow
of the city gates.

It seemed the warrior knew his destination well and that fact
did naught to reassure Kira. Did he mean to be rid of her immediately? Did he make for the slave market that she might at least
bring him some ready coin? One so small as she would not fetch
much of a price, Kira warranted sourly, the very thought per-
versely pleasing her. Should he so heartlessly cast her aside,
'twould suit her well that he saw little gain from the transaction.

But instead, he rode his horse into the courtyard of what
looked to be a domicile. Darkness had fallen and the light of
lanterns gleamed through the arched windows, casting shadows
into the whitewashed yard.

A young boy came and gripped the horse's reins, offering
greetings in a rapid sequence of languages until the warrior responded. Kira fancied she heard Persian trip from the boy's
tongue, but before she could be sure, he had moved on.

The exchange was made in the warrior's tongue until the boy
abruptly shouted a summons into the building. A portly man
filled the doorway a moment later, his manner businesslike as
he evidently negotiated with the warrior.

No imagination did Kira need to guess what was being negotiated. 'Twas insulting to be treated thus, though she

supposed she had been a fool to expect more. And the loss of her innocence had undoubtedly only dropped her value.

If indeed the warrior had seen fit to confide that fact.

No trouble had Kira summoning an image of the retaliation that would be sure to bring from this portly man, or mayhap his customer, on the morrow. Her back had barely healed, but she had little doubt 'twould soon be bleeding once again. And all to fatten the purse of a barbarian.

A barbarian she had been fool enough to almost trust. Kira gritted her teeth defiantly and pulled forward, leaving some distance between herself and the warrior. What had her lack of resistance netted her? Naught but speedy delivery to the house where she would undoubtedly be doomed to slave the rest of her days, in one manner or another.

Curse this Mongol.

A bargain of some kind was struck hastily, leaving Kira surprised that the heavy man had not seen fit to examine her before his purchase. Mayhap he desired her only for domestic tasks. Indeed, though that was a relief, Kira knew she should have expected naught else. Had her father not made her lack of charm evident? And 'twas clear now that this warrior had but toyed with her when he had implied otherwise.

Mayhap she deserved to slave in this man's kitchens for her foolish hopes. But no doubt had Kira that she had just been sold, no less that there was naught she could do about it. Her face flamed as she dismounted before the warrior.

She would not look to the barbarian who had committed this indignity. She would not grant him the satisfaction of seeing her disappointment. Why had she been so foolhardy as to not fight a man like this?

To Kira's astonishment the warrior dismounted and cupped her elbow in his hand. He guided her into the house, the portly man stepping back from the doorway and granting them a paternal smile. Kira's certainty faltered briefly before her conviction redoubled.

He was but seeing her to her quarters. No doubt he expected she would grant him some sweet leave-taking, but Kira had a surprise for this Mongol. He might well have sold her, there might well be naught she could do about that, but she would not fall prey to his rough charm yet again.

They climbed the wooden stairs to the second floor and Kira's confidence uneasily slipped yet another notch. No servant or slave slept upstairs, at least not in Tiflis. She shot a wary glance to her companion, only to find him thoughtfully watching his step. The older man bustled up the stairs behind them, his incomprehensible chatter flowing over Kira as the warrior did not respond. His grip remained warm on her elbow and she wondered if she might have misinterpreted.

But nay. Why else could they be here? He meant to leave her and ride back to his friend. There could be no other reason.

The warrior ducked into a room on the right with a frown tugging at his brows, his gaze assessing as he glanced over the room's contents. The other man trotted around them and struck a flint to light a lamp. The flame cavorted wildly for a moment, sending golden light dancing around the room.

'Twas a fine room and Kira could not help but notice that fact. Larger 'twas than any she had ever known. A wide window there was overlooking a quiet courtyard and surprisingly sweet night air wafted through the opening. Though the pillows stacked in one corner were showing their age and worn in spots, Kira thought them the most lavish she had ever seen. The floor was tiled and swept clean, naught else but a table and that lamp in the room.

Surely these fine quarters could not be for her.

The warrior nodded and the two men exchanged a few terse sentences. This was it, Kira thought. This is where he means to leave me. Her heart plummeted and she could not honestly tell herself 'twas because of the state of the home to which she had been sold. Indeed, the portly man looked quite kindly.

'Twas the thought of the warrior leaving her alone that

troubled Kira, and the realization of that fact troubled her yet more. She had grown used to him, against all odds, and well she knew she would miss the weight of that silent perusal upon her.

Indeed, were she being truly honest with herself, she knew she would miss more than that.

Kira covertly glanced through her lashes to the warrior, just in time to see him dig in his tunic and hand the other man several coins. Her eyes flew open in shock, yet the older man smiled as though naught was amiss. He tucked the coins into his own pocket, waved cheerfully and trotted to the door to disappear.

Kira was dumbfounded. What had transpired? She could not have been sold, for the warrior had paid. Could this be an inn? Had he purchased accommodation that he might abandon her here? Kira spun to confront him, only to find his assessing gaze upon her once more. 'Twas as though he waited for her response and for the first time, his thoughtful manner thoroughly irked her.

"What do you do here?" she demanded angrily, knowing full well that he had no understanding of what she said but needing to voice her frustration. "Why have you brought me here? Who is that man? What manner of establishment is this? And what is going to happen?"

The warrior regarded her for a long moment, then closed his eyes and rested his cheek on his palm in a gesture she recognized well enough.

Sleep.

"But *who* is sleeping here?" she asked tersely, pointing to him and to herself rapidly. She threw up her hands in confusion and a frown flickered across his brow. He indicated Kira, the pillows in the corner and repeated the gesture. Kira frowned in turn.

"And what about you?" she asked. "Do you truly intend to leave me here alone?" He returned her questioning glance blankly and Kira sighed heavily. She pointed to him, mimicked his sleep signal and waved broadly to the world at large.

The warrior pointed resolutely at the same pile of cushions and Kira's breath caught in her chest at the heat in his eyes.

He meant to share her bed here.

"And the other one?" she asked breathlessly. "Where is he to sleep this night? Watching will he be like the others were before?" The warrior propped his hands on his hips and Kira knew he had not understood her question. She made a riding motion, then pulled back the corners of her eyes with her index fingers in a mimicry of the other warrior's features.

She thought for an instant that her warrior almost smiled but the impression was gone before it began.

"Nogai," he said flatly and she assumed 'twas the other one's name.

"Nogai," Kira repeated, adding the sleep gesture and shrugging. The warrior pointed out the window. Kira fancied he indicated the hills beyond the city walls. He added a terse explanation but she knew not what it said. Indeed, it mattered little, for well enough did she understand the situation.

Well enough, indeed, for it seemed she could not keep the heat from her cheeks. She could not bear to ask him the question that filled her mind, and looked down to the tile floor in confusion. Did he mean that they should couple here this night? Had she but imagined that he had granted the choice to her?

The warrior rummaged in his pocket, his movement drawing Kira's reluctant eye. To her surprise he produced a pearl. He rolled the gem between his thumb and forefinger as he caught her gaze. They stared at each other for a long charged moment, and when he finally beckoned, Kira could not have refused him to save her life.

The room was warmer than she had noted on entering it, the sounds carrying from the rest of the house muted to her ears as though they were a world away. Indeed, it seemed once again that there was naught but the two of them in the whole of the civilized world. The warrior's eyes gleamed as Kira slowly closed the distance between them, leaving her feeling as helpless as a fish on a lure drawn ever closer.

She paused directly before him and he held the pearl up

between them without breaking their regard. He rubbed the thumb and forefinger of his other hand together and Kira immediately understood his question.

He desired a value for the pearl. She glanced to the gem for the first time and was startled by its familiarity. Surely this was the gem she had swallowed.

Kira glanced back to the warrior only to find an unmistakable twinkle in his gray eyes. He made an exaggerated swallowing gesture, then pointed to her. Evidently intent on ensuring she did not doubt that 'twas the same pearl, he flattened his palm between them as he had repeatedly asked for the gem and dropped the pearl into his own palm with a dramatic flourish.

'Twas the same pearl.

Kira reached for the gem to value it, grimacing when she realized where it had been and how she had to assess it first. She tapped her own lips and winced anew as she indicated the pearl. Kira could have sworn the warrior's lips twisted with mirth, but before she could be sure, he had bent over his saddlebags.

A tin cup was pressed into her hand as he pulled the cork from a wineskin with his teeth. Kira recognized the smell of the *qumis* as soon as it was opened and shrank back, certain she need never taste that substance again. Despite her reservations, the warrior poured a little into the cup and dropped the pearl into the alcohol. He lifted the cup from Kira's hand, swished the gem around, then tipped the cup toward her.

The pearl glistened from its repose and Kira knew 'twas as clean as it was like to be. She plucked it out of the liquid and slipped it onto her tongue. She closed her eyes and let the flavor of the *qumis* slide away as she concentrated on the cleaned gem.

'Twas sweet, was all she had time to think before the warrior's roughened hand closed around her neck. Kira's eyes flew open and her gaze leaped to his, only to find that twinkle dancing merrily in his eyes. He tightened his grip ever so slightly in mock menace and cocked a warning brow.

'Twas a joke.

Indeed, it had to be, though never had the man made a joke before. Kira caught his eye once more, the telltale crinkling at the corners of his eyes confirming her thoughts. She giggled unexpectedly at this insight into his personality and he wiggled his brows with vigor. Kira was completely unable to check her laughter when his eyes widened dramatically and his grip tightened with mock threat. She laughed aloud and the pearl danced from her lips.

The warrior made some charge over his shoulder as he ducked in pursuit of the gem. Kira shook one finger at him admonishingly, unable to completely quell her smile.

"'Twas your own fault for teasing me so," she accused him laughingly. The corners of his mouth tweaked and he shot her a telling glance as he straightened. Then he sobered with feigned tolerance, sending a mock scowl of disapproval in her direction as he dropped the gem into the *qumis* and swirled it around once more. He shook his head, as though severely plagued by the whimsies of women. Kira swatted him before she thought twice.

But a glimmer of the purposefulness in those silver eyes had she before he dropped the tin cup and reached for her. Kira squealed and ran, making it no more than halfway across the room before she was abruptly scooped off her feet. She laughed again as the warrior easily spun her around into his arms, her laughter fading only when she was looking up into his gleaming eyes.

Kira fell abruptly silent. The warrior's tentative smile fled. His fingers fanned out as he held her closer, his gaze running over her features as though he would memorize every detail. Kira caught her breath at the admiration she saw there, knowing that it could not be feigned, but unable to doubt the evidence of her eyes. The warrior leaned toward her, then hesitated, his silver gaze rising questioningly to hers.

Unable to check her impulse, Kira reached up to twine her arms around his neck. 'Twas all the encouragement he needed and she was folded against his strength before she knew what she was about. His lips were gentle upon hers, firm yet cautious, as though he feared she would rebuff his advance. Kira opened her mouth and leaned against him. She could not have denied his tender assault for any price.

Impossible 'twas that he found her desirable, but time and again he had shown her exactly that. And no doubt had Kira that she desired him. She recalled the weight of him within her and fairly writhed at the memory. Would he come to her again? Did he truly wait only for her invitation or did he intend to join her this very night? Kira was shocked to realize that she could imagine naught but being with him again.

The warrior lifted his head and gazed down at her warmly for a long moment before setting her gently on her feet. He took her hand and tugged her to the table, plucking the pearl from the cup and handing it to her once more.

Business first, Kira thought savagely. Indeed, she could not help but wonder if she was reading too much into his actions when he acted with such single-mindedness. But still, she obediently fingered the pearl, peering at its surface and leaning closer to the lamp to assess its color.

'Twas a fine gem, of that she had little doubt. But how would she tell him its value? Only Persian currency did she know well. Kira's brow puckered. She was not certain even what coin they used here in Constantinople, let alone what currency her warrior might be familiar with trading.

As though sensing her conundrum, the warrior pulled a mélange of coins from his pocket and spilled them upon the table. A small assortment 'twas, though they were mostly unfamiliar to Kira. A pair of gold coins there were that she knew to be bezants, though she knew not their relative value. A trio of silver coins with strange symbols upon them had square holes cut in the center. There were also several thin and bright silver pennies with notched edges that she had seen afore, but knew not the value. Kira's heart sank in defeat just before she spotted the silver dinar.

Good Persian currency, as her father would have said. Kira plucked the coin triumphantly from the jumble and laid it beside the pearl. She held up three fingers and tapped the coin, pointing to the pearl.

Three dinars. 'Twas a good gem. The warrior cocked a skeptical brow and Kira nodded vigorously. How could she tell him how good 'twas?

"'Tis from Oman," she said, waving the pearl beneath his nose and not knowing how much he comprehended. "The best pearls come from Oman. *Oman,*" she repeated deliberately. "And 'tis large—" she made a spreading motion with her hands "—and smooth. Not a blemish is there upon it." Kira turned the pearl under the light so that he might note the perfection of its luster. "And its color is almost white, which is most valuable."

Kira glanced around the room for something with which to indicate color. She shrugged and pointed to the oil in the bottom of the lamp, shaking her head disparagingly at its yellow tone, then pointed to the whitewashed wall and nodded with approval. She held the gem against the wall comparatively and nodded yet more. When she looked back, the warrior nodded in turn and Kira felt a thrill of victory surge through her veins. Had he truly understood her?

He crossed the room to her with long strides and her heart began to pound at his intent. But he merely lifted the pearl from her fingertips and turned to leave the room.

Did he mean to abandon her here? After their embrace, the thought was even more abhorrent than it had been before. She could not let him walk away from her! Kira panicked at the very idea and flew after him to clutch his sleeve. The warrior turned to look down at her with surprise.

"Surely you cannot mean to leave me here," she argued. Kira heard her words fall in a breathless rush but was powerless to halt their flow. "No one do I know in this city and indeed not a coin have I with which to feed myself or—"

The warmth of the warrior's finger fell against Kira's lips

and she fell immediately silent. Her gaze rose tentatively to his, the warmth she found in his regard unnerving her, yet setting her heart to racing once again.

He held his fingers and thumb together, lifting his hand to his mouth as though he ate something, and met Kira's gaze questioningly. She exhaled shakily and granted him a smile.

Aye, she was hungry and she nodded quick agreement. The warrior nodded, pointing to himself, then outside the room. He pointed to Kira in turn, very firmly indicating the room.

She was to wait? But what if he didn't come back? Some of her fear must have shown in her eyes for the warrior resolutely gripped her chin. He pointed to himself, then made a walking motion with his fingers, walking those fingers back into the room. He indicated Kira, then himself, then made the eating gesture again before meeting her gaze inquiringly.

He was going to fetch some food. And what would follow? Kira licked her lips nervously and flicked a finger at the pile of cushions. She pointed to him, then herself, then to the cushions. He nodded, dropping his cheek to his palm.

'Twas not what she was asking. Kira swallowed before she slipped her finger into her fist, pumping it as she had once before. Despite the heat burning in her cheeks at her audacity, she managed to look up to the warrior's eyes.

He shrugged. Kira blinked but once before the weight of his finger landed unerringly on her chest. He tapped her there solemnly, the somber warmth in his eyes fit to drown in before he turned and walked to the door.

It took Kira a long moment to understand, but when she did, she could scarce believe it.

The warrior was granting her the choice.

Kira's heart began to pound and she nearly gasped aloud at his generosity. She had not misread him. Indeed, it seemed she had judged him too harshly. Her stomach skipped unsteadily at the realization that he was a more honorable man than she had yet known or dared to believe.

Kira could not let him simply walk away! She flew in pursuit of the warrior, finding him half-shrouded by the shadows cast across the stairs by the time she breathlessly gained the doorway.

Chapter Eleven

"Thierry!" she cried without thinking. The warrior halted abruptly and she imagined 'twas surprise that flickered across his features as he turned silently to face her. Kira tapped herself on the chest, unable to contain the happiness bubbling up within her.

"Kira," she informed him. "My name is Kira." He inclined his head slightly so that she could not see his expression in the shadows, then his eyes shone as he looked back to her.

"Kira," he repeated softly, a slight question in his tone, the way he rolled the *r* making her name sound strangely exotic. Kira nodded mutely and he shook his head as though amazed. "Kira," he mused, almost to himself. Kira could not help but wonder what he was thinking.

Then he glanced up abruptly, his bright gaze pinning her to the spot. "Kira," he repeated, and quirked one brow as he held up his right hand. "Thierry," he added with deliberation. He twined his index and second finger together, then gave them a resolute shake. "Kira. Thierry," he said resolutely.

Wonder of wonders, as Kira held his gaze in her surprise, for the first time she saw her warrior openly smile.

She gasped at the way the expression softened his features, then ran toward him, unspeakably encouraged by his response to learning her name. He scooped her up triumphantly, his grin widening as Kira laughed with delight and clasped her arms around his neck. Then his lips were on hers, his hands urging her closer, and she gave herself fully to his embrace for the first time. She was his woman. Not a doubt was there lingering in her mind and Kira intended this night to see that Thierry had none, either.

He groaned when she let her tongue meander into his mouth. Something primitive and feminine thrilled within Kira that she could garner such a response from him. Without breaking their embrace, he swung her up into his arms so that he clasped her knees against his chest and strode purposefully back into their room.

Indeed, Kira reasoned, she was not that hungry. Thierry kicked the door shut behind them and Kira closed her eyes when his lips traced a burning path down her throat. She ached with the need to feel him within her. The cushions pressed against her back before she knew they had crossed the room, and Kira savored Thierry's weight atop her. Her man. He unfastened the front of her *kalat* and Kira was surprised to find his fingers shaking.

Nervous he was! Her heart swelled with tenderness at the sign. Surely he could not doubt her response? Kira lifted his hands and pressed a kiss into each palm, stretching up to kiss either corner of his mouth before touching her lips to his. Thierry shivered and Kira could not believe the evidence of her own senses.

This magnificent man desired her but still he granted her a choice. An unbearable sweetness flooded Kira and she could think of naught but laying his own fears to rest.

Kira knelt before Thierry and purposefully set to unfastening his garments. Thierry made to assist, but she pushed his hands away, waving a resolute finger under his nose. The corner of his mouth quirked but he did her bidding, kneeling silently before her as she worked. 'Twas a heady power to have one so much larger than she at her command and the knowledge made

Kira bold. She was well aware of the warmth of his gaze resting upon her and let her own admiration show when she had bared his chest to her view.

She leaned forward and carefully licked one of his nipples. Thierry caught his breath but no intent had Kira to grant him any quarter. She laved the nipple and ran her teeth across it until it tightened defiantly, then turned her attention on its mate.

When they both met with her satisfaction, Thierry's breathing was ragged and his eyes glittered. But still he kept his hands at his sides, and Kira savored the unfamiliar sense of power flooding through her.

For whatever reason, he was granting her control of their loving. And Kira aimed to see that Thierry did not regret it. This night would he know fully how much she desired him.

This night she would seduce him anew, knowing fully what she did.

Kira climbed to her feet beneath his gaze and slowly began to peel off her garments. Thierry appeared transfixed. The admiration she saw in his eyes made her audacious and Kira cast her garments aside with abandon, leaning temptingly close to him as she bared her shoulders. Thierry swallowed carefully when her *kalat* and *kurta* were discarded, his gaze fixed on her bare breasts. Impulsively, Kira teased them to peaks that matched his own beneath his sharp regard. He clenched his hands and deliberately unclenched them but did not make a move toward her.

Kira smiled and shed the rest of her garments, feeling more desirable than ever she had imagined she would. She unfastened the tie in her hair and shook out her plait, letting her hair cascade over her shoulders. Thierry's nostrils flared as Kira pulled his *kurta* and *kalat* over his head, but still he did naught. And when Kira pushed him in the chest with one finger, he obediently rolled back to sit against the wall.

She knelt before him and unfastened his boots, feeling incredibly forward when she tugged his *chalwar* from his hips.

The sight of Thierry's arousal did naught to reassure her that she was not being too bold and her gaze flew uncertainly to his. Thierry smiled and cocked one brow eloquently, signifying that he intended to wait for her lead.

Kira felt her breathing quicken when she reached for his braid. He leaned away from the wall and Kira knelt by his hip, tantalized by his proximity. His hair was thick and silky. Well aware was she that his hand rested directly beside her knee, that her breast fairly brushed his arm. She could smell his skin and the scent taunted her with the promise of what was to come. Her fingers fumbled momentarily but she recovered herself enough to unplait his hair and spread it over his shoulders.

'Twas lighter than she had expected, more chestnut than black in shade, its texture more wavy than straight. Kira brushed its thickness back from his temple and leaned forward to press her lips there.

She could not stop once she had touched him, for the taste of his skin was as intoxicating to her as the most potent *qumis*. She traced little kisses all around his ear and along the line of his jaw. His scent and the heat rising from his skin drove her to distraction and she dared to rest her fingertips on his shoulders. From there they seemed to move of their own volition to trace mirrored paths across his shoulders and chest. Kira caught her breath at the feel of him.

"Thierry," she whispered shakily behind his ear. He shuddered from head to toe at the flurry of her breath there and suddenly his restraint finally broke.

"Kira," he growled as he twisted, but Kira was aware of naught but his hands upon her.

He rolled her summarily to her back and she could not cease touching the smooth warmth of his skin. Kira arched against his weight and tangled her fingers in his hair. She loved his strength, his heat, the unexpected gentleness of his touch. Thierry's mouth closed around her breast demandingly and she cried out at the sweetness of his suckling. She writhed against him and he ducked to assault the other breast, his hands cupping her ribs as he teased her nipples to peaks that rivaled the state of his own. The tension rose within her again and she wanted naught else than to touch and taste him everywhere.

His tongue was in her navel, his hands bracketing her pelvis, then Kira gasped aloud as he moved yet lower. His palms slid over her thighs in an endless caress as his tongue dove between her legs, and Kira found herself shamelessly arching to meet his touch. Only too well did she recall the pleasure he had granted her from that tender point. Indeed, the memory had haunted her and this night she knew she would taste it fully again.

Though she squirmed against him, Thierry granted her no respite from his devilish tongue. Kira's heart leaped in anticipation when she felt again that quickening beneath her skin. Her nails bit into his shoulders and she strained against him in pursuit of that elusive pleasure.

Certain she was that her cry would be heard all the way to Tiflis when it came, but powerless was she against the hot wave that coursed through her veins. She stretched high as she cried out, her hips bucking in an ageless dance that she could not contain. Kira reached fully the crescendo she had but tasted before and fell shivering from the heights to land securely in Thierry's arms.

Had she not been so exhausted, she might have been mortified at her wanton behavior. But then she saw Thierry's slow smile of satisfaction as he loomed possessively over her and she breathed in shaky relief. Kira reached up to touch the side of his face, loving how different 'twas in texture from her own and marveling that this man was hers. She ran her fingers lightly across his shoulders and nuzzled against his chest as he leaned over her.

His feather-light kisses dotted her eyelids, her brow, her earlobe, the underside of her jaw, and Kira fairly purred with pleasure at the attention he was lavishing upon her. Indeed, she nearly felt fit enough to scale those heights again and she opened her eyes to find his gaze sparkling bright in the half-light.

Unable to deny him the pleasure he had granted her, Kira reached up to touch her lips to his. Thierry's hand enfolded the back of her neck, the other cupping her breast. When his thumb dragged leisurely across her taut nipple, Kira knew she had to sample him fully this night. She squirmed beneath him and when he lifted his weight, she purposefully locked her legs around his waist.

Thierry caught his breath, but Kira held his gaze in silent challenge. She smiled slowly and let her fingertip trail provocatively across his lips. He opened his mouth and she continued her caress across his teeth. Thierry bit gently on her inquisitive finger and Kira lifted her hips demandingly against him. His eyes widened at her impulsive mood and she had but an instant to smile before he slipped within her.

Thierry moved slowly, as though he feared to frighten her. Kira willed herself not to be afraid of this natural union. Gentle he was, the concern in his eyes now showing her that she had not been mistaken to trust him. When he rested fully within her, he paused and Kira moved slightly to accustom herself to him. Thierry blanched as he closed his eyes and Kira could not believe the extent of his weakness for her.

She rolled her hips experimentally in a parody of the dance she had learned and watched him grit his teeth. Kira nearly laughed aloud at the possibility that she might be able to please him as he had pleasured her. She arched back and deliberately stretched her arms above her head, dancing as well as she could stretched on her back beneath him.

Thierry's eyes flew open, his eyes blazing with desire. Kira merely granted him a cocky smile and continued her "dance." He reared up onto his knees abruptly and carried her with him, both of his hands clasping around her waist to hold her upright before him. Kira dropped her toes to the ground and stretched high to dance, loving the strength of his grip and the flame smoldering in his eyes.

Thierry tipped back his head and roared as he began to lift

her up and down. The very movement made Kira almost forget to dance, for he rubbed himself against her so that that secret spot was reawakened. She met his gaze and saw the awareness of what magic he wrought gleaming there.

Knowing 'twas his intent, she could not deny him. Kira stretched high, struggling to dance even as the heat gathered within her. She writhed within his embrace as they danced together in a timeless tempo, their pace increasing to a frenzy. Then Thierry arched high and stiffened, his gesture driving him against her so that Kira cried out in his wake and collapsed bonelessly against his chest.

Impossible 'twas to believe that she had feared this union. The promise of coupling thus over and over again fairly made her weak, and Kira closed her eyes against the rise of exhaustion. The man would see she never slept. Kira smiled secretly to herself, deciding that she might ensure he never slept.

But the languor stealing through her in the wake of their loving could not be denied. Mayhap later she would see he never slept, she reasoned as her eyelids drooped closed. Barely did Kira feel Thierry's lips brush across her brow before she slipped into the netherland of sleep within the safe haven of his embrace.

Kira was still sleeping soundly when Thierry slipped reluctantly away from her side. Dawn had come and he had not moved as was his wont, but he could linger no more. The road to Paris was long enough without staying abed all the day. He smiled to himself as Kira rolled over and burrowed into the warm spot he had just abandoned. Indeed, he felt more light-hearted than he had in years.

All because a woman had confided in him her name.

Although 'twas true Kira had granted him more than that. Thierry almost whistled with satisfaction as he hastily dressed, only the fear that he would awaken her keeping him silent. No sound may have crossed his lips, but Thierry was more than aware that his expression was not nearly as stern as usual.

Mayhap 'twas not so bad to see the civilized man revived within him. Mayhap there was another future for him than the one he had hoped for within the Mongol tribe and lost in the blink of a capricious eye. Mayhap something of import awaited him in his homeland.

On this morning it seemed all was possible. Thierry almost considered the tangled mess he had left behind in Khanbaliq, but checked his thoughts just in time. He spared a last glance to the sleeping beauty dozing peacefully on the other side of the room and shook his head.

Even Kira could not heal that wound. Enough should it be that she appeared capable of healing all the rest.

He hesitated on the threshold for a long moment, watching her sleep. Knowing he had no choice but to fetch supplies did little to bolster his resolve to leave. Thierry stood silently for a long moment. Never would Kira know he was gone, for he had noted already that she was a sound sleeper. And should he move quickly, they could be on their way before the sun reached its zenith.

Nogai was undoubtedly waiting impatiently at the gates already. That thought spurred Thierry on and he closed the door to the room carefully behind himself as he departed.

The souk in Constantinople was as colorful and busy as any Thierry had yet seen. Indeed, if he had not such a finely honed sense of direction, he might easily have found himself lost amidst the confusion. All manner of goods were there for sale, fineries collected from all corners of the world, their attributes recited to the thronging crowd by numerous self-assured merchants.

Thierry pushed his way through the crowd and acquired the goods he had need of, ignoring the rest. Dried meat, flat bread, some cheese and dried fruit. Another pair of blankets did he buy, for the air would be growing colder as they traveled farther north. No need had Kira of catching a chill.

His business completed, Thierry swiveled at the savory scent of freshly roasted lamb, thinking to fetch Kira a treat, only to have his attention snared by an inconspicuous shrouded shop.

Round gems gleamed in the shadows and a black-robed man sat nodding behind the display. His beard fell long and white over his chest, his thick eyebrows the same shade, his black turban making his face look more lined than mayhap it was. He glanced up and met Thierry's gaze and those dark eyes flashed knowingly. The man beckoned with a bony finger and Thierry could not help but comply.

The man was a pearl merchant, the richness of the gems arrayed on the dark cloth enough to take even Thierry's breath away. And fine gems had he seen in his days. But never any like these.

Despite himself, he was fascinated by their colors and shapes. Pink pearls there were and even one of palest green, ivory ones and those of outright yellow, and finally those of gleaming white. Not all were round and he marveled at their shapes, some twisted and convoluted beyond belief. 'Twas a sight Kira would appreciate, and half a mind had he to fetch her. Even tiny pearly Buddhas were there and he raised a skeptical glance to the keeper.

"All genuine they are," he declared flatly, touching the Buddhas with a gnarled fingertip. "From Cathay are these. Men there have learned the art of the oyster well. Little bronze statues do they plant in the creatures and the creatures know naught but to create pearls of them, just as they do with grains of sand."

"'Tis amazing," Thierry commented.

The elderly man nodded sagely. "Buddhist, are you? A fine talisman is one of these for a fighting man."

"Nay," Thierry said flatly.

Not yet willing to leave, he let his gaze rove over the display once more and found his attention captured by an oddity of a pearl. On a fine gold chain 'twas, as though meant to be worn around a woman's neck, though the gem was misshapen. Despite its deformity, the pearl had a certain grace, however, and Thierry was intrigued at the way it caught the light.

"Ah," the old merchant breathed. "Fancy the *aljofar,* do you? Have you a woman, then?"

"Aye," Thierry admitted warily.

"Aye, and good luck an *aljofar* is for a mate," the older man confided. "'Tis traditional, you know."

He hooked one finger beneath the chain and let the gem swing before Thierry. Thierry reached out to touch the stone and knew as soon as 'twas cradled within his palm that he had to have it. As a token of his regard for his Kira. Only fitting it seemed to pledge himself to her with a pearl when 'twas pearls that had brought them together.

Pleased with his logic, Thierry dug in his pocket for the pearl Kira had granted him. Yet more fitting 'twas that one gem should be bartered for the other. He offered it to the old merchant, who accepted it with an assessing frown. As Thierry watched, he rolled the gem between his fingers, bit it, peered at it, then met the younger man's gaze.

"Two dinars," he offered.

Thierry shook his head firmly. "Well I am told that it is worth three," he said. The merchant cocked a skeptical brow. "From Oman 'tis," Thierry added, repeating Kira's claim as though he knew exactly the import of it. The merchant's white brows rose and he plopped the gem into his mouth.

This time Thierry knew better than to react. He stood and waited, wishing he could fully dismiss his worry that the man could easily swallow the gem and trick him out of its value. Too much trust did this pearl business require, he concluded sourly, just as the merchant spit the pearl back into his hand.

"So 'tis," he conceded. "Three dinars, then."

"The *aljofar,*" Thierry bargained. The merchant feigned surprise and frowned.

"A precious gift is an *aljofar.* Not a mere frippery to be cast aside when modes change," he argued with a scowl. "This pearl and two more dinars."

Thierry shook his head firmly. "Simply the gem," he bargained.

The old man granted him a wary glance. "For a woman do you want this?" he demanded.

Thierry nodded resolutely. "For *my* woman," he corrected firmly.

The merchant stifled a smile and rolled Thierry's gem across his palm. "Your first woman, then?" he asked in a more welcoming tone.

Thierry cocked an imperious brow. "My only woman," he affirmed flatly. The merchant shook his head and lifted the *aljofar* by its chain once more. He let it swing before him as though considering the wisdom of what he thought to do.

"The pearl and one dinar, then," he offered genially. "An offer 'tis that you will not match anywhere else, for this *aljofar* is worth far more."

Thierry knew from the old man's tone that he would go no lower, but he wanted the gem. He frowned and watched it swing innocently from its chain, as though it deliberately tempted him.

To think that he was considering paying coin for a trinket. When last had Thierry honestly purchased something other than essentials? To turn out hard-earned coin to cultivate a woman's smile was beyond belief.

But 'twas for Kira. And to be granted another sight of Kira's smile. Well Thierry wanted her to have it and already could he envision the gem against her golden skin. 'Twas inexplicable, but there 'twas.

Thierry dug in his pocket for the coin and fairly shoved it at the merchant. The old man bit the coin in turn, then offered the *aljofar* to Thierry with a small smile.

"Well enough do I remember being young," he mused with a twinkle in his eye. "Mind you always hold her in such regard. 'Twill ensure that your lives be long and happy together."

Thierry looked down at the gem in his hand with satisfaction and smiled himself as he met the older man's gaze once more. "I would thank you for both the gem and the advice," he said sincerely. "Well it seems that we have made a good beginning."

The merchant smiled and inclined his head. Thierry was unable to stifle his own smile as he headed back to the inn. He indulged his desire to whistle, certain that naught could go amiss with his world on this day.

Kira was just awakening when he returned. She granted him a sleepy smile before she snuggled beneath the blanket yet again, and his heart swelled.

Impossible 'twas that she could arouse him with such an innocent gesture, especially after their activity of the night before, but Thierry's mind readily enumerated possibilities. He laid his purchases aside instead of packing them immediately away, wanting to linger here but a little longer.

Feeling uncharacteristically playful, he scooped up a pair of blood oranges from his newly acquired stores and dropped beside her on the blanket. Kira opened one eye warily, but he leaned back leisurely to lie beside her. She yawned and stretched and nestled her cheek against him. Thierry felt her gaze upon him as he quickly peeled the orange skins away with his short knife.

Evident 'twas that Kira was hungry, as well, for her eyes gleamed and she soon sat up with interest. The move sent that shimmering curtain of her hair falling over her shoulders and bared the smoothness of her shoulder to his view.

Thierry was seized by a desire to know the taste of that specific spot. Though he well knew he would unable to cease his sampling there. Eternal temptation was clearly the price of taking this witch for his own. Thierry swallowed and carefully schooled the motion of his blade. Nogai would be waiting. They had no time for such whimsy.

Though if nights like this last were any portent of the future, he could scarce complain at the price.

When he offered Kira a segment of orange, a wicked glint lit her eye that should have warned him. Well enough should he know that that expression foretold mischief of the first order.

Thierry but waited to see what she would do. His heart took an unruly skip when Kira simply parted her lips invitingly. Full well did she know how she tempted him, he was certain of it, but he played the innocent.

He carefully placed a segment in her mouth, feeling his desire rise anew when she closed her eyes with undisguised pleasure and her dark lashes fluttered over her cheeks. She closed her lips and he was certain this had been timed to trap his fingertip within their softness. Thierry slowly pulled his hand away.

Kira rolled to her back as she chewed at a fascinatingly languid pace and made a very feline sound of satisfaction in the deep of her throat. When she rolled back to her side, the blanket dropped yet lower, though she seemed not to notice.

She met Thierry's eyes and smiled seductively before she opened her mouth expectantly once again. Thierry separated another segment, astounded to find her coyly beckoning him with her tongue. He halted and she giggled, as though amazed at her own audacity, then curled closer to him. Thierry shook his head and fed her another piece.

Witch. A trickle of juice escaped from the corner of her lips and it seemed he could not tear his gaze away from its path. Thierry watched as the red drop trickled over her chin and disappeared over the soft curve of her jaw.

Little imagination did he need to picture its path beneath the blanket and the realization barely formed in his mind before he impulsively dove in pursuit of its sweetness. Kira giggled, her laughter halting uncertainly when he boldly licked the juice from beneath her chin. Their gazes locked for a heated moment, then Thierry deliberately bent to kiss her.

Kira responded as enthusiastically as she had the night before, though she tasted yet sweeter from the orange. Indeed, Thierry knew he could readily drown in her sweetness once again. His fingers wound into her hair, his appetite for her not nearly sated, and Kira pulled him yet closer.

'Twas only the intrusive thought of Nogai impatiently

waiting that forced Thierry to finally lift his head. Kira was flushed in a most delightful manner, her eyes sparkling bright.

The road was long to Paris, Thierry reminded himself resolutely when she wiggled and her breasts were bared to his view. Her nipples tightened beneath his regard and he swallowed carefully.

Passage on a ship did they need and the tide would be going out, he forced himself to recall. Thierry cleared his throat studiously, torn between his desire and the need to resume their journey. Kira reached up to run a hand gently over his face as though she sensed his indecision, then plucked the second orange from the floor.

Did she understand or was she but toying with him? Though truly if Kira had set her mind upon mating anew, Thierry could scarce escape her. Nor indeed did he want to. Her eyes sparkled with mischief as though she had guessed his thoughts. She held the fruit aloft, shook her head firmly and Thierry knew she had something else on her mind. Fascinated, he could but watch.

"Thierry," she said, laying the flat of one hand on his chest. His heart thumped beneath her hand but her fingertips danced away as she similarly indicated herself. "Kira," she said pointedly.

When Thierry nodded understanding, Kira pointed to the orange and cocked a questioning brow.

She wanted to know the word for orange. It could only mean that she desired to learn to speak with him. Should he teach her Mongol or Frankish? Would she know the difference?

Thierry took the fruit from her and turned it thoughtfully in his hand while he considered the matter. 'Twas Mongol he spoke on a daily basis, Mongol he spoke with Nogai and Mongol she likely should learn. Thierry looked Kira in the eye and intoned the Mongol word for orange.

To his surprise Kira frowned. She explained something rapidly that he could not understand, then pointed resolutely to the orange once more. Thierry repeated the word. Kira shook her head. She tugged the corners of her eyes so that they were tilted and pulled thin as she had once before.

"Qaraq-Böke," she said with her eyes pulled back, then shook her head firmly again. Kira looked him directly in the eye and let her hands fall. "Thierry," she said once more. The challenging glint in her eyes willed him to understand.

Thierry almost jumped at his intuitive grasp of her meaning. Kira wanted to learn Frankish, not Mongol. But how could she possibly know that he had taught her his Frankish name? He stared back at her dumbly, unwilling to trust his intuition.

Kira made a sound of frustration back in her throat and frowned. "Qaraq-Böke," she said again, as though fearing she had mispronounced his name. Her voice faded uncertainly as she watched for his response.

Thierry's surprise that she knew the name the Mongols had assigned to him was so complete that he could not hide his response. Kira shook her head in denial when she noted his understanding. Not Qaraq-Böke, he understood, and wondered if she was denying him. His heart stilled in fear.

Then Kira said "Thierry" again and nodded emphatically.

'Twas not the man but the language she denied. Kira wanted to learn Frankish. Somehow she knew about his name, of that Thierry had little doubt. And she knew that Thierry was his Frankish name. He regarded his woman with newfound respect. She must have gleaned something of that in his expression, for she grinned outright. Kira demandingly pointed to the orange anew, as though he might have forgotten her intent.

"Orange," Thierry supplied.

"Orange," Kira repeated with solemnity. She said the word thrice more, then glanced to him for approval. Indeed, her expression was so hopeful that he could not deny her. Her accent was dreadful, her pronunciation marginal, but Thierry imagined that she might be understood.

At least by him she could be, and he rather suspected that might be the point. He nodded approvingly. Kira said the word several more times as though she sought to memorize it, then her gaze swiveled determinedly back to Thierry's.

No imagination did he need to know that she would want to know more words, and he decided to rein her in before she overstepped herself. Useful 'twould be for them to understand each other and he would not have her exhaust herself with her enthusiasm.

"But ten words a day," he told her. He propped himself on his elbows over her and held his hands open to her when she regarded him blankly. "Orange," he repeated and folded in his thumb.

Kira's evident confusion was replaced by understanding and she nodded emphatically. She tapped the blade strapped to the inside of his arm and he acknowledged a surge of pride. A useful word to know 'twould be.

"Knife," he said. Kira repeated the word carefully until he nodded approval.

But a glimpse had Thierry of that mischievous twinkle in her eye before she framed his face in her hands and pressed a light kiss to his lips. She lifted her brows in silent query and he shook his head bemusedly even as he accommodated her. Witch. Trust her to want to know the name for that.

"Kiss," he informed her.

"Kiss," Kira repeated with such concentration that Thierry could not help but tease her.

"Kiss?" he demanded, arching his brows high as though she had made a request. "Aye, Kira." He swooped down and kissed her, liking the glitter of satisfaction in her eyes when he propped himself above her once more.

"Kiss," Kira said breathlessly. She grinned and snapped her fingers demandingly when Thierry did not immediately comply.

Mayhap 'twas not the best word to have taught her so soon, Thierry reasoned as he bent over her once again. Yet he was unable to quell this lightness that seemed to buoy his heart when she responded to him with such ardor.

"Kiss," Kira whispered against his jaw. Thierry let her roll him to his back so that she was sprawled atop him. He glanced down at her naked buttocks and growled appreciatively. He playfully pinched her. Kira giggled and scrambled up his chest.

"Kiss," she insisted and bent to taste him yet again. Thierry cupped her buttocks in his hands and pulled her closer, more than pleased with this new balance between them. How many nights of Kira's intoxicating kisses would it take to reach Paris?

Thierry suddenly recalled the *aljofar* and decided in that same moment to save the gift for a special occasion. Mayhap Kira's first Frankish sentence.

Mayhap when she learned the name for that even more seductive pastime.

He groaned at his body's response to the reminder and tore his lips from hers, knowing full well that they would never leave the inn at this rate. Thierry reached across the floor and managed to grab Kira's trousers. He wagged them purposefully beneath her nose.

"Chalwar," he said firmly. She pursed her lips in a mock pout.

"Kiss?" she negotiated coyly. Thierry shook his head resolutely and rose to his feet before his desire had him acquiescing to her request. High was the sun and 'twas time enough they sought passage on a ship bound westward.

"Chalwar, kurta, tunic, djellaba," he insisted as he tossed her each item of clothing in turn. He turned to face her once more and gestured toward the hills. "Nogai. Paris." He made a riding motion and Kira exhaled with exaggerated dissatisfaction.

"Chalwar, kiss, *kurta,* kiss," she suggested cagily, laughing aloud when a frown of exasperation crossed Thierry's brow.

Truly they would never leave Constantinople at this rate. Did the woman not know how much her simple kisses affected him? Thierry spared her a glance and, from the glint in her eye, rather suspected that she did.

Though surely if she was dressing, there could be no harm in a few fleeting kisses.

"Aye," he agreed before he thought too much about the matter. Kira glanced up questioningly from donning her *chalwar.*

"Aye?" she asked doubtfully. Thierry nodded emphatically, trying to indicate that *aye* meant assent. Naught had he to fear, though, for clearly she understood. No sooner had Kira fastened her *chalwar* than she launched herself into his arms.

"*Chalwar,* kiss," she reminded him archly.

He gazed down into her sparkling eyes, well aware of the full warmth of her bare breasts pressed against him and the weight of her tiny hands on his shoulders. Irresistible she was. Indeed, when the point was made so compellingly, Thierry could do naught but comply.

And but hope that he could stop with a kiss.

Kira was satisfied enough with her situation to be openly curious when Thierry rode with a definite objective in mind. They met a heartily disgruntled Nogai at the city gates, and she blithely ignored his muttering as Thierry proceeded through the bustle of the town to the market.

Thierry was teaching her his language. Truly it seemed he had claimed her fully after all, and her heart soared with delight.

Kira's nose was assaulted by the strong odor of fish and her eyes widened at the lavish catch displayed in the market stalls. A rare luxury had fish been in landlocked Tiflis and she was amazed by both the variety and sheer amount of fish offered for sale. Like the farmers who seldom ventured into Tiflis she was, for she could not cease her curious peering at such unfamiliar sights.

The cobbled road angled down and the smells grew stronger. The people looked rougher and more men were there in the crowd than women. Without thinking of the matter, she moved incrementally closer to Thierry and felt his grip tighten possessively around her waist. Kira smelled salt and wet hemp and heard the creaking of wood. She was puzzled for an instant by the unfamiliarity of it all, until she saw the bobbing masts of the ships.

Tales she had heard aplenty of these vessels that crossed the seas, but never had she seen one. Indeed, she had never seen the sea. The sparkling water that stretched as far as the eye could see behind the boats fairly took her breath away.

"Are we going to take a ship?" Kira asked as she twisted to look to Thierry. He seemed to be watching for her reaction, for his expression softened slightly when their eyes met. Kira indicated the ships questioningly and he nodded once.

But where were they going?

"Paris?" she asked, but Thierry merely shrugged. He held up one finger and dismounted, passing the reins to Nogai as he strode down the wharf. The pair silently watched him disappear into the crowd, then their eyes met in mutual wariness.

Nogai said something but Kira shrugged that she could not understand. He frowned anew and exhaled impatiently before pointing deliberately to the sun. Kira nodded and Nogai traced a path with his finger where the sun would go over the course of the afternoon. He spread his hand open and glanced to where Thierry had disappeared, then shrugged.

Thierry might be gone for a while, Kira guessed, and she nodded understanding. Nogai gestured to a shady corner of the busy quai and seemed to be indicating that they wait there. Kira nodded and he heaved a sigh of relief. Nogai dismounted and ushered the horses to the space he had indicated.

Kira slipped from the saddle, a little disconcerted that Thierry had so completely disappeared, and retrieved a blanket from Thierry's pack to sit upon. She spread out the blanket, wondering how long he might be, and was startled by Nogai's grunt of approval.

Kira spun to find the Mongol grinning. Before she could question his intent, he produced a curious bundle from his own saddlebag. Kira thought it at first to be a brightly painted box, but nay. Nogai peeled off a thin layer and Kira saw 'twas a pile of such layers. He offered her that first layer and Kira turned it over with fascination.

A painting 'twas on some thin matter like parchment, softer to the fingertip yet stiffer and she fancied more durable. On one side there was a black image she thought to be an Eastern character of some kind, on the other was a colored image of seven golden coins.

She looked questioningly to Nogai and he mutely handed her another card. The black image was the same but the other side carried a colored image of three golden cups. Kira frowned in confusion, her gesture enough to prompt Nogai to explain with enthusiasm.

His words flowed over Kira uncomprehended but she watched his actions avidly. He dropped to his haunches and quickly sorted the cards into four piles. That done, he picked up one pile and sorted it quickly into order. Kira was surprised to see that there was a card to represent gold coins of every number from one to ten.

Fascinated despite herself, she squatted opposite Nogai and spread out the pile of cards with gold cups on them. Similarly, every number was represented there. Nogai spread out the other two piles and Kira noted the same pattern echoed in staffs and what looked to be tree branches.

Unexpectedly, Nogai scooped up all of the cards and mixed their order together. He split a number of them between himself and Kira with alarming speed, leaving the remainder piled in between them. At his imperious gesture, Kira turned over her cards to find an assortment of numbers and images.

A contest it must be. And a way to pass the time while they awaited Thierry. Like chess 'twas, Kira concluded, but the tools of the game were lighter and more portable, making them more suited to the Mongols.

Kira met Nogai's gaze questioningly and he smiled in crooked triumph. His dark brows lifted high, his eyes twinkled and he held up one finger as he began to explain.

Nogai shouted with feigned relief when Thierry reappeared, and Kira could not restrain her laughter. Winning she had been, though she imagined the Mongol had been contriving that she did so. He said something accusatory to Thierry and grinned. Thierry snorted, but his gaze was warm when he offered Kira his hand to help her rise.

She felt her cheeks heat as the recollection of their night before flooded into her mind but Thierry was bending to fold the blanket with businesslike ease. He and Nogai discussed something briefly, the cards disappeared and they began to lead the horses toward the wharf.

They halted beside a bobbing ship and one of the horses balked at being led aboard. Kira could not blame the beast, for one look between the small vessel and the vast extent of the sea was enough to make her question the wisdom of their move.

"Genoa, Paris," Thierry murmured into her ear. Kira glanced up with surprise. He pointed to the ship. "Ship, Genoa. Horse, Paris," he explained.

Kira spared the ship a skeptical glance that she hoped might communicate her misgivings. Thierry folded her hand reassuringly within his and urged her to follow him aboard as he spoke. His explanation was long enough that she understood naught but her name, though his low tone worked its magic upon her.

Had she not already trusted him with unexpectedly good results? Truly, the man saw to her safety and comfort more than anyone she had ever known. And with the promise of more of his leisurely loving, Kira knew she would have been a fool to turn away.

She trusted Thierry. The revelation was not as much of a shock as she might have expected it to be. She was his woman and he treated her with greater deference than many men undoubtedly treated their wives. Surely she could not ask for more. She would remain by his side wherever he chose to ride.

Her decision made, Kira granted Thierry a sunny smile and followed him onto the ship that would take them across the sea to mysterious and distant Genoa.

Chapter Twelve

B<small>y</small> the time the snows were thawing alongside the road to Paris, Kira had missed three bleedings. There was no escaping the fact that she was pregnant with Thierry's seed.

Sick she had been from the second week out on the six-week ship voyage to Genoa, sick enough to not care about anything other than sleep. Nogai had lost a gaming partner and Thierry had lost a lover in her illness. For her part, Kira had lost weight, despite Thierry's efforts to encourage her to eat. Grateful she had been for his warmth when she was possessed by chills in the night and he held her close.

Indeed, she knew not whether she would have had the will to survive without his quiet strength. An unexpectedly playful side of him had she discovered as they lay together in the berth and he taught her yet more Frankish. And his relief when they had reached land and she had managed to smile for the first time in a month had been marvelous to behold. Indeed, 'twas too easy to grow fond of the man. Nary a thought had she spared to her missed bleeding under the circumstances. Surely all would be restored to normalcy once she began to eat again.

But north they rode without cease and still Kira had not bled. That fact had made her start to calculate on her fingers and more than once had she glanced into her *chalwar* for some confirming sign. The second miss was soon enough after their arrival in Genoa that she granted herself the benefit of the doubt.

The miss of the third bleeding left no question. With child she was. With Thierry's child, beyond doubt. Kira fancied she could detect a rounding of her belly and 'twas that that first made her consider the repercussions of her pregnancy.

'Twas not surprising in itself, for Thierry and she had been amorous enough before her illness to well justify the conception of a babe. Indeed, 'twould have been surprising had they *not* conceived, and she wondered if Thierry had considered the matter at all.

Did he desire children? 'Twas difficult to guess, for his wandering life did not appear a suitable one for rearing a family, at least to Kira's mind. But Mongols must have children and she supposed he might think differently than she. Did Mongols raise families the way her neighbors in Tiflis had done? Or did men leave women to that domestic task and simply ride on? Kira knew not and liked that not at all.

Was it truly the same to be claimed as to be wedded? Too late, Kira doubted the Persian woman's word. Indeed, who knew what obligations a Mongol might consider to be his as a result of such a bond? 'Twas clear enough that Thierry's behavior owed much to Mongol traditions, whatever his own lineage. What would Nogai have done with a pregnant woman?

More importantly, what would Thierry do with her? Would he leave her? Kira could hardly bear the thought.

Kira knew not the answers to any of the questions that plagued her and little did the matter aid her sleeping. She was compromised as surely as she could possibly be, and yet no husband had she to claim responsibility for her pregnancy or her child.

Indeed, she might simply ask, yet Kira shirked every opportunity. Only to herself in the night would she admit that she feared Thierry's response. And naught could she deny Thierry, even with all her concerns, when he turned to her in the night. Only one thing did Kira know with absolute certainty, though the fact did little to console her in the aftermath of their sweet loving.

There was no doubt that her sire would be ashamed of what she had become.

Paris.

They were finally here and Thierry could not completely stifle his excitement. Home he had felt since they had first crossed into the lands of those sworn to the Frankish king. Though the sense had faded as they traveled farther north, he knew with increasing certainty that 'twas here, in the land of his birth, that he would find his destiny.

And only the matter of the khan's message kept him from immediately pursuing his fate. With that in mind, 'twas impossible to linger outside Paris. Thierry could do naught but head directly to the king's palace, determined to see this errand behind him. No doubt had he that the khan's message would be politely rebuffed. Indeed, he hoped for no less.

All of Europe beckoned to his ambitions and he was nigh impatient to begin. Well he knew that he had been born at a château known as Montsalvat, and he wondered how he might discreetly find its locale. 'Twas his time finally and Thierry was anxious for his destiny to begin.

Kira looked about with curiosity and Thierry noticed yet again that she was unnaturally quiet. Odd 'twas, the change in her, but he supposed she was yet unsettled by their sea voyage. Indeed, there was a pallor to the characteristic golden hue of her skin that could not be entirely due to the change of clime.

And something he could not quite place had changed in her manner, though he had puzzled over it often. Withdrawn she seemed, private, yet more affectionate than ever before should he touch her. Certainly he could make no complaint about her passion, for she had surpassed even his wildest expectations in their nightly couplings. Though it puzzled him that Kira would not touch him of her own accord, he assumed 'twas something in her upbringing that dictated her behavior.

Dame Fortune had indeed blessed him with a perfect mate.

He dismounted in the courtyard of the king, awed by the majesty of construction surrounding him. Nogai's gaze similarly roved over the high walls of fitted stone and the conical towers looming high above them. Pennants of azure and gold flitted against the winter sky high overhead. Thierry knew he was not alone in counting the sentries along the walls and he found assessment in Nogai's eyes when their gazes met.

"I like not how outnumbered we are," Nogai muttered.

"Diplomats are we, not warriors," he corrected his old *anda*, but Nogai's expression remained skeptical.

"So far," he conceded gruffly as he slipped to the ground.

A man cleared his throat delicately and Thierry spun to find an older man regarding them with evident disapproval. His tunic was as blue as the sky with golden flowers worked upon it, every scrap of his knightly attire perfectly in order. Yet despite the beautifully encrusted scabbard hanging by his side, Thierry knew this was not a man who had seen battle of late. The man scanned their travel-stained and clearly foreign attire with open disdain before he met Thierry's gaze.

"Have you mayhap some business in this courtyard?" he inquired icily, his tone indicating that he believed no such thing.

"Aye, a message have I for the king," Thierry explained, and one silver brow arched high.

"Indeed? From whom might this message be?"

"His most esteemed Second Il-Khan of Persia, Abaqa, son of Hülegü, son of Tolui, son of the Great Golden Khan himself, the immortal and most divine Chinggis Khan, sends greetings to the king of the Franks," Thierry supplied, well recalling the beginning of the missive he had been granted.

To his credit, the formerly impassive guard looked somewhat surprised. "Genghis Khan?" he asked and Thierry nodded. "Have you news of Prester John, then?" he demanded with enthusiasm. Thierry feared to show his ignorance as the man's expectation was evidently so great, but knew not what else to say.

"I know not this Prester John," he admitted warily. The man's lips thinned in irritation.

"A king of the East is he, as all know, who will aid us in defeating the Saracens," he retorted frostily.

"Saracens?" Thierry asked dubiously, knowing naught of this race.

"The godless infidels who have stolen Jerusalem from beneath our very noses," the man confided hastily.

Aha. A question of terms, 'twas, no more than that. Thierry sighed with relief. Indeed, they were back on familiar ground. Well aware of both Kira and Nogai's avid attendance, he felt them relax slightly at his evident relief.

"A proposal this is for an alliance against the invaders of Jerusalem," Thierry assured the man confidently. He removed a scroll of parchment from his *kalat* to illustrate his intention.

"Verily?" the man asked, a new light dawning in his eyes as he eyed the scroll. Well it seemed that his manner thawed slightly when Thierry nodded agreement. "Well can I imagine that the king will be interested in your message, then," he said, and there was no mistaking the haste with which he summoned boys to tend the horses.

"Your horses will be tended," he said crisply. "And I will alert the king's advisers to your presence. A common room is there inside and to your right, should you wish."

With that he turned and bustled efficiently away.

"What says he?" Nogai demanded impatiently.

"That we should wait inside," Thierry replied. Nogai pursed his lips in irritation.

"Truly urban folk are all the same," he muttered. "What feeds this dislike of wholesome air in the lungs? I suppose there is little chance of waiting outside?"

"'Twould be seen as rude, I am sure," Thierry observed tersely.

"Let us hope the matter can be managed hastily," Nogai said begrudgingly with a sigh of dissatisfaction. "This diplomacy is indeed a burdensome task." He spared a telling glance for the cerulean spring sky and trudged reluctantly through the portal in Thierry and Kira's wake.

The summons came none too soon to Thierry's mind.

The common room was noisy, smoky and filled with Frankish knights. Naught was his difficulty with any of this; indeed, it seemed wondrously familiar and had much in common with the atmosphere of a friendly yurt. However, they had been but moments in the room before one knight nudged his companion and gestured to Kira. Thierry had bristled but set his lips grimly, determined not to begin a battle. Outnumbered they were by far, as Nogai had already observed, and naught could he do but glare back at the offending knight.

Obvious 'twas that she was his, but well it seemed to Thierry that no one recognized that fact. He scowled darkly and glowered to no avail as yet more admirers turned an eye on his witch. Thierry was not in the least reassured when Nogai and Kira blithely spread out their infernal cards, clearly oblivious to both the attention they drew and Thierry's dislike of the same.

"The Mongols, you must be." A crisp voice drew Thierry from his dark thoughts and he glanced up to find another guard garbed in that same blue and gold. Tempted Thierry was indeed to greet the man with an enthusiasm far beyond expectation.

"The king will see you immediately," the man intoned. Thierry flicked a summoning gesture to his companions and the cards hastily disappeared. The guard turned and set a quick pace through the smoke, leaving them darting through the common room behind him and out into a high vaulted hall.

As they trudged silently in the guard's wake, Thierry wondered if the others were as awestruck by the evident size of the palace. The boisterous sounds of the common room faded behind them and naught could he hear but whispering footsteps mingling with their own solid trudging. Well it seemed that the labyrinthine corridors twisted off in every direction. Certainly the one they followed was wide enough for eight men to walk abreast and continued on endlessly.

Deeply nervous did it make Thierry to be so thoroughly surrounded by stone and the makings of man. He wondered fleetingly how Nogai could bear it, for that man had little tolerance even of small inns and taverns. Indeed, he had slept on the deck of the ship in fine weather and poor, rather than venture into the hold. Thierry did not dare look back to see the truth lest he give a sign of his own discomfort. The messenger moved with a light step and Thierry knew he had little option other than following this man deeper into the maze.

Kira seemed completely untroubled, a fact that left Thierry feeling that he had somehow fallen short. He knew he did not imagine her curious perusal of their surroundings and wished he could be so cavalier.

Being led into a trap they were. The certainty grew within him until it was unassailable. Though Thierry knew the thought to be a fallacy, still he could not dismiss it. Everything within him distrusted this place and this path.

They climbed two flights of stairs crafted from artfully fitted stone. The steps swept around in a spiral, the like of which Thierry had never seen before. He refused to let his impression of the craftsmanship show and stubbornly kept his features impassive. The messenger pivoted at the top of the stairs, and gestured grandly to a pair of extremely high doors.

"The throne room," he informed them without meeting their eyes.

At an imperious rap of his knuckles, the doors swung open soundlessly to reveal two doorkeepers garbed in that same blue and gold. The messenger fairly skipped across the threshold, evidently expecting them to follow. Nogai made a barely perceptible growl of dissatisfaction in the back of his throat. Thierry took a deep breath, knowing he could do naught but follow suit.

The Khan's message had to be delivered. He squared his shoulders, determined to fulfill his commission, and peered into the room.

The throne room was large beyond his expectations. The ceiling arched impossibly high above, apparently supported by an elaborate arrangement of arches that Thierry knew better than to trust with such a burden. Any fool could see that the ceiling was of carved and fitted stone and he cast it a wary eye. All of the room was beneath the stone, though, and no way was there to enter the room and still avoid the risk.

Liking it naught, Thierry stepped into the room, hoping his perfectly healthy caution of such nature-defying tricks was not misinterpreted by these Franks. An open floor space was there in the middle of the room, flanked by banks of benches that rose higher the farther they were from the center of the room. Courtiers were clustered in small groups here and there on the benches. At the far end of the room and facing Thierry was a dais. A number of men sat there, discussing matters amongst themselves. None of them seemed to be paying any attention to Thierry's entrance.

Neither did they seem concerned about the ceiling, much to his surprise.

Instinctively and out of long habit, Thierry quickly picked out the guards and the exits. Easy enough 'twas to find the guards, for they all wore the same colors, much as the khan's *keshik* guard did. Two guards there were standing slightly behind the king on the dais, another pair at each end of the dais. The two who had opened the doors he would reasonably expect to be armed, as would he expect any number of the courtiers to be similarly prepared to meet a threat.

Two doors were there on the far end of the room. The one below the dais did not appear to lead anywhere of good repute, for 'twas barred and of poorer manufacture. The one behind the king Thierry suspected led to his chambers, for 'twas finely ornamented and marked with those same golden blooms. He shook his head minutely, his sense of being lured into a trap redoubled by his observations.

But one exit. This he did not like, the rising banks of benches to the left and right reminding him only too well of a valley set for an ambush. A valley with but one escape. Thierry liked not that he was the one stepping willingly within the trap. Though he was but an envoy and surely had naught to fear, Thierry felt his pulse begin to race.

"The envoy from the Mongols," the messenger announced when they had crossed the threshold. The words launched an uneasy silence as dozens of murmured conversations halted as one.

The king looked up, pinning Thierry with a glance. His courtiers and advisers glanced up with curiosity. Thierry stiffened and gazed around the room, more than fully aware that he was being scrutinized.

When the whispering began, his pride set him in motion. Let them look, he thought ferociously. Of naught did he have to be ashamed. Thierry strode purposefully down the length of the room, summoning his most forbidding expression as he approached the dais. Only one man was he, but this king would know the might of the Mongol khan.

Thierry paused before the dais, absently admiring the way its design made it virtually impossible to assault the king from where he stood. The leap was too high. No wonder their weapons had not been removed before they were permitted entry. The realization fed his suspicions of the situation, but no time had he to indulge such whimsies.

A man on a diplomatic mission was he. The sooner this matter was completed, the sooner he and Kira could continue with their lives.

And the sooner he could seek out his ambitious dreams. His heart missed a beat in anticipation, but Thierry schooled his response. A task had he to fulfill first.

"Greetings to you do I bring from his most esteemed Second

Il-Khan of Persia, Abaqa, son of Hülegü, son of Tolui, son of the Great Golden Khan himself, the immortal and most divine Chinggis Khan," he began. The king's brows lifted in surprise.

"Frankish do you speak," he observed quietly before a frown flitted across his brow. "And rather well. How came this to be?"

"Many skills have we of which you know naught," Thierry replied, striving to keep his manner and tone consistent with the missive he had been granted. No unnecessary information was he to grant these potential allies, he had been told, in case they became not allies, but foes. 'Twas the strength of the Mongols they should be given to understand and not one concession should he make.

"Indeed," the king commented mildly. Two of the courtiers whispered to each other and Thierry bristled when he saw that they gestured to Kira. The king smothered a smile and Thierry wondered how much of his response had been noted.

"Mayhap you would tell us your own identities afore reading your message," the king suggested.

"Qaraq-Böke am I called," Thierry informed the king proudly, not seeing any reason to discuss his own Frankish lineage. Was he not the messenger of the Mongol khan? "And the blooded warrior Nogai 'tis who accompanies me on this mission."

"And from whence do you issue?"

"We come bearing the message of Abaqa, Second Il-Khan of Persia."

"'Twas not my question."

"But 'twas my response."

The king held Thierry's gaze for a long moment, as though willing him to say more. Thierry remained resolutely silent, knowing full well that he had not answered the king's questions as he had wished.

This prying manner was offensive in itself and Thierry did not feel that he alone should be the one to swallow his pride. A frown darkened the king's brow for a brief moment when Thierry said naught else. The king made a sound that might have been exasperation in the back of his throat before he leaned forward slightly.

"Envoys we have had from the Mongols afore," he confided. "And yet naught has ever come from these liaisons."

"Well might one question on which side the fault lay," Thierry countered flatly.

"One well might," the king agreed readily. "Though truly that is not my point. I would but ask you for some indication that your khan sends this message in good faith."

Thierry unfurled the scroll of parchment he carried, knowing that the text would explain itself more fully than he could.

"The truth lies here, as does the sign you seek," he said.

The king nodded. "Then I would have you read this missive now," he ordered.

Thierry cleared his throat as he stretched the parchment out before him. The moment was upon him and truly he hoped all went well. "His most esteemed Second Il-Khan of Persia, Abaqa, son of Hülegü, son of Tolui, son of the Great Golden Khan himself, the immortal and most divine Chinggis Khan, sends greetings to the king of the Franks."

A clatter of activity diverted Thierry's attention from his reading at that moment. He twisted to find a large group of armed knights entering the throne room. Thierry frowned and met the concern in Nogai's gaze.

Who were these new arrivals and what was their intent?

Did these Frankish people regard diplomats differently than the Mongols did? Was he a fool to assume that they could come and leave here without being assaulted? Well enough had Thierry already seen the difference in their cultures, and the arrival of these knights fed his doubts. Suddenly Thierry was not so certain that their safety was assured and he swallowed carefully, even as he tallied a count of the new arrivals.

"What brings you here?" crisply demanded one of the courtiers.

The older knight who led the group assumed a cavalier air

that Thierry knew was feigned. "Come to see the Easterners, have we," he responded lightly. He was tall, his voice resoundingly deep, his step surprisingly vigorous despite the snowy whiteness of his hair. He carried his helmet beneath his elbow, his sword hanging from his hip.

At their leader's words the others leered at the trio before the king and laughed amongst themselves. Almost might one think they were drunk, but Thierry was not ready to make such an easy conclusion. No reassurance was there in the fact that they were garbed similarly to their leader in mail and tunics with full weaponry.

Thierry acknowledged yet another increment of dread. To what battle did these knights travel? The king gestured to the new arrivals for silence and impatiently waved them toward the benches on either side.

"Provincials," he muttered disparagingly under his breath. His manner indicated that the explanation should have meaning to Thierry, though indeed he could divine naught from the single word. There was shame in dwelling outside the city? Well might he have thought 'twould be precisely the opposite, but no time had he to ponder the matter.

"Please continue," the king insisted when Thierry stood uneasily silent, and he reluctantly returned to his scroll.

"Heavily cursed have both our kingdoms been by that godless union of Mamluk dogs emanating from Egypt and the infidels from Syria, and in this slight we already stand of one accord. Well do we understand that the loss of the city of Jerusalem and the land known as Palestine is a thorn that sticks in the side of the Frankish people, just as the loss of the surrounding plains sorely vexes our tribes.

"We propose a holy union between our armies, that we should attack these territories from opposite sides in a common operation. If by the authority of heaven, we should conquer these people, you should have Jerusalem as our gift."

A murmur of discussion broke out on the dais and Thierry

wondered if 'twas his imagination that made the response sound favorable. Mayhap the matter could be settled hastily and Nogai sent back to Tabriz with the response. Mayhap. Thierry cleared his throat pointedly and the courtiers fell silent as he continued.

"The divine hand is clear in this and well it seems this liaison has been ordained. A sign has been sent to us in the person sent before you, for Mongol he is, yet he speaks your Frankish tongue. Well this seems a portent that our alliance is a blessed one. As if this were not enough, there is yet another sign of heaven's intervention, for this same messenger bears the very mark of your Jerusalem emblazoned upon his flesh for all to see."

A tense hush fell after his words, the expectation more than Thierry thought the missive certainly demanded. But no time had he to puzzle over such cultural differences. The sooner this was delivered, the sooner he could seek his own fate.

As he had been instructed, he unfastened his *kalat* and bared his birthmark to the view of those on the dais.

To his astonishment, the king blanched.

The king then fell weakly back in his chair, the pallor of his complexion making him appear markedly older than he had just moments before. The courtier to his left swore, the one on his right crossed himself vigorously, a young boy appeared to lift a cup to the king's lips.

"He dares to venture openly amongst us," another courtier whispered inexplicably. He stared in openmouthed disbelief at Thierry's bared flesh. Another closed his eyes reverently and raised his rosary to his lips as he mouthed a silent prayer. The last man on the dais clambered to his feet and shouted.

"Guards!"

The cry echoed eerily in the silence that had fallen in the throne room. Suddenly everyone who had frozen in place came to life and the room erupted in activity.

What had Thierry done? This response made no sense. But a glimpse did Thierry need of the guards on the dais drawing their swords to prompt him to draw his own.

"Fool!" bellowed someone far behind when it seemed that naught could make less sense.

Thierry spun on his heel to find the knights who had lately entered the hall leaping down to the floor. They were led by that same solidly set man, who had donned his helmet. Thierry had little doubt 'twas he who had bellowed, for purpose showed in every line of his figure as he closed the distance between them.

"What did you do?" Nogai demanded impatiently.

"No idea have I," Thierry confessed in bewilderment.

"Well it seems that we will have to defend ourselves before we might find out," Nogai observed dryly. The two men's gazes held but for an instant before they backed together out of long-standing habit. A wide-eyed Kira was trapped between the two of them.

"A fine choice of an emissary Abaqa made in you," Nogai muttered with dissatisfaction. He swung his blade and another grunted as his swipe found its mark. "Not long enough are we even here for a meal afore you strike offense. Well it seems the khan might have weakness in assessing diplomatic talents."

No time had Thierry to respond to the accusation, for two guards leaped at him. He swung and missed, then jabbed more successfully. Kira squealed and he pivoted deliberately to keep her sheltered behind him as he dispatched the second opponent.

He cast a dubious glance at the knights now reaching them. On whose side would they swing their blades? Indeed, their role would decide the fight, for should Thierry and Nogai stand alone, they were doomed. Nogai bellowed as he impaled another attacker and Kira fairly crawled up Thierry's back.

"Give me a knife," she demanded breathlessly. Thierry but bared his forearm to her as he kept an eye on the courtier stalking toward him, dagger in hand. Kira snatched the blade. He knew not if she could wield it, but well enough should she try.

Another shout and Thierry fired a glance down the room to find the leader of the knights had dispatched one of the guards from the door with a telling blow. Allies these knights were, then. Thierry's pulse pounded at the revelation. Now they had at least a chance of escaping the clutch of this infernal building.

"Guards! Guards! *Guards!*" One of the courtiers had climbed onto his seat and shouted for aid. The king had disappeared into his chambers behind, several of the courtiers similarly gone. The remainder pulled concealed daggers and swords from their garments and leaped into the fray with a shout. The group of knights worked their way down the floor with methodical ease, steel clanging on steel, until their leader was alongside Thierry.

"Thierry de Pereille are you?" he demanded in a terse undertone.

Thierry nearly missed a parry, so astonished was he by the question.

"Aye," he agreed warily before he could think to do otherwise.

"Fool," the man declared again, his green eyes snapping fire as he dealt a telling blow to another guard. "Though I guessed as much when I heard Mongols came calling. Well might I have thought your sire might have raised you to have more sense than this." He grunted and jabbed his sword into the gullet of an attacker. Thierry struggled to make sense of the enigmatic comment even as he fought.

How could this stranger know his name? And how did he know Thierry's father?

"And who might you be?" Thierry dared to demand, earning himself a sharp glare from the older knight.

"Eustache de Sidon," the man spat. "Were it not for the pledge I took to your father, 'twould be your blood on the floor and deservedly so. Never have I witnessed such brash foolhardiness—"

A roar erupted from the end of the hall as a large contingent of the king's guards spilled into the throne room. The older man beside Thierry muttered something uncomplimentary under his breath that sounded markedly like something Nogai would say. He shot Thierry a scathing glance.

"Get out now," he dictated flatly. Thierry bristled at the order and met that frosty regard with no intent of complying.

"I will not flee like a woman," he snapped.

The other man snorted. "Nay, you will flee like a hunted man," he corrected. "As will all the rest of us now, I wager." He swore eloquently and visibly gritted his teeth, his voice dropping to a growl. "Indeed, I should have trusted the sign more. Had I but known, I would have brought them all." His gaze flitted over the walls of the throne room and he shook his head disparagingly.

"Such an opportunity wasted," he muttered, to Thierry's confusion, then spared the younger man a knowing look. "Well could we have regained the prize this very day," he asserted.

Before Thierry could demand an explanation, the older knight turned and bellowed once more. He raised his blade high as he faced the attackers.

"To the doors, I bid you!" he shouted to his men. They turned of one accord to meet the new arrivals, a collective roar erupting from their throats.

"Of what does he speak?" Kira demanded breathlessly. Thierry shrugged as they were swept forward with the crowd of knights.

"I know not," he confessed hastily. "But for whatever reason, they aid us." Kira tripped and he feared suddenly that she would be undertrodden in the rush. Too small was she to fend for herself in this press. He scooped her up protectively and tossed her over his shoulder, not missing the flash of an impertinent grin.

"Questions later," she advised in a whisper, and Thierry almost smiled. He but gave her knees a squeeze before one of the king's guards broke through the ranks. Thierry swung his blade with vigor and summarily dispatched his assailant.

The army of knights drove through the contingent of guards like a finely honed wedge. Thierry found himself, Kira and Nogai packed into the center of the group so tightly that he had not even the space to swing his own blade. Nogai's alarm was evident, for his nostrils flared agitatedly.

They gained the hall, then the staircase, the group of men pressing relentlessly on despite the cries of those who rose against them. The fan of air did Thierry feel and he exhaled shakily when they passed into the courtyard.

How would they find the horses? Their escape was doomed!

Barely had the fear formed than Thierry saw their distinctively shorter horses saddled before him. How had this happened? Thierry spared a glance to the older man, who grimaced and waved to his beasts.

"Hunted are we," he growled. "Have I not made the matter most clear? Hasten yourself, boy, or I shall truly begin to question whether you might be your father's son."

Nogai had already mounted and Kira was in Thierry's saddle an instant later.

"But seven short horses like this did I find, milord," a young boy informed Thierry solemnly as he made to mount himself.

"But seven have we," he confirmed tersely. He turned his back on the impertinent lad and swung up behind Kira.

"And fine creatures they be, milord." The boy bobbed a bow. "Fine thick coats have they and well it seems they must be well suited to travel—"

"Beauregard!" the older man bellowed impatiently from atop his own charger, and the boy winced. "Well I bade you be *mounted* when we arrived!" The boy's eyes widened in a manner that left no doubt as to his identity and he scurried toward a smaller pony.

"Aye, milord, but I had to confirm we had found all the foreign beasts," he explained hastily.

"I care naught for your excuses!" the man shouted, scooping up the boy with more care than his tone might have led one to expect. "I bade you find the Mongol's beasts—surely seven is plenty, even if 'tis not all." He dropped the boy into the saddle before him and gave the riderless pony a hearty swat across the rump.

"Hasten yourselves!" he bellowed once more.

Thierry dug his heels into his beast's side and whistled, sending the others running along with them. The troop of knights barely cleared the gates before shouts rang out from within the fortress behind. Thierry's heart nearly stopped when he saw the market carts and old farm horses cluttering the street, knowing with certainty that the king's troops would be upon them before they reached the city walls.

To his astonishment the townsfolk seemed well accustomed to this sort of interruption, for a bellow from Eustache sent them hurrying out of the path. The cry was taken up by the others. Nogai winked at Thierry before he lent his voice to the fray. The horses were given their lead and the cobblestones echoed with the thunder of their passing.

"Surely they will pursue us?" Thierry demanded. The older knight shot him an indulgent glance and ruffled the hair of the boy seated before him.

"Beauregard has a way with knots and harnesses that may keep them behind us," he commented with a wry smile. The boy grinned proudly at his master's praise. Thierry jammed his own helmet on his head, acknowledging he would believe that when he saw the evidence, and pulled Kira resolutely closer.

When they passed beneath the walls of the city without intervention, the knights hollered victoriously. Thierry released the breath he had not known he was holding and deliberately loosed his grip on Kira's waist.

He noted with pleasure that they set a course to the south where he had felt so attuned to the land. His relief must have been tangible, for Kira grinned up at him as she slipped his knife back into his scabbard. She curled closer to him and pulled his cloak about her against the late-afternoon air. Too comfortable she looked and Thierry was prompted to jolt her just a little. When next the knights bellowed, he raised his own voice so ferociously that she covered her ears with mock fright.

"Kiss," she whispered. Thierry brushed his lips across her brow, his gaze seeking out the leader in the throng of knights.

"Later," he murmured into her hair and felt her pout.

But more important matters were there afoot now than the exchange of kisses. Not only had Thierry to discover what had happened in the king's throne room, but he would know how this knight knew his name. And what did this man know of his father? Well it seemed the man avoided his gaze as they rode, but determined was Thierry to learn the truth of the matter when they halted for the night.

Chapter Thirteen

Kira liked not that Thierry had declined her a simple kiss of reassurance. And not enough was it that he had said "later," a word she had learned and liked little in itself, but his very manner was aloof. His lack of interest in her did not bode well, to Kira's way of thinking, for well she knew that she could not hope to conceal her pregnancy from him much longer.

Indeed, had he already noted it? Was that the reason for his disinterest?

She fretted as they rode and he said naught else to her. Darkness fell and Kira shivered in the chill, yet still the knights continued along the silent road. They rode without shouting or even speaking once the city was behind them, their passage through the quiet countryside almost soundless in itself. There was naught but the hoofbeats of the horses on the dirt, the occasional cough, the periodical jingle of the trap. The moon rose and Kira huddled closer to Thierry's warmth, not daring to hope when the lights of a building bobbed in the distance.

But stop there they did. A gate opened as they drew nearer and the knights rode directly within the building's embracing walls of one accord. Nary a word was said, the gate drawn up virtually on their heels and secured against the outside.

A great walled courtyard they stood within, a tall building

to one side and the walls enfolding all within their protective embrace. Golden light and the scent of roasted meat spilled out of the building. The horses stamped in the courtyard, their breath making white plumes in the air as the young boys dismounted to tend them. The men spoke quietly to each other as yet more men and boys appeared from within to aid with the tasks at hand.

Thierry lifted Kira to the ground and she knew not what to expect. The white haired man who had shouted so much joined them, as did a heavyset man who had come out of the building. The three men conferred hastily, their words too low and quick for Kira to comprehend. Thierry listened and eventually nodded in agreement.

To what? The heavyset man snapped his fingers and a pair of women in those trailing skirts Kira had noted throughout this land hastened toward them. Thierry brushed his lips across Kira's brow once more and waved her toward the pair of women without any explanation. They smiled invitingly but she was not convinced of their sincerity. Accompany these strangers? Where and to what purpose?

"But, Thierry—" Kira protested, turning to find that Thierry had already walked away. She picked out his figure where he walked with the other two men, his head bent low as he listened. Kira suddenly felt more alone than she ever had before.

A hand landed awkwardly on her shoulder and Kira glanced up to find Nogai's expression surprisingly sympathetic.

He said something she knew to be a joke, even though she could not understand, and winked reassuringly. Kira smiled despite herself. He tapped the pocket where she knew he kept his cards and wiggled his brows questioningly. Indeed, Nogai must feel even more lost than she.

Encouraged, Kira nodded and gave Nogai's hand a squeeze before she turned to accompany the two women. Whatever their intent, there was naught she could do to fight it alone. Mayhap if Thierry trusted them, she should do so, as well.

Mayhap if Thierry had appeared to give the matter some consideration, Kira might have had more confidence in that conclusion.

The women's dastardly intent proved to be that of offering Kira a bath.

So delighted was she at the possibility that she could not be coy. Half afraid they were teasing her with the steaming tub, Kira clasped her hands together and looked longingly at the steaming water. One of the women laughed at her hopeful manner as she nodded.

"Aye, the tub is for you," she said.

"Well it seemed you might desire one after your ride," affirmed the other. Her eyes twinkled merrily for a moment, then she pinched the bridge of her nose theatrically.

"Aye, you know the truth of it." Kira laughed along with them, her pleasure at the prospect making it impossible to take affront. A bath. 'Twould be heaven itself to scrub this grime from her skin.

'Twas only when Kira was nude in the tub and the women disappeared with her clothes that she began to doubt the wisdom of her decision. Were they to leave her here with naught to wear? But nay, they returned before the water had cooled and urged Kira out of the tub. They offered her a long-sleeved white *kurta* that fell to the floor and Kira smiled in recognition of the familiar garment.

"*Kurta*," she said, but the women frowned.

"Nay, this is your chemise," one corrected. "My old one, actually, but 'twill fit you better." Kira repeated the word to herself and mentally chastised herself for speaking out so hastily.

"And your kirtle," said the other in a more kindly manner as she held out a bundle of cinnamon hue. Kira accepted the heavier garment and shook it out, surprised to find it of much the same cut as the one she had already donned. 'Twas the weight of the fabric alone that changed the garment's name? Curious 'twas, but she pulled it over her head as they indicated.

To Kira's shock they tugged on laces at the sides of the garment until it fit her figure snugly. She looked down at herself in amazement when they nodded approvingly, knowing she could never show herself in public in such a manner. Indeed, there was naught left to the imagination by such a scandalous garment.

The women tut-tutted, though, and coiled Kira's hair back with businesslike ease despite her discomfort with her garb. They draped a sheer wisp of cloth about her throat and more over her head and hair, tucking the ends into a stiffened circlet placed atop her head. Kira regarded them skeptically when they stood back to admire their work.

Surely no one appeared in mixed company like this?

The kindly woman's expression brightened as though she recalled something forgotten, and Kira almost applauded her memory. Surely there was a good bit of cloth missing. At the very least, she had need of *chalwar* and a djellaba to cover this indecently tight garment.

To Kira's astonishment the woman offered naught but a pair of leather shoes.

Kira shook her head firmly and lifted the hem of the kirtle and chemise to show her bare ankle. "Am I to have no *chalwar?*" she requested politely. The women frowned and Kira struggled to find a way to explain. "To cover my legs," she finally said. The two of them discussed the matter in excited whispers, turning of one accord to grant Kira indulgent smiles.

"We wear no such garment," they informed her.

This did not bode well, to Kira's thinking. Surely it could not be so? The women shook their heads and chattered too quickly to be comprehended, then finally lifted the hems of their own garments.

Their legs were similarly bare.

The sight made Kira yet more aware of the loose chemise brushing against her bare thighs and buttocks. No other conclusion could she make than the obvious one, and though she resented that these women had assumed her to have the same occupation as they, she could hardly blame their error. Indeed, without vows between them, was she truly any better than Thierry's whore?

They urged her to the door and Kira concluded that she was not to be granted a djellaba either. Well it seemed that simple modesty was not assumed to be one of her traits, and her color flared high as they descended the stairs to the common room.

Just as they reached the floor and Kira was painfully aware of the regard of the company of men upon them, another entered from the courtyard. The cold gust of air swirled around her bare ankles and made her shiver after the warmth of her bath. Kira felt a telltale prickling and knew without looking that her nipples had beaded. The sight was surely visible through the shockingly fitted cloth and she felt yet more self-conscious at the realization.

Crimson with mortification, she kept her gaze resolutely on the flagstone floor and followed the women as she was bidden.

"Kira."

Even the awe in Thierry's voice would not compel her to look up, for certain was Kira that he was as appalled by her transformed appearance as she. Had she any hope of being considered his only woman, that meager possibility had most assuredly been destroyed by her appearance in the garb of a whore.

"Kira." Thierry's finger was gentle beneath her chin. Though she was upset, Kira could not turn away from him. She reluctantly lifted her gaze to his, surprised to find no censure in his silver gaze. That her clothing did not trouble him was surely all the answer that she needed to confirm her status. Kira felt her tears rise and she shook her head weakly. To her astonishment, there was admiration in Thierry's gaze when it locked with hers once more.

"Nay, Kira," he murmured. "Be not so distressed. Your garments were worn and 'tis best you dress in the Frankish manner."

"But 'tis so different," she protested, knowing she referred to more than the garb itself.

Thierry shook his head. "Yet flattering to you all the same," he mused affectionately.

To be told that the garb of whores suited her was far from the confirmation Kira sought from him. A single tear escaped the trap of her lashes but Thierry gently wiped it aside with his thumb. A small smile played over his lips and he traced one finger lightly down her cheek as though he feared to touch her.

"You are beautiful, Kira," he whispered. Kira closed her heart to the aching tenderness in his voice.

"But the others—"

"Nay." Thierry interrupted her firmly, turning her chin with one warm fingertip so that she was compelled to look into his eyes again. "None is so lovely as Kira," he reiterated with a slight emphasis on her name.

'Twas enough to dissolve her reservations, at least for the moment.

There was no mistaking his pleasure with her appearance and the very fact of that made Kira's heart beat faster. Thierry found her fetching above the others. Whatever role she might play in his life, Kira could not deny that his appreciation pleased her. A flame there was in his eyes and she well knew that he desired her in this moment. It seemed not for the first time that there were no others than the two of them and her heart swelled with pride that this man should have chosen her.

A man made a raucous comment and she jumped at the proximity of his voice. Kira's color flared yet higher at the realization that they stood amidst a veritable army of men, and her gaze flicked nervously to Thierry's. His smile widened slightly, but he did not yet usher her to the board. Embarrassed anew by the lack of modesty of her garb, she raised her hands hesitantly to cover her breasts in the hope that he might understand.

"But, Thierry, 'tis so immodest. I fear to have any look upon me so revealed," she protested.

"Nay, Kira," Thierry murmured. Much to her surprise, Thierry took her hands within his and lifted them away from her. He pressed a kiss to the soft skin on the inside of first one wrist and then the other. A shiver raced over Kira's skin from the sensitive point and she felt her hand quiver within his grip.

"No shame should you have, beautiful Kira," he whispered against her flesh. Undeterred by her shiver, Thierry's lips nudged against her hand and he pressed a kiss into her palm. He straightened before her and folded her fingers over the spot he had kissed, as though her grip could hold his embrace captive there.

Kira smiled at the whimsy of his gesture and it seemed that the hall was cold no longer. Thierry placed her hand on his elbow and escorted her to the long table where Nogai and the leader of the other men already sat, seating her alongside him as though she were the shah's consort herself.

'Twas only much later, when the hall was filled with the sounds of snoring men and Thierry dozed contentedly beside her, that Kira dared to give herself a hard look. She felt the dampness between her thighs, the weight of Thierry's hand on her waist and the absence of any token or vow taken between them. No consolation was it that when Thierry touched her or granted her a tender look, she forgot all else but the magic wrought between them.

But that did not change the truth of it. Kira stared at the ceiling and forced herself to form the thought. She was Thierry's whore and all others knew it. 'Twas time enough she faced the fact herself.

Kira folded her arms about herself in the darkness, hating the kind of woman she had become. Unbeknownst to all who surrounded her, she let her tears creep silently over her cheeks and wondered what would be the fate of her child.

Thierry felt that he recognized the old château reposing on the hill before them ten days after they rode out of Paris. They had ridden hard, especially after that first night, and put the leagues rapidly behind them. The company of knights had also kept from the main roads and Thierry suspected their leader thought they might be pursued.

Old Eustache had confided naught else, much to Thierry's annoyance. "For home, with all haste," had been his anthem these days and when Thierry saw the dark gray edifice ahead, he suspected home was precisely where he was.

He urged his mount deliberately forward in the ranks until he was riding alongside the old knight. Eustache granted him a wary glance but said naught.

"Is this our destination?" Thierry asked.

The other man snorted. "Know you not?" he asked disdainfully.

"Nay, or I would not ask," Thierry responded tightly. He fancied the other man smothered a smile.

"Montsalvat 'tis called," Eustache supplied finally. Thierry felt Kira turn to look up at the forbidding facade of the fortress but did not look away from the older man. Montsalvat. The name he knew well from his sire's tongue, the name of the place where he had been born. Thierry's heart leaped in anticipation.

"And 'tis here you call home?" he asked.

Eustache shot him a sharp look. "Aye."

Realizing that the man was being unnaturally communicative, Thierry decided to ask more. "What happened in Paris?" he asked, watching the knight's expression close stubbornly.

"Naught have I to say of that, if indeed you do not know," he replied tersely.

"Will they not follow us here?" Thierry demanded.

The old knight snorted. "Have they a whit of sense, they will." His lips thinned grimly. "But we will be ready."

"'Tis more than clear you know something more of this matter," Thierry observed.

"And evident that you do not," the older man replied.

"And equally evident that 'tis a factor of import I do not know," Thierry snapped in growing annoyance. "Surely if you knew my sire, you would feel some compunction to confide in me this truth."

The older man's eyes blazed with unexpected anger. "Surely if I knew your sire as I did, I would respect his decision."

"What decision?" Thierry demanded.

"I will say naught of it," the older man retorted. "Mind the road!" he shouted suddenly over his shoulder to his knights. "Singly will we pass, if you please." With that, he urged his horse ahead of Thierry's mount and the conversation came to a frustrating halt. Naught was there wrong with the road that two could not ride abreast and Thierry knew Eustache was avoiding his questions.

But why? Suddenly Thierry realized that 'twas when he had revealed his mark that all had gone awry.

"What is the import of my birthmark?" he shouted at the back of the man ahead of him. Eustache stiffened, telling Thierry he had found the crux of the matter, but naught did the older man say.

Eustache touched his spurs to his mount as though he would outrun the question, but his opponent had no intent of being so easily avoided. Stubbornly Thierry kept his horse hot on the heels of the knight's destrier and they began the climb up the steep road to the fortress well ahead of the others.

"Tell me, Eustache," he called, but no sign did the knight make he had heard. "Well do I know that you know the truth of it. Confide it in me."

Eustache touched his spurs to his mount in response and raced up the twisting road to the gates.

"Would you have me pay the price of my life for your stubborn silence?" Thierry demanded impatiently, to no avail. Eustache reached the barbican gates and passed beneath the shadow of the tower with reckless speed.

"My father's mark is exactly the same," Thierry shouted as he rode into the bailey behind him. Boys came running from the stables as Eustache leaped from his destrier's back. The beast panted from its exertion but the older knight merely cast the reins impatiently aside.

"What means this cursed mark?" Thierry asked in frustration as he followed suit. Eustache glared at him.

"'Tis no *curse* to bear the mark of your line," he spat indignantly. Thierry sensed the thread of the tale.

"What line?"

"Ask your sire," Eustache ordered in disgust as he turned away.

"I cannot," Thierry retorted. The older knight spun on his heel and granted him a wary glance.

"Dead is he?" he growled. He propped his hands on his hips and Thierry imagined the matter meant more to him than he might be willing to reveal.

"I know not," Thierry admitted. Eustache's eyes narrowed.

"Then you had best find out," he concluded harshly, and turned away once more.

"Well do I know that you know this tale!" Thierry shouted as the other man stalked to the portal to the hall. "And well do I see that you hold my father in regard! Is it not a travesty of your respect for him to not confide this in me?"

That question struck the flint.

"Travesty?" Eustache whirled around furiously and stomped back across the bailey to confront Thierry. So angry was he that Thierry wondered what he had wrought with his accusation, just before he found a meaty finger poked into his chest.

"Travesty? Well would it be a *travesty* of respect to tell you this tale, boy, and had you a whit of sense about you, you would know it. Twenty-one years past, afore the Yule, were you born in *that* tower—" the finger jabbed to the château behind the indignant Eustache "—and not four months later a fire was lit in *this* very bailey that you might be granted the full legacy of your line." The finger swept to encompass the deadened grass in the bailey and returned to wag beneath Thierry's nose as Eustache's voice dropped. "Your sire chose to wait."

"What say you?"

"He granted you *naught* of your legacy at your birth or your naming," Eustache clarified, slowly enunciating each word. "Well had he paid the price for its burden and he wanted you to make the choice yourself of shouldering its weight."

"Well, I would choose it now," Thierry asserted firmly, folding his arms across his chest. "Tell me the tale."

"You know naught of what you speak," Eustache sneered. "All my knighted life I have served your family, and even now, in tending this keep, I hold to the word I granted your sire and his sire before him. Can you not see that confiding in you this tale would be the greatest travesty of all? Your sire chose to be the one to confide the tale in you himself, and well did I know of his intent." Eustache took a step away and resolutely held Thierry's regard.

"'Tis out of respect for your sire that I decline your request."

With that flat assertion, Eustache turned to walk more slowly to the hall. The other knights passed through the gates then, the jumbled activity of their arrival doing naught to clarify Thierry's thinking on the matter. Had his father declined him as heir? It sounded not that way, but he knew not what to think.

"What if he is dead?" He blurted out the question afore he thought. Eustache spun slowly and met his gaze assessingly.

"Then your legacy died with him," he said so softly that Thierry had to strain to hear the words.

Nay. It could not be. Destined he was for greatness and well he knew it. This was his chance! No one could steal that from him and Thierry would not permit another opportunity to be lost to him by some whim of the fates.

"Time do we waste!" he cried to the older man in undisguised frustration.

Eustache grimaced. "Time has been wasted afore," he said. "My word did I give to your father."

His father.

Khanbaliq. Thierry's mind wrenched back to those days and those angry words even as Eustache disappeared.

Surely Dagobert still drew breath. Surely 'twas not too late to seek him out and hear the fullness of the tale. Anger raged briefly within him that his sire had not already granted him the tale of his legacy, until a thought dismissed the accusation before it could fully form.

Likely 'twas Thierry had stolen the opportunity for his father's confidence by leaving so abruptly those long years past. He released a long, slow breath and turned to face out over the hills, blind to the stunning view as he remembered his departure from Khanbaliq. Thierry winced in recollection of the accusations he had hurled at his sire that fateful day and rubbed one hand across his brow. He halted mid-gesture as a thought abruptly occurred to him.

Was this what the shaman had meant when he had said that Thierry's success would be sacrificed by his own hand?

If Kira had thought Thierry distracted before, 'twas naught compared to his manner after his argument with the older knight on their arrival. He was upset beyond anything she had seen before and she wished she knew what to say.

Indeed, though she had understood much of old Eustache's words, his talk of tales and legacies was a complete enigma to her. Kira suspected that Thierry knew little more than she. Though somehow it all had to do with his curious mark.

He frowned, lost in his own thoughts, as they were shown to a large room in the tower. Kira waited but no others joined them and she felt a thrill of pleasure that they were to have some privacy. A civilized place this Montsalvat was undoubtedly. Time enough 'twas that they reached one.

A box made of drapes sat in one corner of the room and Kira regarded it with curiosity. When 'twas evident that Thierry was not in the mood to explain Frankish matters to her, she investigated on her own, leaving him scowling at the floor.

She pulled back the drapes, not knowing what to expect. To her surprise, 'twas merely a place for reposing, from all appearances. Cushions were scattered across the raised base of the box, those heavy drapes hanging all around. Kira felt the bottom of the box, pleased to find it quite soft beneath the blankets.

Privacy, in truth. She smiled with satisfaction as she tugged the drapes closed once more. A strange contrivance 'twas, indeed, though with the coldness the stone floors took in this country, it mayhap was quite sensible. And well was she ready to have Thierry to herself during the night.

"'Tis a bed, Kira," Thierry informed her, his voice unusually flat.

She spared him a glance to find him no more happy than he had been moments before. Well could Kira do something about that. And mayhap 'twas time to show him that she could grant him more than one might expect from a whore. She purposefully closed the distance between them and stretched to her toes to frame his concerned face in her hands.

"Nay, Kira," he said, shaking his head slightly as he frowned. Kira ignored him, reaching up to smooth the furrow from his brow with a gentle fingertip. She shook her head in mock disapproval and he smiled absently at her antics.

"Everything will be fine," she told him solemnly, wishing she was articulate enough in Frankish to tell him yet more. "'Twill all work out in the end," she added confidently, telling him precisely the opposite of what she had been feeling these past days. But clear 'twas that he needed some reassurance, and mayhap if she played the role of wife and mate, he might see the appeal of the idea. Impulsively she stretched up and kissed him gently.

'Twas the first time she had initiated a kiss, although she had demanded many, and Kira rather liked the sensation. Thierry responded naught for an instant, telling her that she had surprised him, as well.

Kira deliberately nudged her tongue invitingly against his and gained the response she sought. Thierry inhaled sharply and lifted her against him as he deepened his kiss. Kira pulled him closer with satisfaction, rubbing his neck soothingly and liking the way the tension was easing from him.

Something there was that she could give Thierry. Something more than sexual release, for here she gave him comfort. And more, he accepted it from her. She dared to take encouragement from that meager offering. Mayhap he did hold her in higher regard than the Persian woman had implied that all Mongols held their women. Kira closed her eyes and dared to dream that one day she alone would be Thierry's woman.

Though she needed not his love, for love had already left its furrows in her back.

She smiled softly when he lifted his head and he traced her cheek with that roughened fingertip again. A habit 'twas becoming, and one Kira rather liked. She nestled her cheek against Thierry's palm contentedly.

"Kira, I must go down to the others for a time," he explained quietly. Kira nodded understanding. She could not restrain the urge to rub her fingertips speculatively over her lips as she watched Thierry go, unable to completely stifle her budding optimism.

Mayhap she could be Thierry's woman alone. Should the thought not have occurred to him as yet, she would endeavor at every opportunity to make it so. Indeed, Kira could not imagine that their thoughts were not as one when she met the warmth in his silver gaze. Dare she even wonder whether he already thought of her alone?

'Twas almost too much to be believed, but Kira dared to indulge her whimsy. She spun about the room happily, pausing to poke at a trinket box or a tapestry in gleeful disinterest. Here would they stay, she fantasized, here would they make their home, simply the two of them together. The two of them and their babe, and mayhap more babes after this one. 'Twas fitting that they stay here at Montsalvat, where Thierry had been born, himself. And 'twas a place she suspected that she could find amenable, as well.

Kira closed her eyes and imagined telling Thierry of the child. Mayhap 'twould be all the impetus he needed to cast aside his wandering ways and settle here to live. Mayhap he would be delighted that they had wrought another so soon.

Mayhap he would feel as wondrous of the new life forming within her as she did.

Mayhap. Kira's eyes flew open and her gaze landed on Thierry's saddlebags. Did she dare to make her desire known? She hesitated for but a heartbeat before deciding to unpack his belongings. Liked it here, Kira did. More, she would raise her child here within these sturdy gray walls. She would lift her babe high and show him the wonder of the view from this perch high above the land, let him fill his lungs with the scent of the sea.

What better way to show Thierry thus than to spread about his belongings as though they lived here in truth?

The rationale was inescapable and Kira set to her task with relish. The blankets she shook out and folded atop the bed. Thierry's brass pots and cooking implements she arranged neatly on the cold hearth. She ensured that they were clean, though she did not imagine he would cook anything here. Already the smell of roasted meat rose from the hall below to tempt her stomach and Kira found herself happily humming at her task.

His silk *kurta* that she had worn that long-ago night came next from the bag. She rubbed her nose in its softness and draped it over a stool with a smile of reminiscence. Always would she remember those first little fishes.

On the morrow she would wash their garments, Kira resolved, reaching into the bag yet again. A small bag she retrieved and assumed it contained coin. But nay, 'twas too light and its contents not bulky enough. With a frown Kira spilled the contents out into her palm and caught her breath at the sight.

'Twas an *aljofar*. She would have known the token anywhere.

A gift for a bride. The very fact that 'twas hidden away told Kira in a heartbeat that 'twas not meant for her.

Having the evidence for what she feared most cradled within her palm unnerved Kira more than she would have expected. Indeed, she felt that she had been dealt a telling and unexpected blow by this discovery. Would Thierry not have given the token to her already if he had meant her to have the gem?

Kira's hand shook at the truth of that and she hastily dumped both the pearl and its chain back into the small sack. Her vision veiled with tears and she shoved the bag back into his saddle-bag. Bittersweet was the realization of how much she had longed to have Thierry as hers and hers alone.

Wanted Thierry as her husband and the father of her children, Kira did, and now that 'twas not to be, she dared to fully voice her desire. One man, one woman, as 'twas ordained to be. And she had thought mayhap…

But nay. Kira had imposed her own beliefs on her perception of the situation and seen only what she wished to see. No promise had Thierry made to her. No more did he seek from her than a man might expect from a whore. A fool she had been to tease herself with other possibilities. Had the Persian woman not made it clear that these Mongols took many wives and held not one above the others? Had she not been warned?

Could this sweet longing she felt to be with Thierry alone be love in a different guise? Well it seemed it shared the same serpent's bite as her father's love. Though in truth, the teeth dug deeper this time for all that they did not scar her flesh.

Had she fallen in love with Thierry? If so, it seemed she had gained precisely what she deserved for daring to have faith in tender emotions yet again. Kira dropped to sit on the stone ledge of the window, knowing the truth when she heard it. No sweetness was there in the realization that she loved Thierry as she stared down at the rumpled bag. Only too well could she still see that plumply expensive *aljofar* in her mind's eye and well Kira knew she would never forget it.

A token for another woman.

A token of Thierry's regard that she was not destined to wear.

And never would Kira wear one, even as a token of another man's regard, after bearing a child out of wedlock. No doubt would there be that she was no longer innocent. A life of shame stretched out before Kira and she found she liked the taste of it naught. She stared blindly at the small sack perched in the bag and suddenly realized the folly of what she had done in unpacking his goods.

Nay, she thought wildly. It must be precisely where she had found it. Observant Thierry was beyond belief and he must never know she had seen what he had hidden from her. Kira forced herself to recall the sack's original position and unsteadily put it back just so, then cast a nervous glance around the room.

Better 'twould be if Thierry had no idea she had opened the saddlebag. Her hands shook as she folded the blankets but she would not falter in this task. Kira inhaled shakily and choked back her tears as she carefully repacked his belongings. 'Twas obvious that Thierry had come to the land of the Franks to fetch his bride.

Indeed, it mattered naught whether her belly rounded or not, for he would soon cast her aside, one way or the other. Fretted she had for naught all these nights. Only a matter of time was it before Thierry cast her aside. And whither then? She knew not and could not bear to speculate about raising their child alone.

Despair welled up in Kira's heart as she completed her task and weak tears spilled over her cheeks unchecked. She dashed at them with her fingertips before she realized the futility of the gesture and sighed raggedly in acceptance of her fate. Would that she had never met Thierry. Would that she were back in Tiflis.

Kira sniffled, then hastily crawled within the comfort of the draped bed, wishing it truly could render her invisible to the world.

"Tell me not that you have troubles in this paradise," Nogai commented sardonically. Thierry glanced up from his wine as his friend dropped to sit beside him, and scowled into the red liquid anew.

"Well it seems that I must seek my sire," he muttered.

Nogai's brows rose. "First a family, now a sire. Suddenly your kin are being conjured from naught so quickly that I cannot keep a reckoning of them all." Thierry's glance slid sidelong but Nogai was innocently draining his own tankard.

The Mongol tapped the empty pewter demandingly on the board and grinned when it was promptly filled.

"Fitting it seems that you would be in haste to leave the first decent place we have quartered," he commented.

"Montsalvat meets with your approval?" Thierry demanded tersely, indicating that his tankard also be filled. Drink aplenty was what he needed this night, for only with oblivion might he escape his memories.

"Aye," Nogai concluded with satisfaction. "Aim to sleep under the stars this night I do, as is fitting for a man. Have you seen the goats? Sturdy stock have they here and able herdsmen they must be. Even with the liability of this tower, 'tis an amenable place."

"Should you like it so well, you will undoubtedly be welcome to remain in my absence," Thierry responded sourly. He did not bother to acknowledge Nogai's glance of surprise.

"Truly you mean to leave?"

"I must seek my sire," Thierry growled.

"Ah." Nogai took a long draught of wine. "Have you any inkling where he might be?" he asked with apparent idleness.

"Khanbaliq," Thierry supplied tightly. Nogai choked in a most satisfactory manner.

"Khanbaliq?" he demanded in open astonishment. "Know you how far that is?"

"Aye." With greater precision than Nogai might guess did Thierry know the distance, for he had traveled it and he suspected Nogai had not. Without the endorsement of the khan, 'twould take a full year to reach Khanbaliq. And then what? Another year to return to the land of his birth? All to hear a tale he might have been told years past. All to hear a tale that might mean naught.

Or might mean everything. Thierry indulged himself with a venomous glance to the taciturn Eustache, who stubbornly ignored him.

Cursed man. Two years was Thierry to waste over this matter. Yet little choice had he. Thierry's sense that his destiny hung in the balance and that this tale could tip the scales could not be denied.

"'Aye,' says he, as though 'twere no farther than the town below this fortress," Nogai snorted into his tankard. He fixed Thierry abruptly with a bright eye. "What of Kira?"

"What *of* Kira?"

"Does she ride to Khanbaliq?"

Thierry's lips thinned. "Kira is my woman," he said tightly, as though that explained all. And to his mind, it did.

Nogai, however, snorted with undisguised skepticism. "And enchanted will she be with the sight of another ship in such short order, you can be sure," he commented dryly. Thierry refused to indulge him with a response and the two drank in silence for a long moment.

"Have you considered," Nogai began finally in a measured tone, "that such a trip might be difficult for one so small as she?"

He would *not* leave Kira behind. 'Twas unthinkable, and truly Nogai overstepped himself in even suggesting such a thing. Thierry bristled at the very thought and turned a chilling eye on his *anda*.

"What do you suggest?" Thierry demanded coldly. Nogai spread his hands carefully.

"Only that it might well be safer for Kira to remain here. Not so strong is she as Mongol women and well might she welcome the opportunity to wait behind such sturdy walls."

Everything within Thierry clenched at the very idea. Two years without Kira? Impossible. And naught would happen to her on the road—he would personally ensure her safety. Whereas here, who knew what fate might befall her?

"Kira is stronger than you know," he retorted frostily. Nogai raised his brows but said naught, philosophically taking a sip of his wine instead.

"When do you plan to commence?" he asked mildly some moments later. Thierry drained his tankard and banged it on the board yet again.

"On the morrow, with first light," he informed his *anda* tightly. "Well it seems that time is of the essence."

"Aye," Nogai responded with an easy grin. "Imperative 'tis that I should have some decent *qumis* in short order, instead of this thin swill that passes for drink in these parts." He drained his tankard, showing no trouble in swallowing the "swill," before he banged it on the board with a roar and a wink.

Chapter Fourteen

Not reassuring at all was the fact that Thierry did not return.

Kira curled alone under the coverlet within the secure embrace of the draped bed and watched darkness descend over the room. Thierry did not come. Raucous sounds rose from the hall below, their volume increasing as time passed with aching slowness and still Thierry did not come. The smell of the meat reached a peak and faded away to naught, yet no tread of a foot in the hall outside did Kira discern.

She huddled deeper within the blanket's warmth and wrapped her arms around her stomach, as though she would comfort her fledgling babe. Alone they were, and they had best become accustomed to that fact. Indeed, Kira might not even have the bed to hide within once Thierry discovered her state. An expensive indulgence it must be and she could not imagine that one would waste such richness on a pregnant concubine.

But what choice had she other than to stay? No coin had she with which to smooth her way back. And where would she go? Back to Tiflis? Indeed, she could not imagine that her sire would even welcome her there should she arrive with her belly swollen with child and no husband in tow.

The *aljofar* had value.

The traitorous thought held a certain appeal, though Kira's

ethics rose in instant denial. She nibbled her lip in indecision. Did she dare?

Recollection of precisely who had compromised her had her flying out across the room and rummaging in Thierry's saddle-bags. Tears pricked Kira's eyes as the gem tumbled out into her palm, but she resolutely blinked them away. Precisely how much value did the pearl carry? Was it indeed worth betraying the man she had grown to trust, however mistakenly?

Kira closed her eyes and placed the gem on her tongue.

Sweet. She stifled a curse and spat the pearl out with disgust.

A plague on the man for buying such a good gem! She cast the necklace away from her, not caring where it fell. How could he manage such a feat? *Naught* did Thierry know of pearls and yet he still acquired an exquisite *aljofar* for his bride. Unfair 'twas, and her indecision rose yet higher at the evident value of the piece. Kira stalked irritably across the room and back to cast an accusatory eye over the pearl. The gem winked innocently in the light cast by the moon where its chain had snagged on the saddlebag.

'Twas worth good coin, that cursed pearl. Kira crossed the room reluctantly to lift it from its perch and let it swivel slowly from its chain before her. Good coin. Coin enough mayhap to buy passage to Constantinople. The gem gleamed invitingly as though it would tempt her to make the choice, but Kira shook her head and heaved a sigh.

'Twould be wrong. She could not do it. Thierry had parted with hard-earned coin to acquire a worthy gift for his bride and no place had she to intervene. The *aljofar* was not hers to take, one way or the other. Kira was but a whore who had made the mistake of conceiving, and well would she have to bear the burden of her error alone. She slipped the pearl slowly back into the small sack and replaced the entirety within the saddlebag.

Naught had she but the garments on her back and her own resources. Precious little they seemed indeed to see a way for herself and a babe, but somehow Kira knew she would ride the storm.

And as long as she could, she would keep Thierry's protection. Even if he could grant her naught else.

'Twas with the first light of the dawn that Thierry crept up the stairs. Not too drunk was he to have forgotten that Kira had not eaten, though admittedly he had recalled the fact rather late. His steps were rather more unsteady than he expected as he made a swerving path down the corridor, offering in hand. He scowled even as he wondered whether Nogai had spoken aright.

Had they been so long without *qumis* that they were less than they had been? Nogai had fallen asleep on the board from the red wine, and well enough did Thierry know 'twas not his wont.

Was Kira making them both soft?

The twinge of guilt Thierry felt when he nudged open the door and found the room within silent did naught to reassure him. Not even Kira's breathing could he discern and well he knew that his hearing was better than that.

Impossible that he was becoming an urban man. Impossible that he could not carry his *qumis*. Impossible that he could not discern the sound of a sleeping woman's breathing when she lay so close. Thierry stalked into the room in poor humor and fairly dropped the crockery of stew onto the table by the hearth so that it clattered noisily. Let Kira see the fullness of the man she had chosen. He burped fruitily, amplifying the sound with satisfaction.

Naught stirred.

'Twas disconcerting. Fear rose within him and he wondered suddenly if Kira inexplicably might have abandoned him. No reason had she, but still the room was too quiet. Thierry spun around in panic and surveyed his surroundings, finding his saddlebags precisely as he had dropped them.

Not a good sign was that. Indeed, it appeared that naught had stirred since his departure and the matter did not sit well. Thierry's eyes narrowed as he found no sign of Kira, and his gaze landed on the bed. 'Twas the only place where Kira could be concealed and he strode across the room and ripped open the drapes.

Time 'twas they were on the road to seek his sire, and he told himself that 'twas that impatience alone that fueled his anxiety.

Kira slept curled in a tight ball. Little cat. Thierry released his breath slowly in relief and forced his fingers to loosen their grip on the drapes. He stood and gazed upon her, unaware of the smile that transformed his features as he leaned against the bedpost.

His Kira. Thierry's heart wrenched at the fragility of her. So tiny she was. Her breathing was soft enough that he fancied she barely breathed at all. No wonder he had not heard her, for she made virtually no sound. Only too well did he recall her illness on the ship, and the hand that would have urged her awake froze mid-gesture.

Was Nogai right? Would he threaten Kira's health by taking her on a journey that was sure to be arduous? Thierry reached out one tentative fingertip and gently smoothed the hair back from her temple. He admired the luscious sweep of her dark lashes upon her cheek and found his fingers trailing over her skin in a caress.

How could he bear to be without her for two years?

There was not just Kira's health to consider, though. Only too well did Thierry recall the gleam in men's eyes when they had looked upon her, and his hand clenched involuntarily. They could be set upon by bandits on the long road to Khanbaliq. Kira could be hurt. Worse, she could be raped or even killed.

How could Thierry live with himself should he be responsible for bringing her to such a fate? How could he bear to see her hurt?

What if something should befall him and she was left alone with Nogai? Would Nogai protect her? Thierry hoped so in the same moment he prayed Nogai would not see fit to claim his strong yet delicate little cat for his own.

Was that not the Mongol way? Thierry's gut twisted in indecision and he paced impatiently across the room. No sooner had he put distance between them than he was drawn back to gaze down at her as though she kept him on an invisible lead.

Witch, he thought affectionately, tempted by the luscious swell of her rosy lips. He sat carefully on the side of the bed and leaned over her, fancying that she sensed his presence when she immediately turned toward him.

What if some evil fate befell both Nogai and Thierry, leaving Kira truly alone?

Thierry's gut went cold and he shoved to his feet, the thought sobering him more than two nights' sleep. Had not old Eustache pledged his hand to Thierry's family? Would that old knight not see Kira protected? And safer she would be here, within the walls of the fortress Montsalvat, than anywhere on the open road he might take her. Eustache had said they were prepared to greet any pursuers from the crown, and the forces Thierry had already seen quartered here convinced him.

'Twas the only sensible path to take, despite his own misgivings. Thierry must think of Kira and her safety, not simply his own baser desires.

But how could he tell her that he did not abandon her here? Two years was long enough that any woman might have doubts. Would she believe any promise he made? Thierry propped his hands on his hips with dissatisfaction as he stared down at her once more.

Would she cry at the news? Thierry's innards writhed at the possibility. Never would he be able to leave without her, should she cry. But he could not endanger her. Thierry pressed a hand to his temples.

Would that he could be assured that she would be safe in his company, for his heart vehemently protested any other solution.

But nay. 'Twas illogical to jeopardize such a fragile creature so, purely for his own whimsy. Some of his possessions Thierry would leave that Kira might know he intended to return.

'Twas the way it should be. She would understand. Thierry's vision blurred as he stubbornly set about his packing and he forced himself to think of his return. Once he knew of his legacy, he would return and take Kira to his side once more. His woman she was and even the breadth of the Mongol empire could not change that simple fact. His fingers fumbled when he came upon the small pouch with the *aljofar*. He hesitated for a long moment, finally letting the chain and gem tumble into his palm.

Well should he have given Kira the token already. Thierry spared a glance to the bed, knowing that if she had awakened, he would have granted it to her now.

But nay. Kira slept on, oblivious to Thierry's anguish, and loath was he to awaken her for such an indulgence. And then he would be forced to explain all to her. Thierry jammed the *aljofar* into its pouch.

Witch. So completely had Kira ensnared him, yet she blithely slept while he wrestled with his feelings for her.

And what were his feelings for her? Strong indeed was this urge to see her safe, yet Thierry would not grant it a name lest he be compelled to look it fully in the eye. He thought of his parents, and for the first time considered that there might be a difference between claiming Kira as his woman and making her his wife.

But nay. Foolish whimsy that was. 'Twas all the same. The woman warmed his bed and knew the safety of his protection. What more could there be between man and woman? What more might one desire of a union?

Thierry thought unexpectedly of the way she had offered him comfort before he had gone down to the hall the night before and decisively snapped his saddlebag closed.

Mayhap 'twould be better that he was without her for a while. Mayhap this softness she had launched within him would disappear, should she not be constantly before him.

Mayhap that softness was not something to be distrusted. The taunting voice of temptation would not abandon him readily this morn, it seemed, and Thierry shoved restlessly away from the bed.

Enough. A task had he to perform and though 'twas one he would rather avoid, he would see the matter through. His father he would seek, his legacy he would know, his woman he would return for when all was completed.

And he would grant her the *aljofar* on his return. Thierry grimly shoved the pouch containing the gem deep within his *kalat*.

Despite his resolutions, he could not help but pause before he left and look down on her lingeringly once more. Would that he could commit her features to memory. Would that he could safely take her with him.

Would that he did not have to go.

Kira sensed the difference in the room as soon as she awakened. Something was amiss. She rolled over and peered out through the heavy drapes, squinting at the brightness of the sunlight that flooded the room.

Clear 'twas that Thierry had not returned to her, for she had not felt his warmth throughout the night, but there was something else gone awry. As soon as her eyes adjusted to the morning light, Kira saw that one of Thierry's saddlebags was gone.

It could not be. She flew from the bed, tripping over the cursedly long chemise these folk wore, and tore open the top of the remaining bag. His blanket, his cooking utensils, his tin cup, all were gone. Indeed, this bag was virtually empty and she wondered why he had left it behind. One blanket there was only.

Kira rummaged in the hidden shadows of the leather bag and encountered something hard. She drew it out into the light and bit her lip when she realized she held the knife Thierry had granted her once before. That time he had given her a means of protecting herself when he sent her home alone.

The message was clear enough to Kira's mind. Well it seemed he gave her the same means once again. Which could only mean that Thierry would be gone for a time. Kira sank to the floor beside his bag and turned the blade over and over in her hands.

Mayhap he was gone for good.

Mayhap 'twas his way of telling her to be gone when he returned.

And he had not even awakened her to tell her of his decision himself. Truly she had been a fool to expect anything else.

She would not cry.

How could he leave her without saying adieu? How could he abandon her here in this remote fortress with solely a short dagger to protect herself? How could he not have known that she bore his child?

Curse him! In a rare burst of temper, Kira swatted the saddlebag viciously and sent it rolling end over end across the stone floor. The blanket tumbled out and unfolded itself, another tin cup rattled as it danced across the flagstones. Kira scooped up the empty bag, shook it savagely and cast it against the far wall in disgust.

'Twas then that she realized what else Thierry had taken with him.

The *aljofar* was gone.

Thierry had gone to fetch his bride. The moment she had dreaded was upon her. Kira had been dismissed.

An overwhelming sadness threatened to engulf Kira but she stubbornly bit down on the tide. She would *not* cry. She would not be disappointed or hurt. Had she not known from the outset that he was Mongol? Had the Persian woman not warned her of their ways?

Had she not known better than to put her faith in him?

No matter that she had done precisely that. No matter that Thierry had not treated her in the manner she might have expected from a Mongol. No matter that he had been kind and considerate of her beyond anything or anyone she had ever known. Mayhap that just made the inevitable more bitter to swallow.

'Twas the cruelty she had originally expected from him, rendered all the more cruel by the kindness he had shown her first.

Curse him.

She was an abandoned whore who was with child. Kira jabbed her chin into the air determinedly. She owed her child more than wallowing in self-pity would earn him. Was his sire not a proud and tall man?

But she would not raise her child here in this place that brought a gleam to Thierry's eye. To this fortress she knew he would return. Mayhap he fetched his bride to bring her back here. At the very thought, Kira hauled the heavy kirtle over her head and began to hastily lace the sides.

Whatever the price, Kira and her child would not be here to greet him.

Thierry and Nogai were leaving the village perched on the side of the hill below Montsalvat when Thierry realized another party rode along the serpentine road toward them. He and Nogai exchanged a look and Nogai frowned.

"Think you that they follow from that king's court?" he demanded suspiciously. Thierry did not like that he had no ready answer, nor did he like that the party was too far away to be readily identified. His first thought was for Kira sleeping far above and he knew he could not simply ride away without knowing more.

"I would know their intent," he said, relieved when Nogai nodded agreement. They ducked into the shadows alongside the only tavern in the ramshackle village and waited impatiently for the others to approach.

As they sat, Thierry watched his horse's ear twitch complacently and reviewed what he had seen. The party was extensive, which did not bode well to his mind. But there seemed to be no haste to their progress, a fact both annoying and puzzling.

Surely invaders would approach quickly and attack before any guessed their intent? To that end, surely attackers would arrive in the night. But this road led to no other destination than the fortress. Well it seemed that Montsalvat would soon have guests, of one manner or another.

And Kira he had left alone within the fortress walls. Thierry

stifled a foreboding sense that these riders came on a mission
he would not like. Nogai settled himself back into the shadows
with his usual calm and spared Thierry a telling glance.

Aye. Thierry gritted his teeth. They would simply have to
wait, even though these riders seemed to be taking far too long
to reach the town.

Well it seemed that he had lost his patience for waiting,
among other things, these past few weeks.

"Töde!" called an imperious voice when Thierry thought
he could surely remain quiet no longer. 'Twas a voice that
Thierry remembered well and he stiffened instinctively at the
sound, despite all the years that had passed since he had last
heard it raised.

It simply could not be.

"Do pick up the pace, Töde. I would cross the threshold of
Montsalvat yet again before I expire." The rumbling growl was
so achingly familiar to Thierry that he closed his eyes for a long
moment to regain his self-control. He felt Nogai's inquiring
gaze upon him, but could not summon the words to explain
through the midst of his surprise and confusion.

"Never is time wasted on caution, milord," a younger
voice replied.

"Time aplenty have we already wasted on this trip and I
would sit at a warm hearth with a cup of brew in short order."

"Our homeland 'tis, Töde, and safer than you might think,"
an equally familiar but feminine voice added persuasively.

It seemed that Thierry could not summon the air into his lungs.

Here. Now. Naught had he decided of what he would say,
what he would do, what he would ask, having fully expected
to have the width of a continent to summon his thoughts. But
the moment was upon him already and naught was there he
could do but face its demands as well as he was able.

Thierry straightened slowly and turned, the knowledge of
what he would see not lessening the shock a whit. He took a

deep breath and urged his horse out of the shadows into the road as the arriving party drew alongside.

The closest horse whinnied in surprise and took a double step. This drew the attention of the Mongol who rode alongside, his hand dropping to his blade with predictable speed.

Thierry moved naught as he met the steady gaze of his sire.

"You!" Dagobert inhaled sharply and hauled his destrier to an abrupt halt.

The others jostled to a halt and all fell silent. An expectant silence filled the crooked road, but Thierry could neither speak nor look away from the recollection in his sire's eyes. Dagobert squared his shoulders suddenly and his expression turned forbidding. In that moment Thierry knew he would have to be the first to speak and hoped he could do so. He cleared his throat, the clamor of his heart making it difficult to find fitting words.

"Hello, Father," he said simply.

The quiet words hung in the silence and it seemed the very earth held its breath. His sire's expression melted not a whit and Thierry feared that his greeting would garner no response at all.

A movement caught his eye and he noted his mother's presence for the first time. In the same instant he saw his father's restraining hand on Alienor's forearm and well understood the meaning.

This battle was betwixt the two of them alone.

Thierry noted the signs of his father's aging in the morning sunlight and endeavored to calculate how long it had been since they had exchanged heated words. Five years? Six? Thierry could not be sure, but well did he know that his sire's memory of that day had not faded, either.

He had been young indeed when he had ridden out of Khanbaliq in anger. And had sworn he would never return.

The hostility sat between them as surely as if the argument had only just been voiced.

"What are you doing here?" Dagobert demanded tightly.

"I might ask the same of you," Thierry retorted, his tone

colder than he might have intended it to be. His father's nostrils flared slightly, the only outward sign of his anger, and he glanced up at the brooding fortress with almost a casual air.

"This is my home," he asserted stonily. "I would ask again, what brings *you* here?" The challenge in his eyes was unmistakable. This was not Thierry's home.

"I had thought I might find something of home here myself," Thierry maintained proudly. His father lifted one fair brow.

"No legacy have you here," he said flatly.

The memory of what Eustache had said filled Thierry's mind. The realization that his sire had deliberately chosen to deny him his heritage cut like a well-honed knife.

"So I have been told. No idea had I that you were so ashamed to have me as your son," Thierry commented bitterly. His mother gasped, but both men paid her no heed.

"Not half as ashamed as evidently you are of having me as your sire," Dagobert snorted.

"No shame have I in my lineage, even if my own sire would deny me," Thierry argued.

"Ha!" Dagobert charged. He urged his horse forward as the color rose in his neck. "'Twas not as I recall your last words to me," he spat venomously. "Or mayhap you find no shame in having a 'coward' as your father?"

Thierry felt his own color rise at the reminder. "I was young and spoke in haste," he said defensively.

"Oho! In haste indeed did you speak, not to mention that in haste did you leave," his father countered. "And nary a word in the years between. Have you not a shred of compassion for your mother's worries, at least?"

"Well I understood that you were relieved to see the back of me," Thierry snapped, his anger finally beyond constraint.

"Me? And what had my concerns to do with any of this? Headstrong you were from the first and determined that you alone knew what was for the best!"

"Headstrong?" Thierry repeated angrily. "'Twas not I who

deliberately denied my only son his rightful legacy! Tell me, Father, am I a bastard born? Is that what lies at the root of this?"

"Thierry!" Alienor breathed in shock. Dagobert's eyes blazed and he spurred his mount yet closer to his son.

"Were you not my own spawn, I would take a lash to you for speaking thus of your mother," he spat.

"So you claim me, then?" Thierry demanded proudly.

Dagobert's head jerked up and his silver eyes blazed. "Always have I claimed you as my own," he retorted.

"Indeed?" 'Twas Thierry's turn to arch an inquiring brow. "'Twas not what old Eustache told me."

Dagobert's features paled despite his tan and when he spoke, his voice was strained. "Eustache could not have told you that I denied you, for he knows better."

"To deny me my legacy is not to deny me?" Thierry snorted in disgust. "Indeed, it seems you play a game of words with me, milord."

Dagobert's eyes flashed. "I denied you *naught!*" he fairly shouted. "Claimed you as my son and heir I did all those years past." He jabbed one finger through the air to the fortress high above. "There in that bailey under the spring moon did I claim you as my own son!"

"Then what of this legacy that all speak of in whispers?"

"'Tis naught for you to concern yourself," Dagobert insisted stonily. He turned slightly away. Rage rippled through Thierry as he realized that his father still had no intention of confiding in him the tale.

"Has it to do with this?" he demanded, tearing his *kalat* open to bare his mark with a vicious gesture.

Dagobert looked up with evident reluctance. The tension crackled between the two men until Dagobert glanced away from Thierry's mark and swallowed carefully. "What do you know about that?" he asked quietly.

"Well enough do I know that you sport one much the same."

Dagobert shrugged with feigned nonchalance. "'Tis a birthmark, no more, no less," he maintained calmly. Even with the years between them, Thierry knew his sire lied.

"'Tis a birthmark that nearly saw me slaughtered!" he cried. His father's eyes widened in shock. Thierry felt a surge of satisfaction that his point had been made.

"Where?" Dagobert demanded tightly.

"At the court of the king in Paris," Thierry supplied proudly, savoring his father's astonishment.

"You bared your mark there?" his sire asked incredulously. Older he looked, though his new appearance of vulnerability did naught to cool Thierry's anger. "Well does it seem that *you* cannot be called a coward," Dagobert charged. "Although mayhap a *fool* would be closer to the mark! Know you what you have done in this? Know you what you risked?"

"How could I? 'Tis a *birthmark,* no more, no less," he taunted. His father's jaw tightened.

"Fool!" he spat. "Know you what you have risked by such foolishness?"

"Evidently not!" Thierry shouted in exasperation. "How could I know when all refuse to confide in me the tale?"

Dagobert glared at him and his lips thinned. "Always did I mean to tell you the tale. When you were older."

"I *am* older," Thierry retorted. "And your reticence has nearly seen me dead."

"'Twas you who called me a coward," his sire accused. Thierry glared back at him, having naught with which to explain away those angry words. "Well did I understand that I was simply some coward with the good fortune to have fallen upon your mother at an opportune moment," Dagobert continued when Thierry did not speak. "And now you would ask of me a tale of your heritage."

"Dagobert," Alienor chided under her breath, but Dagobert's expression did not soften.

"'Twas precisely that the boy charged, as I well recall." His eyes narrowed as he looked to Thierry once more. Thierry winced at the familiarity of the words, wondering how he could ever have been so cruel.

"I erred," he said simply. Dagobert's eyes flashed angrily.

"Quickly indeed does that confession come for all the years spent awaiting it," he said tersely. "Should I not know better, I might conclude that you were solely concerned about your status as heir. Have you seen Montsalvat and decided you fancy it better than roaming ceaselessly over the hills?"

Thierry impaled his sire with a glance. "I seek no more than to know the truth of something that might see me dead," he maintained tightly. "Indeed, it seems little enough to ask of a father."

"I would tell you the fullness of the tale, were you not clearly leaving Montsalvat," Dagobert answered stiffly. Thierry met his father's gaze slowly.

"I ride only to seek you out," he said quietly and saw the surprise register on his father's features.

"Why?" Dagobert demanded.

"Eustache did I ask for the import of my mark. He declined to tell me the tale out of deference to you." Something eased in his father's expression, encouraging Thierry to plunge on and ask the question to which he most feared to hear the answer. "He bade me seek you out," he confided hoarsely. "I would ask you myself whether you had disclaimed me by not granting me the fullness of this legacy."

"Never."

Dagobert's flat denial hung in the silence between the two men so long that Thierry wondered if he had imagined the sound.

So long had it been. And for what? Heartless words exchanged in anger. Surely his sire knew that Thierry did not truly believe him a coward.

Was it possible his father had not swept Thierry from his heart?

"And well it seemed that I owed my sire an apology," Thierry added quietly.

Then Dagobert shook his head and dismounted hastily, closing the space between them with hasty steps. Thierry knew not his intent, but echoed the older man's move lest his father think even less of him. Their gazes met again when they were but a pace apart and Thierry did not dare to hope when his father laid one hand heavily upon his shoulder.

"Never would I deny you, no matter what charge was made in anger," Dagobert asserted with quiet resolve. "My son are you, blood of my blood and fruit of the vine. One night long past, I claimed you as my son and heir in the bailey at Montsalvat. I but left the decision to you whether you would assume the burden of the family legacy."

"What *is* my legacy, Father?" Thierry demanded softly. His sire frowned into space for a long moment, then met his son's gaze once more.

"Well do you know that we share a mark in common," he said quietly. Thierry nodded. "A mark 'tis of our lineage and the heritage of our bloodline." His voice dropped and Thierry had to strain to hear the words, even though they stood but an arm's length apart. "Well might you have heard tell of the lost kings of Rhedae, the forgotten kings whose line was divinely chosen to rule."

"Aye."

Dagobert's gaze grew serious and Thierry fancied he saw sadness in those gray eyes. "A line of kings wrongfully displaced by usurpers and overthrown from our rightful role. Long centuries have passed, each with their attempts, some noble, some covert, to regain that which we have lost, to regain that which is our rightful legacy. Each attempt has been a failure. I watched my sire die in battle and took the pledge at his hand that very day."

Dagobert sighed heavily. "I, too, failed at the task and nearly lost all I held dear in the transaction. 'Twould have been too much to pay for something mayhap no longer within our grasp, for well it seems to me that the days of regaining lost legacies are passing. Such doings are of the matter of myths and fireside tales and not a way for a man to earn his way. Centuries has it been and oft have I wondered if the blood royal ran too thin in my veins to see the matter successfully resolved."

He cleared his throat carefully and looked into Thierry's eyes once more. "When we had retreated to Montsalvat and were besieged, well we knew that the fortress would fall to the invaders. Alienor and I decided to stay but long enough to grant you your name. 'Twas when you should have been granted the burden of your legacy according to family tradition, but I—" Thierry watched in amazement as his sire shook his head wonderingly and smiled sadly "—I could not so readily commit you to a path I feared to be folly.

"That night, beneath the stars at Montsalvat, I claimed you as my son, granted you my name and bestowed upon you the choice of whether to take up the family quest or not. Never had another in our line done this for his heir, but times change and opportunities fade, and I would not see you pay a high toll for what might well be whimsy."

The lost kings of Rhedae culminated in him. Silence reigned between them for a long moment as Thierry fought to make sense of his father's words.

'Twas impossible to believe, yet the tale struck a chord of truth within him that told him his sire spoke aright. Of a line of kings was Thierry. Of a rightful line of kings destined to rule by divine choice. Here was the meaning of his mark. Here also was the grand destiny he had envisioned for himself, should he but regain the crown.

Quickly Thierry reviewed what he had observed in Paris and the vigor with which those summoned by Eustache had taken up his cause. A lost line of kings. Never would Thierry have imagined this to be his fate, but even now, his pulse quickened at the prospect.

"Make no mistake, Thierry," Dagobert said with utmost seriousness. "Never did I imagine 'twould be so many years before I told you the fullness of the tale."

"No fault was it of yours that I would behave so foolishly.

'Twas that quest that drove you from home, not cowardice as I charged," Thierry guessed intuitively and his father almost smiled at his low words.

"'Twas that, indeed," he admitted. "Already had I lifted my hand to the battle and failed. A hunted man was I in these parts and well had my desire grown to see many more days in Alienor's company." He spared a crooked smile over his shoulder and Thierry followed his gaze to find his mother's eyes glazed with tears. Dagobert's voice dropped to a confidential whisper.

"'Twas Alienor's desire once she had saved me from certain death that I live long enough to see my son become a man." The two men looked into each other's eyes once more and Dagobert lifted his other hand to rest companionably on Thierry's shoulder. He tightened his grip and summoned a smile that warmed the silver of his eyes.

"And so I have," he said softly. "So I have."

The two men looked away for a moment, Thierry struggling to clear the tears from his vision. His father cleared his throat gruffly.

"Not easy is it for a man to admit when he is wrong," Dagobert added quietly. "And I would not be churlish enough to hold words spoken in haste against you." No mistaking his pride was there and emotion rose in Thierry's throat fit to choke him. Dagobert's grip tightened on Thierry's shoulder. "Glad I am indeed that we chose this time to come home."

Home. Thierry followed his father's gaze back to the heavy stone walls and knew exactly what the older man had meant. Naught did he recall of this place, but still Montsalvat invoked a powerful magic in his heart.

'Twas here he wanted to raise his family with Kira, he realized suddenly. 'Twas here he wanted to make his home. Well did Thierry know that he had not imagined Kira's comfort with the old keep. Here would they set down their roots.

A sudden thought disturbed Thierry's thoughts and he glanced to his sire in alarm.

"Why do you ride home now?" he asked urgently. "Is something amiss? Are you ill?"

Dagobert shook his head slowly, his calm expression soothing Thierry's fears as naught else could. "Nay," he said finally, squinting as he looked up to the high walls. "'Twas a dream that set us on our way west."

"A dream?" Thierry prompted. His father nodded once, then turned to face his son.

"Aye," he confirmed solemnly and his grip tightened slightly on Thierry's shoulder. "A dream that the time to regain what we had lost was upon us again."

Thierry's heart soared at the import of the words. 'Twas *his* time! 'Twas from Montsalvat that he would launch his attempt to regain his rightful legacy.

A thrill tripped through Thierry at the thought that his destiny was once again within his grasp, and he stifled a grin of anticipation. From here would he hold court over his domains that he had no doubt he would regain.

Were the knights not already loyal to the cause? Had not Eustache and the others already risked their hides and their reputations to save him from certain slaughter in Paris? He would lead them to the victory they desired, the victory they had hoped for all these centuries. He would grasp his legacy with both hands and make the old tales ring true.

The blood of two divinely appointed lines of kings mingled in his veins. Was this not everything of which he had ever dreamed? Not a doubt was there that he would succeed, for destiny was on his side.

Under Thierry's hand, the lost kings of Rhedae would soon be found again.

Chapter Fifteen

"Did you travel alone?" Alienor interjected hastily. Thierry returned reluctantly to the present at her question.

"Nay, I did not ride west alone," Thierry admitted warily. He indicated his silent friend, still sitting astride his mount in the shadows. "My *anda*, Nogai." His parents nodded, and greetings were exchanged in Mongol.

He knew he should tell his parents of Kira. Suddenly Thierry was nervous beyond recollection and he unexpectedly feared that they would not approve of the woman he had taken to his side.

"Just the two of you were there?" his mother inquired politely.

"Nay," Thierry conceded awkwardly. "My woman was there, as well."

He did not miss the look his parents exchanged. "Your woman or your wife?" Dagobert asked in a precise tone of which Thierry well knew the import. He straightened and deliberately looked his father in the eye.

"Indeed, there is naught of difference betwixt the two," he maintained stonily. His father arched one brow high and made to speak, but Alienor intervened.

"What is her name?" she asked in an obvious bid to avert an argument.

"Kira," Thierry supplied, feeling suddenly in poorer temper

than he had expected. "Persian she is," he added for no explicable reason.

"And lovely, I am sure," his mother said quickly. Thierry fancied she spoke thus to keep his father from interjecting but he flatly refused to meet the older man's gaze. "Mayhap we could meet her," Alienor suggested. Thierry's gaze flew to his mother's in dismay.

Kira meeting his parents? The idea was more disturbing than it should have been.

What if they did not approve?

"She is not here," he said. His parents looked confused and his rationalization for leaving Kira behind suddenly seemed inane beyond compare. "Small she is and delicate. Well I thought that I would have to go to Khanbaliq to find you, so Kira I left in Eustache's care—"

"You left her alone at Montsalvat?" his sire demanded tightly. Thierry did not miss the agitation in his father's tone.

"Aye, for safer she will be there," he began, but got no further.

"Safer? But with you she was in Paris?" his father demanded skeptically.

"Aye," Thierry agreed warily. "My woman is she, as all know."

Dagobert leaned closer and his eyes gleamed. "Tell me how you left Paris," he ordered.

Thierry shrugged uncomprehendingly. "We fled, for as soon as I bared my mark, we were attacked."

"Fled with Eustache?" Dagobert insisted tersely.

"Aye," Thierry responded irritably, still not seeing the way of things.

"Fool!"

To his complete astonishment his sire wagged one indignant finger directly beneath his nose. "Addlepated fool!" Dagobert spat and whistled impatiently for his attendants. "Surely I raised you to have more sense than this!"

The charge was so reminiscent of precisely what Eustache had said in Paris that Thierry was momentarily taken aback.

"Eustache said they would be prepared," he protested.

"It matters naught," his father snapped before he turned away.

"Töde! Make the horses ready immediately! We ride on to the fortress with all haste!" Dagobert muttered an expletive under his breath. He spared his son one eloquent glance of disgust before he spun and hauled himself back into his saddle.

"Surely they can defend the fortress—" Thierry said to his mother. Alienor leaned over to grip Thierry's hands for a long moment.

"He but fears for your Kira," she confessed quickly before releasing his hands and hastily turning her mount. Already had Dagobert given spurs to his horse and Thierry was left staring after them.

Had Eustache not spoken aright? Had he left Kira in danger?

"For Kira?" Thierry was in his own saddle in an instant. "Why? What risk has she at Montsalvat? Safe she should be there." Thierry's heart went cold but evidently no answer was he to have. The rest of his father's retinue followed in the older man's wake, naught but a cloud of dust left before Thierry.

"What does this mean?" Thierry shouted in frustration. He spurred his beast and raced to catch up to his sire. "What is the threat to Kira?"

"Haste must we make," Dagobert called impatiently over his shoulder. "You have but to think upon the matter to see the truth. Poorly indeed does it serve the king's interest to leave any of us breathing. 'Twas that alone that had me flee my homeland. 'Twas that alone that bade me grant you a choice in taking this legacy."

"What is the price to Kira?" Thierry demanded again as he stood in his stirrups, already half certain he knew the answer.

"Your Kira may be forced to bear the price of being the woman of the fruit of the vine," his sire said enigmatically.

Kira could not be in danger because of his mark alone. 'Twas preposterous.

"Nay!" Thierry retorted sharply. "Safe she is at Montsalvat! 'Twas why I left her there. Naught has this to do with her.

Naught." His father shook his head slowly as Thierry drew up alongside, sympathy dawning in the older man's eyes as he regarded his son.

"We can only hope that 'twill not be too late," he advised.

The very words set a chill through Thierry's heart, but no more could he ask, for his sire was already digging his heels into his mount.

Had he abandoned Kira to some cruel fate? It could not be thus, but Thierry feared that he had done precisely that. Surely naught could have happened in the short span of a day. Surely Eustache would protect Kira, he thought wildly, urging his horse on with renewed vigor.

Surely this legacy of his that promised so much could not steal away the one person he held most dear.

Kira was over the wall and a dozen steps down the slope before she realized that she was being watched.

She stopped abruptly and clutched her bag to her chest, not at all liking the look of the two dozen men who confronted her. Half-hidden they were, lurking in the shadows of boulders and leaning against the trunks of trees, but their eyes gleamed.

And every eye was fixed upon her.

Kira's pulse took off at a gallop. She stepped cautiously backward, knowing full well that she could not scale the cursedly smooth wall. Jumping down had been one matter, but now she was truly stranded on the outside.

Mayhap leaving Montsalvat had not been a well-conceived plan.

One man stepped forward, the ripple of his cloak revealing a sliver of azure and gold that fairly stopped Kira's heart.

Knights from the court in Paris. One look into the steely gaze of the one who approached her with relentless steps told Kira that this was no social call. She panicked and turned to run just in time to see old Eustache leap from the wall in her wake.

He bellowed and drew his blade before he hit the ground.

Kira was certain she had never been so glad to see another mortal in her life. The knight stalking her shouted a response. Kira spun to see his blade clear its scabbard as well and knew instinctively that this would be a battle to the death.

With her as the spoils.

Eustache shot her a glance and Kira instantly understood. She scurried out of the way and leaned against the chill of the heavy wall, wincing when the blades clashed for the first time. She opened her eyes and was relieved to find Eustache was yet unscathed. The men backed away from each other and circled. Kira licked her lip, her gaze drawn unwillingly to the figures lurking in the trees. Something cold took hold of Kira's stomach when she realized the import of their presence.

Should Eustache best this cold knight, he had yet twenty-three more to conquer before he earned her freedom.

How could she have been so foolish?

"Eustache de Sidon, are you not?" the cursedly agile mercenary inquired conversationally.

"Aye, 'tis my name," Eustache responded with a vicious swipe of his blade that belied his age to Kira's eyes. "Heard tell of me, have you?"

The mercenary cocked a skeptical brow. "Aye, plenty have I heard of you and your liege lord over the years."

"Many years has it been since my liege lord passed away." The lie fell so easily from Eustache's lips that Kira knew he had told it before. Was that why Montsalvat had been left in peace?

"Passed away?" the foreign knight inquired mildly. "Mayhap passed away over the hills." He backed Eustache determinedly across the deadened grass with a renewed attack. Kira felt her hands rise to her mouth. The two men danced across the dawn-tinged ground, more evenly matched than she might have guessed.

Suddenly the mercenary tripped over a stone and lost his balance. Eustache took advantage of the opportunity to lunge forward. The knight swore and twisted, managing somehow to raise his blade with lightning speed. Kira gasped when the sword slid between Eustache's ribs and surprise lit the older man's features. Eustache swore vehemently and backed away, the other knight watching with eerie steadiness.

To Kira's astonishment Eustache took a deep breath and lifted his blade once more.

"En garde," he said with icy precision.

Even Kira's inexperienced eyes saw that the stakes had been raised. Eustache fought now for his life and his vigor was astonishing. Their blades clashing with deafening force, they crossed the clearing back and again.

Eustache's blade caught the other knight across the cheek and those impassive features contorted in pain. The foreign knight swore as a trickle of red meandered over his skin. Anger tightened his lips but Eustache had already jabbed again. The knight twisted and the tip of the blade but traced an ineffectual line across his throat. He roared in fury and lunged, slamming Eustache's blade so hard that the sword clattered across the few stones embedded in the grass.

Too far away to be readily retrieved. Kira dared to take a step in pursuit but two of the other foreign knights drew their blades and stepped over the sword.

Eustache drew his dagger in a flash as the knight swung for the final blow. Eustache kicked out and caught the other knight's ankle. The mercenary swore again as he lost his balance, but his blade still found its mark.

Kira's heart stopped as Eustache fell, the length of the knight's sword buried in his belly. She waited but he moved naught.

'Twas over. The foreign knight ignored Eustache, calmly inspecting his own wound.

This could not be. Eustache could not be gone so quickly. Kira's gaze flicked over the party of foreign knights in trepidation.

She swallowed in anticipation of her own fate. And her foolishness had cost Eustache dearly as well!

To her astonishment Eustache suddenly leaped to life. His dagger caught the morning light as it arched toward the other knight's chest. The mercenary shouted in outrage and jerked away. Eustache buried the blade in his shoulder with a grimace of pain and wrenched the blade downward.

His grip loosened and he slowly slid bonelessly back against the dirt, his features lifeless in truth now.

Well it seemed that the pounding of Kira's heart might deafen her when she met the cold gaze of the foreign knight. The cursed man smiled a most predatory smile and she knew naught good was in store for her.

The sun was well past its zenith when they passed beneath the barbican again. All seemed normal, but Thierry liked it not. Dagobert shouted for Eustache as they gained the bailey, but Thierry had no interest in finding the older man. All of his fears focused on Kira. Never should he have left her alone. He leaped from his saddle and dashed up the stairs to the solar.

'Twas empty. Thierry tore open the bed curtains to find that space similarly voided.

She was gone.

It could not be. Thierry turned over stools and prowled the room angrily until he saw that his other saddlebag was gone. Kira had left him.

Impossible it seemed, but the chilling truth could not be denied. He dashed back down the stairs to find a frown on his sire's brow.

"None have seen Eustache all day," Dagobert said with dissatisfaction.

"Kira is gone," Thierry said flatly.

"Something is amiss," Dagobert concluded. He snapped his fingers and raised his voice. "Search the grounds! Summon all to the task! The lady's life may be in danger!"

There was a scurry of activity as the men within the hall left to do Dagobert's bidding. Thierry fought against the tangle of emotions within him as he struggled to make sense of it all. Why would Kira have left him deliberately?

And what would he do if she was lost to him? Already there was an aching hollow within him and he yet knew not her fate.

To his surprise he found his mother's hand resting on his arm. Thierry looked up and found sympathy in her eyes.

"Well I think that you hold your Kira in regard," she said softly.

"Aye," Thierry agreed roughly. The press of his mother's fingers increased slightly.

"And yet she is not your wife."

"'Tis the *same*," Thierry insisted, knowing all the while that his mother was not convinced.

"Mayhap 'tis the same to you," Alienor said smoothly. "But is it the same to your Kira?"

Was that why Kira had left? Did she think he did not care for her? The very thought made everything turn cold within Thierry. Well should he have given her the *aljofar*. Well should he have told her the truth.

He could only hope that he still might have the chance.

"Here!"

The cry brought Dagobert and Thierry simultaneously to the guard post on the curtain wall. Dagobert muttered a curse and stepped immediately back from the scene below.

'Twas Eustache lying below, bloodied and dead. Thierry studied the older man's corpse until he located the telling wound. Swordplay. Several men were gathered around Eustache and looked to be making preparations to lift him back within the fortress walls. Thierry's gaze lifted over them to scan the ground and the periphery as he sought some sign of Kira's passing.

Had she come this way?

Thierry met Nogai's gaze. The Mongol nodded thoughtfully, visibly tracing the bloody trail marking the path where Eustache's body had been hauled.

"Dragged behind the rocks and trees was he, milord," the

man who had accompanied them supplied tersely. "'Twas why the sentries did not spot him sooner. 'Twas Beauregard who saw him."

Thierry looked at the men below and spotted the young squire whose hair Eustache had ruffled in Paris. His jaw tightened at the signs of the strain the boy had borne, for his eyes were red rimmed and his countenance ashen. 'Twas evident the boy had worshiped Eustache, and 'twas a cruel blow that he should be the one to find his hero thus.

"And the lady?" Dagobert asked. Thierry's gaze flew to the other man in time to see him shake his head slowly.

"Not a sign of her, milord," he confessed. Thierry saw sympathy dawning in the man's eyes and hastily looked away.

Not a sign. Mayhap not to him.

Thierry's gaze meandered over the jutting rocks and meager trees that covered the slope on this face of the mountain. Some small sign he sought that Kira yet lived, though when he spotted the broken branches, he thought at first his eyes deceived him.

Then he saw another snapped branch, a bevy of stones disturbed from the places they had long rested. The evidence was there and widely scattered enough that it could mean only one thing. A number of people had passed this way. Nogai lifted a finger and pointed to the same broken branches that Thierry had noted.

"Mayhap as many as twenty," he muttered. Thierry nodded, feeling his father's questioning gaze upon them both, but did not elaborate.

Only too clearly did Thierry recall the way they had departed Paris. Now that the fullness of his heritage was clear to him, he understood the king's response. Indeed, 'twas much like the thinking of Abaqa to eliminate all threats to one's hegemony.

But why this way? Why come to the wall, kill Eustache and leave without approaching the fortress itself? It made no sense to so quickly abandon an objective.

Unless... Thierry's heart chilled as the only answer became

clear to him. Kira was the missing clue. Eustache had died defending her. Eustache had failed and they had taken Kira. Mayhap someone recalled that she had been with him, mayhap they sought to draw him out without sustaining the casualties necessary to storm an old fortress like this one.

It mattered not what their intent was. The more Thierry reflected upon it, the more certain he became. Kira had been abducted and he could not leave the matter lie.

"Where are you going?" his father demanded. Thierry glanced over his shoulder and saw the approval in his *anda*'s eyes.

"To fetch my pack," he said simply. "'Tis evident they have taken Kira," he added grimly and turned away.

"Wait!" his father cried and Thierry halted unwillingly. "We will summon a party to go with you. Already had Eustache made preparations for battle." Dagobert paused and swallowed carefully. "Should you choose to accept the fullness of your legacy, well might this be the time to stake your claim," he added quietly.

All eyes fell to Thierry and he felt the will of those surrounding him. All their lives had they hoped and worked for the return of the rightful king. For years had this moment been their dream and for long Thierry had thought it might be his.

The time was ripe. His own ambitions were within his grasp.

But he could think of naught but Kira. Assembling a war party would take time, time that might be critical to her safety.

Thierry was surprised to realize that that fact mattered to him more than any ambition he thought himself to have. Should he be with Kira alone and be important to her, it would be enough to satisfy his ambitions.

This task he would do alone.

"Nay," Thierry said flatly. "This is betwixt this king and me."

He paused for a moment and acknowledged the concern in his father's expression. Nogai stood silently and Thierry knew his old friend understood his choice to go alone. "Let the man see the manner of opponent he has engaged," he added quietly. Something flashed in Dagobert's eyes, but Thierry turned hastily away, mentally composing a list of all he might need.

If they had harmed Kira in any way, he would see they sorely regretted the day, he resolved grimly.

'Twas dusk before Kira saw her chance.

The foreign knights had set a killing pace once mounted on the horses hidden at the mount below Montsalvat. That she was increasingly farther away from the fortress and any chance of aid did naught to reassure Kira, especially since the knight who had killed Eustache had yet to relinquish his grip upon her wrist.

They halted to let the horses drink from a passing stream and Kira dared to take a chance.

"I beg your pardon, sir, but I fear I must relieve myself," she said meekly. The knight granted her a skeptical glance and Kira was grateful to feel her color rise. More credence would that lend to her tale. She dropped her voice to a whisper. "I fear I may not be able to hold my water much longer," she confided.

"Troublesome bitch," the knight snarled. He dismounted all the same, hauling Kira in his wake. She struggled to give no sign of the thrill of victory coursing through her. The knight moved no farther and Kira's hope faded.

This would not do.

"Sir!" she declared in a scandalized tone. "Surely you do not expect that I…that I should, should…here amidst your men." Kira's cheeks heated yet further at her own audacity and several men around them chuckled.

"Oho, a lady fine have we," chortled one. Kira's chin shot up proudly and the knight who held her wrist granted her an assessing glance.

"For pity's sake," he snorted when she thought he might not give in. He turned and plunged into the woods, the chuckles of his men lending impatience to his step.

She would have to be quick about it, should she make the

most of this chance. 'Twas dark in the shadows of the trees, yet still Kira played the demure maiden.

"Please, sir," she implored as she fingered the hem of her kirtle. The knight's lips set stubbornly and he turned his back upon her.

"Make haste, woman. Far have we to ride this night," he growled.

Had it been Thierry before her, Kira knew well he would have missed naught of what she did. She could only hope that this knight was less observant.

A man shouted and the knight's head turned. Kira's heart leaped. 'Twas her chance and likely the only one she would get.

Before she could question her impulse, Kira scooped up a broken tree branch. She crept up behind the mercenary, feeling it took a week to close the distance. She barely dared to breathe as she raised the heavy branch high. Kira swung it at the back of his skull with all her might. He turned, evidently hearing some hint of her presence, but had only time to open his mouth before the branch crashed into his brow.

He crumpled to his knees, his fingers grasped wildly for Kira's kirtle. Terror flooded through her. She danced out of range of his grip and raised the branch high. The knight curled his lip in a snarl. Kira panicked. He was going to summon the others! She swung the branch and squeezed her eyes closed so that she wouldn't have to see the damage she wrought.

The branch hit the ground with a thud. Kira had missed.

Something whistled past her ear. Her eyes flew open in time to see the knight lunge forward, then suddenly stop mid-gesture.

The shaft of the arrow buried in his throat quivered for a long moment, then he fell face-first onto the forest floor.

Kira gasped and spun on her heel. Everything within her dissolved at the sight of Thierry's grim countenance and she thought her knees might give way. She took a gulping breath of relief and he held up one finger for silence as he stepped to her side.

"Are you hurt?" he demanded with blazing eyes. Kira shook her head, not trusting herself to speak. Thierry slipped one hand into the hair at her nape, the warmth of his fingers there reassuring her as naught else could.

Thierry was here. She was safe, despite her foolishness. Kira willed her heart to slow its pace.

"Woho, Gunther! For whose relief do you take the wench?" The men laughed in the clearing beyond. Thierry stiffened, then crouched lower, his eyes narrowing as he peered through the forest growth.

"I will fetch him," another growled. "Is he not the one in such a rush to return to Paris?" The other men laughed amiably and the sound of the horses in the stream carried to Kira's ears.

"How many?" he whispered.

"Twenty-two," Kira supplied.

Thierry nodded, then a footfall in the brush brought his head up with a snap. He shoved Kira behind him and drew several arrows from his quiver. The silhouette of a knight appeared and Thierry moved so quickly that the arrow was planted in his chest before Kira saw Thierry draw his bow.

The knight grunted and fell, the thick carpet of leaves muffling the sound.

"Jean-Luc! Tell us not that the wench accommodates you both!"

A trio of men burst abruptly into the woods, but Thierry dispatched them with similar efficiency. Kira gaped at his skill, but he merely spared her a wink. He grasped her hand and tugged her hastily farther into the woods.

A cry rose behind them and Thierry ducked behind a tree, pressing Kira into the tree before him. He leaned against her protectively and silently threaded another arrow into his bow. Kira did not dare breathe lest she give their location away.

Thierry was completely motionless.

"What is this?" cried another man in dismay.

Another swore and Kira glanced up to see a third cross himself. They were close, too close for her comfort, but still Thierry waited.

"Who could have done this thing?"

"Where is the woman?"

"Naught did I hear."

A babble of outrage rose from the cluster of men. Kira felt their gazes rise to scan the forest and she closed her eyes, willing herself invisible. The scent of the cedars flooded through her and she hoped against hope that they would not be discovered.

Thierry had pursued her! Despite her fear, the thought sent a thrill through her. Was it possible indeed that he cared for her?

"Naught do I see," whispered another man. Awe there was in his voice. "How do we track a silent foe?" The group of men shuffled their feet in response to his question.

"Is the woman worth seeing our demise?" demanded another.

"But what will we tell the king?"

"Back to the fortress should we go!" cried one man. His suggestion was not greeted with enthusiasm.

"Nay! We should ride directly to Paris!" snapped another and Kira sensed this one would take the lead.

"Fool!" spat the first. "I would not darken that portal with this task unfulfilled."

"Mayhap you would not, but I fully intend to do so," the second man maintained frostily. "Any who would rather ride into battle uninformed are free to accompany you on your futile mission. Mayhap you will even manage to survive." A ripple of dissent rumbled through the company of knights.

"Uninformed?" argued the first man. "'Tis more than evident what we were bidden to do."

"Hardly that. Well you know that Gunther alone knew the fullness of the deed," the second knight snapped. "Without Gunther, we are best to return," he maintained haughtily.

"We need not a foreigner to conclude business here—" The first got no further before he was summarily interrupted.

"Have you not a whit of sense in your head?" the second knight said impatiently. "Can you not see that this is but a fairy tale we chase? The old king is becoming whimsical. Enough 'tis that we have ridden all the way to this cursed southern country, without wasting yet more time here."

"But this southern lord covets the crown."

"Plenty of others are there closer to Paris who covet the crown," sneered the second. Assent rippled through the ranks at that assertion.

"But he bears the mark of the old kings of Rhedae," the first knight objected, some of the vigor fading from his tone.

"Indeed," his companion said skeptically. "And you have laid eyes upon this mark?"

"Nay," the other admitted reluctantly.

"Nor have I," the second insisted, a telling confidence in his tone. "And that fortress does not inspire my fears. Poorly kept 'tis, for all its reputation, and any fool knows that a major battle of any kind, never mind a play for the crown itself, requires a fat purse. There is no threat in these southern hills."

"But the woman—?"

"Was not fetching enough to merit the trouble."

Kira might have gasped at his bold assertion, but Thierry's lips were suddenly warm against her ear. "He lies," he whispered, the fan of his breath making her warm all over.

"But what shall you tell the king?"

"Did you see this Mongol in Languedoc?" the second knight challenged his companions. Kira watched yet another knight bend over one of the fallen men and snap the shaft of Thierry's arrow. He turned it speculatively beneath the second knight's nose, though that man showed no sign of relinquishing the fight.

"'Tis said the bow is their weapon of choice," this new knight asserted calmly. "And this is fashioned unlike any arrows I know."

The second knight held his gaze for a long moment, then snatched the arrow from his hand. He snapped the shaft twice more, then cast the pieces on the ground. "I went to Montsalvat and found a deserted keep," he asserted boldly. "Save Eustache de Sidon who lay dead from this arrow. Unfortunately, it seemed the old knight and his men were deceived by those he took in."

"And the Mongols?"

"Mercifully, we caught sight of them riding south on the road and gave pursuit," the knight responded smoothly. "Sadly, several of our companions were lost in the resulting exchange, but the Mongols—" he lifted one finger "—were chased along the road and into the sea just south of Mont-salvat." His voice dropped and he eyed his companions speculatively.

"Which of you will call me a liar?"

The other knights avoided each other's gaze as Kira held her breath.

"The Mongols might return," one finally protested weakly.

The second knight laughed skeptically. "Only to hang your sorry hide," he retorted and leaned closer to the objector. "Think well, Didier, whether you would be more afraid of him or of me," he murmured before he straightened and cast an eye over his companions. "Be not fools. Subscribe to this tale and we shall all be paid in short order. Have you no desire to be paid and sleep well in your own beds?"

The question seemed to decide the matter for most of the knights. They nodded amiably to themselves, reassuring each other that their choice had been the right one.

One alone hung back from the others, his gaze rising to scan the trees. Kira's heart stopped when he seemed to look directly at them.

The knight who took the lead turned back, but he needed to say naught to his doubting companion. Kira heard the whistle of the bow and saw alarm cross that knight's features as he turned to find the man he had just argued with falling to his knees. Two more knights glanced back, their mouths opening in surprise. For a long moment, it seemed they could not move, then they turned and bolted as one from the woods.

When Kira gasped and doubled over, Thierry feared he had lost all he had gained. He glanced up to confirm that the knights were indeed gone, the jingle of their destriers' trap carrying to his ears.

"Kira? Are you hurt?" he asked and heard the thread of panic in his own tone. She shook her head, but the tears in her eyes when she straightened reassured him naught.

"You must tell me, Kira," he insisted. "Where are you hurt?" Kira inexplicably shook her head.

"'Tis the babe that kicks, 'tis all," she whispered. Shock enfolded Thierry. The babe? Kira carried a babe? Impossible 'twas, but when she drew back and met his gaze, he saw the truth reflected in her eyes.

"A babe?" he whispered. "But how?"

Kira smiled sadly. "In quite the usual way, I would imagine," she said, and her color rose becomingly. Thierry stared at her for a long moment before the questions erupted in his mind.

"But why did you not tell me?" he demanded finally. Kira tried to pull away, but Thierry tightened his grip around her.

"I feared you would not be pleased," she confessed quietly. Her lashes dropped demurely and Thierry cupped her chin gently, compelling her to look to him. Fear there was lingering in the depths of her dark gaze and intuitively he knew its source.

"Kira," he chided. "Never would I raise a hand against you." Tears filled Kira's eyes, though her doubt was still clear. "No man strikes a woman whom he loves."

The words had an unexpected result, for Kira abruptly pulled away and averted her face. "You know naught of what you speak," she maintained tightly. "My sire loved me well."

"Yet 'twas he who scarred your back?" Thierry guessed. Kira's only response was a nod and he felt his lips tighten. "No love is that, Kira," he said, but she did not respond. The silence hung thickly between them, then Thierry dared to touch her stomach. 'Twas rounding slightly, much to his amazement, and he marveled that he had noticed naught of the change.

"What of the babe?" he demanded urgently. "How far along is it?"

"But four moons along is it, as I figure, and I know not the import of its restlessness. No good can it bring, I am sure."

Four moons. Pride flooded Thierry and he stifled a smile. The child was his. Kira bore the spawn of his seed.

"Mayhap you have but strained yourself this day," he suggested. Kira's gaze flew to his and he lifted his brows encouragingly. "Come home and we shall ask my mother's advice."

"Your mother?" Kira asked breathlessly. Thierry nodded.

"Aye, a long way has she come to meet my bride." When he might have expected a smile, Kira turned abruptly away. "Kira?" he asked, but she resolutely ignored him.

And naught else did Kira say the entire way home to Montsalvat, though more than once Thierry caught her speculative gaze upon him.

Was it possible that Kira desired not to be his wife?

Chapter Sixteen

'T was too much to be pampered within the great curtained bed, knowing all the while that Thierry's bride would soon arrive and cast Kira from this luxury. Could they not see how they made her ache inside with their consideration? Did Thierry's mother not guess how much it hurt to have her compassion, knowing all the while that it would soon be stolen away?

Kira rolled over and ran one hand over her eyes. 'Twas not that which troubled her most and well she knew it. More vexed was she by the thought that Thierry would soon be with another. Only too cruel was he to tease her at night and hold her close when they both knew their time together to be fleeting.

Had Thierry been right about love? Well it seemed that his affection bore its dark price, much as her father's had done. Kira concluded that the bite of the lash was easier to bear. She opened her eyes and stared about the solar, gasping in surprise.

Thierry stood against the wall some ten paces away from her.

Curse the man for his silent passing. Kira exhaled shakily and eyed him warily.

"I thought you asleep," he said quietly. Kira shook her head and felt her color rise.

She was unaccountably reminded of the first time she had laid eyes upon him. She felt the weight of his regard upon her and knew not what to do. When Thierry straightened slowly and deliberately stepped toward her, it seemed her heart would stop.

"Feeling more hale?" he asked as he sat on the edge of the bed. One finger rose to stroke her cheek and Kira shivered beneath the warmth of his touch.

Would that he would wed her. The scandalous idea shocked even Kira for daring to think it and she averted her gaze that Thierry might not guess the direction of her thoughts.

"Aye," Kira agreed. His fingertips wandered over her cheek, her throat and traced a path to the curve of her belly. Even through the bed linens, Kira swore she could feel the touch of his skin against hers and she closed her eyes against unexpected tears.

"A value for a gem do I need this day," Thierry said slowly. Kira looked to him in surprise. He lifted a fine chain and the *aljofar* dangled from his finger before her.

'Twas the gem from his saddlebag. Kira licked her lips carefully as she schooled her temper. How could he bring this gem to her for a valuation? More crass was his move than she believed him capable and she inhaled indignantly. Thierry's lips curved in a tentative smile when he noted her surprise and Kira could not believe his audacity.

"How dare you?" Kira demanded in a low voice that shook with outrage. "How dare you bring me this pearl to assess?"

How could he insult her thus by asking her to value his gift for another? Well it seemed he twisted the knife in the wound and Kira would hear no more of his prattle. She rolled over so that her back was to him and drew up her knees, not nearly satisfied by the way his smile had abruptly disappeared. Kira's hands clenched into fists and she wished there was some way she could hurt Thierry de Pereille in truth.

At least as savagely as he had hurt her.

"Kira!" he whispered.

Kira fancied she heard surprise in his tone and mayhap a tinge of injured pride but she refused to indulge her whimsy.

No tender feelings had this man for her. That much had been clear for a long time had she simply had the sense to see what was before her.

She was a fool a hundred times over.

"Kira, what is wrong?" he asked, his breath warm against her ear.

Should he truly wish to know, Kira was angry enough to illuminate matters for him. She rolled over, enjoying the way he recoiled from the fury in her eyes. Kira propped herself up on her elbows and stared down the mighty warrior of whom she had once been afraid.

"What is wrong?" she echoed indignantly. "Here I lie with your child in my belly and yet you torment me with your bride's bauble. Have you not a scrap of compassion in your soul?" Thierry looked momentarily blank. Kira snatched the pearl from his grip and waggled it beneath his nose.

"This *aljofar,*" Kira replied hotly, having no patience with his games. "Know you not what you hold? 'Tis a gift for a bride alone and none other. I would not watch you grant this to another woman and cast me aside for the crime of conceiving your child. Not alone did I manage that task, yet you would cast me out like a common whore."

"How do you know I would give this to my bride?" Thierry asked in confusion.

Kira acknowledged a niggle of doubt. Was it possible that he knew not the import of the gem?

"'Tis an *aljofar,*" she explained patiently.

"Aye. Well do I know what the gem is called."

"Know you its import, then?"

"What import?" Thierry asked, and his scowl deepened. "'Tis a token for a woman, evidently."

"Nay." Kira shook her head firmly. "'Tis more than that alone. An *aljofar* is a traditional gift from man to wife on their wedding day a gift to celebrate their vows and bless the match with good fortune."

To Kira's consternation Thierry smiled crookedly. "Then 'tis an apt gift indeed," he said smoothly. He lifted the chain toward her once more and the pearl rocked invitingly. "Would you not value the gem for me?"

"I would *not* value the pearl you would grant your bride," Kira snapped. She would have rolled over again, but Thierry grasped her arm.

"You would wear it, then, without knowing its worth?" he asked. Kira glanced up to find a puzzled frown marring Thierry's brow. When he spoke again, his voice was so low that he fairly undid her resolve to turn him away. "In truth, Kira, I do not understand your objection."

It could not be. He could not have said that he intended for her to wear the *aljofar*. Mayhap she had misunderstood him.

But she had to know for certain. Kira swallowed nervously.

"To whom would you give this gem?" she asked, feeling her voice was far too unsteady under the circumstances. Thierry shook his head indulgently and pulled her closer.

"Kira," he chided in a warm undertone. "Know you not that this *aljofar* is for you?"

"Tease me not," Kira protested, but the warmth of Thierry's fingers spread to span her arm more determinedly and his gaze bored into hers.

"No jest is this," he said solemnly. "Always has it been for you but I found not the right moment to give it to you."

"What of your bride?" Kira demanded.

"My bride has yet to accept my offer." Pain flickered through Thierry's eyes and he leaned so close to Kira that she could smell the heat from his skin. "Well it seems that she will keep me begging in her bed."

Kira's heart skipped a beat.

Thierry intended to wed her? It could not be. But a glimpse of the sincerity in his eyes told her 'twas so, though Kira still fought against the conclusion. She would not believe what she most wanted to hear for fear she saw something where 'twas not.

"I thought you were to wed another," she protested weakly, but Thierry shook his head with maddening slowness.

"I would wed you," he said firmly. Kira's pulse rose in her ears

"But—" she protested. Thierry dropped one hard finger to rest gently against her lips and silence her words. Her gaze flew to his and he shook his head slowly.

"But *naught,* Kira. Will you accept my *aljofar* and be my wife?"

Kira's gaze slanted to the gleaming pearl and she forced herself to breathe evenly. "Stole the gem, you did," she accused in a last effort to prove her earlier conclusion right. Too much 'twas to believe that Thierry would be hers alone. So long had she wished for exactly this that Kira could not believe 'twas her heart's own desire Thierry offered her. "'Tis the bounty of an attack or some pilfered tribute you offer me, in truth," she charged wildly.

"Nay, Kira," Thierry replied with a resolve that told her he spoke the truth, though his next words challenged her conclusion. "Bought with hard coin 'twas."

She spared him a disparaging look. "Never would a Mongol buy a gem with hard coin," she charged flatly. Thierry arched a single brow high.

"And never had I until I saw this pearl in Constantinople," he confessed with utmost seriousness. "This I knew I had to see grace the lady who holds my heart."

Kira's heart pounded at this revelation. But a glance to Thierry's expression told her he spoke the truth. Thierry loved her. She eyed the pearl and let her heart flood with hope that happiness might truly be hers.

"But a token 'tis, Kira, and naught compared to what you give to me, should you consent to take my hand." An appeal there was in his deep voice, an uncertainty that Kira had never expected to hear from him and of which she could not bear the sound.

Thierry still knew naught of her feelings. Kira looked at the gem and lifted the chain from his hand with trembling fingers. She rolled the gem between her fingers consideringly and felt Thierry's breath against her ear.

"Marry me, Kira, and I will cherish you with all my heart and soul."

But one doubt remained in Kira's mind and she could not avoid giving it voice. "My father cherished me," she said quietly. Thierry's features immediately grew stern and he braced himself over her. His hands framed her face and he stared down into her eyes.

"Your sire knew naught of love," he said urgently. "Never will you know abuse at my hand and never will I stand by to let another harm you. I love you, Kira, and that you may take as my pledge to see you safe and well."

'Twas an opportunity she could not refuse. Kira looked up into Thierry's eyes and smiled as she reached up to smooth the frown of concern from his brow.

"Well it seems to me that this pearl is beyond price should it carry such a pledge from you," she whispered unsteadily. Hope flickered in Thierry's eyes.

"Nay, Kira," he murmured. "Should you accept the token, 'twill be but the setting for the richest treasure of all."

Should she accept the token. Still he knew not what she desired. Kira reached up and framed his strong jaw in her hands, wanting no more than to erase his doubts.

"No greater honor can I imagine than to be your bride," Kira said softly. "In truth, I have loved you long and wanted naught other than this."

Relief flared in Thierry's eyes and he scooped the gem jubilantly from her fingers. He slipped the chain over Kira's neck and smiled down at her as he traced the line of the gold chain against her skin.

"My Kira," he murmured wonderingly.

Kira smiled outright at his pleasure. "My Thierry," she corrected impudently and threw her arms happily around his neck. He was here and he was hers. Truly she could ask no more of the fates.

"Kiss," she demanded mischievously, readily recalling one of the first words she had learned in Frankish.

"Aye, a kiss would be in order." Thierry's eyes sparkled as he agreed.

"Mayhap more than one," Kira teased. Thierry tipped his head back and laughed outright for the first time that she had ever heard him do so. No time had she to wonder at his happiness, though, for he was quick to comply with her request. Indeed, the force of his arms closing around her was fit to take her breath away, but Kira cared naught when she tasted his lips upon hers.

For her was the *aljofar,* Kira thought triumphantly. She arched against Thierry with pleasure as she tasted the kiss she had feared she would live without for the rest of her days.

For her was Thierry alone.

* * * * *

Don't miss the next exciting volume in
**MEDIEVAL LORDS & LADIES
COLLECTION,**
Mediterranean Heroes.
Available in December 2007 from M&B™.

If you've missed any of the volumes in the *Medieval Lords & Ladies Collection*, you can have them delivered straight to your door:

Book Title/Author	ISBN & Price	Quantity
1. *Conquest Brides* Julia Byrne & Elizabeth Henshall	978 0263 85881 5 £5.99	
2. *Blackmail & Betrayal* Juliet Landon & Elizabeth Henshall	978 0263 85882 2 £5.99	
3. *War of the Roses* Sarah Westleigh & Joanna Makepeace	978 0263 85883 9 £5.99	
4. *Christmas Knights* Joanna Makepeace & Elaine Knighton	978 0263 85884 6 £5.99	
5. *Exotic East* Anne Herries & Claire Delacroix	978 0263 85885 3 £5.99	
6. *Mediterranean Heroes* Claire Delacroix & Paula Marshall	978 0263 85886 0 £5.99	

Please add 99p postage & packing per book
DELIVERY TO UK ONLY

Post to: End Page Offer, PO Box 1780, Croydon, CR9 3UH

E-mail: customer.relations@hmb.co.uk

Please ensure that you include full postal address details.
Please pay by cheque or postal order (payable to Reader Service).
Prices and availability subject to change without notice.

Order online at: www.millsandboon.co.uk

Allow 28 days for delivery.